W

S0-AEG-220

# DATE DUE

JAN 0 5 2020

# HOBNAIL AND
# OTHER FRONTIER STORIES

# HOBNAIL AND OTHER FRONTIER STORIES

## A CENTURY OF THE AMERICAN FRONTIER

## WITH A FOREWORD BY *NEW YORK TIMES* BESTSELLING AUTHOR TOM CLAVIN

# EDITED BY HAZEL RUMNEY

**FIVE STAR**

A part of Gale, a Cengage Company

Farmington Hills, Mich • San Francisco • New York • Waterville, Maine
Meriden, Conn • Mason, Ohio • Chicago

Hobnail and Other Frontier Stories: Copyright © 2019 by Five Star Publishing, a part of Gale, a Cengage Company.
Kanta-ke © 2019 by James D. Crownover
Rata Remembers © 2019 by Paul Colt
The Times of a Sign © 2019 by Rod Miller
Legend © 2019 by Johnny D. Boggs
Arley © 2019 by Wallace J. Swenson
Grogan's Choice © 2019 by Lonnie Whitaker
Boxcar Knights © 2019 by Steven Howell Wilson
The Bells of Juniper © 2019 by Vonn Mckee
Frank Rule and the Tascosans © 2019 by John Neely Davis
When Tully Came to Town © 2019 by Richard Prosch
The Caves of Vesper Mountain © 2019 by Greg Hunt
Hobnail © 2019 by Loren D. Estleman
The Assassin © 2019 by Patrick Dearen
Apaches Survive © 2019 by Harper Courtland
Spanish Dagger © 2019 by W. Michael Farmer
The Way of the West © 2019 by L. J. Martin
Return to Laurel © 2019 by John D. Nesbitt

## LIBRARY OF CONGRESS CATALOGING-IN-PUBLICATION DATA

Names: Clavin, Thomas, writer of introduction. | Rumney, Hazel, editor.
Title: Hobnail and other frontier stories : a century of the American frontier / with an introduction by Tom Clavin ; edited by Hazel Rumney
Description: First edition. | Waterville, Maine : Five Star, a part of Gale, Cengage Learning, [2019]
Identifiers: LCCN 2019025062 | ISBN 9781432864330 (hardcover)
Subjects: LCSH: Western stories. | Frontier and pioneer life—West (U.S.)—Fiction. | American fiction—21st century.
Classification: LCC PS648.W4 H63 2019 | DDC 813/.087408—dc23
LC record available at https://lccn.loc.gov/2019025062

First Edition. First Printing: December 2019
Find us on Facebook—https://www.facebook.com/FiveStarCengage
Visit our website—http://www.gale.cengage.com/fivestar/
Contact Five Star Publishing at FiveStar@cengage.com

Printed in Mexico
1 2 3 4 5 6 7 23 22 21 20 19

# TABLE OF CONTENTS

Table of Contents

# FOREWORD

## BY *NEW YORK TIMES* BESTSELLING AUTHOR TOM CLAVIN

In the nineteenth century, as people moved west so too did the American frontier. Initially, to the European explorers and the settlers who soon followed in the 1500s and 1600s, North America was one big frontier. It was literally uncharted territory: to the Spanish on the West Coast the land appeared to spread east forever; to the English on the East Coast the frontier to the west seemed to have no end. The concept of "frontier" may not have been created by those first European visitors, but it did become an ideal to be passionately pursued and embraced in a land of seemingly infinite potential.

In the 1700s, the first frontier for those most keen on taming and settling on large swaths of land was what awaited on the other side of the Appalachian Mountains. When Daniel Boone and others cut their way through the Cumberland Gap, they found forests and fields teeming with game and fertile fields begging to be farmed. With Ohio, Kentucky, and Tennessee being settled, it was time to move on, the frontier now beckoning from the other side of the Mississippi River. Especially in the nineteenth century, that boundary separating "civilization" from the frontier kept shifting enticingly west, to the Missouri River, to Texas and Kansas and Nebraska, to Colorado and Utah, to New Mexico and Arizona, until finally, with the wagon trains and telegraph lines and railroad tracks, all of the Lower 48 was connected.

The Oklahoma Land Rush of 1889 was the last great burst

of pent-up energy on a frontier waiting to be claimed. A year later, the U.S. Census showed that the "frontier line," a point beyond which the population density was less than two persons per square mile, no longer existed. With that Frederick Jackson Turner, director of the U.S. Census Bureau, announced that the American frontier was closed. From then on, we've just been filling in the gaps.

Of course, there had been a pesky problem for people looking to embrace the frontier and all its beauty and challenges—the presence of native inhabitants. It cannot truly be said the frontier was virgin or pristine if people already lived in it. And what strange, incomprehensible creatures, ones who looked and dressed differently, spoke any number of languages, performed bizarre rituals, were blithely unaware of land ownership, and who fought with savage brutality. As the frontier shrank throughout the nineteenth century, so too did the world and future of American Indians. The process of exploring and settling and civilizing the frontier was also one of conquest that bordered on—or perhaps simply was—genocide. For most white men and women, the frontier kept moving westward, but for America's original residents the frontier was a circle that kept getting smaller and tighter until only the reservations were left.

Sadly, there could not have been another way. The clash of cultures was too loud and harsh for all to survive and prosper and enjoy the opportunities the frontier offered. Increasing the pressure in the 1800s were the waves of immigrants arriving at the docks of major cities, especially on the East Coast. Some were welcomed by those who had come before; others aimed rickety wagons west, searching for the vast open spaces and big skies that would have been unthinkable options in their native Ireland, Germany, or Italy. America offered promise and the frontier was a promise within a promise. Helping to hammer together many of the communities that suddenly popped up out of the ground like prairie dogs west of the Missouri were people who also spoke different languages but shared that deeply American desire to forge a new life on the other side of the horizon. Perhaps a reason why the immigration issues of today are so intense is that we no longer have that seemingly limitless horizon because, as Turner declared in 1890, there is no more American frontier.

To understand where we were in the nineteenth century and then how we got here can be an academic exercise. Much more enjoyable, though, is to read stories set in that period. Writers' imaginations remain a limitless horizon. But while this may serve especially well practitioners of science fiction who write about worlds we do not (yet) know—a new frontier that may indeed be endless—stories about the American frontier must read and feel authentic. No longer is there a gullible public on the East and West Coasts who will swallow whole the exaggerations, embellishments, and outright fabrications of the dime-store novelist. Today's readers of fiction about the West want to be entertained, yes, but they also want the research, the facts, the authenticity that satisfies intellectually as well as emotionally.

That is why a collection such as this one is necessary as well as a welcome addition to bookshop and library shelves (and Kindles). Each story, from James D. Crownover's "Kanta-ke," set in the very early 1800s, to John D. Nesbitt's "Return to Laurel," taking place as the frontier was becoming history, portrays a piece of America, a specific time and place rendered clearly in addition to action and the beating hearts of characters. In Paul Colt's "Rata Remembers," we are given a unique perspective on the dawn of the Texas Revolution. In "Legend" by Johnny D. Boggs, we are offered a different view of the dime-store novel and its impact. The first sentence in Lonnie Whitaker's "Grogan's Choice"—"Jake hated to think about leaving the dog"—is such a gripper one has to keep reading.

Among other benefits, in Richard Prosch's "When Tully Came to Town" we learn about the inner workings of a mid-1870s newspaper office. In the story "Spanish Dagger" by W. Michael Farmer, we not only learn what Spanish dagger is, and its significance, but enjoy such appealing passages as, "Jordon's face was peaceful, close to smiling, eyes closed. He looked like he was taking a nap except for the black, half-inch diameter hole between his eyes." And of course, one feels all around better for having read anything by Loren D. Estleman, and "Hobnail" in this collection adds to his reputation as one of our finest writers in any genre.

Let's face it, the first goal of this collection is to satisfy the appetite of discerning readers of western fiction. The stories cited and the others in this gathering do that. But when the last sentence has been devoured, we have a sense of having spent a century on the American frontier, when it was still full of promise and an undiscovered country . . . and scary and dangerous and occasionally violent. Well-written and authentic stories give us that picture, full of colors and shades and big enough to cover the entire canvas.

**Tom Clavin** is the author or co-author of eighteen books, among them the best sellers *Dodge City, Halsey's Typhoon, The Last Stand of Fox Company,* and *The Heart of Everything That Is.* The forthcoming *Tombstone* (February 2020) will complete a "frontier lawmen" trilogy that includes *Wild Bill* and *Dodge City.* Visit tomclavin.com for more info.

# A Century of the
# American Frontier
# *1800–1855*

★ ★ ★ ★ ★

# KANTA-KE
# BY JAMES D. CROWNOVER

★ ★ ★ ★ ★

# I
## THE BATTLE OF THE SHAWNEE ARMADA

*1800*

*In an unnamed tavern somewhere in old Pittsburgh sat two Dutch-men of Quaker ancestry . . .*

The first time we noticed him, he was standing in the door to the tavern—more accurately, he filled the doorway, his head above the lintel and only glimpses of light indicated that the door was behind him. I admit to being well into my cups and only heard the noise of his first challenge, but understood it the second time, "I can whip any two o' ye lubbers wi' one hand an' never spill me ale," he roared, waving his tankard and sloshing beer here and there.

"Never thee mind the sailor, Jemmy Hall, play thy dice," Jobe Pike, my hunting partner, demanded. I shook the leather cup and dumped the dice on the table. Jobe chuckled. "Ye lost again, Jemmy, boy," and turning to the serving wench called, "Two more, me girl, Jemmy is buying again."

"And that is the last I will buy tonight," I vowed.

The wench filled our tankards and leaned between us to set them on the table, pressing her ample bosom against Jobe's shoulder and revealing a goodly amount of cleavage for his appreciation.

A tankard slammed down on the table and the sailor grabbed the woman's arm, "Gie me thy pitcher, wench." Holding her by the arm, he grabbed the pitcher and turned it up, spilling ale down his beard and shirt while the woman struggled to be free.

15

Jobe stood and faced the giant. He could have walked under the sailor's outstretched arm with room to spare. "Turn the woman loose," he demanded.

The sailor looked down at the little man and grinned. "That I will, mate." He loosed the woman and with the same motion, slammed Jobe beside his ear with the back of his fist, sending him flying across the table, wiping out two tankards and upsetting the table.

There I sat, holding my mug and no place to set it, so I stood and slammed it into the face of the giant, spoiling his foolish grin. He staggered back a step or two and his eyes widened when he noted that I was fully as tall as he and maybe a stone heavier.

"Thee must not pick on wenches and little men," I said. The pewter mug had collapsed and trapped my fingers against the handle. It would not shake off.

My opponent grunted and sprang at me, arms flailing. I ducked his first swing and met his other fist with my trapped hand. His fist hit the mug and dislodged it from my fingers. It felt like my little finger had stayed with the mug. The way my other three fingers stung when the ale sloshed on them, they must have lost some skin too, but there was not time to look.

Our Sinbad charged, his lowered head striking my chest; arms about my waist pulled me to him and we fell to the floor. I kneed him in the groin and grabbed both his ears to keep his teeth away from mine. He was not as light as other men I had fought, but I was still able to throw him off and rise to my knees. As he came to his knees, I hit him with my injured fist. The blow hurt me more than him.

He grinned when his huge fist connected to my jaw and the world turned blurry. Just before it faded completely out, a pitcher crashed down on my opponent's head.

I awoke lying across the back of the sailor and hearing a low humming in my ear. Sitting up at last, I found the wench sitting on the floor with Jobe's head cradled to her bosom, softly humming and rocking. *They always go for the little man, and here I sit, hurt just as bad—bleeding even—and no one cares.* I stood, and immediately looked for a chair. As my knees folded, someone slipped a chair under me and stayed my return to the floor.

Someone clapped me on the shoulder, "Great fight, friend."

"Never seen nothing like it," another voice said.

"Ah-h-h, two giants and a midget go at it and a woman saves the day," a third disappointed patron said.

My little finger was still attached, but with a new crook in it. There was not much skin from my knuckles to my nails and blood dripped from my fingertips. I wrapped the hand in as clean a cloth as could be found.

The sailor stirred and groaned and the crowd grew quiet, watching the big man return to the land of the living. "Wha' 'appen?" Sinbad's lips were swelling and it was beginning to affect his speech.

I nodded at the battered pitcher on the floor beside him, "That pitcher fell on your head." It lay on its side in a pool of ale. The big man picked it up and took a long pull from it. I declined his offer and he drained it. "Hafa go." He lunged up and teetered in the general direction of the door.

Jobe was showing little improvement in his condition, and it looked like it would be a long recovery for him. I stood and he winked.

"I am going to bed," I said and caught the door when next it spun by.

Outside, the cold fresh night air revived me somewhat and by feeling my way along the wall, found the corner of the building. My first step around the corner brought my foot against an obstacle and I fell across somebody. From his smell, I knew it was not the first time tonight I had fallen on him.

"Wake up, sailor, and go to your ship." He was lying facedown and I shook his shoulder. No response. When I tried to turn him over, my hand brushed the hilt of a knife. The blade was buried between his ribs and there had been little bleeding. I began shouting, "Murder!" It was a long time before a lantern came from the tavern and shone on the scene. The sailor was dead and I was the primary suspect.

Jobe had recovered enough to come see and when the constable arrested me, whispered, "I will have horses ready behind the livery."

The constable shackled me hand and foot and led me to the gaol. "Hold this lantern, prisoner, while I find the right key." He fumbled with the large key ring until he had the right key and unlocked the door, pulling it open. I shoved him in hard and slammed the door, turning the key to lock it. The key ring came apart, scattering keys everywhere. No time to look for the shackle key, I shuffled off down the alley to the back lots and the horses.

"Can thee not get thy shackles off?" Jobe asked.

"No, not in the dark and without making a lot of noise." My horse looked back at me when I sat down sidesaddle. "Shut up and get going before I crack thee one." I'm daft if she did not snicker.

They would expect us to ride south and west, so Jobe led us north beyond the farms and into the Pennsylvania woods. We stopped in the midst of a windfall about midmorning.

"A fine fix this is, no food, no guns, no tools to break thy shackles. What are we going to do? I tell thee now, Jemmy Hall, I will never come to Pittsburgh again. Zanesburg is as much civilization as I will ever want," Jobe vowed.

I laughed. "Mayhap it will be Holderby's Landing if the ale is good and the fur prices fair." With my head and fingers aching and my ankles and wrists chafing, I had to agree with him. "Is not tomorrow the Sabbath? Then the good people will surely go to meeting and stay the day. We shall borrow farmer Fleming's forge and tools and remove these shackles like the angels did Paul and Silas."

Jobe grunted his disgust, "Then we will gather our horses at Holderby's and gear and take the path to Kanta-ke with our silver in our purses."

It would be the first time we returned to the hunt with money in our pockets. There was no place in the wilderness to spend it, so when we came and sold our pelts, we stayed until the money was spent, then returned to the hunt without a shilling to our names. Two hungry men lay on their horse blankets and nursed aching heads. My chafed ankles and wrists and skinned fingers added to my discomfort.

Midafternoon, we moved back toward the settled country and found a farm likely to have a forge and waited for the dawning of the Sabbath. Just before dawn, the farmer came out and turned the calf out with his milch cow, hitched up the buggy, and returned to the house to put on his Sabbath clothes. Soon, they departed; husband, wife, and covey of kids, two boys dangling bare feet off the tailgate.

Hardly had their dust settled before we were in the shed starting the forge. The hinge pins on the ankle cuffs were easy to punch out, but the wrist cuffs were a problem. The farmer would be puzzled when he came back to find his forge warm, but he would understand the next spring when he plowed up the shackles we buried in his field. We took the smallest ham from the smokehouse and left silver for payment. Hard cash in a farmer's hand was as rare as ice in Hades in those days, so we knew he would be happy with it.

"Sneaking about like a murderer chafes as much as those cuffs did," I said to Jobe.

"It is the *truth* of the matter that is important, not what some sheriff *thinks*," Jobe replied. "Ye could hire some barrister to plead thy case and he would take thy silver and horses and traps and guns and present thy case to the judge and shrug when the judge pronounces thee guilty withal. And when thou art hung and dead, he will demand thy clothes for final payment and thou wouldst go before thy maker naked as the day thee were born. Let us return these horses, get our gear, and go."

Two days gone, and the innkeeper had our gear for sale, though we were paid up on our rents. The remorse he showed was for getting caught, not his sins. We left him with the hope that the thrashing he got showed him the error of his ways.

We stole a boat and set it adrift where the young Ohio River turns north in a great loop before it dips south and west in the hope the good sheriff would pursue it while we tramped west through the woods to the river where we had cached our canoe. We thought it prudent to pass Zanesburg with its lovely Betty Zane and its Fort Fincastle in the dark and go on to Holderby's Landing where our horses waited.

Several times in our journey, we were saluted by Indians on the northern shore. They were mostly Shawnee with a few Wyandot and Mingo thrown in. Their bows were not powerful enough for their arrows to reach us, and we taunted them until in one group, a white man in British costume stepped out and shot at us with his musket. The shot fell fifty yards short.

It was surprising how much more accurate our guns were after we changed to rifled barrels and Jobe scrambled to return the Lobster's salute. "Hold steady, Jemmy, while I aim," Jobe said. He scooted down and propped his gun on the gunnel while I back-paddled to hold the canoe steady.

The soldier fired again, cutting the shortfall by half.

The crack-bang of Jobe's shot made me jump and we watched a moment as the shot flew. The Lobster threw his hands up and fell and a second later we heard his cry.

The greatly disturbed Indians gathered around the fallen man and he must have said something about being exposed to the fire, for they suddenly looked our way and ran for the woods, leaving the wounded man to fend for himself. He rolled to his knees, sat up, and climbed his rifle. Crimson stained the back of his white pants from mid-thigh down.

Jobe grunted, "Damme, through and through, it missed the bone."

"He must have moved after you fired," I said sarcastically. We moved on and the Indians came out yelling and gesturing until Jobe scooted down and aimed again.

"Just like magic, they are gone," Jobe said, and we laughed.

We had to go with the river, and the afternoon after our encounter with the British officer, we were again accosted by a larger band of Indians, mostly women and children and a few old warriors. They showed more respect for our guns than before. The river here flowed south, then looped in a big bend and flowed north before again bending south. Before we were out of sight, the Indians were running into the woods, intent on cutting across the neck to greet us again.

"Why do they not get a canoe and come out to meet us?" Jobe asked.

"Who says they do not have one? And do thou really want them to?"

"Just one boat at a time, I mind." We rounded the bend and could see where the river swept on around to the north.

"That is thy idea of a good fight, not the red man's. Their idea of a good fight would be a half-dozen boats converging on us from all directions, which they would gladly do . . ." I stopped mid-thought and turned the canoe sharply for the shore, "Dig deep, Jobe."

In the wilderness if one does not react instantly to an urgent call, he could find real trouble. Jobe dug deep with his paddle and we shot under the overhanging limbs of a willow thicket at the end of the tongue of land. When we were well hidden, he asked, "What is it, Jemmy?"

"How many warriors were in that crowd?"

"Not many . . . thou thinks mayhap the warriors are in an armada!"

"Let us wait and see." We held the drooping willow wands and waited. Our wait was frightfully short, for racing around the bend from behind us came two large canoes with six painted warriors in one and eight in the other. The only weapons they carried were their knives and tomahawks.

Jobe stared. "Damme, Jemmy, damme."

"Shoot the near boat at the waterline," I whispered, "I'll sink the other." They were beyond us before we were ready and both shots were hurried.

"Ready on three," Jobe said, "one . . . two . . . three."

The two shots sounded as one loud bang and we were enveloped in a cloud of smoke trapped under the thick trees.

Cries from the river told us our shots had been on target. Both boats were sinking and the bullets had taken effect on three of the passengers. Jobe's shot had broken some of the frame and we heard the gunwale snap and the boat spilt its occupants into the waters. My target was still afloat, but the confusion on the boat had caused it to turn broadside to the current. The bow pointed straight at us and I took another shot along the near side, hoping to open a long gash in the birchbark skin at the waterline. It must have worked, for the canoe listed to that side and turned over, spilling its occupants, who were swimming in all directions to get to a shore. We had little time to watch them, for two more canoes loaded with men swept into the scene of the fight from downstream, a British soldier in the middle of each boat, with a musket.

"You get the far Lobster this time, the near one is mine," I said. We both aimed and Jobe counted down again, and again the shots sounded as one. Jobe's target slumped forward and the musket tilted overboard before anyone could catch it. My target, alas, was unaffected, though the Indian just behind him fell over and began his long journey to the Happy Hunting Ground.

The smoke was thick and choking around us, and it was a wonder that we had not been discovered because of it. I reloaded quickly and searched for my target. He must have been lying on the bottom of the boat, for I could not see him, though his space in the canoe was not occupied. "Laying down, art thou? Well, we will see about that," and I aimed at the waterline below where he had sat. When Jobe was loaded, I fired. A hole appeared just above the waterline and crimson flowed from it.

"Thou got him," Jobe said.

A splash drew our attention and we saw the last of the other dead soldier as he sank into the river. There were shouts from the lead boat and the front man was pointing at something to our left. Apparently, the wind had released smoke from the willows and the boat was going straight into it. The second boat nosed into the willows downstream from us and we shot out of our cover into the open water. There was no need to urge haste.

Without taking time to turn the boat around, the downstream canoe backed out of the willows. Jobe fired his pistol into the bottom of the boat. As they spun around to parallel our course, I stuck the muzzle of my rifle against the side of the canoe and fired. It blew a large hole and struck the legs of the warrior kneeling there. Hands grappled for our gunnel and Jobe slashed at them with his dirk while I tried to paddle us away from their grip. Abruptly, we were free of the sinking canoe and warriors were swimming for the shore. Jobe began reloading his weapons.

The fourth canoe was flying across the water, closing the gap between us too rapidly for escape. "Hurry, Jobe," I called and spun the canoe crossways of their path. My pistol shot struck the front man in the boat and he fell back against the man behind him, the resulting upheaval rippling the length of the boat. It lost way but remained moving enough to strike us amidships. The bow of the light canoe crumpled just as Jobe fired a load of birdshot into their midst. I heard our boat gunwale crack and saw water flowing to my feet.

Several of the enemy had eaten their last meal as a result of Jobe's shot, and the remaining were too injured to do us damage. We pulled away as the enemy canoe sank.

"Head for the south shore, Jobe, before we sink also," I called. By the time we got to the shore, water was above my ankles and the bow was entirely out of the water. Jobe jumped out and pulled the boat up on the shingle. I hopped out to lighten the load and push the boat as far up on the shore as we could. A hatchet blow on the back end of the canoe allowed the water to escape, hopefully before it ruined anything. We reloaded as fast as we could with an eye out for unwelcome visitors.

The forest was quiet in the gathering gloom of twilight and far across the waters we heard echoes of the wailing of widows, mothers, and sisters for their lost warriors. It was a haunting sound.

# II
## THE CACHE

"What do we do now?" Jobe asked as he shouldered his pack.

"I do not know, but we better do it fast, or we will be the favored guests at a Dutch roasting. One battle we have won, but it is sure we will not win the war."

"Better cache this gear and run," Jobe said. "I figure we are twenty leagues to Holderby's by land and forty by the river."

Looking over our supplies, I could see little we could afford to leave behind. Our one bow to personal comfort would be the keg of fine rum, but that was all that was easily dispensable. "We cannot carry these packs and outrun any pursuit. Our canoe is useless and here we stand on the horns of the dilemma when we should be moving."

"Here is an idea," Jobe said. "Why not leave them the rum?"

I laughed. "Then our journey would be a pleasant walk through the forest."

"Better would be a cruise down the river," he said. He emptied a pack and, opening the powder keg, poured its contents into the pack.

Perceiving his intent, I opened the rum keg as he filled the powder keg half full of water. It took only a moment or two to pour half the rum into it. "Rum, water, and gunpowder," Jobe said with a chuckle, "A deadly combination if the powder stays dry."

Before we refilled the rum keg with water, Jobe said, "Hold there, Jemmy," and handed me our canteens. When both were filled, as solemn as a wake, we each took a swallow of as fine a rum as money could buy in Pittsburgh, and each picked up a keg and plunged into the brush. Jobe was leading and stepped into a hole up to his chest, left by a rotted stump. It turned out to be fortuitous for us.

"How did thou dig a hole so fast?" I asked.

"Fie on thee, hand me up."

"Is there room for thee to set thy keg down in the hole?"

It took a lot of grunting and scooting, but he finally managed to get the keg on the ground. "Can thee set this keg down too?"

"No, and I be on me way out." He stood on the keg and climbed out of the hole. I lay on my stomach and lowered my keg into the hole. It would not slide down beside the first keg, so it sat on top.

Already, Jobe was pushing soil into the hole and soon the hole was filled and in the midst of a bowl-like depression. From other places, we gathered armloads of leaves and twigs and laid them over the bowl. As a last incentive, we sprinkled a cup of rum around on the leaves over the hole. To find the cache would be as child's play to the Shawnee.

Our efforts to cover our tracks in the dark were clumsy at the best, but we had to make it look as genuine as possible. We gathered our packs and started our trek to Holderby's Landing, the cries of the mourners fading away.

"When do ye think they will come?" Jobe asked.

"About sunrise. That is when we will turn around." When it was light enough, we made our passage as invisible as possible and made a wide circle to come back to where our boat lay. From the brush, we could see three canoes pulled up on the shingle, with three people guarding them. The one nearest us was a woman.

"Must have been a bad squaw," I whispered. "Look at the rope around her neck." We were preparing to rush the two men when a call and shouting from the woods drew their attention and they trotted off.

"Now!" Jobe grunted and we ran to the near boat. The woman saw us and ran to the other canoes and pushed them into the river. We heaved our packs into the canoe and pushed it into the water. Jobe was about to cut the tether that tied the woman to the bow when she rushed by him and climbed into the boat amidship, forcing Jobe on the other side to hold the boat level to keep it from swamping. He looked at me with a grin and hopped into the bow. No two men ever paddled as we did. We cruised between the two freed canoes and Jobe secured the tether rope from one while the woman grabbed the other and tied it to the gunwale, rocking us precariously.

"Be still," I demanded.

There was the cry of a small voice and the woman picked up a bundle from between her feet. "We have a passenger and a stowaway, Jobe."

"Do not bother, keep paddling."

The woman sat with her back to me, nursing her child. In polite company, she would have been shamed as naked, for the cloth she wore would not cover her body. It was an unfortunate thing I sat behind her, for she stank—*worse* than an Indian. The thought jolted me, she could be diseased and affect us both. The bottoms of her bare feet were black and crusted. Her thin frock did not hide the welts on her back. Indeed, there were smatterings of blood on the cloth. Her dark hair was a tangle and even from my seat a few feet away, I could see lice crawling, and nits.

Jobe caught a moment and turned to the woman and spoke the Shawnee greeting, to which the woman looked up at him, but did not respond. Jobe blanched, and asked, "Dost thou speak the King's language?"

"What is the matter, Jobe?"

"Her eyes are blue."

It actually took my breath away; we had heard of white captives and seen some who had grown up Indian and happy to stay that way, but this was our first contact with a captive white woman, and it took a few minutes to digest the facts.

"Dost thou speak the King's language?" Jobe repeated. Again to no response.

"Dost thou speak Dutch?" I asked in the language.

After a moment, she nodded her head, but still did not speak. Jobe had turned around to paddle and did not note the nod. "She nodded her head, Jobe, guess she speaks the Mother Tongue." I spoke in Dutch so she could understand and we spoke that language from then on. We were going north in one of those eternal loops this river makes and as we approached the head of the loop, our passenger became agitated and we saw a village. It was set so the villagers had a long view both upstream and downstream.

"That must be the village of her captivity, Jobe. Lie down, woman, and hide thyself." I said it three times before she seemed to comprehend and lay in the bottom of the canoe.

We stayed midstream and very few people came out to watch. There were only two canoes on the bank and I noted there were no warriors in sight. This was a small village.

"All the warriors must have gone upriver to do battle with us," I said. "Little do these people know that all thoughts of war have left their warriors and that they are drunk and stranded across the river. We will get to the Kanawha before mid-afternoon, Jobe. This woman needs some attention, so let us go up that river to our old camp."

"I think thou art right," Jobe answered in English. "I would hate to be downwind very long." He must have gotten a whiff or two.

"Do thou suppose it is a disease?"

"A disease of squalor," he replied.

We paddled well into midafternoon before the mouth of the Kanawha River came into view.

I spoke to the woman, "We are going up that river over there and camp where thou can wash and eat."

She nodded. It was the first time we thought she understood what we were saying. We turned up the Kanawha River and hid the two empty canoes. About a mile up that stream was a small stream that came in from the left. Its mouth was hidden by the willow thicket around it and the only way it could be found was by tracing it from the land. Jobe and I had used it several times and never been bothered by the natives. We found our lean-to intact and unmolested and the long pool in front of the camp looked very inviting.

Jobe and the woman jumped out, and while Jobe pulled the boat to the bank, the woman disappeared into the woods.

"She is not running, is she?" I asked.

"No-o," Jobe said, and pointed to the bundle still in the boat.

We unloaded our gear and began looking through it for things we needed for the woman. It was a good thing, for once, that Jobe was fastidious and wanted to stay clean. He had even bought soap for his weekly baths and I sat out a bar of it with our new shears (we had traded off our old pair for lead) and two new blankets. There was also the buckskin we had brought along. She could make herself some moccasins.

Jobe took up his bow and disappeared into the woods while I lit the fire.

The woman returned and began gathering wood to stock the firepit. The baby gave a little cry and she retrieved it from the canoe and sat on a stump near the firepit nursing the child. I wondered if she was giving enough in her condition.

"I need to cut your hair," I said, picking up the shears.

She nodded and looked at me with those blue eyes. "All," she said.

"All of it?"

"All of it, *all of it.*" Her anger took me aback, but I was glad she agreed with me, and I began snipping and throwing the clippings into the fire. When I paused, she felt of the one-inch long hair that was left and demanded, *"All of it."*

I looked at her and smiled, "Very well, milady." More rummaging in our packs produced my cup and razor and I lathered her head and shaved it to the skin. When I finished, she lay the child down, ripped off her ragged garment, and slammed it into the fire.

Her paps were pink where the baby had suckled, but the rest of her body was incredibly dirty. She was so thin. Her ribs and shoulder blades stood out. How she could still nurse her baby, I will never know. It was obvious the child was hungry most of the time. She grabbed up the soap and a cloth and walked into the creek. Amidst the welts from her knees to her neck were old scars that had healed in some fashion. She had been a captive for a long time. Her nudity in my presence was not untoward under her circumstances; indeed, she needed help in order to get clean and doctored.

When she began washing, I busied myself and set a kettle of water on the fire to warm for the baby's bath. I set a kettle of dried beans cooking for the morrow and turned my attention to the baby. His clothes were not nearly as dirty as his mother's and he was reasonably clean also. His thick black hair showed positive parasite infection and would have to be removed when his mother returned. *Another half-breed. Lord help us and help this child.*

She was still scrubbing her body. "I could wash thy back." My call startled her as if she had forgotten anyone else was around. She almost smiled and almost blushed and then nodded. When I waded out to her, she stood up, her back to me, and handed me the soap and cloth over her shoulder. I began where she had washed her shoulders and very carefully washed away as much of the dirt and old blood as I could. She still had pain when around the fresh wounds. She took the cloth when I had cleaned down to her waist and indicated she could take care of the rest. She still spoke very little, but did tell me her name was Arabella Big Horn and her baby was Curly Big Horn. We called her Belle. She fit into one of Jobe's new shirts and fashioned a skirt from one of the blankets.

Jobe got a fat doe and we stayed there three days, the woman alternating between baths and feasting. We could tell she was stronger and the baby was more content.

"Damme, Jemmy, another half-breed," Jobe whispered once

when the child was nursing.

Canoes leave no tracks nor spoor and we do not know how Belle's Shawnee husband found us. I knew of him when he struck me between my shoulder blades with the blunt end of his tomahawk. I fell with the man on my back pulling my head up by the scalp lock he was intent on taking. His knife had just begun its cut when Belle screamed in anger and plunged a long knife into his lung. My world went black.

I awoke and sat up in time to see Belle heave the man into the canoe. She tried to shove it into the creek and collapsed, sobbing. I stumbled to the boat and saw the naked man lying there on his back, a horrified expression on his face and the bloody end of his phallus protruding from his mouth. I retrieved one of the spare canoes after I had pushed the bier into the current of the river and vowed never to provoke that woman to anger.

We had paddled all night and reached Holderby's near noon the next day—and lo and behold, we had no more than stepped ashore than Jobe was engulfed by the wench from the tavern. Belle peeked from under her scarf in surprise. I could not help but laugh.

We had left Pittsburgh hastily, not waiting on our friends, Jake and Drewery Moss, another hunting outfit, to join us. They had originally come through Cumberland Gap with the rest of the Tar Boilers and lived at Boonesborough for a while, then moved off on their own. Dicey Vincent had run away from her husband and convinced the two of her love for Jobe and they gleefully agreed to take her to him. They passed us while we camped on the Kanawha.

Jobe's enthusiastic welcome must have dampened their fun. Parson Holderby pronounced the wedding vows, whereby Dicey gained a second husband.

It was our intention to leave Belle at Holderby's to return to the towns, but she would have nothing of it because of her shame of having a child. We had to buy two horses for the women to ride.

# III
## KANTA-KE

Holderby's love for silver was fortunate for us for we got bargains on the few items we needed before returning to our hunting grounds. He should have paid *us* to take that sorry keg of rum he sold us. We only stayed a day before moving on out of reach of the constabulary that would have me hanged for murder.

There was a decided coolness between Dicey and Belle at first, but the sight of Belle's scars and the wiles of the baby soon warmed Dicey's heart and they became friends. Belle's modesty returned and we saw her bathe no more. As time passed, she became more at ease with us and talked more.

Our adventure in Pittsburgh had caused us to return to the wilderness midsummer instead of the late fall just before prime fur time. As a result, we had much idle time on our hands. Our "home" was in a walled-up shelter cave on a ledge above the valley floor of a creek that fed into the Licking River. On our first hunt, we had built a cabin and we returned from running our traps one day to find it burned to the ground and our furs carried off on the backs of our horses. That was when we moved up the bluff to the cave. It was large enough to house us on one side and our horses on the other. Dicey was put off by the cave and betook herself to campaign for a cabin. We showed her the ruins of our cabin and Belle convinced her the cave was much safer.

Our quarters were walled up to the ceiling with a stacked

rock wall, and Jobe and Dicey decided to plaster it with mud. They got dirty as pigs and we suspect they took more pleasure in washing off in the creek than anything. When they finished, the wall looked like a part of the earth, effectively hiding our home.

A lot of time was spent in gathering firewood, for it would be sure that we would need much more of it with the women and child. We had built a fireplace and chimney in the back of the shelter when we discovered that the smoke was drawn through a crack high on the wall instead of finding its way out the mouth of the shelter. We never found where it emerged from the ground, but were thankful it was not nearby.

The discovery of a beehive in a red oak some distance from the cave moved me to harvest some honey and beeswax. The women were to send Jobe with containers when he returned from his hunt. Meanwhile, I took my axe and began chopping the tree down.

A sixth sense develops in the wilderness that tells you when danger is near and after half an hour, I got that feeling of being watched.

"Jobe, over here." There was no answer, so I resumed chopping only to have a stronger feeling of eyes on me. With my pistol in my belt, I searched unsuccessfully for a visitor. When I returned to my axe, there not twenty feet away sat a mountain lion, tail twitching and mouth watering. It was plain to see he had a hunger for honey. Keeping one eye on my visitor, I resumed chopping on the tree. Just before the last few chops brought the tree down, I stopped to rest and contemplate my visitor's intentions. Would he share the honey, or was he going to demand the whole crop? There he sat, tail still twitching and a little drool in the corner of his mouth. It was a curious thing and I sailed a wood chip at him just to see what would happen.

The chip had not stopped bouncing when that lion sprang at

me. I had no time for defense with axe or gun, but threw up my fist at his face and rammed it down his throat. The force of his leap bowled me over and I plowed a trench with my head and shoulders with that cat on my chest, gagging and choking on my arm. Blood oozed from his mouth. It was mine. The axe had flown away with the force of his leap and my pistol was gone. The lion stood on my chest, his hind paws clawing for traction to remove himself from me. If he got free, I would be dead, so I kept my fist balled up. His struggles became feeble and he fell over and died with my arm still in his gullet. I passed out.

". . . and that is how I found him, laying there asleep with that lion sleeping beside him, his head on Jem's arm," Jobe was telling the women. "Only the lion was not resting his head, he had Jemmy's whole arm in his mouth, all the way to his elbow.

"That horse almost had a runaway when he smelled blood and cat, but I held him long enough to get a rope on that lion's hind legs and hold Jem while the horse pulled until the lion spit that arm out. He wanted to keep going, but I caught him and laid Jemmy across the saddle. A breeze must have stirred the trees, for that honey tree gave a groan and fell almost on us. Those bees swarmed us and me and horse needed no more incentive to leave the area."

I looked up from the tabletop and grinned at them, "I got ye some honey, miladies." Their pallor puzzled me, until I remembered my arm. It must not look so good. I tried to raise it and the pain caused me to faint again.

When next I opened my eyes, it was to find out what that snip-snipping was and why it was stinging my arm. There was a strong smell of rum in the room, and a pale and determined Dicey was trimming ragged skin from my arm.

Belle was holding my arm still and patted my shoulder, "Hold still, Jemmy, we will be through in a moment."

"Here, Jem, suck on this." Jobe stuck a rum-soaked rag in my mouth.

The snipping stopped and Dicey said, "We have four long cuts to sew up, Jem, and it is going to take some time. Jobe, give him a strong drink and hand me a cup."

The rum was fiery, but not near as fiery as the rum she poured in one of those cuts, returning me to my dreams of lions and honey and pain. When next I heard their voices, Jobe was saying, "One down and three to go, Jemmy, me boy." I bit hard on the cloth.

It was a relief to wake in the night on my pallet. The room was quiet and dark save for a glow from the fire. Soft breathing told me someone was lying behind me, but I neither knew whom nor did I care. The fire drifted away into darkness.

Cool hands touched my brow and Belle was saying, "He has no fever."

"But he does have a hunger," I said.

"We are cooking thy meal as ye speak, Jemmy," Dicey replied.

Curly cooed and kicked on the pallet next to me. There was a sleeping space between us.

"How do thee feel?" Belle asked.

I took stock of myself. "My arm hurts and my mouth has died."

Dicey laughed. "Warm saltwater will help, Belle—or hair of the hound that bit him."

"I shall give him saltwater, the rum is low." Belle smiled at some secret they shared.

"How much rum did I drink?" I asked.

"One cup per cut," Dicey said. She and Belle giggled.

"O-o-oh? And how much did *thou* drink?"

"Only one cup . . ." Belle began.

". . . per stitch," Dicey said and both of them laughed and laughed.

I groaned. "Is there any rum left?" My question only made them laugh harder. Nobody relished a trip to Boonesborough for that rotten whiskey those Tar Boilers brewed.

"There is half a keg left," Jobe said as he entered. "I had to take it away from them before they were out on the floor and I would have had to finish their sewing," he added. "The stress on them was such that they were stone sober when they finished. Indians could have carried all of us away that night, we were so tired."

"That night? Thee means last night, do thou not?"

"Night before last, Jemmy."

I had slept through a whole day and two nights and not even known it. On the third night after, I awoke with a burning fever and one of the cuts on my arm was hot and tender to the touch. It was infected and nothing could improve my condition. Belle and Dicey conferred and Belle disappeared for a while. When she returned, the two conferred again and came to me. "We have another cure, but it will be uncomfortable for thee."

"Something has to be done or I will lose my arm or worse," I said. "Go ahead and try."

They stretched my arm out and Dicey leaned on my upper arm, "Mostly so thou wilt not see," she said.

They cut the first stitch at my elbow and wiped the flux and gore away. After working with it awhile, they reapplied the stitch and wrapped the place up. Other than a little pressure relief nothing changed with my arm. Belle still cooled me with wet cloths to keep the fever down. Late in the night, something stirred in my arm and it felt like something between an itch and a tickle. I stirred, with the intention to scratch only to find that a string restrained my good arm. Immediately, Belle awoke and asked, "What is it, Jemmy?"

"My arm—"

"Do not scratch, it is the cure working. As long as it tickles, it is curing thee. If it stops, we will have to open the wound again." Thus began a time of torment, but the arm began improving and my fever subsided little by little. Belle and Dicey monitored my arm closely and when the tickling stopped, they opened the wound a little bit and took out two dark elongated eggs. We put them in a cup and watched them turn into—for me—beautiful blue-tail flies. From that time on, the arm healed up nicely.

Jobe and Dicey harvested much honey and wax and we had the luxury of candles. Belle had watched over and cared for me that whole time. When I was well enough, she made to move back to her bed, but I asked her to stay and she has. I know little of love, but much of a brave and true heart.

# IV
## AUX ARCS

*1803*

The Great Warrior Path is a trail between the Shawnee and Cherokee lands. It is used by the two tribes to raid upon each other, for they were ever enemies. In the fall of the second year of the women, a large force of Cherokee warriors bent on raiding the Shawnee was accidentally met on the Great Warrior Path by a large force of Shawnee warriors hunting Cherokee scalps. The woods were full of Indians hunting Indians and both sides killing whites when they found them. Hunting was impossible. In the middle of all that fighting, a small Shawnee party found our cave.

Jobe finished reloading and licked his front sight. "Did not take them long to discover our rifled guns covered more ground, did it?" We allowed the Indians to drag away a fallen warrior— one less for us to bury.

"It will not be long before the rest of the tribe gets here and our goose will be cooked," I said. "We need to leave now."

"We are nearly ready," Belle called. They had loaded the packs while we held off the Indians. The last thing we wanted was to be cornered in this shelter, and we found that a long passage could be made from the stable along the cliff face and behind huge boulders. The first thing we did with a new horse was to train him to use the passage.

"We leave at sunset," I said. Meantime, we fashioned a bomb out of gunpowder and gravels and hung it in the chimney with a trip-string attached to a partial keg of rum. It would drop the bomb into the fire.

"Sure hate to use up that powder," Jobe said.

"We have enough left and it will serve us well." We sent the women to the stable to wait on us.

"Here they come, Jemmy." There were eight of them spread in an arc, and if we stayed too long, the fight would be hand-to-hand. We shot the two Indians closest to the stable with our pistols, leaving the rifles loaded and ready.

"Run, Jobe." We both rushed to the stable and moments later watched as the savages entered the cave. Two entered our living rooms and shortly gave a shout that brought the rest of the warriors. Their happy chatter was cut off by a terrific explosion that blew out the wall of the house. The interior wall leaned, rumbled, and collapsed inward, burying the victims.

"Rest in peace, vermin." Jobe did not care for Indians. "Where to now?" Jobe asked, though he well knew.

"West," I answered. And thus began a trek of several months across the wilderness. We crossed many frozen rivers that winter, including the Mississippi, and followed a trail we found going southwest until it came to a small white settlement on the banks of a clear-running river and at the eastern foot of a range of hills. Several men came out to meet us while women stood in doorways, little eyes peeking from behind their skirts.

"Welcome, strangers," one man said in the King's tongue.

"Thank you," I answered. "What is this place?"

"We call it Flee's Settlement after the man that greeted us when we got here," another man said. He extended his hand and we shook. "Come on to the settlement, you can use old Flee's cabin, he'll never use it again." They turned and led us into the midst of the cabins.

"Tar Boilers—and away out here," Jobe whispered in Dutch.

As if in answer, one of the men said, "We left Boonesborough when it got too crowded there. Game's a lot more plentiful here."

"In those hills?" I asked pointing to the mountains west of the settlement.

"Yes, the Ohs Arcs Mountains, home of the Osage Long Hunt—and the white men of Flee's, if we do not get caught."

"Just like Kanta-ke?" Jobe asked.

"Ju-ust like it," another man answered. "Say, would you have any tobacco on you? Our crop froze out."

"Because he was too damme lazy to pick it, and his wife did not have time," Jobe hissed under his breath.

"Say, what year is this?" one of the men asked.

"Nought three a couple of months ago," Jobe replied.

"Is Adams still president?" another asked.

"Lost to Jefferson in nought one," I said.

"Jefferson, huh? Partial to Washington, meself,"

"Me too," I agreed. They plied us with questions about things in the east, but none of it seemed to be very important to them. None of it affected their lives. It was even doubtful that they knew they were in Spanish territory and not the United States.

We arose a few days later aware that some sort of disturbance was going on in the settlement. Several of the men were facing a man on horseback in a strange uniform. He was backed by several foot soldiers with long muskets and bayonets. Jobe and I stood behind the corner of a cabin and listened. The officer was speaking English with an accent so heavy as to be unintelligible. I understood part of it the third time he said, "You are all trespassers and I place you under arrest in the name of His Imperial and Royal Majesty, Napoleon Bonaparte, of France. Surrender your arms and prepare to leave this place."

"Damme Frogs." Jobe hated Frenchmen.

If the grins on the frontiersmen faces did not mean anything to the officer, they said volumes to the two of us.

The officer turned and rode aside and called an order to his men, who brought their guns to the ready. As they prepared to aim at the next order, Jobe shot the officer off his horse and the frontiersmen greeters charged the soldiers. I shot the sergeant standing beside the squad, but that was the last chance to use a gun in that mix-up.

Our two women took our rifles and began reloading them while we joined our comrades, dirk against bayonet. It was a bloody fight, but the French soldiers held no advantage over hardened frontiersmen, and soon the battlefield was quiet.

Dicey and Belle handed us our guns, looked us over, and declared our wounds paltry. They hurried past us with bandages and hot water to help the wounded. Not a Frog was standing, nor did any need bandages.

"Great fight, Jemmy Hall," Jobe shouted and threw his hat in the air. We looked around, but there was nothing more to do except bind the wounded. One man in the settlement died from his wounds.

It seemed we had gone as far as was practical. South of Flee's were vast empty lowlands full of swamps and forests, and west was the Osage hunting ground of Aux Arcs. Hunting was good in and out of the hills, and the hide harvest was generous. Our neighbors proved to be good people we could share our lives with, even though they spoke a strange English tongue. Jake and Drewery Moss joined us two years later.

Belle and Dicey both proved fruitful and it was not long before two Dutch cabins were brimming with children. We continued the Long Hunts every winter, contending with every manner of Indian, the Osage being most numerous and bothersome. Every year or two we hauled our furs to St. Louis, always taking enough men that no one bothered us. We never lost a fur.

## AUTHOR'S NOTE

There were at least three regions all tribes set aside as holy and hunting grounds; He Sápa (Black Hills), Aux Arcs, and Kanta-ke. No tribe, clan, or individuals were allowed to live permanently within these areas. As a result, they became dark and bloody battlegrounds.

Frontiersmen in the northern colonies were not contained by a mountain barrier, but traveled west on the Ohio River before the pioneers of the southern colonies discovered the Cumberland Gap.

Flee's Settlement, at the falls of the White River, continued to grow. It was in the territory of three nations, Spain, France, and United States, and part of three territories, Louisiana, Missouri, and Arkansas. The Ozark Mountains remained an isolated, almost trackless wilderness into the twentieth century.

Inside every major event in history are hundreds of smaller events performed by men and women with little notice from the historian. **James Crownover** believes that these unnoticed people and the aggregate of their labors are the essence of any great event in history. These are the people he wants to recognize and write about.

★ ★ ★ ★ ★

# Rata Remembers
## by Paul Colt

★ ★ ★ ★ ★

*Me llamo Rata.* I know no other name. As you know, we rata keep our tales to our own kind. We take our daily comings and goings, feedings, mating, and sleeping with no need to remember them in stories we repeat among ourselves or recite for the benefit of others. We live on the fringes of other societies, scavenging for scraps, foraging where we are not welcome. This is our lot in the larger order of life. I come forward with this tale for it is an extraordinary remembering. I am gifted among rata, though the events I observed in these days are beyond even my understanding. Still I observed them. They ring loud in the passage of many seasons. I remember the old mission. I cannot escape the memories witnessed there. I tell them here that perhaps you may hear, remember, and understand. Not many of your kind survived to tell this tale. None witnessed these events as I did.

I came to the mission in the time of the sandal-feet friars. Here our days passed in peace, so long as we kept to the dark places when the two feet were about. The mission afforded many places we took refuge. Corners under the sinks in the scullery, between and under casks in the wine cellar, and dark recesses of the stable with its loft. I favored the wine cellar and stable. I preferred the soothing scents of white oak barrels and straw to the harsh wet scent of lye soap under the sinks. Still, all these places afforded safety and refuge.

Caught in the open by day, one might be forced to scuttle

away from some two feet with a broom. These risks, however, were small for one such as I, gifted in guile and craft. I easily avoided them, by simply abiding the rhythm of the bells. Bells called the friars to a place they call chapel for morning prayers and evening vespers. I ventured there once. A golden place, colored in light, scented in beeswax and the long past presence of some perfumed smoke. There they prayed and sang their hymns, announcing times safe for foraging. Safe from the sandal feet, not so from *El Gato*.

El Gato roamed the mission day and night between naps. Big and black with yellow eyes, the cat moved with stealth on pad-ded paws. Padded yes, but armed with sharp claws and long pointed teeth. The cat regarded us as natural prey to stalk and pounce upon at any moment. We foraged with ears and noses alert. Always we hewed to our defenses, a nearby safe haven and knowledge of El Gato's habits. Did I mention he sleeps? He does. He prowls from one nap to the next at various times and places. Knowing his habits freed us to forage when the bells proclaimed the proper times.

That is not to say our feedings never encountered the cat. The monster was quick and cunning. We lost more than a few of our number to his prowling. Still, in the natural order of things, it thinned the colony, making the food supply more plentiful for those of us clever enough to survive. Did I mention I live by guile and craft? I do. And so I minded El Gato's habits. His presence merely added spice to my foraging adventures.

Adventure we did. Feeding in the refectory where we found scraps from the table. Table scraps could be most tasty, though their presence uncertain. One day the refectory might yield a bountiful banquet. The next swept spotless to famine. Thank-fully the stable was certain to be stocked with grain for the livestock. There could be found burlap sacks. These we opened by gnawing a small hole in the threads, releasing a feast. If one chose his sack wisely, many days might pass before his sack was selected to feed the stock. Did I mention clever begets wisdom? It does. My sack always made the choicest selection.

At various times, barefoot *peones* came to the mission. Here they were greeted by the friars with gracious hospitality and generous feedings. Peones squat in the dusty plaza to eat their fill of frijoles and tortillas. By night we foraged the scraps they dropped. These were as tasty as refectory fare and never swept clean. What is a little dust to such splendid repast? *De nada.* So passed halcyon days in comfort and plenty little troubled by small risks. All in peace and serenity until the day of the coming.

The coming arrived on winter chill. Winter was expected. This one intruded with unfamiliar sights, sounds, and scents. It came with many two feet in blue coats and fine leather boots. They called themselves Texians. They brought with them heavy iron trees, felled on wooden caissons. These they hoisted to the top of the mission walls with heavy ropes accompanied by much shouting and grunting. Sacks of round iron fruit were carried and stacked in their place along with wooden kegs handled with much care. The kegs reminded me of the wine casks in the cellar. They smelled not of sweet grapes and white oak. These smelled of bitter salt, offering no temptation to feed. In days, the mission walls bristled with iron trees the two feet called cannon.

I thought all this curious. I might even have welcomed the change for the foraging that fell from the plates of so many new feeding two feet, except for the air. The restful peace of the friars given way to groans, curses, and sweat. Unlike the gentle friars, these two feet were rough and coarse with sweat scented of something unknown to me. A sour odor flavored the air with promise of some grim tension. I turned this unfamiliar taste on my tongue. In coming days, I would learn to know it more and well.

More Texians arrived with the two feet I called Big Knife. In the days that followed, I heard him called Bowie. He carried his blade as one in authority. The motley rabble who came with him wore moccasins, shabby boots, buckskins, and ragged sweat-stained filthy clothing. Big Knife Bowie climbed the mission walls and walked among the cannon trees, nodding some silent approval. These two feet too smelled strange. The scent of some impending danger grew stronger with these new arrivals.

El Gato is a danger I understand. Two feet danger too is well known to me. I rely on guile and craft to serve me well. I am confident in the face of these dangers. This new danger I did not understand. This danger visited on the two feet. Could cannon, knives, and fire-sticks of every length and size make a craft to protect them? I sensed no confidence in these, only strange sour scent. I sniffed more change in the hot dusty wind. Change with foreboding known to your kind.

Twelve nights foraging passed. With so many mouths to feed, victuals grew scarce. We noticed the paucity of droppings and scraps we found to quench our hunger. A young long knife arrived with still more two feet in blue coats and fine boots this time mounted on horses. These horses filled the stable and ate into the grain supply. It would not be long before even your humble Rata would feel the pinch of hunger.

The young long knife Texians called Travis carried his blade with the air of one in authority. Big Knife Bowie regarded Long Knife Travis with suspicion. I sensed tension between them. I puzzled over it, searching for something in my experience to explain it. Two male rata might come to such feelings over mating rights to a female in season. Little got in the way of such feelings, little save for a danger such as El Gato. Would these two put aside their mating fits for the danger gathering like clouds building before a storm beyond the mission walls?

Five forages later I encountered a new threat. A raccoon sat brazenly on a table in the plaza. These creatures possess voracious appetites. It would consume still more of what little was left to us to eat. I watched for a time, curious the raccoon did not forage in the night as was their custom. It slept. At the coming of day, I took refuge in the stable loft where I could observe the intruder. It did not forage. It did not take shelter. I grew suspicious. Could the raccoon be dead? A tall two feet I had not seen before rolled out of his sleeping blankets nearby. He approached the coon, carrying a long fire-stick. I brightened at the prospect he might shoot it. They are voracious foragers, you know. Such was not to be. This two feet picked up the coon and placed it on his head. I twittered with laughter, quickly catching myself lest I give away my presence to El Gato. This coon would not challenge us for food. This coon gave his skin for two feet's cap.

Fifteen forages passed amid the bustle and commotion of much preparation. The blue coat two feet marched and drilled with their fire-sticks. They took turns climbing the walls to tend the cannon trees and watch. Big Knife Bowie's two feet watched and waited. Watching, searching, always on the lookout. Somewhat more must be coming. But what?

The sixteenth night I foraged in the stable at a discarded grain sack. The sack, empty for the purpose of feeding horses, contained kernels caught in the seams and spilled where the stable boy tossed it. It made a meager meal; but in these days, a meal was a meal and all to be taken for it. As I licked up the last lap, I noticed quiet. Quiet sounded alarm, sending my instincts a twitter. Somewhere in the darkness a horse stomped. Straw rustled some response. *El Gato?* One never knows in such cases, but one so gifted as I never takes chances. I scampered through a chink in a stall door just as the monster struck. Dare

I say my tail slipped through outstretched claws? Did I mention I am quick? I should. I ducked between a horse's hooves and I scuttled up a beam to refuge in the loft. Had El Gato anticipated my hiding place, he might have cut me off before I could reach it. As it happened, I knew where I was going. The cat did not.

As morning broke, I settled into my hole in the stable loft. I caught my breath, heart pounding in my breast. The encounter closer than I cared where the cat might be concerned. It was then I noticed two feet scrambling in every direction bent to some grim purpose. No laughter, little talking, some shouting. Blue coats and Bowie's ruffians took positions on the walls; some with fire-sticks, others near the cannon trees. It was only then I observed in the gray light of dawn, two feet in red-breasted coats, more than your humble rata could count, massed in the distance beyond the walls. This must be the reason for all the preparation, watching, and the source of the strange scent given off by the two feet. But why?

A rider wearing gleaming black boots and much gold braid across his red-breasted coat approached the gates on a great white horse, carrying a white flag. He exchanged words I could not hear with Long Knife Travis. The rider wheeled his horse and galloped off to rejoin the red-breasted line in the distance. Word murmured along the walls in hushed tones. I strained to hear. *Santa Anna*. What means this Santa Anna? Soon enough I would know.

Long Knife Travis turned to the nearest cannon. The two feet there touched a smoking taper to it. A fearsome roar of fire and smoke made my heart stop. A blast force of sound washed over me, blinding me with an acrid flash of terror. The cat, the cannon, my poor heart; the beat scarce contained in my breast. Bitter smoke scent hung in the air cleared on the breeze, leaving something behind. A scent that did not wash away in the wind. I sniffed. I tasted. The scent I did not recognize mingled with my own terror. I now knew it for fear. Fear only grew stronger with waiting and watching through the long days of preparation.

That night I foraged in the refectory. I found precious little to feed on. Crumbs of bread and cheese. Scared and hungry, I took shelter in the wine cellar. What followed fairly frightened the life out of me. For days and nights smoking thunder rained out from the mission cannon. More thunder rumbled in the distance as a summer storm gathering force. The air above whined in great screaming rushes. Powerful thumps shook the earth, rattling hollows in the pit of my stomach. I judged these the fruit from Santa Anna cannon called ball and grape. Grape. These grape made no wine. They sloshed wine in the casks above me. Thick adobe walls trembled and cracked. Dust fell from the rafters and hung in the air as a fog. The smell of fear tasted bitter and strong. Soon other scents flavored the fetid air. Choking powder smoke, iron blood-smell mingled with sweet, putrid death.

Starved after days of constant bombardment, I ventured out. The refectory yielded no food. Massive holes gaped in the roof. I took a chance on the stable. There I found a little grain and made way to my hole in the gray light before dawn. As I scampered across the loft I came upon a lump of shattered remains. The hackles at the back of my coat stood on end. El Gato lay twisted, barely recognizable, a grotesque mask in death. I remembered the fearsome threat he once posed. No more. Fighting two feet show no mercy to the living, even those who have no part in their fight. I cannot say I mourned my former adversary, though I noted but for the trickery of fate, the dead might have been me. Guile and craft gave no quarter to the forces unleashed in this fight. I hurried to my hole.

By the first light of dawn, I looked over the plaza and along the walls. Everywhere death lay by destruction. The plaza pocked in craters. Walls cracked and breached. Two feet bodies lay where they fell. Wounded huddled bandaged and bleeding. Still two feet stood at their stations. I recognized Long Knife Travis and the Coonskin called Crockett. I did not see Big Knife Bowie. Beyond the walls, storm clouds of Mexican black boots moved about as shadows covered over by rising dust; they drew up a great line on all sides.

I sensed more fighting to come. Why? Why do these two feet kill each other? Why? Are they not the same kind? Rata do not kill our own kind. Oh, we males may fight over breeding rights. Such things improve the species. But here there are no breeding rights. El Gato was our natural enemy. He would kill us for food. That we understood. But here there is no food worth fighting over. Here there is only blood and gore and horror visited upon one's own kind. As I ruminated over these disturbing imponderables, a clarion call split the morning stillness. A guttural roar rose from the ranks of the red-breasted line in the distance as it surged forward.

Thunder smoke spewed a storm of ball and grape on the Mexican advance, throwing great gouts of dirt against pink and blue morning sky. Coonskin Crockett and two feet on the wall fired their long-sticks and reloaded at a fevered pace. Smoke hung a blue haze over the walls. The Mexican advance faltered. The Texians rallied their cries, pouring still more fire and thunder on the assault. I sensed a sweet hint of hope.

The Long Knife Santa Anna mounted on his great white horse rode to the fore of his line. Gold braid flashed on his red-breasted coat. He circled his horse, brandishing his knife gleaming in sunlight. The Mexican line stiffened. Raising a primordial roar, they rushed forward. Texian cannon and fire-sticks rained shot and charge on the Mexican line, ripping gaping holes in their ranks. Still the Mexicans came, more filling holes for the fallen. Texian thunder could not blunt the attack spurred on by this willed force Santa Anna.

Attackers battered barred mission doors. Red-breasted coats threw ladders against the walls, cracked and breached by days of bombardment. They climbed faster in number than the fire-sticks could reload. Coonskin Crockett used his fire-stick to push a ladder off the wall, sending those climbing screaming their fall. Climbers on other ladders made it over the wall. More red breasts followed with a roar. Long Knife Travis drew his blade to meet attackers breasting the walls. He impaled one at the top of the wall and pushed his ladder away. Those climbing the ladder behind howled as they fell. Black boots clamored over the wall at Long Knife's back. The first red breast leveled a pistol. It spit fire and smoke. Long Knife Travis fell, his blade clattering off the wall, broke in the fall.

I sensed peril in the harsh scents of powder smoke fog. Day or no, I scurried down from the loft and raced for the only safety I could think of, the chapel. There the light was no longer golden, no longer colored in hues. Colorless gray cast a pall over the once warm restful setting. Beeswax and any remembrance of perfumed smoke too were gone. Here I smelled more dread, blood tasting death, and bitter smoke. Battle sounds raged in the plaza beyond the adobe. I hid beneath a bench near the place where friars prayed. I have no understanding for the meaning of their prayers, but from what little I knew of them, it seemed some were needful that day.

I heard running feet. Desperate Texians poured through the chapel doors. They stacked heavy wooden benches against the doors and took cover behind other benches, bracing for further attack. Fire-sticks and long knives leveled at the chapel doors. Boots sounded beyond. A heavy ram battered iron bound doors. Stout doors held, bowed, splintered. Red breasts poured into the breach. Texian fire-sticks erupted, deafening roar filled the chapel. The first Mexicans fell. Others filled the doors in their place. Long knives and fire-sticks turned clubs met the rush. Mexicans fired pistols and thrust fire-sticks bright with blades fixed. Texians fell. Blood-splattered death flowed all around.

Smoke burned my eyes, sulphuring the air, resting bitter harsh on my tongue. The chapel filled with blood scent and death. No safety here, my guile screamed. I scampered through a hole behind the altar before the black boots could do me harm. I ran to a sewer drain under the wall. Dark and wet, I welcomed human stench that did not kill. The sewer emptied beyond the walls. I raced to refuge, hollowed out in the roots of a nearby cottonwood tree. There I listened to the waning sounds of battle.

Cannon fell silent. Assault ladders stood here and there, stark sentinels now to mission doors thrown open to receive the conqueror's quest. Smoke spread a pall over the battle-scarred mission. Dust clouds churned by storms of black boots colored the smoky underside dun gray. Two feet shouts mingled triumph with death throes. Fire-sticks, pistols, and knives finished the grisly work of total defeat. Battle sounds faded away to the moaning and wailing of the wounded and dying.

Presently a new sound thrummed from within. Drums. I peeked my nose above my hole to a curious sight. Heavily armed red breasts marched by twos behind the drummer. These were followed by the Coonskin Crockett and a few other Texians. All these were accompanied by still more armed black boots. Last the gold-braided Santa Anna mounted on his white horse followed them out to the mission wall. There Crockett and the other Texians were lined up with their backs to a still-standing section of mission wall. Mexican black boots drew up in rank. Santa Anna ordered aim. The drum rolled. The Texians stood firm. Santa Anna raised his long knife. The blade flashed. Black boot fire-sticks charged. The Texians fell, Coonskin no more.

I let go a breath I'd forgotten I held and wondered at what I witnessed. These Texians fought and fell bravely, no chance against so many. Why did they fight? Even your humble rata knew when to run. Why did they die? Why? It must be something for your kind to know. Clever that I am, I confess I cannot know. I do know such a fight must be remembered. I tell you this tale so you may know; and remember the old mission they call . . . Alamo.

**Paul Colt** takes a fanciful departure from his critically acclaimed, award-winning historical dramatizations and western fiction to offer a unique remembrance of the Alamo. Inspired by his wife, Trish, "Rata Remembers" is Paul's first short story.

★ ★ ★ ★ ★

# The Times of a Sign
# BY ROD MILLER

★ ★ ★ ★ ★

The truth of it is, that advertising sign on my place of business ain't nothin' but bullshit. It says:

FOR SALE

MULES & OXEN

BREEDING STOCK

Now, anybody with a lick of sense knows mules can't breed. Leastways not so's it amounts to anything. Besides, most all of them that needs it is gelded, anyhow. And the only ox worth a damn is a steer, which as everybody knows can't breed neither—they just plain ain't got the tools for the job.

It all comes down to that fool sign painter I hired way back when to make the sign. Had he put a little flourish or fancy or some such between them last two lines it would've worked out fine. But when I complained, he said he was too busy for such nonsense and wouldn't do it 'less I paid to have the whole thing done over.

But with things the way they is in Independence, and as they have been since I first hung up that sign, I been sellin' every mule and ox I can get growed up enough to pull a wagon as quick as, well, I can get them growed up enough to pull a wagon. So, I guess it don't make no never mind about that sign.

You see, it's like this. Independence is the place where most folks wantin' to set out for the western territories—Oregon and California and whatnot—gets outfitted. Then there's all them freight trains wheelin' down the Santa Fe Road like they been doin' for years. Fact is, that Santa Fe Road is why I'm in the mule business in the first place. I got into the ox business later, but that don't matter for now. What you want to know is how I came to be doin' what it says on that sign I'm doin', so that's what I'm a-goin' to tell you.

Before I go on, I reckon I had best clear up that sign business. See, we do sell breeding stock—brood mares that will birth baby mules if bred to a jack—but we don't sell jacks no how, no way, them bein' the very lifeblood of my business—and we sell cows that'll produce passable calves that might make an ox one day. And we don't sell no bulls, neither. Good Durham bulls that throw sizable calves ain't that easy to come by, so when we get a good one, he ain't goin' nowhere.

'Course I don't let on that the mares and cows we do sell is the ones that ain't quite up to snuff, but that's just horse tradin'.

I already told you my name is Daniel Boone Trewick. No relation to ol' Daniel Boone his own self, but my daddy thought him a hero and thus hung the name on me. Most everybody calls me Boone, save my wife, who calls me Danny—which I don't prefer, but it's what she called me back when we was young and I guess she can't get over the habit.

What I ain't told you is that I got a partner in this here business, his name bein' Juan Medina. Now, Juan, he's a Mexican from out in California I hooked up with, but that was before . . . Aw, hell, I guess I had best quit ramblin' and just start at the beginning of this here story.

What happened was, me and a girl name of Mary Elizabeth Thatcher was sweet on each other back when we was young—me bein' about sixteen at the time, and her bein' fourteen or maybe fifteen. This bein' back about '39. Her daddy was Reverend Thatcher, and he had no use for me—or any other boys, of

which there were plenty—sniffin' around young Mary Elizabeth. One day up in Liberty, where we all lived, we was in the
reverend's carriage house sittin' in a buggy gettin' to know one
another, you might say, when the reverend caught us at it.

Well, he yanked me out of that buggy and went to wailin' on
me, which was not to my likin'. So, with me havin' got my
growth up to where I was of a size where I didn't have to take
such from anybody, I returned the favor.

Hangin' there on a peg on the wall was a singletree, which
sort of fell right into my hand, and I walloped Reverend
Thatcher upside the head with it. He went down like a poleaxed
steer in the slaughter yard and Mary Elizabeth started in to
yowlin' like a scared cat and the reverend was layin' there with
blood pourin' out of his head like used grass and water out of
the back end of an incontinent cow and me seein' nothin' but
trouble to come from it all, I lit out of there and hit the road for
Independence and never looked back. Never even slowed down
to say goodbye to my ma and pa nor nothin', which didn't matter much on account of them havin' so many other kids
scratchin' around the place that they might not even notice I
was gone anyhow.

'Course, I didn't stay around Independence long, on account
of it bein' near enough to Liberty that the Clay County law
would certain sure come there lookin' for a murderer. Per-
chance, there was a freight outfit ready to pull out for Santa Fe
and they hired me on as a herder. So it was that I come to
spend day after day a-horseback on an old high-withered
swaybacked nag of theirs, chafin' my backside on a worn-out
Mexican saddle they found for me somewheres, followin' a
bunch of oxen that they took along to take over for them that
lamed up or tired out and needed a rest from them big freight
wagons they pulled.

I had no notion at the time of my leavin' what I was to do

with myself once I got to Santa Fe—my only purpose was to avoid gettin' strung up for killin' Mary Elizabeth's daddy. But somewhere along the way, I took up thinkin' about them mountain men and free trappers that I'd read about and had seen from time to time in Missouri on their way to someplace or another, and thought to look into becomin' one of them. When we got to Bent's Fort out on the Arkansas, there was some of them mountain men hangin' around, and listenin' to their stories made me want to try that way of livin' for sure. 'Course bein' young and dumb and all I had no idea how to go about doin' such a thing, but it was in my mind.

Anyhow, after makin' it on out to Santa Fe and collectin' my pay—which amounted to more money than I ever held in my hand at one time before—I heard tell there was mountain men livin' up at a place called Taos, on account of them bein' up there and out of the way, the Mexican government left them alone.

So it was off to Taos I went. Once I got there, I met up with a fellow with a wooden leg named Pegleg Smith, who, I was told, was one of the best of the trappers ever there was. Him and some others let me know right off that the times when a man could make decent livin' trappin' fur in the mountains was gone. Pegleg his own self was lookin' to keep his belly full in other ways, one of which was goin' partners with a man makin' whiskey that come to be called Taos Lightnin' by them that got struck by it.

But at present, Pegleg and Old Bill Williams and some others was outfittin' for a trip out to California to steal horses and mules and bring 'em back to Santa Fe and sell 'em at a handsome profit. They asked me along with the promise of a share in the takin's, and me havin' nowhere else to go and nothin' else to do at the time, seein's as my becomin' a trapper wasn't in the offing, I did so.

Even bein' in Mexico as I was, there was too many Mexicans in on that horse-stealin' deal to suit me. I could see right off it weren't so, but I could not get rid of the notion that those people was by nature lazy and shiftless. And then when we got to this place called Abiquiu, there was this black man name of Jim Beckwourth came along. Me and him ended up in a dispute when he told me to do some thing or another and I let him know that where I come from, white folks *give* orders to his kind, not *take* 'em. Near as soon as I said it, I found myself on my back with his foot planted in my middle. But it turned out all right on account of he was one of them—a mountain man and trapper, I mean—and he was one of them that cooked up this here foray to California we was settin' out on.

And if it weren't bad enough to be in cahoots with Mexicans and a black man, a ways up the trail we hooked up with a bunch of Indians—Utes they was—and one of 'em, called Wakara, was as much in charge of things as was Pegleg or Old Bill or that black fellow Beckwourth.

I'll tell you, they got a whole different way of doin' things out there than what I growed up with here in Missouri.

Well, anyway, we went on out to California followin' a wandering road that Mexican traders used. That path has since come to be called the Old Spanish Trail, even if it ain't that old and it ain't Spanish. We stole thousands of horses and mules and jackasses from California ranches and brung 'em back, just as planned—save for leavin' what must've been a thousand dead horses layin' out in the desert from pushin' 'em too hard, so as to avoid bein' overtaken by a posse of them Californios. I'll tell you, I seen things on that trip I never even knew to dream about, and was involved in all manner of adventures.

But all that's a story for another time.

There is one part I got to tell, and that's how Juan Medina came to be here in Missouri in this business enterprise of ours.

See, Juan is a Mexican from California and he worked on one of them ranches we stole horses from back then. 'Cept he wasn't there at the time we did it on account of him bein' in jail owin' to a dispute he had with the brother of a girl he was sweet on, which ended up with him bein' locked up 'til they sprung him to ride with the posse that was chasin' after us.

For reasons he'd rather I not talk about, he left off with that posse when it give up the chase and he followed us and throwed in with our outfit. Him and me spent a heap of time together on the trail and he learned enough white-man talk from me to where we could palaver some. Him bein' a hand with horses and mules the like of which you ain't never seen gave me an idea—I took a notion to take my pay for that horse-thievin' trip in mares and jacks—*yeguas y machos,* Juan celled 'em—and drive 'em back here to Missouri and raise mules.

There was always plenty of plowin' and whatnot to be done on Missouri farms, and some of the outfits headin' out the Santa Fe Road used mules, so I figured sellin' off what mules we could raise would be easy enough and make us a right smart of money besides. And I had seen right off that them California mules we stole was a hell of a lot better than what was raised here in Missouri back then, and it was all on account of them California *machos.* They was big, strong jackasses and they throwed big, strong mules.

Juan, he had nothin' else to do and nowhere else to go so he allowed as how he'd come in on the deal. I wasn't all that sure about throwin' in with a Mexican, but I seen how good he was handlin' critters, and he knowed a hell of a lot more 'bout *machos* and mares and mules than what I did, so I reckoned it was worth the risk.

What I didn't know at the time was what was 'bout to happen back in the States. I'll tell you more on that later on.

Anyhow, by the time we got that herd back to Santa Fe, I had talked it all over with Pegleg Smith and Old Bill Williams and them, and we had come to terms on my share of the takin's. Juan, meantime, had picked us out a nice string of mares and *machos*—some of 'em he'd had a hand in raisin' back on that California ranch he come from. I ain't sayin' how many head I got for my share, as that ain't no man's business but my own. Juan, he didn't get nothin' as he wasn't part of the outfit, but I took him on as equal partner anyhow.

You will recollect that I had gone out west with a freight outfit on the road to Santa Fe. But, fact is, I spent the whole trip in a cloud of dust followin' the spare oxen and, besides, I wasn't payin' all that much attention. So, I didn't have but a smidgen of knowledge about the road, and sure as hell could not pass myself off as an expert. But I knowed it took them ox trains two, two-and-a-half months to make it out from Missouri and I figured it would take them about as long to get back here. But we had no oxen and wasn't pullin' any wagons, and horses that ain't under harness or saddle can travel at a quicker pace, so I figured me and Juan ought to be able to get our herd back here to Independence in somethin' less than two months. We sold off some of our stock to buy supplies and pack outfits to haul 'em. We sure as hell didn't buy no pack animals, as we had horses and jacks enough to carry what we needed and then some.

We strung the critters carryin' packsaddles together head to tail and let the rest run loose, as we knowed they would stay in a bunch and not wander off 'less somethin' spooked 'em. Headin' southeast out of Santa Fe, the road winds through the mountains and over Glorieta Pass 'til strikin' the Pecos River and some fords called somethin' like *San Jose del Vado* and *San Miguel del Vado*. Don't know what them Mexican names mean, but I recall Juan sayin' it was somethin' about them namin' them crossings after some Mexican saints.

Juan and me decided to lay over in Las Vegas for an extra day, that bein' about the only town that amounted to much between where we was and where we was goin'. We fed up good in them bean parlors there, not knowin' when we'd again have occasion to eat food cooked by someone who knew what they was doin'. See, neither of us was much of a hand at the cookfire. Oh, we could put the scorch to enough provisions to keep ourselves alive, but it ain't like what we fixed was worth eatin' otherwise.

Whilst we was havin' dinner the day before pullin' out, a trail-worn old man—I say old, but lookin' back, he likely hadn't more'n forty years on him—stepped inside the door and looked around in the dim light in the place 'til seein' us.

He wandered over to our table. "You the young fellers got that bunch of horses and jackasses out yonder?"

I nodded.

He stood, waiting for more, shifting his weight from one foot to the other. I sliced off another forkful of meat and went to work chewin' it. He watched me, looked at Juan, and back at me. He shifted his weight again and cleared his throat. "Mind my askin' where you-all are takin' them?"

I watched him as I chewed and swallowed. "Why might that be of interest to you?"

The man shuffled for another moment. "Mind if I sit down?"

I nodded toward the empty chair he stood behind and set my knife and fork down. It didn't look as if he was goin' away anytime soon, so I figured I might as well pay him some attention. "Well?"

Again, he cleared his throat. "I'm lookin' to get back to the States."

"There's plenty of freighters on the road most anytime," I said.

"I know it. Thing is, I been a bullwhacker and mule skinner

66

on them trains more times than I care to remember, and I've had my fill of 'em."

I could see how that could happen. It's a hell of a long road and the monotony and drudgery of it all can wear on a man. And that ain't even takin' into account the risk of mishaps of one kind or another, or a run-in with Indians.

Turned out the man had family up in St. Joseph and wanted to get back to 'em. Leastways that's what he said.

"You ever drove any loose stock?"

"Oh, hell yes. I was a herder on a couple trips out and back years ago, 'fore I got a place on a wagon. I can pack a mule or horse and throw a passable hitch. Ain't no expert at it, but I get by."

"Me and Juan, we can handle all that. The drovin', too. It ain't like we need any hired help."

"I ain't askin' for no job. All I'm after is a way to get home. Travelin' that road alone ain't smart. You-all take me along, I'm more'n willin' to pull my weight with the work to be done. Keep me mounted and fed is all I'm askin' you to do. I'll even do the cookin' if you-all want."

After talkin' it over with Juan, we decided to take him on. Come the morning, we rustled up an old saddle and bridle at a wagon yard and added some extra supplies in the way of foodstuff. After a last café breakfast, we readied to leave. Our new man was leanin' against a tree out where the herd waited when me and Juan rode up leadin' a packhorse. I led it over to where he sat, untied a knot, and tipped the saddle off to where it landed at his feet.

"Pick yourself out somethin' with four legs to cinch that onto," I said.

He had already made his choice, as he walked right over to a leggy sorrel mare and slipped the bit into her mouth and slid the headstall over her ears. After getting her saddled, he helped us finish packing and loading.

We pulled the last diamond hitch snug and strung out the pack animals and swung aboard our mounts, with Juan holdin' the lead rope for the string.

The new man squirmed into his saddle, lookin' for a comfortable seat. Then, "You boys decided where you-all are goin'?"

"What do you mean?"

" 'Fore long—I'd make it about twenty miles—we'll come to a place called *La Junta de los Ríos*. Get there, you got a choice to make. The road branches there and you-all can take what's called the mountain route, or the Cimarron route."

I pulled off my hat and scratched my head. "I don't know nothin' about that. Only thing I know is when I come out here, we followed the Arkansas River and went by a place called Bent's Fort."

"That'd be the mountain route."

"What's the difference 'tween that and the other'n—what'd you call it, Cimarron?"

"That's right. Cimarron route. It's a good ways shorter, save you some time. Cuts off a big loop up through the mountains. Meets back up with the Arkansas not too far from where the road leaves that river."

I thought it over. I looked to Juan, but he only shrugged. Could be he didn't savvy all what the man said, or could be he had no more idea than what I did.

"What would you do?"

The man slid his greasy hat up his forehead 'til it perched on the back of head. " 'Twas me, I'd go the mountain way. It be longer, but there's good graze and water most all the way. They call the Cimarron the 'dry route' and it's for a reason. Plenty of times out that way there ain't no more water than what a man could spit."

That decided it for me. "We take the mountain road, then.

These critters has already had more'n their share of goin' without enough to drink. I thank you for the information." I nodded at Juan and he set out with the pack string in tow. "By the way," I said to the man as we waited to push the loose stock onto the trail, "that boy's name is Juan. I go by Boone. What's your name?"

He looked at me and pulled his hat back down over his forehead. "You can call me Conley."

So that's what we called the man from then on. Don't know to this day if that was his first name or his last, or if it was his name at all, but it's the only name I know.

Things went along without much of anything happening. We just plodded along the road up through Raton Pass and on down onto the plains. Looking to the east, there wasn't a thing to see but empty. Now, I wasn't raised in no mountain country, but for the past many months I hadn't never been out of sight of mountains, and bein' mostly in amongst 'em. Even them big ol' dry lakes out in the desert that the Mexicans call *playas,* which was the flattest places I ever seen, was surrounded by mountains. Anyway, the emptiness of bein' in a country without no mountains again was a mite strange.

We passed freight trains on the road to Santa Fe now and again, and overtook some on the way to the States. We'd share a camp on occasion with the freighters and there was a few men among them that seemed to know Conley. But no one of them ever went out of his way to act friendly to the man. I had no notion of why that was and did not ask.

Conley, he turned out to be the kind of man who didn't do a thing 'less he was told to. Oh, he would do pretty much anything he was told, and do a passable job at it, and whilst his cooking wasn't anything to brag on, it was way ahead of what me or Juan could've done. So, while havin' him along was a help in some ways, he wasn't the kind of a man you'd want to be in harness with any longer than need be.

I came to think that even more so when we laid over at Bent's Fort to let the horses rest for a time. And I came to know why none of the bullwhackers that knowed him wanted anything to do with him. One day I was sittin' in the plaza there at the fort listenin' to men tellin' stories—some of them the same old mountain men and same old tales that put me in mind to take up fur trapping—when a man who looked to be from a freight outfit squatted down beside me.

"You're the one herdin' horses, ain't you."

It wasn't really a question, so I didn't say nothin' to him. He knowed who I was, so I just waited to see what he wanted of me. He waited a bit as I looked him over, then invited me to find someplace quiet to talk. We walked over to where the powder house was, as there wasn't anyone hangin' around there, and I leaned against the wall listenin' to what he had to say. He allowed as how he was wagon master on a bull train, and had run several such outfits out and back on the Santa Fe Road.

"You got a man name of Conley with you, ain't you."

Again, it was not a question, so I waited.

"Was I you, I'd keep an eye on that one. See, I've had him in my employ before, so I know him."

"What might it be that I should watch out for?"

The wagon master glanced around to make sure no one was near enough to overhear. "Conley's a thief."

"A thief? What's he steal?"

"That's the thing. He ain't like no other thief I ever seen. It's like he can't help himself. He'll steal anything. Even trinkets and such that won't do him no good at all."

I thought over what he said. Then he said more.

"He stole money and such, like you might expect. And we caught him pilfering out of the stores on the wagons. But he'd steal about anything. Take little keepsakes and doodads out of another's man's baggage. We booted him out first chance we got, soon as we could run him off where he wouldn't starve to death." He scratched his beard and kneaded his chin. "Like I said, sometimes it's like he can't help it. So was I you, I'd watch him, for it is my notion that a man who'll steal when he don't even have to will steal for sure when he sees it to his advantage."

I extended a hand to the wagon master and, as we shook, thanked him for the information. I allowed as how we would watch Conley extra careful. Then I looked up Juan and passed along the caution.

Things went along just fine for weeks as we trailed them mares and *machos* along the Arkansas. We come to several places where Conley said there was crossings for them that took the Cimarron way, and after that there was more freighters on the road. We chose to stay clear of them most times, and kept a close watch on our man Conley whenever we camped with them.

After a time, we reached the Great Bend, where the Arkansas takes a more southerly course and the road leaves the river and goes on east towards Independence. The country was startin' to look more like home, what with more and more trees a-growin'. We laid over at Council Grove, where I was told there'd been a treaty of some kind made with the Indians there. There was one big, old tree folks called the Post Office Oak on account of there bein' a hollow place at its bottom where you could find letters and messages and such left in there. Some had names wrote on them and was undisturbed by others, and some was just messages of a general sort meant for anyone who cared to read them. Some told about bein' on the lookout for someone who run off, children that got carried off from their folks, news about weddings on the trail, Indian troubles, and all manner of things.

I pawed through the stack of letters there and was nearly

surprised right out of my boots to find a folded-up page sealed with wax that had wrote on it in a fine hand, if faded some, *Daniel Boone Trewick.*

It took some time to catch my breath and gather my wits about me. I could not fathom any reason why there should be a letter for me there, or who might have wrote it. I broke the wax seal and unfolded the crisp sheet. The writing inside filled a portion of the page. My eye went first to the name at the bottom, and again I was discombobulated to read *Mary Elizabeth Thatcher.* I went on to read what she wrote.

*Danny,*
*I do not know what has become of you. It crossed my mind that you might have taken the Santa Fe Road in your haste to be gone from Liberty after the unfortunate circumstances of our parting. I hasten to tell you, should this missive find its way to your hand, that there was not then, nor is there now, any reason for your continued absence from Clay County. No doubt you were concerned for the well-being of the Reverend Thatcher, but I can assure you that Father is well. Any lingering difficulties between the two of you can, I am confident, be settled satisfactorily and I pledge my heart to see it so. If you hold any feelings for me, please return at first opportunity and with haste to me in Liberty.*

*Yours,*
*Mary Elizabeth Thatcher*

That whole deal rattled my brain so that I ain't got much recollection of what went on the next few days. All I remember is that we kept trailin' them mares and jacks along the way to Independence. I had no firm notion of how to proceed with my plans once I got there, and that letter from Mary Elizabeth only addled my brain more. I reckon that's part of the reason why what happened next happened.

We was camped along the trail within sight of Blue Mound when things took a turn for the worse. We was all three rolled in our blankets sleepin'—or so I thought. We never posted a guard on account of the horses bein' content to graze and rest through the nights and us havin' no notion of any danger of any kind in that part of the country.

But when I rolled out of my blankets in the morning, it was a mite later than usual, there bein' no smells in the air of Conley cookin' breakfast or makin' coffee. I sat up and scoured out my eyes with my knuckles and looked around. The campfire had gone cold, without even a wisp of smoke risin' from the ashes. There weren't no sign of Conley. I stood up and hollered for Juan to wake up. We walked out to where the horses was pastured and there weren't but about a third of them there. There wasn't no other way to think about it, save that that sonofabitch Conley had made off with them in the night.

We talked over some what to do. We found the track where he took them out of there, and it appeared he was settin' a northern course toward St. Joe, but there was no tellin' how long he'd hold to that direction or if he'd only talked about St. Joseph now and then as a way to throw us off. What with Juan bein' a whole lot better tracker than me, we thought to put him on Conley's trail whilst I pushed on to Independence with what horses and jacks we had left. That was one thing—Conley hadn't stole a single one of them jacks—he only took the mares.

Then we thought better of sendin' Juan off in pursuit. What with him bein' Mexican and all, and his English bein' somewhat lacking, we decided he might find himself in more trouble than he could handle should he be accused—by Conley or on general principles—of bein' the thief.

Which brings up somethin' that might matter in the circumstances. Them horses was stolen by me and them others way back in California. But that was Mexico, and this is America, so it likely wouldn't matter. But I had tucked away a bill of sale wrote up and signed by Thomas L. "Pegleg" Smith, declaring me the rightful owner of them animals. He even had it attested to by some make-believe official of the government in Santa Fe. Still, even with that paper in hand, folks might not be inclined to believe Juan, him bein' Mexican and all.

So I set off after Conley and my mares and left Juan to wait where we was. Well, not exactly where we was—we determined to push a ways farther off the trail, where him and them horses would be less likely to be found by anybody. If he was found, well, all we could do was hope for the best.

It turned out Conley held true on a course towards St. Joe and he made no effort to throw me off the trail. But he was movin' fast, so I was glad to have brought along a spare horse on a lead, which allowed me to move at a good pace over the prairie, stopping only for a few hours' sleep in the dark of the night.

By the time I hit Fort Leavenworth, Conley wasn't but a couple of hours ahead. There was men at the fort—soldiers and civilians both—who had seen him with my horses, and said he could yet be gettin' them across the Missouri River on the ferry. With promise of a reward, I hired on two men who looked like they knew their way around a scrape. When we got to the river, the man who kept the ferry—name of Cain, as I recall—said Conley and the horses couldn't be more than half an hour gone, as he had just tied up after returnin' from the last trip haulin' him over. I don't know where Conley came up with the money to pay the man, but he had it from somewheres.

We caught up with Conley pretty quick. One man wrangling a herd of horses ain't no match for three men horseback. My two men stayed out of sight behind the herd and I hurried off through the woods to get ahead of the thief. His look of surprise when he saw me sitting horseback on the trail turned to fear before despair overcame him.

"Boone, I—"

"—Shut up, Conley. I don't want to hear it."

He looked around and I could see he was mulling over making a run for it. But then the men from Fort Leavenworth rode up and I could see he was resigned to his situation.

One of the men said, "This him?"

I nodded.

The other said, "Well, hell, we might just as well get on with it."

It sickened me to hang a man, but we left Conley dangling from a red oak tree and rode away. Hanging from his neck by a loop of whang leather was a piece cut from a saddle skirt with the words HORSE THIEF scratched on it.

We got the horses ferried back across the river and those two men offered to help me get the horses back to the Santa Fe Road.

"No, gentlemen. I reckon if that sorry sonofabitch Conley got them up here, I can get them back."

What cash I had been carrying was now in the hands of the ferry man, so I allowed my helpers to take a mare each from the herd. Pretty good pay for a day's work, I thought. Even if the job required stringing up a horse thief.

I found Juan without no trouble and we set off for Independence, which I figured to be two, maybe three days away. We made it in two.

Me and Juan spent a few days riding around the country and located suitable pasture that was there for the taking. It was a different deal in town, where I had to put the horse herd up as security for a bank loan to buy land in town for a barn and pens and an office.

As you might imagine, most all them mares had already been serviced by them big jacks on the trail somewhere between here

75

and California, and was carrying foals, so our first crop of mules was already on the way. Them *machos* did their job that year, and every year since. So did that herd of mares, as have them we've added since.

By the time we got that first bunch of mules raised up and Juan got them broke to drive, things had changed in Independence. What we figured to be a ready market among freighters was still there. But in the meantime, all kinds of folks from the east was headin' west, most bound for Oregon and some for California. We couldn't raise mules fast enough, and every team that left our barn left behind a hefty profit. That's when we got in the ox business, bringin' in some big Durham bulls from back East and breedin' them to lanky longhorn cows brought up from Texas, and whatever other cows of a suitable size we could find hereabouts. We been at it ever since, sellin' every mule and ox we can get raised up to a proper size for work.

Which brings us to that damn sign. I confess that slab of wood daubed with paint is right handsome, even though it's showin' its age all these years later. And it has sure done its job. But, like I said, the way it looks makes it look like we're sellin' mules and oxen for breeding and there sure as hell ain't no such thing. Sticks in my craw. I could have had a new sign made over the years but never did. Fact is, as much as the damn thing bothers me, I like the look of it. And plenty of folks stop in to ask about it, just like you did.

So that's the story about that sign, and I don't know what else I can tell you. Well, there is one more thing. After we got settled in and doin' business, I made my way across the river to Clay County and on up to Liberty, where I made my peace with the Reverend Thatcher. It took some talkin', but I done it. It didn't take much talkin' at all to convince Mary Elizabeth to marry me. The reverend allowed as how she was too young for it, but she was past sixteen and as stubborn as one of my mules, so he finally gave in. Hell, he even read out the rites for us. The passel of kids that's come along since has been to his likin' as well.

As for me, I've been content and have not ever once been tempted to take another trip on the road to Santa Fe. And, no matter how much I admire the horses and mules and *machos* out that way, I sure as hell ain't been back to California.

Four-time winner of the Western Writers of America Spur Award, **Rod Miller** writes fiction, history, and poetry about the American West. His writing has also been honored by Western Fictioneers, Westerners International, and the Academy of Western Artists. Find him online at writerRodMiller.com, Raw hideRobinson.com, and writerRodMiller.blogspot.com.

★ ★ ★ ★ ★

# Legend

# BY JOHNNY D. BOGGS

★ ★ ★ ★ ★

# I

"Kit, look what we got." The pockmarked Dragoon waves the penny dreadful over his head, motioning for the small man to step closer to the fire.

"You ain't gonna believe it." The sergeant also beckons the scout. "Alyicious found it in a grip over yonder."

Lowering his coffee cup, the St. Louis Frenchman whispers to the soldiers, "*Mes amis,* this is a mistake you make. He will not wish to see these . . ."—and sighs—"*mensonges.*"

"You're just jealous, Leroux," the sergeant says. "On account nobody's never writ nothin' 'bout you."

"*C'est la vie.*" With a shrug, Leroux focuses on his coffee. It is not his place to argue with Dragoons or imbeciles. He is paid as a scout and guide, just like the small man who turns his gaze from this never-ending country of red rocks, harsh winds, and a river, more mud than water.

Leroux stares at his cup, empty now, and waits, hearing no footsteps, but even if dead twigs carpeted the ground, no sound would be heard. Kit Carson walks like a ghost. The Dragoons grow excited, alerting Leroux that Carson approaches the fire.

"See what we found," the pockmarked one says again.

Carson remains quiet.

"It's a book," the sergeant says.

"I ain't that ignorant," Carson says.

"But it's about you," the one holding the book says.

Now, Antoine Leroux raises his eyes.

In front of the fire, but not too close, for he has learned to stay in the shadows, Carson cocks his head.

The sergeant points at this gaudy, cheap . . . book? No, Leroux could tell them that a book is *Le Père Goriot*. A book is *Les Trois Mousquetaires*. A book is not . . .

"*Kit Carson, The Prince of the Gold Hunters,*" the sergeant reads aloud, as best as he can. "*Or, The Adventures of the Sacramento: A Tale of the New Eldorado, Founded on Actual Facts.*"

Out of the growing darkness, Carson—short but solid, with long, stringy hair and grizzled face—moves closer, incredulous at the slender volume the sergeant shoves forward, like a scalp or a jug of Taos Lightning. Carson's gray eyes bore through the bold letters and brassy illustration before he stares at the soldiers.

"Somebody writ a book 'bout me?"

"That's right," the pockmarked Dragoon says. He bends his head to make sure of the name and says, "Charles E. Averill."

"Chargin' two bits for it," the sergeant adds.

"Charles E. Averill," Carson says. "Don't recollect meetin' no Charles E. Averill." He stares at Leroux. "Do you?"

Leroux smiles gently. "Names rarely stay with me. And *Capitaine* Averill did not write about me."

"He's a capt'n?" Carson asks.

"They are all *capitaines*. Unless they are *colonels*." A joke, which no one understands.

Squatting, Carson rubs the stubble on his chin. Leroux can read the hesitation in Carson's face. The small man turns back into the gloaming, wets his lips, and stares once more at the book, before finding Leroux. That look passes quickly, and Carson's Adam's apple bobs; he draws in a deep breath, and asks the question Leroux dreads.

"Would one of you boys mind readin' that thing . . . ?" Carson sticks a gnarled finger at the twenty-five-cent piece of garbage.

*A man like Kit Carson knows of many dangers, but not this kind,* Leroux thinks sadly, *but you would have made the same request were you illiterate.*

The sergeant stares at the novel. "Well, it's a thick book." Which it isn't. "And . . . dark is coming fast . . ."

"And," another young Dragoon adds, "won't we be moving out? Keep after those savages?"

"We got what we came after," Major Grier says. He points his flask toward the grave. "We return tomorrow."

Leroux whirls toward the commander. "The baby remains missing," he says.

"I know that," Grier snaps. "But we have no forage for our horses, not enough rations for our men, and winter is fast approaching. We will deal with the Jicarillas later and avenge . . ." The sight of Carson's glare silences him.

Grier has lost his nerve, has no taste for pursing Indians in a cold, barren Hell, yet Leroux finds no fault in Grier. The major had been shot during the attack on the Jicarillas' camp. If that ball had not struck a suspender button, Grier could lie dying in his bedroll or already be buried beside the woman they had been ordered to rescue.

"Read the story, Sergeant," another soldier says, and Leroux realizes others have gathered around the fire. Even the New Mexico Volunteers, who speak passable English if at all, want to hear.

"Well . . ." The big man wets his lips, turns the cover. The dreadful shakes in his hands. He says, "Chapter One," and starts stuttering over something before a German immigrant who has joined the Dragoons tells him what he's attempting to read isn't important and to get to the story.

" 'From the Old South clock,' " the sergeant begins, too soft, too uncertain. He's goaded to read like a man. After clearing his throat, he continues. " '. . . and the State House bell chimed the hour of nine.' " No interruptions. The sergeant gains confidence. " 'The living word of Boston's—' "

"Boston?" Carson says, not quite a bark, for Carson rarely raises his voice. "I ain't never been to Boston. Been to Washington City . . . taken a train . . . but didn't get to Boston."

The sergeant blinks repeatedly. He stares at the page, and scans down and up the columns, moves to the next page, turns a page, focuses again on the cover to make sure he's reading the right book, flips another page, skimming now, another, another, swallows and says, "I think this fellow's name is Harry." He thumbs through more pages. "There's a Eugene here." He digs deeper inside the novel.

Leroux holds up his tin cup. A jug is being passed around, and the German, leaning on a rock, has the rum. He splashes some in the Frenchman's cup. The sergeant is halfway through *Kit Carson, The Prince of the Gold Hunters.* Leroux does not yet sip the liquor, but offers an explanation.

"They are Easterners. Young. They will leave Boston eventually and strike out for California. After many adventures, they will meet Kit Carson, befriend him, and he will save many lives."

Even Grier studies Leroux. "You have read this?"

Leroux laughs. "No, Major." How could he explain to these men? Charles Averill is no Balzac, no Dumas. No Dickens or Thackeray. Certainly no Hugo. "It is a blood-and-thunder. They are all pretty much the same."

"I ain't no prince," Carson says. "And never hunted no gold. Iffen I ever found any, I sure wouldn't let nobody know 'bout it . . . not from all the mess 'em emigrants has caused of late in Californy, and just gettin' there."

"Read the story," Grier orders. "From the beginning."

He says this to appease Carson. The sergeant flips back to

the beginning. He reads.

Leroux remembers.

# II

*Sitting in the inn, sipping brandy, enjoying the fire and the song the raven-haired señorita sings in Spanish.*

The door opens, and Major William Grier enters, lets his eyes adjust to the darkness, and spies Leroux.

"Antoine." The major speaks brusquely. "Trouble. I need your services."

The song has ended, and a *ranchero* begins talking to the singer, showering her with Spanish praises, and she smiles, a most charming sight. Sighing, Leroux sips his brandy and nods at Grier.

"Indians raided a train near Point of Rocks," the major says. "Part of Aubry's caravan."

Leroux knows Francois X. Aubry. Who doesn't in New Mexico Territory? A wiry, young, fearless man with French ancestry, too, only his from Canada, not Leroux's St. Louis.

"Aubry wasn't with them," the major says. "At least, not from what we've learned." Grier looks around, as though hoping someone will bring him a drink, but few pay attention. "This man White—I cannot recall his Christian name—had a dozen or more wagons he was bringing to Santa Fe to open up a mercantile. Aubry sent Calloway ahead to fetch fresh mules."

Another familiar name. William Calloway, Aubry's wagon master.

"This White, he didn't want to wait," Grier continues. "So he and his party rode out with Calloway."

"Aubry let them?"

"I'm sure Aubry told White it was a damned fool idea. They're east of Point of Rocks when Jicarillas hit them. One boy lived, must have played dead. After the Indians rode off, he

85

crawled to Point of Rocks. Hugh Smith, who happened to be on his way to Washington City, found the boy. They all hightailed it back to Santa Fe."

"When did this happen?" Leroux asks.

"Best we can figure from what the boy said, the twenty-fourth."

Leroux smiles his saddest smile. "*Mon ami,* there is nothing to be done but . . ." He makes the sign of the cross.

"The boy says the Jicarillas took women with them," Grier says. "And a kid: White's wife, her baby daughter, and a colored woman who must've been the girl's nanny."

The brandy sours on Leroux's tongue. He rises from his chair, turns to find his coat and hat, as Grier keeps talking.

"I have a company ready to march. Captain Valdez of the Volunteers has forty men with him, and a battery of six-pounders. A courier rode in from Santa Fe this morning saying that the Indian agent and Aubry have put up a thousand dollars each to ransom the women or pay for their return, at least Mrs. White and her kid."

Leroux cares not about the reward, or even the pittance he will collect from the Dragoons. With such a head start, the Jicarillas will be hard to find, and he already knows who has led this raid. Lobo Blanco. The Llaneros band of the Jicarillas has been raiding since the Americans arrived in the territory. Ferreting out Lobo Blanco will be a challenge. And finding the women and child?

"Point of Rocks," he says, absently finding the St. Christopher dangling from his neck. "That means we must ride through Rayado."

# III

Kit Carson has arrived.

Not in person, not yet, not the way Charles Averill tells his story, but the heroic young aristocrat from Boston is gazing upon a portrait of, in Averill's words, "the famous hunter and adventurer of the Great West" . . . "hardy explorer" . . . "daring guide" . . . "hero of prairie and forest" . . . "prince of backwoodsmen."

The sergeant's voice has turned hoarse, even though noncommissioned officers in the 1st U.S. Dragoons are supposed to be able to yell for weeks on end. He pauses to wash down the dryness in his throat with rum.

*Averill is nothing but a hackney writer,* Leroux can imagine his father saying, yet Averill has pretty much described Kit Carson to perfection.

The soldiers begin cheering. One even dares to slap Carson's tough shoulders. Carson smokes his pipe, stares at the fire.

"You're famous, ol' hoss," the pockmarked one says. "I knew you were legend, but, to have a book writ about you, now that's somethin'." He waits for the sergeant to pass the jug along.

The jug does come into the Dragoon's hands, and *Kit Carson, The Prince of the Gold Hunters,* rises to the sergeant's bloodshot eyes. He has trouble finding his place in what's more pamphlet than book.

"It is said that there is a steamboat on the Mississippi and Missouri," Leroux says, "that is called the *Kit Carson.*" Which makes him realize that someday there will likely be towns, marble and bronze monuments, and perhaps other ships, plus parks, mountains, rivers, and forests named after this Kentucky-born, Missouri-bred legend.

"A steamboat is not a book," the German says.

*"Oui,"* Leroux says. He thinks: *But a steamboat never speaks.* He wishes he had never suggested that Grier stop at Rayado.

# IV

*Josefa holding the baby under the portal of the adobe home in Rayado. What a beautiful woman.*

By the corrals, Major Grier and Captain Valdez speak with Carson while Leroux, holding the reins to his horse in one hand, removes his hat and bows to Carson's wife.

"For what reason have you come for my husband this time?" Josefa asks in Spanish. Barely out of her teens, she appears to be with child again, but though married to Carson for perhaps six years, life has not aged her. Her hair is glossy black, parted down the middle. An oval face, unblemished by the sun and dry winds, perfect eyebrows, aquiline nose, rounded lips, she could have had any of Taos's finest, but she, and her father, chose Kit Carson. Her dress is blue. Her eyes are sad.

With a shrug, Leroux answers, *"¿Qué más . . . ?"*

The baby squirms. Josefa looks at her husband, then back at Leroux. *"Vaya con Dios."*

*"Desde siempre,"* he says as she disappears inside the dark adobe home. But there is no God where he is about to ride.

By the time he leads his gelding back to the soldiers, Carson is lugging blanket and saddle toward a mule.

One of the Dragoons snorts and spits tobacco juice onto the ground. "He don't look like much to me, Alyicious. A slight breeze'll blow him away."

As Leroux swings into the saddle, he remembers Carson telling a story once, so he uses the last line on the foolish soldiers, trying to effect Carson's own drawl.

"I reckon he ain't the Kit Carson you was lookin' for."

# V

If they let the sergeant keep reading, they will be thawing out in the spring before they reach the end of *The Prince of the Gold*

*Hunters.* Besides, his slurs of Averill's words and his monotone has sent some Dragoons and Volunteers to their bedrolls. The sergeant has no objections to relinquishing command of the dreadful. The major shakes his head when his troops seek him to narrate. The German points and says, "What about him?"

Leroux starts to decline, but Carson speaks.

"Go on, Antoine. Read it." He laughs bitterly. "Ain't like I can."

The book moves through the blackness. Leroux lets the novel hang there as he peers across the fire. Carson tamps the pipe, which he has not smoked for better than an hour. "Go on," Carson says again. "Get 'er done."

# VI

*The land looks flat, but is not. The grass looks dead, and is. The bodies, what's left of them, leave soldiers puking.*

Carson has been here at least an hour before Leroux guides the major's command ten miles beyond Point of Rocks.

Captain Valdez's Volunteers cross themselves, mouth prayers. A few even cry.

Wolves have dug up the dead from shallow graves covered hurriedly, scattering carnage from that feast more than a hundred yards.

Leroux hobbles his gelding and moves through the bones and litter—bridles and harnesses that have been cut, clothes and other items carried by the wind into cactus, chests and crates broken open, wagons burned or reduced to kindling. Behind him, the major and the Mexican captain order burial details.

Carson squats and stares off to the southeast.

"You see the stone wall?" Carson asks without looking back at Leroux.

"I did."

"Indians built it, hid behind it, then ambushed 'em."

"Lobo Blanco gets smarter all the time."

Carson spits between his teeth. He has pulled a weed and twists it around absently with his fingers.

"Who buried these men?" Leroux asks.

"Barclay be my guess," Carson answers. "Wagons, oxen, mules come down the Cutoff, found what happened." He points. "Kept movin' toward Mora Creek."

Alexander Barclay, decent enough for an Englishman, runs a way station on that creek. They would have found the bodies, buried them quickly. Who could blame them? Fearing Lobo Blanco's Jicarillas might still be around, few men would have even made an attempt at covering the dead.

"They have made finding the Jicarillas' trail harder," Leroux says.

"Lobo Blanco didn't leave much for Barclay and his boys to mess up," Carson says.

Leroux breathes deeply, slowly lets it out. "The women? The child?"

Carson tosses the twisted stem of grass to the ground. With a sigh of weariness and age—though he has not quite reached forty years—Carson stands. "I don't know," he concedes.

# VII

The naïve young wayfarers from Boston, now in a rugged land east of Sacramento filled with "pesky" redskins and treacherous barbarians, have found Kit Carson, whom they all know as "the prairie-ranger, the scout, the gold-discoverer . . . whose name the Union rings," Averill writes.

" 'Yes and no, stranger!' " Leroux reads. " 'You *do* see Kit Carson, *plain Kit Carson,* mind you.' "

He reads to the chapter's end. "My God," Carson whispers.

Leroux folds the book, keeping his place with his forefinger.

The pockmarked Dragoon laughs. "You do have a 'lynx-eye,' Kit."

The German says: "But you don't talk like that."

" 'Cause he don't talk at all," the sergeant says.

"Keep reading," Major Grier orders.

Carson shrugs. "Might as well."

The book is opened again, but as he finds his place, Leroux considers that this Averill must have interviewed someone who knows Carson.

Leroux corrects himself. *Nobody knows Kit Carson.*

Yet Carson's smile is always "good humored," his countenance is typically "calm and quiet," and while the dialogue is overblown, the descriptions trite, the story convoluted and often crass, much truth can be found in Averill's prose—not that Leroux will seek out *Secrets of the High Seas, Pirates of Cape Ann's Secret Service Ship* or anything else by Averill.

# VIII

*At the edge of the first Jicarilla camp they discover, Carson breaks open horse apples, then curses. They are still days behind.*

The major, who has lost his patience, yells, but a biting gale drowns out those words.

Carson inches his way off to the southeast; Leroux moves from the northwest. Scouts Dick Wootton and Tom Tobin, who have joined the command, read the ground two hundred yards from camp.

Carson is legend, but Tobin, Wootton, and Leroux know this country well and have earned deserved respect as trackers. Yet this brutal land refuses to give up its secrets.

"How many directions?" Leroux asks Carson when they meet.

"South, southeast, southwest."

Leroux tilts his head toward the opposite directions. "North, northeast, northwest."

"At least they ain't goin' up or down." Carson walks to the approaching major, who reins in his horse.

"They split up here, Major." To be heard above the wind, Carson must yell. "Two, sometimes three, headin' ever' which way."

The major's mouth opens, and his lips try to form words, but nothing comes out.

"They will, most likely, circle around at some point, join together," Leroux explains.

"But figurin' out which way they wanna go will take some doin'," Carson says.

"By Jehovah, we could be wandering around this godforsaken land forever," Grier roars. "We don't even know if that damned woman is with them."

Carson opens his hand to reveal a piece of torn calico, yellow with green and white polka dots. "She's with 'em."

"And the child?"

Carson shrugs. "Maybe so." He moves to his mule. Leroux finds his gelding. They mount and ride, one north, one south, knowing that Lobo Blanco will continue to gain ground while they search for the right trail.

"Eventually," Carson tells Leroux, Wootton, and Tobin, "Lobo Blanco'll figure we quit the chase. It'll be hard-doin', but it's gotta get done, boys. We gots to get 'er done. For the women, and the little girl."

Sometimes, it feels pointless. Find a chip in the rock that might have been cut by an unshod pony's hoof. The droppings of a horse. The tiny ditch that could have been caused by an Indian urinating. A strand of blond hair on a cactus. Another piece of calico. Until the train turns, and they know that the Jicarillas are not traveling north. Unless they turn around again. Until they find where the Indians have rejoined and made another camp.

And then? Pony tracks leading in myriad directions. Another trail lost. Hours wasted. The trail found, only to disappear inside some canyon, vanish at a mesa, or be blown away by the wind that grows icier with each passing mile.

"Never," Carson says, "in all my years have I found a trail this hard to follow."

"The soldiers want to turn back," Leroux says.

"Let 'em. I ain't."

# IX

A prairie fire has sent panicking buffalo into a deadly charge, and the heroes face certain death under the hooves of those big shaggies, but Kit Carson, that prince of gold hunters, uses flint and tinder to start another fire. The backfire stops the raging inferno, and turns the stampede. Again, Kit Carson has saved the day, and as Averill's hero begins speaking to those young adventurers from Boston, the Dragoons still awake, still sober enough, to be listening, cheer the Kit Carson who sits away from the others, away from the fire.

"By grab, Kit," says the pockmarked kid. "Did that really happen? Did you save 'em from gettin' trampled?"

Leroux stops reading to rest his voice. Carson says nothing. Over the past hour, he has not even grunted.

Carson stares at the fire, never acknowledges the questions.

"Maybe I should stop for the night," Leroux says. "We have a long way back home tomorrow."

"Go on," Carson says. "Ain't but a little more left."

After wetting his lips, Leroux finds his place, and reads.

# X

*Fording the Canadian River and following the trail southeast. Only to find the Jicarillas have turned back to the river, forcing scouts and soldiers to cross the frigid waters again—fifteen miles from where they crossed earlier. Damning Lobo Blanco. Damning themselves. Damning the days lost.*

A week . . . ten days . . . twelve. Exhaustion and boredom leave Dragoons and Volunteers irritable, dirty, discouraged. Nothing but bread to eat. No fires at night, no coffee, just a thin bedroll to keep warm. Horses and mules feel no better. Nor do Leroux, Wootton, or Tobin. Only Carson seems more alive than dead.

*On the outside,* Leroux begins to think.

"Buzzards!" The pockmarked Dragoon reins in and points.

Dick Wootton sees the black birds taking flight. "Ravens," he corrects.

Already, Carson lopes his mule to where the ravens have been roosting.

"What is it?" Grier demands, and hearing no reply, turns his horse toward the cottonwoods.

"Rest easy, Major," Leroux says, but does not face the officer. His eyes follow the *cawing* ravens' flight.

Grumbling, Grier slackens the reins. A few minutes later, Carson emerges from the trees and rides to the soldiers.

"Camped here," Carson tells the major. "Ashes still hot."

"Mrs. White?" Grier asks.

Carson holds up another ripped piece of calico.

"The kid?" Leroux asks.

Carson nods. "But no sign of the Negress."

"Well . . ." Grier doesn't know what to say.

Leroux points. "Ravens."

"Yeah," Carson says. "They're camp followers, Major. Eat what they can, what the Jicarillas toss away. Follow 'em black birds, we find what we been huntin'."

By the end of the day, after forty bone-jarring miles, they camp in another cottonwood grove, the leaves long fallen, but hope returning to sleeping men.

At dawn, they set out at a hard trot toward the Canadian. In the distance, Tucumcari Butte beckons them. Carson is too far ahead to be seen.

Leroux smells smoke. Carson gallops back toward the soldiers, slides the mule to a stop, and waves. "It's Lobo Blanco's bunch, boys. We've found 'em. Give 'em hell. Follow me." The mule has already been jerked around. Carson holds a Hawken rifle in his right hand.

Wootton and Tobin charge after the scout.

Yes, yes, Leroux spots the Indians. No woman. No child. One old Jicarilla waves arms over his head.

Major Grier's voice is lost. His mouth opens, but it is Leroux who speaks.

"They might want to parley," Leroux says. "Ransom the woman and her little girl."

"I . . ."

A heavily bearded Dragoon rides forward. "Major, we can't just sit here."

Carson gallops back. "Come on, you sons of bitches. Come on." Without waiting, he tears back toward the camp.

The bearded Dragoon throws his saber into the dirt. "For God's sake!" he yells.

"Hell." Leroux realizes his mistake. The Indian waving his arms is a decoy. Touching the gelding's ribs, Leroux says,

"Quickly, Major. Attack. Attack."

The bullet almost knocks Grier out of the saddle.

# XI

All's well that ends well. Villains conquered. Kit Carson's vow fulfilled. The stolen child recovered. A wedding to be planned. Enough gold to satisfy everyone. And a sequel, *Life in California; or, The Treasure Seekers' Expedition,* to be published—probably already in mercantiles across the United States and her territories—in pamphlet form.

"Well," the German says after Leroux closes *Kit Carson, The Prince of the Gold Hunters.* "That was something."

"Was any of it true?" the pockmarked Dragoon asks.

Carson stares without blinking.

Once Leroux stands, he stamps his right foot to get the blood circulating again. As he looks around, he realizes that most of the men have retired. The major walks away. A few Dragoons and two Volunteers sleep on the ground, no pillows, no blankets, but it has been an exhausting day. Tobin and Wootton remain on guard duty, having not heard one word of Averill's blood-and-thunder.

Slowly, Carson rises, steps out of the shadows toward Leroux.

# XII

*Leroux sees the hole in the major's coat, hears the panicked gasps. Grier's face loses all color. Wheeling in the saddle, the major slaps his chest.*

But there is no blood.

Grier's fingers enter the breast pocket, withdrawing the gauntlets. A flattened lead ball topples into the sand.

"Charge, Major," Leroux pleads. "Charge." He can wait no longer. He is as much to blame for the delay as Grier. The gelding explodes into a gallop.

Behind him, Leroux hears the trumpeter's call.

Jicarillas have crossed the Canadian. One floats in the reddish-brown water. Fires still burn. A few horses and stolen livestock from Aubry's wagon train wander about. Carson stands over the body.

Sickened, Leroux slides out of his saddle and moves toward Ann White. He does not need to try to find a pulse, but he does anyway.

"She was a brave woman," Tobin says. "Tearing up her dress and all, trying to leave sign for us to follow."

Carson bites his bottom lip.

"Imagine the hell she went through," Wootton says. "By thunder, just look at her."

She lies on her side, the bloody point of an arrow protruding from her chest, the yellow, green, and white calico dress hardly recognizable. A month ago, she must have been pretty. Now . . . her open eyes reveal misery. Hardships line her sunburned face. Death is supposed to bring peace, but her features exhibit eternal agony. But none wants to think of everything Ann White has endured these past weeks.

Leroux closes her eyes, and curses himself.

Some Dragoons and Volunteers swim their horses after the Jicarillas. Muskets fire. Men yell.

"Search for the baby," Captain Valdez orders in Spanish. Yet Leroux knows the girl will never be found.

Their mission is a failure. There is nothing to do but bury the dead.

# XIII

Crackling wood and popping coals are the only sounds. The wind has stopped completely, and no snores can be heard, no rippling of water from the river. Eyes around the campfire stare at the small scout as he stops in front of the Frenchman. Carson extends his hand.

Leroux passes the novel to the scout, who glares at the cover, and that artist's fancy interpretation of a gallant knight, part Homer, part Hercules, all legend. In the darkness—dawn is but a few hours away—Leroux sees the flames reflecting in Carson's eyes. He can also see the tears.

Perhaps Carson will talk later, but not here, not in front of the Dragoons. Yet Leroux knows the thoughts troubling Carson. He can hear the scout's words in his head.

*Do you think that woman read this, Antoine? And that she knowed I was around these parts, and that she prayed I'd come to her rescue? And I did come. But . . .*

The gray eyes fall to *Kit Carson, The Prince of the Gold Hunters*, and then the twenty-five-cent dreadful drops into the fire. At first, it smolders. The illustration of Kit Carson darkens, pages curl and with sudden violence, flames dance across the cheap pamphlet, devouring the words of Charles E. Averill.

Carson does not witness the funeral pyre. He has vanished in the darkness.

"Damnation, Leroux, I don't get that at all." The pockmarked Dragoon stares at the mass of ashes that once was *Kit Carson, The Prince of the Gold Hunters*. "He gets a book writ up about him, and he burns it. Don't make a lick of sense. By grab, that's Kit Carson. He's a livin' legend."

*"Oui."* Leroux speaks in French, but the Dragoon would not have understood even had he used English. "But even a legend can be cursed with something called humanity."

**Johnny D. Boggs** is an eight-time Spur Award winner from Western Writers of America. He lives in Santa Fe, New Mexico, with his wife and son. His website is JohnnyDBoggs.com.

★ ★ ★ ★ ★

# ARLEY

## BY WALLACE J. SWENSON

★ ★ ★ ★ ★

The rough-knuckled fist hit Arley's ear without warning, and the blaze of light behind his eyes flared as hotly as the anger he felt for not anticipating the blow. His brother, seven-year-old Jacob, crashed to the floor with him as the bench they sat on fell over. To Arley's relief, Jake scuttled on hands and knees to temporary safety under the table.

"Squintin' at me'll get you one of them . . . ever' goddamned time," his father shouted, the words slurred. The gaunt man, sallow and rheumy-eyed, slammed his whiskey jug down on the table and rose unsteadily to his feet. "Now get the hell outta here ya worthless whelp . . . 'fore I stomp yer guts out yer scrawny ass."

Experience drove Arley toward the door, but he chanced one backward glance: his mother, disheveled hair bound in a rag, stared back, her brimming eyes gleaming yellow in the light of the single lamp. Jake's hand appeared above the table's edge and snatched the corn cake he'd been savoring; an instant later, the hand reappeared and grabbed Arley's cake as well. Arley barged out the door and shoved it shut behind him.

The smell of river mud came to him on a chill breeze as he hurried toward the gray, weather-beaten barn. This day had gotten off to a bad start and had steadily gotten worse. But now, sixteen hours later, he was too tired to care, and all he felt was gnawing hunger and fear. The best he could hope for tonight would be his father passing out, or being too drunk to cause any damage if he came looking. Or worse—Arley's fists clenched and his heart raced—the drunken pig would turn his attentions to his mother. Jake would hide—he was good at that—but the youngster would then have to listen to what went on and wonder.

That morning, a mid-April Saturday in 1855, had dawned clear and calm on his thirteenth birthday, but he hadn't expected the date to make the slightest difference in his day. Even with good equipment and a stronger back, young Arley would've been hard-pressed to grow much of anything on such a hardscrabble farm—to say nothing of producing enough to feed a family of four. They lived on nine poor acres; all that remained of the original seventy his grandfather had wrested from the wilderness along the Illinois River starting in 1820. The higher, more productive ground now belonged to their neighbor, Axel Holverson, sold to him piecemeal for money, then wasted by Arley's father on whiskey and gambling.

Before the sun cracked the horizon, Arley had risen from his nest in the barn to milk the cow and turn her into the pasture. For some reason, the normally placid beast put a foot in the half-full bucket and tipped it over, soaking his trouser leg and filling his brogan for good measure. He was relieved his father had already left for work in town.

With the milking finished, after a fashion, he headed for the corncrib while two hungry sows and their thirteen shoats grunted impatiently in their pens. Their beady eyes tracked his steps across the yard, and he smiled to himself despite his sticky-wet pant leg and squishy foot. He enjoyed feeding the pigs and had once said as much. His father's ridicule of such a notion only made the rowdy swine more appealing to him. Arley knew whose company he preferred. The pigs lived downhill toward the river and fifty-eight paces from the house. He knew the exact number because counting them helped focus his mind when weariness fuddled his brain; house to barn took forty-five. He reckoned today might be just such a day. Besides daily chores, the garden needed work, and he had to finish planting the field corn—or else. He'd been warned.

Two separate, plank-sided, half-covered pens provided shelter for the two sows while their offspring, weaned weeks ago and each weighing over two hundred pounds, ran free inside a rail-fenced area next to them. They ate a lot and he was glad they'd soon go to slaughter. The older sow grunted her impatience and tossed her enormous head back and forth as he approached the three-foot fence; the two full buckets of shelled corn banged his legs. He dumped the first into her trough while the younger sow in the next pen assaulted a split-log partition that separated the four-hundred-pound animals. Watching her out the corner of his eye, Arley hurried to get the agitated beast her ration. Last year's harvest had been poorer than usual so he held back on their feed. He and his mother had worked the sums and decided to feed more to the weaned piglets. For his diligence, his father had given him a hot-tempered warning not to lose any and an emphatic punch to the chest that still pained him.

After another trip to the crib, he stood outside the larger pen. There the troughs lay at right angles to him so he couldn't simply dump the feed over the fence. Leaving one bucket on the ground, he climbed the planks and shoved his way through the rambunctious animals. They followed his every move, snouts jostling the bucket of corn as he struggled through them. He knew to keep moving lest one of the feistier beasts took a nip, or worse, knocked him down. He'd overheard his father tell his mother about some hogs upriver eating a man; they'd gobbled up everything but his skull. Arley had halfway believed the story despite his father's tendency to stretch the truth; maybe more than half—the story still haunted him once in a while. He dumped the corn along the trough in one sweeping motion and made for the rail. Six or seven of the larger pigs butted and bit their way to the food, their smaller brothers and sisters squealing in protest.

Just then, a barefooted and smiling Jake appeared carrying a wicker egg-basket. Arley pointed at the second bucket of corn. "Hey, Jake, put them cackleberries on top the corner post and hand me that bucket." Stretching, Jake carefully placed the basket, and then grabbed the bucket handle with both hands. For a few seconds the boy's perpetual smile changed into a determined grimace as he heisted the bucket into Arley's grasp.

"Heavy," Jake said and grinned. With his bony elbows poking through a ragged shirt, and his charity trousers reaching only halfway down his clothes-peg shins, he had no more reason to be cheerful than did Arley, but he always seemed to be.

Mr. Holverson had once used the word *enigma* to describe Jake. Arley had sounded out every "in" word listed under "I" in his mother's *Webster's* before finding it in the "E's." A riddle it said. It still didn't make much sense. He dumped the corn, and then scrambled out of the way to climb the fence and face Jake. "Do you think you could carry half a bucket from the crib?"

"Long as I don't have to put it in there." Jake glanced warily at the black-spotted animals.

Arley had warned Jake away from the pigs, the youngster's skinny body a guarantee he'd lose any contest for control of the bucket. "Nope. Just get it here and I'll do it. I've got to haul water."

"Okay." Jake picked up the bucket and sauntered away.

The sows needed about ten gallons of water each: four trips from the well with two, three-gallon buckets swinging at the ends of his neck yoke. The hogs would get what they needed when he turned them into the rough riverside pasture in the afternoon. Next year Jake might be big enough to carry water—

half-buckets to start. At least that's what Arley hoped. He dumped the first two buckets about the time the sows had each finished bolting six gallons of corn, and their eagerness to get a drink made the drudgery of packing it a bit more tolerable. It wasn't hard to imagine a smile on their faces.

Trudging across the ground on the second trip, his gaze wandered over the hard-packed farmyard. Their house, such as it was, stood midway between a two-story barn on the right and a tangled mass of charred wood surrounded by a scorched stone foundation to his left. A tall chimney stood tombstone-like at one end of the mostly burned remains of his grandparents' house. Burned down in the night, they'd both died inside, and Arley had heard whispers that the fire had been set on purpose; hushed conversations that ceased whenever he came close enough to hear. He remembered moving from Bittsburg, the town a mile east where his father worked in the clay pits. His father had promised to rebuild the burned-out shell, and they'd moved into the hovel the black field-hands had once lived in.

The shack, squat, square, and sad-looking, had been built by the field workers using whatever they could find, mostly refuse and driftwood washed up on the riverbank. The flat roof leaked. Centered in the front wall, a rough-hewn plank door hung slightly askew on three leather straps, and the two small windows on either side—the only ones in the house—didn't have glass, instead filtering the light through sheets of mica. At-tached on the left side, a lean-to clung desperately to the wall; storage for firewood and coal, plus a few tools and a place for Arley to sleep during the hot summer months. The two-story barn had been built with more care, as had all the other outbuildings: chicken coop, pigsty, corncrib, and smokehouse, but neglect showed everywhere. The Negro workers' shanties in town looked better.

Back at the well again, he twice lowered the bucket into the musty darkness, the windlass squeaking wood-on-wood. Then he shouldered the yoke and walked back to the pigs. The sows now lay in the morning sun on the clean cornstalks he'd put down the night before. They'd seek cover in the roofed section come afternoon. The covered part stayed warm in winter, and he'd once tried sleeping there instead of in the cold barn. The nose-burning stench of ammonia, and the cloying air made it a one-time experience. But it wasn't just the warmth that had drawn him to spend the night; the pigs seemed to appreciate what he did for them: cold, clean well-water, scoops of corn—hard-won using a hand-cranked shelling machine, pitchers of skim milk and whey, and clean, dry stalks to root around in and sleep on. Last year they'd gotten three and a half cents a pound for the eleven hogs they sold, over six dollars apiece, and he knew how important they were. He poured the water into the trough.

On his way back to the well, two dozen chickens followed, all scolding him as he walked. Jake must have opened the coop. They'd been fed yesterday, so today they got nothing, but they didn't know that. At the well, they clucked to each other for a minute or so, and then wandered off. Back at the pen, a beaming Jake stood waiting with the corn bucket. Arley glanced at it; three quarters full. "Ain't you the mule?" He ruffled the boy's sandy hair. "Good job. Now go find a hoe and get after the garden." Jake took a deep breath, widened his smile, and ambled away.

Arley hated to work his little brother so hard, but there was only so much one person could do. He fed the corn to the voracious pigs and then took the empty buckets back to the crib. He winced at the meager amount of corn in the catch box; two days' worth maybe, certainly no more than three. Then he'd have to spend three or four grueling hours turning the crank on the hungry red corn-sheller while Jake or his mom fed it cobs.

His shoulders started to ache just thinking about it. That would have to wait; the last acre and a half of feed corn had to be planted, and there was only one way to do it: one hole at a time. He headed for the house to get something to eat and tell his mother he was ready to pull the board.

Liesl Dachauer punched the pan of dough down again and breathed the sour smell of starter that wafted up. She then covered it with a piece of dingy linen. Two large loaves of sourdough bread would go into the oven in an hour and a half. She hated the thought of telling Arley he'd have to go to town today for more flour, but she'd used almost the last of it. If her husband demanded pancakes in the morning, she'd be in for it if she couldn't make them. The thought had no sooner formed than Arley walked through the open door. "Did you see Jacob?" she asked.

"Yup. He's pestering some weeds out back."

"He does a pretty good job for a seven-year-old." Her heart felt it when Arley slumped onto the rickety bench across from her and folded his arms on the uneven tabletop. He looked at her with old-man eyes. "I can pull a piece of dough off this batch and fry it if you'd like. A spoonful of treacle on top?"

Arley nodded. "And maybe a small piece of ham? We have to finish that corn today. Pa said—"

"I know what he said. Nothing would come of it if that last acre waited until Monday." The look in his eyes spoke to her folly, and she sighed as she lifted the cloth and pulled off a fist-sized lump of dough. "Cut a little off the side of that ham. The fat will do you better than the lean today." She put a skillet on the hot stove and dropped a dollop of lard into it before working the wad of bread dough into a flat cake. The smoked meat hung in a corner of the cramped room, and Arley soon returned with a small piece of meat. "I hate to tell you," she said, "but we're out of flour, and you'd better go to Stringham's first thing. I don't want your father to catch you."

"He knows I go to town."

"But it irritates him if you're not working." She dropped the flattened piece of dough into the hot grease. "No sense offering him an excuse—he finds plenty."

Over the strenuous objections of her Irish Catholic father, Leisl had married a rowdy braggart, Klaus Dachauer, convinced she could settle him down. At first her constant attention to his slightest whim had worked well: Klaus's skill earned him a promotion at the pottery, affording them a decent place to live, and Arley was born. Soon after his birth, Leisl became pregnant again. Maybe it was too soon, because the child was stillborn, and then she lost yet another one. Klaus blamed her and bolstered his insulted ego with a whiskey jug, and punished Leisl by keeping her pregnant. That led to her father dealing Klaus a severe and public beating, and the die was cast. She couldn't know for sure, but in her heart, she believed Klaus had gotten the last fiery word. His drunken misbehavior eventually relegated him to working with the Negroes in the clay pits for a dollar and a half a day.

After Arley finished his meal, she took two dimes out of an old soda tin and laid them on the table. "Get three pounds of flour and a box of salt. Tell Mr. Stringham I don't need cake flour." Arley looked at the two coins and then up at her. "I know it's too much," she said, "but for your birthday, I want you to get two sticks of candy each for you and Jake." Arley grimaced. "Don't worry," she said. "We'll keep it a secret."

"But Jake can't keep secrets."

"He will if his second piece of candy depends on it." She put her hand on his shoulder and squeezed. "Now go."

The road to town went close by the Holversons' farmhouse,

and as Arley had hoped, Mr. Holverson was out in the barnyard. Klaus hired Arley out to the friendly Swede in exchange for the use of a boar every June, and they used Holverson's mules to plow in the fall. "Off to town, we are?" the farmer called in his melodic Swedish accent as Arley approached.

"There and right back," Arley said. "I've got a bit more corn to plant."

Holverson hustled across the yard to the front gate. "I tell your father he was welcome to my planter."

They'd lost their two-wheeled cart and one of a matched pair of mules to the sheriff for debts, and one animal trying to do the work of a team took its toll; the remaining beast now struggled just to pull an empty, wobbly-wheeled wagon. "I know," Arley said with a sigh. "He says we can do it by hand."

"We?"

Arley shrugged. "Yeah."

Holverson shook his head. "Sometimes it is a wonder."

Just then, Mrs. Holverson came out of the house, her apron a-flutter, and hurried to join her husband. Though Arley really liked the farmer, he was truly fond of his wife. "Hello to you, Arley," she said. "How is your mother?"

"Baking bread this morning." He grimaced. "Then we're going to plant corn."

"That is not woman's work," she said, and scowled at her husband before looking back at Arley. "You can stop for a few minutes?"

"Better not." Arley nodded towards the gathering clouds to the west. "If we could get it planted, it just might rain on it."

"Then tomorrow. Today is special day so I bake you a cake." Her husband raised his eyebrows. "He is thirteen years today," she said.

"Aw, no longer the boy."

Mrs. Holverson snorted. "Foolishness." Then she touched

Arley on the arm. "Sneak along in the afternoon. And bring sweet Jacob."

"I'll try. It depends . . ." He shrugged.

"I know," she said, her eyes misting. "I know."

"Better git." Arley raised his hand and hurried away.

Mrs. Holverson didn't wait long enough to speak to her husband because her words reached Arley clearly. "I take both those boys, and I hurry," she said to her husband.

"Yaw, that's for sure," Mr. Holverson replied.


Arley made the trip to town and back in less than half an hour.

Jacob stood beside his mother at the table, his eyes gleaming with expectation. "I *can* keep a secret, Arley," he said firmly as soon as Arley reached the table. "Lemme see what ya got us."

Arley tousled Jake's hair, and handed the string-tied package to his mother. "Nineteen cents." He put a penny on the table.

She carefully untied the knot, took a six-inch ball of string off a shelf, and added the day's prize to it. Then she folded the dirt-brown paper open. Jake's eyes opened wide and his jaw dropped as she picked up several pieces of stick-candy. Arley caught the spicy scent of mint. "Nine?" she asked.

"A man at the store paid the extra half-dime," Arley said. "I think he works at the pottery. He had chalk on his shoes like Pa." He paused a moment. "What's a *dickensurchan*?"

"Dickens's urchin. Two words. Where'd you hear that?"

"That's what the man said to Mr. Stringham. 'Give the boy five more. He looks like a dickensurchan.' "

"A boy in a story written by Charles Dickens, an Englishman. A very hardworking and smart boy."

"Was it all right to take them?"

"Of course. That man thought you were worth it." She turned to Jake. "Now I want you to tell me what we talked about while Arley was gone."

Jake furrowed his brow and bit the inside of his lip, his smile gone. "This is our favor and Pa will be mad if he doesn't get one but he has his own favors so it's fair and we won't tell." He took a deep breath and his smile returned.

"I'm impressed." His mother pinched his cheek. "But I wasn't expecting so many. And just so you can enjoy a sweet another day we'll put five back until then. Okay?"

Jake's smile struggled to hang on.

"No later than Monday," his mother said and held out two sticks. Jake brightened again and reached for them.

Just then a high-pitched squeal reached them from outside, followed immediately by several spine-rippling screams. Fighting pigs! Arley bolted through the door, and raced down the hill to the pens—his father's warning echoed clearly in his mind. The rail fence rattled alarmingly, and he reached it to find all thirteen hogs crowded against the planks. He'd seen squabbles erupt over a share of corn or a bucket of turnips, but this seemed different somehow, more frenzied. Blood smeared the faces of several pigs.

His mother arrived with Jake. "What's wrong?"

"They've got something in the corner," Arley said helplessly, then held onto the top rail and leaned over.

She grabbed his arm. "You can't go in there. Nothing to do but let them fight."

"I know, but . . ."

"Is that my egg basket?" She pointed at some mangled, yolk-smeared wicker.

Just then, one pig broke out of the pack and scampered to the back of the pen, hotly pursued by another. The second hog charged past on the right, and the first one turned left, its eyes rolling, wild and crazy-looking. From the pig's mouth hung the rear half of an animal with blood-smeared tawny-brown fur. "They've got a raccoon," Arley shouted when he saw a flailing ringtail. Three more pigs took off after the two at the back, squealing so loud it hurt his ears. He shook his head and pointed at the corner post. "Jake left the basket there this morning to give me a hand."

"And the raccoon smelled it," his mother said. "Egg-robber."

Two more pigs broke off, running side-by-side; one with intestines trailing from its mouth, the guts still attached to the raccoon's front half clamped in the jaws of the other hog. The remaining pigs, all smaller, packed the corner, shoving, biting, and butting, the noise now a series of grunts and the occasional angry squeal.

"I forgot," Jake said, looking sadly at his mother.

"Not your fault, I told you to," Arley said. "An accident."

"Just that," his mother said and pulled Jake to her side. "And it's over and done. How many eggs?"

"Four." Then Jake's eyes opened wide. "But I only looked in the coop," he said hopefully.

"Then there'll be more, and those four won't be missed." She studied the milling swine. "I don't see anything too bad. Pigs *will* bite each other."

"You think that's good enough?" Arley asked.

"You can slosh a bucket of water over a couple of them. The blood will wash off and no one need be wiser. Besides, how often does he come down here to look?"

Arley raised his eyebrows and shrugged.

"Exactly. It's done. Let's go enjoy the candy, and then we'll plant corn."


Arley glanced up at the gathering clouds, and then took up the strain on a rope looped around his chest. He pulled until the tail end of the ten-foot-long dibber board drew even with his mother's foot and she stopped him with a word: "Hit." Seven, two-inch round holes, eighteen inches apart, penetrated the centerline of the heavy plank. His mother, walking down the left side, poked through each opening with a blunt wooden rod, and Jake, on the other side, then dropped three kernels of corn into each hole she made. When she said "Go," Arley advanced the plank again, the weight of the board dragging dirt into the cavities. To the end of the field and back, his legs trembling with exertion, Arley concentrated on keeping the rows straight, crooked ones were a beating offense. "Hit." "Go." "Hit." The time between his mother's calls got longer and longer as Jake tired, and Arley cursed his father for not allowing them to use the mule. "Got you, no need wear out the damned mule." Arley visualized his father's sneering face. They finished with about an hour of daylight left. Jake and his mother hurried to the house, both hugging their chests against the cold; Jake's smile long gone.

Arley put the board and dibber pole in the corncrib, and then went to look at the pigs. His bucket of water earlier had done the trick, and he saw no flowing blood, nor any trace of the clumsy raccoon; nothing of the morning's carnage except for scattered remnants of the wicker egg-basket. He breathed a sigh and walked up to the well. When the sky had clouded over, he'd decided to leave the pigs penned for the day. Now he wasn't so sure that had been a good decision. Which was worse, chasing pigs or toting water?

After watering the hogs, he carried a bucket of coal and some wood into the house, and then got the cow from the pasture and milked her. Counting the forty-five paces to the house, he went inside, slumped down on the floor by the black iron stove, and leaned back against the crudely daubed wall to wait.

He wanted to quit, but the family's survival depended on him and his strong back. That it ached chronically from the hard work and regular beatings had to be put aside. Fleeting memories of a better life used to help him a little, but those thoughts came less frequently, and now he simply wanted to sit still. Nobody ate until his father came home; another brutally enforced rule.

Home by dark meant his father might be almost sober, but after that his state of drunkenness increased with each passing minute. Arley's stomach had been cramping for hours when his father, carrying a jug, stumbled into the house at ten o'clock. He sagged onto his kitchen chair, and Arley's mother scrambled to her feet, then took a pan of corn cakes and five small slices of fried ham from the warmer oven and put them on the table. From atop the stove she got a covered pot of red-eye gravy, gave it a stir, and put it by his plate. She then stepped away from him. He speared the ham slices with his fork, dropped all of them on his plate, and then arranged five of the eight cakes around the outside. After pouring gravy over the lot, he put the pot down beside his plate again and looked directly at Arley, his eyes mean, his brow lowered.

"Come to the table, boys," his mother said quietly.

Arley got up, his hunger overwhelming his caution, and sat down on the tableside bench. Jake sat beside him and his mother took a seat opposite his father. Jake, head lowered, eyed the three cakes as his mother picked one up and put it on his plate. He grabbed it with both hands and nipped a tiny bite before putting it back down. She gave one to Arley and took one herself. "Is there any gravy left, Klaus?" she asked.

Arley's nape hair bristled, and he stole a sideways glance at his mother.

"Who needs it?" Klaus grumbled and sniffed a snotty nose.

"The boys. They finished planting the corn today, just as you wanted."

"Damn . . . good thing." He picked up the pot and half-threw it across the table. "None for bright-eyes." Arley sensed his father's gaze. "Heard he was foolin' 'round in town."

116

"I needed flour, in case you wanted pancakes in the morning."

"That don't take all day."

"He was only gone half an hour. And we all worked hard today—all day." She picked up the pan and glanced inside. "You've left nothing."

Arley cringed.

"Goddamn right. I take what I want," Klaus paused, "when I want it."

"Arley can't work as hard as he does without eating. You treat that mule better than him."

Arley glanced at his father, swallowed hard, and then stared at his mother, horror-stricken. *He'll kill you.* The rough-knuckled fist crashed into the side of his head without warning and he flew backwards, taking Jake and the bench with him. Jake scuttled under the table on hands and knees as Arley scrambled to his feet.

"Squintin' at me'll get you one of them . . . ever' goddamned time," his father hollered, his words slurred.

Arley ran for the door and looked back as he grabbed the latch. Terror etched his mother's face, and helplessness swarmed over him as his father picked up the whiskey jug and slammed it onto the table.

The man struggled to stand, gripping the table's edge. "Now get the hell outta here ya worthless whelp . . . 'fore I stomp yer guts out yer scrawny ass."

Arley darted out and pushed the door shut, his mind in chaos. This had all happened before so why did he feel such a panic? Why did this time feel so different? In the barn, he kicked some inferior grass-hay into a loose pile, burrowed into it, and pulled a mildewed piece of canvas over his head. The cold, clammy, and unyielding ground met his bony butt, and he pulled his knees to his chest. The vision of his mother's face denied him

117

exhaustion's numbing solace and he trembled in his isolation.

His baby brother Percy had died the day after Christmas; he'd watched him die of starvation: wasting away slowly, surely, and silently. He knew about two tiny ones before that; and three or four that he'd never seen, born long before they were ready and taken away by Mrs. Holverson, who came over to help. Was his father doing the same thing to him as he'd done to Percy? The storm-chilled darkness sent shivers through his body, and his stomach cramped again.

He could have run away, and his mother had told him many times to do just that. But what then for her and Jake? Tears stung his eyes. *What then?* His exhausted brain searched for something, anything that made sense. And then he heard the door drag across the dirt. He turned back the canvas and peered over the edge.

His father, raised lantern in hand, stood just inside the door, leaning on the frame, his bleary eyes fixed on Arley's. "Took care . . . of the hag," he said with a sneer, and wiped one eye with the back of his hand. "Jake run off . . . I'll find 'im." His gaze shifted around the barn for a few seconds, and then he hung the lantern on a wall bracket. Arley's breath caught as his eyes followed his father's to a three-foot-long, three-inch-thick oak singletree leaning against the wall by the door. On each end, iron bands held harness rings, and in the middle, a heavier band for the chain ring all added weight to the heavy wood. He clambered to his feet still clutching the canvas, barely able to breathe.

His father reached down and grasped one end of the rigging, his eyes never leaving Arley's face. *Took care of the hag.* His father's words screamed in his head, and he released his pent breath with a gasp. The image of the wild-eyed pig that morning appeared, and the icy fingers of fear seized his heart—it was the *same* look. The singletree rose shoulder-high as his father staggered forward, and then it swung in a wide, looping arc toward Arley's head. He threw the canvas and ducked. The heavy implement crashed into a stall post and the rings clanged against the bands. His father stumbled sideways and fell facedown in the dirt, losing his grip on what Arley now saw as a weapon—a murder weapon.

Arley snatched it up, and then faced his father, who pushed himself to his knees, both hands tightly clenched. Narrowed eyes looked back, unblinking, and yellowed teeth showed behind snarling lips. "Time to go see Percy," his father growled, and started to get up.

Arley could not remember the first blow, nor the second, or third. Only after his arms would no longer lift the heavy oaken bar did he see what he'd done. He dropped the bloody tool alongside the misshapen head and battered, blood-soaked body at his feet. Bile rose to the back of his throat and brought him to his knees as his stomach rebelled. The powerful stench of unleashed bowel forced what little he had in his stomach to gush onto the dirt. *What have I done?* He stared at his bloodied hands and clothes and shuddered as his fingers stuck together.

His heart slammed hard against his chest when his piece of canvas floated past him and settled shroud-like over the dead-still body. A hand gently touched his shoulder.

"Get up, Arley," his mother said.

He took a shuddering breath.

"Come out of here." She pulled on his arm. "Come out."

He stood up, legs numb and unsteady, and she laid his hand on her shoulder. "Hold on to me." She paused to grab the lantern, and then led him outside and into the cool fresh air; living air. He stopped, then slowly and completely filled his lungs. "What have I done?" Swallowing hard, he choked back a sob. "I'll burn for this."

"You did what you had to do," she said softly. "And nobody

here will judge you."

For the first time he looked at her. Blood seeped from her left ear and flowed freely from a two-inch cut over her swollen left eye. She carried her largest butcher knife in one hand. "Jake?" he asked.

"In the corncrib."

"What are we going to do?"

"*You're* going to do nothing more here."

"We have to tell the constable."

"I'll take care of that. You're going to take Jacob to Mrs. Holverson. She and I have talked before so she knows what to do. And then I want you to go south—Tennessee maybe, or Georgia. Find work and stay there."

"But I don't know anything."

"You wouldn't be here today if you weren't smart and strong, Arley."

"But I killed my—"

"Because of *my* weakness he was your father, and because of his own, he turned into an animal. He meant to kill all of us tonight."

"But—"

"You saved your brother's life, and mine. I will not see you punished for that. And please, please don't make yourself pay for it either." She stared at him a moment with her one seeing eye. "It was not your fault. You had no choice. Do you hear me?"

Arley nodded, and then looked down at his bloody hands. "I've got—"

"That will wash off. Everything will, and no one's the wiser. Go to the well and do that, then go change into your other clothes before you get Jake. I'll be along in a minute."

He started to speak.

"I'll take care of this. Now go!" She shoved him towards the house.

Less than an hour later, with seven dollars and thirty-eight cents in his pocket and a bewildered Jake in tow, Arley stopped at the end of the cornfield and looked back at his home. He could not think of it any other way even though his mother had told him to forget it existed.

"Will Gramma Holverson be awake?" Jake asked.

"Yes."

"I know Ma said she'd be happy to keep me awhile, but I'm not sure."

"I am. She told me so only yesterday."

"No fib?"

"No fib." Arley turned and had taken one step when Jake grabbed his hand.

"Is that Ma?" He pointed back toward the house.

The yellow light of a lantern bobbed across the farmyard, away from the barn and towards the river. There it stopped for a few seconds and then moved back to the barn and disappeared.

"Well, is it?"

"I don't know, Jake. Maybe she's got belly business."

"Oh."

Arley stood a bit longer. *Why'd she go to the river?* Then the light reappeared at the barn door. There it stopped for several seconds before moving towards the river again. Move, stop, move, it stuttered across the ground towards the water for another couple minutes. And then, well short of the river, it stopped again. Arley squinted into the darkness, waiting for it to continue, and then his scalp clutched when the high-pitched screams of several hogs ripped the night. His heart stumbled when Jake grabbed his leg and hung on tight. "Another raccoon," Jake whispered, "or something else?"

At that instant, lightning defined the western horizon, and a blast of cold air whipped their clothes. *The knife. The river. They'll eat everything but the head.* The image of the savaged egg-robber swarmed his mind and then vanished as quickly as it had appeared, leaving nothing but black. "Could be that," Arley said as he pulled Jake off his leg, "or the storm we got coming." Thunder muttered as the two boys turned away and hurried before the wind.

**Wallace J. Swenson** was an award-winning Idaho native who lived in the Upper Snake River Valley. He is the author of ten novels.

# A Century of the
# American Frontier
## 1855–1875

★ ★ ★ ★ ★

# GROGAN'S CHOICE
# BY LONNIE WHITAKER

★ ★ ★ ★ ★

Jake hated to think about leaving the dog. Goddamned copperhead, anyway. Shep's head had swelled up like a dead hog in the sun. Only minutes ago, he had bolted after a cottontail at the edge of the river and stuck his head into the brush, wagging his tail. Then came the hurt yelp. Next thing Jake Grogan saw was Shep shaking the snake like a rag.

In seconds the venom hit. Shep dropped the snake and began pawing at his muzzle. Instantly, Jake pulled his pistol from the pommel holster. The injured serpent tried to slither back into the weeds, but one shot from the Colt Dragoon left the twisting snake's body in search of its missing head.

Jake shoved the pistol in the holster, sprang from the saddle, and rushed to Shep. He stomped the snake's head with his bootheel and kicked it into the weeds.

"Easy, boy." Jake wrapped his arms around the shepherd-mix and carried him a few yards to the river and laid him at the water's edge. Shep lapped hard at the water but threw it up.

Jake cut incisions across the fang marks with his Barlow and sucked out what poison he could. He cupped river water in his hands and dripped it over the inside of Shep's lips, which had turned from pink to white. His glassy eyes were beginning to swell shut.

He knew dogs had a lot of fat in their heads that would absorb the poison and slow down the effects, but if Shep didn't drink water he would die of thirst in the August Missouri sun.

In 1868, Jake was the only dentist between Lexington and Kansas City, that is, the only one who had actually graduated from dental college. And on this afternoon, he was headed to an emergency call for someone who was very dear to him.

Earlier that morning, a cowhand from Sam Chilton's cattle spread had ridden into town with news that Sam's daughter, Esther, had a swollen jaw. "Doc, she's got a knot big as a pawpaw, and she's in considerable pain."

It was the same girl with the yellow hair that Jake had seen with her parents in Lexington just weeks after General Price's troops had forged west after the second battle there. They were riding in a horse-drawn wagon when Jake straggled into town still wearing Confederate gray.

"Mr. Chilton says if you're not there by tomorrow, he's going to let Sledge pull her tooth," the cowhand told him.

The image chilled Jake. A few months before, Chilton's young blacksmith, Sledge, had pulled a tooth and broken the jaw of a cowhand in the process. The man would never speak right again.

"Tell Chilton I'll be there tomorrow and not to let that blacksmith near her." It was twenty-five miles to Chilton's and even if Jake rode until dark, camped along the way, and was back in the saddle by first light, it would be late morning before he arrived. And Jake still had two patients in his office that he couldn't abandon.

The cowboy traded horses at the livery stable, and Jake gave him a small bottle of laudanum, with written instructions on how to dose it.

After Jake had finished with his patients, he packed his medical satchel with dental instruments and supplies: rubbing alcohol, clove oil, alum, cotton, ether, and laudanum. He also wrapped up some biscuits and sausages left over from breakfast, ground coffee, and lucifers, and stowed them in a bailed boiling pot. By late afternoon, he mounted up, whistled for Shep, and they left Lexington.

Back on that day, four years ago in Lexington, Sam Chilton had seen Jake, too, and his stare wasn't charitable. When his yellow-haired daughter gazed back at Jake, he heard Chilton say as he snapped the horse reins, "He's deserter-scum, Esther. An unworthy coward. Pay no attention to the likes of him."

A deserter, yes, but after the battle at Pilot Knob, Jake had seen all the killing and maiming he could stand and vowed to escape at the first opportunity, even if it meant being branded a coward. It wasn't his skill as a dentist the Confederate States of America wanted when he was drafted—he was assigned the worst head wounds, and he stood side by side with the surgeons as they sawed off limbs. One night he just slipped out of camp and disappeared into the darkness.

Months passed but he never forgot the girl's face. How she looked at him. Her blue eyes and her yellow hair. She was sixteen—too young for him, at twenty-one. But things had changed a year later, at a pie supper to celebrate the end of the war.

Most of an hour had passed since Shep was bitten. Shep was too sick to travel, but Jake couldn't bear the thought of abandoning him, unable to defend himself from coyotes or even buzzards. He had heard buzzards would attack helpless animals that weren't yet dead.

The sun was low in the sky, so the buzzards would be roosting, but not the coyotes. The vision he imagined gnawed at his gut: Shep alone and stalked by snarling, circling coyotes. A plaintive sigh slipped out as he gazed toward the western sky. "Lord, I don't ask for myself, but I pray that You be with Esther until I can figure what to do with Shep. And please don't let that blacksmith get near her before I get there. Amen."

Something on the river caught his attention. Shafts of sunlight filtered through river willows and sycamores casting shadows and a golden glimmer on the water. Upstream, a canoe emerged from the shadows—with an Indian paddling.

Thoughts swirled through Jake's mind. An Indian in these parts? The Missouria and Otoe tribes had all but vanished in the Indian Wars or were moved onto reservations years before. But sure as hell, here was one.

Brown as a nut, the Indian paddled from a kneeling position. He steered the canoe toward Jake and stopped at the shore a few yards away. He stepped out, pulled the canoe onto the bank, and stood erect—tall and sinewy. His hair was dark and fell from the middle in a natural part to just past his ears, and his eyes were black as midnight in a cave. His age was difficult to discern—thirties, perhaps.

Jake thought of his Colt in the holster on his horse, but as the Indian approached wearing only moccasins, a breechcloth, and leggings, Jake could see he was not armed.

"Aho," Jake called out, using one of the few Chiwere words he knew.

The Indian smiled broadly, and in perfect high diction said, "You use the common language, but do not worry, my friend. I speak English, and I mean you no harm." The resonance and tone of his voice echoed confidence. His smile seemed almost indulgent.

The Indian gestured toward Shep. "Your dog has been bitten by a serpent." Without waiting for a reply, he knelt next to Shep.

Jake stiffened. "Be careful, now, Indian."

"Nature teaches beasts to know their friends."

Jake considered the Indian's response and then said, "Only two kinds of folks around here quote the Bard—cardsharps and shysters. Which are you?"

"Neither, friend. My Christian name is Jonah Smith, and I

can help your dog. What may I call you?"

"I'm Dr. Jake Grogan."

The Indian raised an eyebrow. "A medical doctor?"

"I'm a dentist. I was on my way to an emergency call when Shep was bitten."

Jonah Smith nodded in response as he gently touched the dog's snout. A shaman divining an evil spirit. Without looking at Jake, he said, "I think the copperhead did not deliver a full bite."

"How do you know it was a copperhead?" Jake's tone was skeptical.

"The copperheads come to the river at dusk to hunt and drink water." Jonah Smith smiled, looked up, and held his gaze on Jake, seemingly assessing his worth or intelligence. "You have cut the bite, that is good. I will make a poultice out of thorn apple leaves to draw out the poison."

"Thorn apple?"

"Jimson weed." Jonah Smith patted Shep's head. "I will be back shortly, my dog friend." He turned and strode past his canoe, a brown shadow disappearing in the river underbrush. It was eerie how silently he moved.

Twenty minutes later the Indian returned with a fistful of green plants in one hand and two round river stones in the other. Looking at Jake, he said, "I will crush the Jimson weed for the poultice with these stones. I will need your bandanna."

"Jonah Smith, why are you doing this act of kindness?"

"Because I hate to see an animal suffer . . . and I heard your prayer."

Jake started to respond, but hesitated. Words failed him. He looked down and began untying his neckerchief. When he looked up, the Indian was smiling—that same all-knowing smile. Jake handed him the neckerchief and said, "Jonah Smith, I would be obliged if you would fix that poultice."

Jake backed away and watched as Jonah Smith gently applied crushed leaves to Shep's snout. Shep raised his head several times, but each time the Indian soothed it back down with soft-spoken native words Jake did not understand.

After Jonah Smith had secured the poultice with the bandanna, Jake said, "I'm going to camp here tonight and figure out how to transport Shep. I'm fixing to brew a pot of coffee if you would care for a cup."

With the mention of coffee, Jonah Smith showed the first sign of emotion. His eyes widened and a smile appeared, but it was different. To Jake it seemed to be a sociable, friendly smile.

"Thank you, I would like some coffee. It is well that you are staying here tonight. Your dog will be improved tomorrow, but he should not try to walk a long distance. I can show you how to make a travois so you can travel with him."

"Again, I am obliged to you."

"You are not in my debt. I could, perhaps, find a rabbit to go with that coffee, if you would not mind company."

After a meal of roasted rabbit and biscuits, the Indian and the dentist sat in silence staring at the campfire and savoring the last of the coffee. Jake puffed on a cheroot. In the distance a couple of owls were calling and frogs croaked along the river. Shep labored in his sleep, twitching a paw and making muted yelps, as if exacting revenge on the snake.

In the reflection of the firelight, the Indian had a mystical air. It seemed to Jake that he might begin chanting some strange incantation—like the words he uttered while ministering to Shep. Jake exhaled smoke from his cigar and then broke the silence.

"Now, I am really curious, Jonah Smith. Just where in the hell do you come from? You speak English like a professor, yet you dress like your ancestors, and you suddenly appear on the river to help my dog."

Several moments passed, and Jake wondered if the Indian would respond, when he said, "My ancestors are from Missouri. My father died when I was young, and my mother and I traveled west with Mormons. She became one of many wives to a cruel man who spoke of a god I did not understand. I ran away but was taken to a reservation. There I was taught by Jesuits." After a short pause, he added, "It is time to sleep now."

Jonah Smith wrapped himself in his blanket and said no more.

The next morning Jonah Smith was gone. But next to Jake's mare were two long poles cut from saplings, lashed together with cross limbs and rawhide strips. And covered with Jonah Smith's blanket. He had left his blanket to transport Shep. Jake shook his head and said, "Thank you, Lord, for sending Jonah Smith."

Miraculously, Shep was able to stand and walk. He drank some water but turned his nose when offered some rabbit scraps.

On the trail, thoughts of the strange Indian and concern for Shep faded into the task ahead. Jake worried that Esther was suffering and hoped the laudanum was making her pain tolerable. If not, he feared Chilton would allow the blacksmith to intervene.

It was midday when Chilton's large barn and two-story frame house came into view a half-mile away. The place was far enough off the main road that it had avoided damage during the war, and Chilton had been mercenary enough to supply beef to both sides. The war had all but ruined agriculture in Missouri, but now Chilton was prospering from increased prices and access to a railway spur to Sedalia.

A couple of hounds barked but kept their distance as Jake neared the house. He dismounted and assisted Shep off the travois and coaxed him to walk. Wobbly at first, Shep padded several yards to the shade of a post oak and lay down. "You stay here, boy."

Hearing footsteps, Jake looked up and saw Sledge, the blacksmith, striding toward him. Sledge's gate had a swagger, and his face was fixed in a confident sneer. His black hair looked as if he had dunked his head in a watering trough and slicked it back with his fingers. Perhaps nineteen or twenty years old, and a half-foot shy of six feet, he stopped arm's length from Jake. Too close. The boy's odor drifted aggressively through his sweat-soaked chambray shirt.

Jake offered his hand, but the blacksmith crossed both arms over his chest. His arms, huge from pounding out horseshoes with a sledgehammer, bulged against the shirtsleeves rolled above his elbows.

Jake took a step back. "You got something on your mind, Sledge? If you do, be quick about it because I have a patient inside waiting on me."

The sneer still on his face, Sledge said, "It took you long enough to get here. I could have had that tooth out yesterday." He nodded toward Shep. "If you hadn't been dragging that dog you might have gotten here sooner."

Jake's jaw tightened, and he met Sledge's eyes with a glare. "And broken her jaw, too."

Sledge dropped his arms and clenched his fists just above his waist. The sneer was now an angry stare. "You better tread lightly, tooth doctor."

"What are you saying, Sledge?"

"I don't chew my cabbage twice."

Jake turned his back to the blacksmith and retrieved his medical bag from his horse. He saw Sam Chilton open the door to the porch. From behind Jake, Sledge said, just loudly enough for Jake to hear, "And don't be getting any ideas about you and Esther." Jake kept walking without looking back. "Did you hear me, tooth doctor?"

Chilton met Jake at the door. "Thanks for coming, Doc."

Inside, Chilton led Jake to the parlor where Esther was sitting in a chair wearing a dress that would have been suitable for a church social. Her golden hair, which looked as if it had been recently washed and brushed, covered her shoulders in a cascade of shiny waves. She would have been the picture of health, but her eyes were red, no doubt from tears and lack of sleep. And her right jaw, which she cradled with her hand, was horribly swollen.

She attempted a smile as Jake entered. "Thank you for coming, Dr. Jake." Her voice was weak.

"That's okay, I just wish I had gotten here sooner. Did the medicine I sent help?"

"At first, but now it doesn't seem to help much. I took the last dose a couple hours ago."

"Mr. Chilton, would you please assist me by getting a small pan and a towel?"

"I'll tell my wife. She's in the kitchen making dinner."

"Thank you, sir."

When Sam left the room, Jake took both of Esther's hands. "I am sorry we have to meet like this, darling, but I'm going to help you get well."

He gently touched her swollen jaw and could feel the heat of infection, and that slightest touch made her wince. "Sorry, Esther. I'll be as gentle as I can."

He unrolled the cloth wrap that held his dental instruments onto a nearby table. "Esther, open your mouth as wide as you can and lean your head toward the window so I have some light."

He dabbed the inside of her mouth with clove oil, and with a probe he tapped on the surrounding teeth to make sure he had found the offending tooth. When he tapped the most likely suspect, Esther groaned.

"Sorry, Esther. You have infection from a lower molar abscess that appears to be coming to a head. It has to be drained. If Sledge had pulled that tooth, you likely would have ended up with blood poisoning that could have killed you."

Esther's eyes widened, and she uttered a fearful moan.

"But don't worry, I'm here and you are going to be all right."

Sam returned with the towels and dishpan in time to hear Jake's dire prediction.

With the probe, Jake applied light pressure to the swelling, and pus erupted into her mouth.

Esther screamed and gagged and began spitting and hacking the corruption from her mouth. Jake grabbed the pan and held it in front of her. Between gasps, Esther blurted, "This is so foul."

"Mr. Chilton, if you would assist again, a glass of water with a half teaspoon of salt in it."

"Now, Esther, this is gonna be painful, but it will make you feel much better." He told her to hold the pan and then made a small incision with a lancet to enlarge the opening in the abscess. He pressed on the swollen jaw. Esther moaned and began spitting more blood and pus.

After she rinsed her mouth with the saltwater, Jake placed an alum pad on the incision to stop the bleeding

"Dr. Jake, the pain is much improved."

"It was the pressure that was causing most of the pain. The tooth may have to be extracted, but I want the infection to subside first. You'll need to come to the office for the rest."

Sam, who had been observing from a distance, said, "I'll get your mother."

"Jake," Esther said, "I can't thank you enough."

"You can thank me by letting me speak to your father about us."

As he spoke, Jake noticed Esther's eyes begin to glisten, almost dreamlike. He suspected it was mostly lack of sleep and the lingering effect of the laudanum . . . but perhaps not completely.

"Oh, yes, Jake."

A dog's howl from outside snapped Jake back to earth. "That was Shep. And he's hurt!"

Jake bolted to the yard. The smell of burnt flesh hit his nose and smoke was rising from Shep's hide where his fur had been scorched. And Sledge strolling toward the barn carrying a branding iron and a pistol—Jake's Colt. Without another thought, he charged toward the blacksmith. As Sledge turned around, Jake tackled him to the ground. The gun and the iron fell from Sledge's hands.

The two men wrestled on the ground each trying to gain the upper position. Jake landed a glancing blow to the jaw with little effect. Sledge wrangled his legs around Jake's waist and clutched Jake's throat in a viselike grip. "Now, you're done for, tooth doctor."

From the porch, Chilton yelled, "Let him go, Sledge."

"Daddy, help him! He's going to be killed."

"Get my shotgun, Esther," Chilton said, and rushed to the fight.

Jake pried and scratched against the death grip, but Sledge's hands were like a steel trap. He was on the cusp of blacking out when he saw a brown blur lunging at the blacksmith. Sledge screamed in agony and released his grip. Shep had locked on Sledge's ear and was shaking his head, the same as he had shaken the copperhead.

Sledge knocked Shep away and screamed, "Goddammit, he chewed off my ear." Blood spewed from the side of Sledge's head where only ragged gristle remained. Enraged, he grabbed Jake by the throat again.

Esther came to a running stop and pointed a double-barrel ten-gauge shotgun inches from the blacksmith's face and pulled back both hammers. "Let him up, Sledge, or so help me God, I'll blow your head off." Sledge released his grip.

Chilton took the shotgun from his daughter but kept it cocked and pointed at Sledge. "Now, get up, get your things, and get off my property."

Esther dropped to her knees in tears next to Jake "Please be all right."

Jake, still struggling for breath, said, "I'll be okay, but I need to check on Shep."

Sledge yanked off his shirt and pressed it to his wound. He glared at Jake. "This isn't the last of it, tooth doctor."

Chilton motioned toward the barn with his shotgun. "I said I want you off my property. And if you are still in the county by tomorrow, I will swear out a warrant for your arrest for attempted murder."

"He attacked me—it was self-defense."

"That's your side of the story. We have three witnesses here who see it differently."

Sledge spit on the ground and headed to the barn holding the shirt to his ear.

Shep was lying under the post oak tree licking his wound as Jake and Esther checked to make sure he wasn't too badly injured. While Esther was patting Shep's head, Jake untied the blanket from the travois and laid it next to Shep. Maybe some of Jonah Smith's healing power remained in it.

After Sledge rode off on his only possession, Chilton convinced Jake to spend the night to tend to his daughter's tooth and not chance being ambushed by Sledge.

Although Chilton had come to respect him as a dentist, it had taken longer to accept his daughter's fondness for Jake. After supper, he allowed that it would be permissible for Jake and Esther to sit together on the porch swing, with Shep as the only chaperone.

In the quiet moonlight, Esther kissed Jake on the cheek and nestled her head on his shoulder. She sighed and said, "I have dreamed of a night like this."

Jake touched her hand and said, "but not a *day* like this."

Esther didn't respond. She had fallen asleep leaving Jake with his thoughts. *It had been a lifetime in a day.*

**Lonnie Whitaker**, a retired federal attorney, works as a freelance writer. His novel, *Geese to a Poor Market,* won the Ozark Writers League Best Book of the Year award. His stories have appeared in magazines, anthologies, and *Chicken Soup for the Soul.* His children's picture book, *Mulligan Meets the Poodlums,* was published by Little Hands Press.

★ ★ ★ ★ ★

# BOXCAR KNIGHTS

## BY STEVEN HOWELL WILSON

★ ★ ★ ★ ★

This story takes place in the years following the American Civil War, c. 1868

"Now, Marshall! Grab the damn rung!"

"Don't swear!"

"I'll stop damn swearing when you damn grab the damn rung!"

They had practiced this. They had watched for days, hiding in the fence row just north of Danville Station, watching the cars go by, learning the different types, memorizing the location of ladders, footholds, hatches, and access doors. They had climbed cars on the siding by the light of the moon, to get a feel for it. Two weeks they had studied. Marshall had insisted they know everything there was to know before they made their first attempt at hopping a freight.

Two weeks, and now the cussed little sumbitch was going to lose his nerve and leave Carl alone on a train to Indiana.

The train was gaining speed, and Marshall, running, still hadn't worked up the nerve to take hold of a ladder rung and haul himself up. Carl, having gone first, had seized hold, found his footing, and scrabbled up to the top rung, where he now glared with disdain at his best and only friend. Was he going to have to jump, and possibly break his own neck, just so he could convince Marshall to try again?

He held out his hand. "Grab the rung and grab my hand. It's

now or never!"

Chestnut eyes wide with fear, Marshall took a deep breath, shot out a trembling arm, grabbed the rung, and swung himself onto the ladder, a hand reaching to clasp Carl's. Marshall yelped as the train's momentum seized and wrenched him, but he was on the car.

"Hold onto my belt," instructed Carl, and he swung down and began to inch along a narrow, treacherous lip of steel, towards the open door.

Ordinarily, Carl didn't give orders. Marshall was the planner. He was the one who knew things. He read books. He listened attentively when old Sister Hapgood taught lessons. He organized the other boys and girls in activities to keep them busy, out of her hair, and unpunished.

But Marshall was at a loss when it came to physical activities, dangerous activities, like climbing a rock face, or swinging into the lake from a rope . . . or hopping a freight. Carl tried not to make too much fun of his friend's lack of physical courage, against the day he would have to confess to Marshall that he, Carl, couldn't read. He knew it was going to be on Marshall to teach him.

Someday.

The door loomed open in the fading October sunlight, a black hole amidst the cool red and gold splashes painting the car. The climb was easier once they reached the door, its ribbed surface providing handholds, or at least fingerholds. Carl inched his feet, a hip's width at a time, sideways toward his goal. Marshall's knuckles dug into his spine.

"Ease up on my belt!" he shouted against the wind.

"If I ease up, I'll fall!" Marshall yelled back into his ear.

*Great, the kid's probably afraid of falling, along with everything else. He's probably all froze up and can't move a muscle.*

"Okay, here's the door," he called out. "You go in first."

"I can't!" said Marshall.

"You have to. If I get inside, and you're hanging out here, I can't help you. Climb behind me, then take hold of the door-frame."

Marshall grabbed too hard onto Carl's belt, pulling him back and almost making him lose his hold on the open door. As Carl's body jolted and recovered his balance, Marshall's hand, making for the door, missed and grabbed his shoulder. Fingernails dug hard into Carl's flesh.

"You're doing good," Carl winced, promising himself that, if Marshall corrected him and said he was doing *well*, he would pitch them both to their deaths on the tracks.

Marshall was too distracted to correct him.

"Now take hold of the door. I'm going to move us both over."

Struggling with the weight of an extra boy on his back, albeit a scrawny one, Carl dug toes in against a rib of the door and levered them both toward the opening. Marshall, hanging on, was lined up with it.

"Now, let go of me! Drop to the floor!"

"But—"

*"Drop!"*

*And don't roll out the other side of the damned car!*

But Marshall did not drop. He snaked an arm around Carl's waist, holding Carl in a stranglehold, and fell onto his butt on the floor of the car. Carl's butt landed on Marshall, his spine wrenched by the fall, and he called out three of his favorite words at the air.

The boys spent the next half minute recovering their breath, taking stock of their body parts, cataloging their injuries, and assuring themselves they were still alive.

After that work was complete, Carl asked, "Ya got anything to say for yerself?"

"Those words you said aren't Christian."

"Neither is pulling a feller down on his ass when he told you to let go!"

"I was scared!" protested Marshall. "And please stop saying those words."

"Ass!" bellowed Carl in Marshall's face. "Ass, ass, ass!"

Marshall dropped his eyes and swallowed. "I hope Jesus's grace will keep you out of the flames."

"Fer now, maybe some of Jesus's grace will find us a comfortable place to sleep."

"That's blasphemy," protested Marshall. "Don't take His name in vain."

Carl sighed out loud and stood, not enjoying the process. His wounded back complained in language that might have given Marshall a stroke. He surveyed the dark space about them, wishing they had had the chance to steal some candles. His eyes made out the wooden slats of crates, stacked three high and tied to the walls of the car. A narrow passageway between two rows seemed the only form of shelter they would manage. He wondered idly if any of the crates contained something that could be used for bedding, but then they had no way to open them anyway.

"We'll have to just hide out as best we can at the end of the car," he said to Marshall. They had deliberately selected a car near the front of the train, as they tended to be loaded first, and fuller. They were less likely to be entered by rail hands soon.

Marshall dropped to a cross-legged position on the dusty floor and settled himself against a crate where he could look out at the thin sliver of moon peeking through the clouds. "Well," he sighed, "at least we got away from Sister Hapgood. I think we were gonna get a lot worse than locked in the basement this time."

Yesterday evening, Marshall had lost his temper and shouted at Sister Hapgood, right in front of the other orphans in the

Baptist Home. She had promised to "wear the flesh off" Marshall's body with a switch. "And you'll be taking your punishment next to him," she had promised Carl. Carl hadn't complained or asked any questions. Of course, he would be punished too. They were always punished together, usually because Carl had committed the infraction, and Marshall had tried to stand up for him. The usual punishment—for stealing, for lying, for falling asleep during lessons—was to miss dinner and be locked in the basement for the night, to sleep if one could sleep. The basement of the old farmhouse, which the church had adopted as an orphan asylum, had a low ceiling— Carl's head brushed its beams, and he was not full-grown. It was dank and filthy, with a dirt floor. Mice and rats were often spotted, and, where there were rodents, there were snakes, hungry for a meal. Carl didn't mind snakes. Marshall was deathly afraid of them.

If a child had a history of escaping the basement in search of better sleeping arrangements, then he was chained by the wrist to the wall, fastened to hooks. No one knew if the hooks were original to the farmhouse—used to restrain slaves, perhaps?—or if Sister Hapgood had ordered them installed.

Corporal punishment was not exactly rare, but it was saved for extreme cases. Sister Hapgood would have used it more often, but the church pastor, an older man named Brooks, valued moderation. Indeed, it was Pastor Brooks's influence that had reduced Sister Hapgood's promise of immediate violence to a threat to be carried out the next morning—after Marshall and Carl had spent another night in the basement.

Marshall and Carl had left the orphanage that night.

"Why ya always mouthin' off at that old bitch anyway?" Carl asked as he took a seat opposite his companion.

"You're family."

Marshall said it with a shrug, as though it were obvious.

"I ain't yer family!"

Marshall's face did not fall, but it settled into that look of quiet, patient suffering that told Carl he could heap as much pain as he wanted on his friend. There would be no anger, and no retribution, only profound sadness.

Damn Marshall's sadness anyway!

But Carl softened his tone and continued, "I mean ya only met me a few months ago. I can't replace the family ya lost. I'll never be enough."

"That's plain. You're a pretty poor replacement."

Carl reared back and let his foot fly into Marshall's knee, eliciting a yelp.

"But you're all I've got," said Marshall as he rubbed his wound.

Marshall's parents and younger sister had died in the War Between the States, which had ended just three short years ago now. His daddy had been a Confederate soldier . . . for a little while. He had died of measles before seeing any action and was buried in a mass grave . . . somewhere. His mama had got sick and died before she could collect his pension. The Confederacy had died not long after. She still would have had a pension from the U.S. Army, but now she was dead. A lot of people had died during and after the war. There was no food. They were burned out of their homes. Soldiers had torched the Marshall's family's cabin the night they learned his daddy was dead.

All of this history, Marshall had confessed to Carl during sleepless nights, either in the cramped boys' room upstairs, or in the basement. Well, sleep had evaded Marshall. Carl had been cheated of sleep by Marshall's never-ending personal history lessons.

Now, Marshall looked to be ready to launch into another one.

"Before Mama died, she told me—"

"Oh, not another dad-blamed story!" moaned Carl.

"She told me there's nothing more important than family, to go and find mine," finished Marshall, undeterred.

"And all ya found was me."

"She meant to find my uncle in Evansville."

"And we're on our way to find him," said Carl, "courtesy of the Christian charity of the Tennessee Railroad."

Marshall snorted. "How can it be Christian charity when they don't know we're here?"

"The Lord moves in mysterious ways."

"Not that mysterious, he doesn't."

Carl felt around in his pockets, hoping to find a scrap of tobacco left to smoke. Coming up empty-handed, he swore under his breath and then asked, "You sure that uncle o' yours is gonna help us?"

"He's my mama's elder brother, and I've got no one else. He pretty much has to."

"He don't have to take me."

"I told you, you're my family now. He'll take you in. Besides, he'd be getting two anyway, if—"

Marshall choked on the end of his sentence, but he didn't have to finish. Carl knew that his sister had died within minutes of his mother, of the same illness. Their bodies had been too starved to fight it off, there being little food to spare in the refugee camp they had landed in, outside Danville. From there, the orphaned Marshall, a boy not yet tall, with no beard, had been shipped off to the state-funded, church-run orphanage.

Six months ago, Carl had been brought to the same orphanage, a wild boy with fiery hair and coal-black eyes. Nobody knew where he had come from, or who his parents had been. He had just been found wandering on the road. If he remembered a home and a family, he wasn't talking about them. He didn't know his own age, and he might have been old enough to go to work, had there been work. Someone had decided that he was young enough for the church's care.

When Marshall pressed Carl for his story, he was told to mind his own business. He had come to learn that, if he wanted to be friends with the only boy his age in the asylum, he'd best do just that. And so he did. He didn't like it, but he did it.

"It don't help to think about the past," Carl said now.

Marshall nodded, blinking away tears. "You're right."

"Guess we should get to the back of the car and try to sleep."

"Reckon so."

Marshall did not know how long he had been asleep when the weight of the world landed on his chest.

Awakening, breathless and in pain, he quickly realized that it was not the weight of the whole world, but rather the weight of one of its occupants, a wiry figure, smaller than himself, dressed in a ragged but heavy coat. Muscular, canvas-clad legs squeezed Marshall's middle until he feared his ribs might crack, and something cold and sharp pressed the exposed flesh of his throat.

"Best you make yer peace with the good Lord, white boy," croaked the voice of the figure.

Marshall held his breath, wondering if he would ever draw another. He was pinned. There was no option for resistance. He tried to whisper, "What do you want?" but his voice was apparently still asleep. Only a squeak came out. He said a silent prayer that such an undignified sound might not be his last, swallowed carefully, and was making to speak again when what he now realized was a well-used Bowie knife was yanked from his throat. A familiar hand had seized the wrist of the attacker. Marshall looked up to see Carl's arm wrapped around the stranger's throat.

Struggling under the weight of the new arrival, Marshall pulled away until he saw an angry, brown face, teeth clenched, mouth curled into a snarl. The black boy pulled his knife hand close, dragging Carl's arm with it, and sunk his teeth into Carl's flesh. Carl recoiled but brought his unbitten arm forward to knock the knife from the attacker's hand. Before he could get in close enough to restrain his opponent, however, the black boy drove a knee into Carl's groin, then shoved his doubled-over form backward.

Marshall cried out in alarm as his friend came dangerously close to the open door of the moving car. Carl steered his fall enough to avoid ejection, but his head struck the door frame with a sickening crack. He collapsed and did not move.

"Carl!" Marshall shouted again, coming to his feet. He did not have time to examine Carl's injuries, however, for the new arrival was moving to reclaim his knife. Marshall was not as accustomed to fighting as Carl apparently was. There had only been much younger boys at the orphanage with him, and fighting was not Christian anyway. In this case, however, with both their lives in danger, he had little choice in the matter. He flung himself at the black boy, impacting him low, and wrapping arms around muscular legs, bringing him down hard.

His opponent, apparently more familiar with close combat, quickly used leverage to throw Marshall onto his back, landing once again on top of him. He raised a fist to strike. Marshall raised one arm to block the punch, and grabbed at the boy's chest with the other, hoping to get hold of his coat or shirt and gain the upper hand. His hand thrust under the coat and seized something soft and warm, like—

"Good Lord!" Marshall snatched his hand away and stared aghast at his opponent, who seemed suddenly amused.

"What's the matter? Don't got any fight left?"

"I can't fight you, you're a girl!"

"Ain't stopping me," said the girl, and brought her fist down hard against Marshall's jaw.

He tasted blood, and wriggled, trying to get away. "Stop that!" he barked. "I'm not going to fight you."

"Real gentleman, huh? Well they bleed red like everyone else, I hear." She drew back to strike again.

Marshall heaved his hips up hard and threw her off him. As the girl scrambled for her knife, he held up two placating hands. "Stop! Why are you doing this?"

"This is my place," she hissed.

"We didn't know," Marshall said, looking sideways at the still-unmoving Carl. "We just got on the first open car."

The girl's eyes narrowed. "A open door usual means they's somebody already here. And what you doin', gettin' on a car full o' crates? Don't you know you could get smashed if they fall? Yer s'posed to get in a empty car."

"But you're here."

"Ain't no empty cars."

"Well then—"

"Shut up!" snapped the girl.

"We didn't know to look for an empty car," said Marshall quickly. "We don't know anything much about riding the rails, except what a friend who'd done it told us."

She appeared to relax ever so slightly. "Reckon ya don't look like reg'lar hoboes."

Marshall attempted to look disarming. "First time. I promise." He nodded at Carl. "We're just a couple of orphans on the run."

"Couple o' dumb orphans," replied the girl.

"A couple of dumb orphans, yes," agreed Marshall. "But we're not here to hurt you or try to take your space. Now, could you put down the knife, so I can check on my friend."

The girl considered it, then nodded.

Marshall crossed carefully to Carl's prone form and knelt. The other boy was breathing, thank God, and stirred with a groan when Marshall shook him.

"Carl, can you hear me?" Marshall asked.

"Uhnh," said Carl.

"Do you know who I am?" Marshall asked this because his only experience with a person who had been knocked unconscious had happened when little Sonny Lacy had slipped on a rock and hit his head at the swimming hole. Pastor Brooks had asked the boy if he knew the names of people around him, by way, Marshall supposed, of making sure his brains weren't all smashed up inside his skull.

"Yer a pain in my ass," muttered Carl, and rolled over to his side, facing away from Marshall.

"I guess he's okay," Marshall concluded. He looked back to the girl. "What's your name?"

"Venus."

"Venus? Nice name. She was a Roman goddess, in mythology."

"It's a boy's name," said Venus, gesturing with her still-raised knife.

"If you say so." Marshall leaned back against a crate next to Carl and settled down to sit, legs outstretched. "You're tough for a girl."

"I'm tough for a boy, too."

"I would agree with that. How did you get here?"

"I run away from a plantation."

"You were a slave? But they outlawed slavery."

"Not 'fore I run away they didn't. And outlawin' slavery don't make a lot o' difference to a colored girl on the rails. I might as well be a deer for 'em to shoot and eat."

"Why did you try to kill me?" asked Marshall.

Venus rolled her eyes. "Weren't gonna kill you. Just wanted t' scare ya."

"Why?"

"Get rid of ya. So ya won't turn me in."

"We don't want to turn in anyone. We just want to get to Indiana. Besides," he added, "turning you in would mean letting someone know we're here. That would be kind of stupid of us, don't you think?"

"Guess maybe. But ya don't look too smart, so I ain't bettin' my life on you."

Marshall ignored the insult. Girls insulted boys. It was the way of the world. He didn't know why and hadn't asked in many years. "Why are you dressed as a boy?"

" 'Cause on the rails, ya don't wanna be a girl. Ya keep yer head down and yer knees together." She paused and looked him over, finally taking a seat opposite him as she did. She situated herself cross-legged with perfect balance. Once she was comfortable, she asked abruptly, "Ya got money?"

"No. We weren't allowed to have money in the orphanage."

"Well, I ain't gonna give you nothin' if you don't have money."

"I haven't asked you for anything."

"Every boy asks every girl for somethin', sooner or later."

For a moment, Marshall was confused. Then her meaning overtook him. He spluttered, "I—are you talking about . . . ?—I would never presume to ask you for that!"

Now she looked at him in disbelief, head cocked to one side. "What's wrong with you? Ain't you a proper boy?"

He had no idea what she meant by "proper," but he answered, "I—I think I am. It's just . . . well, it isn't right for a gentleman to ask a young lady—"

Venus threw back her head and laughed out loud. "I don't know about you, Mistah Gentleman, but I ain't no lady."

"Well . . . well, I'm not asking for . . . that. Do you really take money for—?"

"I take money however I can get it. Sometimes men gives it to me for lettin' 'em get between my legs for a few minutes."

"That's awful!"

She shook her head. "You ain't no kinda hobo, gettin' all flustered talkin' about a little brush."

"I'm not a hobo. I'm . . . I don't know what I am. But I won't take liberties with you."

"What about your friend?" She looked over at the sleeping Carl. "He got any money?"

"No."

Lips pursed, she said, "Too bad. He's pretty, like a pony or a li'l puppy."

"Boys aren't pretty."

"Sure they is. You are too, kinda. If ya do get hold of any money, I won't say no."

"Um . . ." Marshall felt his face grow hot. He could think of nothing to say but didn't want to be rude to a young lady. "That's a very kind offer."

Venus swore quietly and shook her head, then she rolled easily onto her side. "I'm gonna get back to sleep now." She held up the knife. "But don't get any ideas."

"Not a one," agreed Marshall. He scooted closer to Carl, verified that his friend's skin was warm, and that his breathing was still even, and then he lay his head down on his elbow.

Marshall was awakened before dawn by the sound of Carl groaning unhappily. He lifted up on one elbow to see the silhouette of his friend in the faint light from the door. Carl sat with his knees raised, his head resting on them. His hands were knotted at the back of his neck. He was still in pain.

"Headache?" asked Marshall.

"No thanks, I've got one."

"I kept an eye on you overnight."

"Good, it's comforting to know was somebody here to wake me up and tell me if I died." He looked at Marshall, clearly aware of his friend's displeasure at the remark. "Thanks. Don't mind me. I'm cranky on account of this hole in my head."

"I checked. You don't have a hole in your head. At least not any new ones."

Carl looked across to the sleeping form of Venus. "Did you kill him?"

"No. And he's not—"

"Did you get his knife away?"

"No, but you should know—"

"Jesus!" hissed Carl, and he was on his feet, jumping to where Venus was, grabbing for the knife clutched at her breast. She awoke as he touched her and, with the thrust of one hand, knocked Carl flat on his backside.

"Get his knife!" shouted Carl.

Venus leapt to her feet and, brandishing the knife, made to carve Carl some new openings from which to blow hot air.

Marshall jumped between them, grabbing Venus's arm. "Don't," he said. "He's not going to hurt you. He just woke up and he's confused."

"He ain't confused," said Venus.

"I ain't confused," said Carl.

Defeated, Marshall threw up his hands. "Well, then, by all means, let me step out of the way, and you two fight it out. I'll continue on to Indiana with the survivor."

Both seemed to consider this seriously.

"Or," Marshall went on, "you could both realize that nobody here wants to hurt anybody, and maybe we can help each other."

"Tell that to the boy with the knife," said Carl.

"He's not—"

"I only got my knife up on account o' you tried to steal it!"

"I only tried to steal it on account o' you tried to slit my friend's throat!"

"*All right,*" shouted Marshall, "*stop!* Carl, this is Venus. Venus, this is Carl. Venus is a runaway slave and a professional hobo. Carl is a runaway orphan and a professional troublemaker."

Carl sighed. "Hello."

"Hey," said Venus, who still did not put the knife away.

"Where were you a slave?"

"Kentucky. Ran away and wound up in a contraband camp."

"Contraband camp?" asked Marshall.

Carl, no doubt pleased to know something Marshall did not (for a change) explained. "Places where escaped slaves and freed men could go to live, and some white folks would look out for them."

"Ours was at Camp Nelson," said Venus. "Union camp. We thought we was safe, but the Union soldiers turned us out. Most folks died. I learnt to hop freights."

"Among other things," said Marshall.

"Don't go gettin' high and mighty with me, boy," said Venus. "You two don't look like nothin' to me but poor white trash. You ain't no better than me."

" 'Than I,' " corrected Marshall.

"Oh, good, Marshall. Torment the boy with the knife," said Carl.

"He's not—"

"Hey!" Venus cried, leaping to her feet. In two steps, she had her hand on Carl's shoulder and was pulling him back, away from the door where he had moved to sit.

"Get off me!" barked Carl as he fell onto his back.

"I'm savin' your damn life! What did you think you were doin', hangin' your legs out like that?"

"I was just getting some air."

"Gettin' your damn legs cut off, more like, if we come upon a hillside, or if the door rattled shut. Don't you know nuthin'?"

"I think we've established that we don't," said Marshall.

"And don't go puttin' yer face in the door, ya scenery bum,"

Venus went on to Carl. "Somebody sees ya, they'll come toss all of us off the train, and they ain't gonna slow down first!"

"Sorry," said Marshall. Carl just looked angry.

"What you goin' to Indiana for, anyway?" asked Venus.

"My uncle lives there."

"He got money?"

"I don't know. A little, I guess."

"Make you a deal. I'll look out for you two, teach you how to get around on the tracks. You give me money when we find your uncle."

"Maybe we don't need you," said Carl.

"You still got yer legs 'cause o' me. You two'll be picked up by bulls before the day's out if I don't help you."

Carl looked at Marshall. "What are bulls?"

"See?" asked Venus. "Bulls is railway police. You keep out of their sight."

"You're right," said Marshall. "We really could use some help."

"Glad one of you got the brains to see it." Venus glared daggers at Carl.

"When we get to Indiana, I'll see what my uncle can give you. A meal at least."

"Speaking of which," said Carl, "where do you find food around here? I'm starving."

Venus shook her head. " 'Less you knows somebody on the crew that's got a lunch pail, we ain't eatin' till this train stops."

"How soon is that?"

"Dunno. Never rode this spur before." She said irritably, "Just settle back and see what you can see."

They were silent for a while. Venus, staring out at the racing scenery, began to sing. She had a clear, melting soprano, and her song was about the joys of meeting Jesus in Heaven.

"That's pretty," said Marshall. "Where'd you learn to sing?"

"Got to learn to do somethin' when you're riding. Hoboes don't set idle."

"I thought that's what hoboes done best," said Carl.

"Proves you don't know nothin'. Tramps set idle. Hoboes work. And when they ain't a job in front of us, we do somethin' useful. I sing. People like it."

"I like it," said Marshall. "Please don't stop."

Venus looked to Carl, as if for a second opinion.

"Do what you want," he muttered. "I don't care none."

Marshall's muscles had internalized the rhythm of the tracks, so much so that he barely noticed the vibrations of the floor beneath him. What motion he did register had become comforting to him, soothing his tired limbs and tortured mind.

It was evening again, and he relaxed, alone, against the stack of crates near the open door, mindful of Venus's warning to keep out of sight.

In the darkness, there was not a lot to see outside—dark shapes flying by, like giant bats, or midnight storm clouds, hulks of old houses and barns, dying trees—or were they dying? Everything looked dead in the darkness of this night. But then there were the houses whose windows were warmed with the glow of lamplight, pale orange and radiating heat into the evening. Marshall was almost warmed by it as well, and by the thought of being in a home again, after years in camps and the drafty old orphan house, where Sister Hapgood allowed a coal fire only first thing in the morning. Nights, she said, should be cold to encourage sleep and godly quiet.

Marshall wondered what it must be like to sit at the dinner tables of those houses, to eat warm, buttered biscuits and salted ham, pickled green beans put away by a grandmother who smelled like smoke and pine oil, later to stroll the town main street, lit by gas lamps, its dust held down by the evening dew.

What were the people in those houses like? Was there a father, upright but tired from a day's labor in the field, or angry, drunken, and stumbling? A mother with hands reddened by chores, warm and ready with a comforting arm, or shrewish, criticizing, ready to complain? Were there children? Were they well-behaved, with maybe just a hint of mischief in their eyes as they plotted an adventure? Or were they spoiled and brattish? Or bullies with hateful gazes? Did they have dreams of greatness and riches, or were they defeated from the start, aware that the world had nothing to offer and would take any meager portion they chanced to have?

From the far end of the car drifted moaning sounds. Marshall recognized Carl's voice from nights when dreams were not pleasant, and sleep did not come back after they visited, and from nights when dreams were pleasant and . . . well, it wasn't proper to think on such things.

Not long after, Carl returned to Marshall's side, his red hair ruffled, still buttoning his shirt as he sat down.

"What were you doing?" asked Marshall.

"Talkin' to Venus."

"Must have been quite a talk. I didn't hear any words."

"We said what we needed to."

"Guess she told you she's a girl."

Carl snickered. "She didn't have to."

Marshall looked away, not wanting Carl to see the look on his face, not sure of his own feelings.

After what may have been thirty seconds, Carl said, "What?"

"I didn't say anything."

"That's why I asked. When you don't say nothin', I know there's trouble. What's itchin' you?"

"You . . . you acted on your lustful impulses—with that innocent girl."

Carl snorted. "She ain't innocent, trust me."

"It's not Christian."

"See, that's why I need you here—when she spread her legs, I forgot to ask if it was Christian to put my—"

"Shut *up*! I don't want to know what you put where! You should be more godly."

"Like you?"

"Like Jesus."

"If I run into him, I'll ask his advice on what to do in that situation."

"You'll only run into him if you pray."

"Then I guess I'm on my own."


Evansville, Indiana, was the most despair-ridden place on Earth. There seemed to be dust on everything, as if the owners of the town had gone out one day, expected to return that evening, and been instead ambushed or—more likely, given the territory—scalped and left to die in the blazing sun. In their absence, everything had accumulated dust—even the people they had left behind—and now, Evansville was just the corpse of a town that used to be lived in and cared about. The people remaining— dusty shadows—were merely abandoned playthings.

"Your uncle lives here?" Venus asked Marshall as they shuffled, hungry and sore, down the town's main thoroughfare.

"If you call being in this place 'living,' " muttered Carl.

"Beggars can't be choosers," said Marshall.

Venus returned the suspicious glance of a man sitting on his unclean front porch. "I ain't a beggar. I work for a living."

Carl answered with an irreverent smirk that would have got him slapped by Sister Hapgood.

"It's not much," said Marshall, "but if my uncle will put us up, I guess it's home."

"Y'all damn near broke your necks to get *here*," wondered Venus. "Which o' you fools—"

"The Bible says not to call a man a fool, Venus."

"Okay, Reverend Marshall, which one o' you mush-headed *idiots* came up with the idea to hop a freight to come here?"

"We got the idea from Phil," explained Carl. "He was a, I guess you'd call him a kind of a stray, come to church one Sunday and asked if there was work. Pastor Brooks gave him a job trimmin' back the blackberry brambles out back, so's we could have a proper Sunday School picnic someday."

"We helped him," said Marshall. "He told us he had been a Confederate soldier."

"Pretty much all o' them lookin' for a job now, if they're able to stand up straight," said Venus. "Fair number of 'em hoboes."

"Phil had been with General Jo Shelby's division in Texas," Marshall went on. "Seems the general and his men decided, when the war ended, that they were going to just keep going south—to Mexico—to avoid capture by the Union."

"They make it?" asked Venus. "Did they get away?"

"Doesn't sound like it. Phil wasn't a hundred percent sure. But he broke away. He wanted to try and make it home to Maryland."

"Virginia's as far as he got," said Carl. "They found out who he was, the Army did, and they took him away from our place in chains. But not before he told us all about ridin' the rails from Texas."

Venus laughed under her breath, low and caustic. "God musta handed you a extra dose o' luck, that he got took away. You damn fools done fell for a jocker!"

"A what?" asked Marshall.

"Listen, they ain't many women on the rails, right?"

"Present company excepted," said Marshall.

"Huh?"

"He means 'ceptin you."

"Right. So, hoboes bein' mostly men, well, they get horny—"

Marshall went pale.

"You okay?" asked Venus.

"He cain't hear words like that," put in Carl. "It aches his Jesus bone."

"Well that's how they gets, reverend. Ya can't change men." She looked ruefully at Carl. "Or boys. Anyway, jockers needs some company, so they go for the next best thing to a woman, a fresh, smooth, boy."

"That's disgusting!" said Marshall.

Carl was silent.

"They sees a boy who ain't on the rails," said Venus, "but maybe's a little unhappy. They tells him tales of mountains made o' candy and places where gold grows on trees."

"And boys go with them?"

"You come."

"By ourselves."

"Ya still fell fer the pitch."

"I don't think Phil was a pervert," said Marshall.

"For his sake, hope he weren't. Hoboes, most of 'em, don't like to see a young'un took advantage of. So they takes care of any jocker they catch at it. Y'all would do best to stay away from anyone who seems a little too friendly."

"How do you stay safe?" asked Carl.

"I sticks to the young ones what decides to take up the life on their own."

"He decided," said Carl, pointing to Marshall. "I just followed him."

"You just follows him everywhere?"

Carl shrugged. "Till I get a better offer."

"Well, we made it here, didn't we?" asked Marshall. Before she could say it, he added, "Thanks to you, Venus." He stopped and pointed. "There's the post office. Let's go find out where my uncle lives."

The man in the post office had no good news for them. When Marshall gave his uncle's name, he shook his head. "Sorry, son. You're a few months too late." He seemed a kindly man, middle-aged, eyes warm behind small, wire-framed reading glasses, a neat, gray beard decorating his chin. "We had the smallpox."

"He's dead?" asked Marshall, his face blank, almost as if it didn't know the word.

The postmaster nodded. "The whole family. Too many families. It's hardest on the children."

Marshall just stared at the floor.

"What about his house?" asked Carl bluntly. Venus had waited outside, not wanting to attract attention.

Marshall looked at Carl in surprise, but Carl said reasonably, "If the whole family's dead, their property would be yours."

"Oh, were you family?" asked the postmaster.

"He was my uncle."

"I'm so sorry. And I'm sorry to tell you that the house went to the bank. He owed on it. Most people do, 'round here. I reckon no one knew he had a nephew. Any personal effects likely went to the church. You could ask—"

"No," interrupted Marshall. "Thank you for your . . . time. There's nothing we need."

Carl followed him out of the small building and into the street where Venus waited.

"Sorry about your uncle, Marshall," Venus said as they walked back to the train station.

"Thanks. I never knew him. It's hard to mourn a stranger." He stopped and looked at the sky aimlessly. "But now I suppose I'm really an orphan." He turned to Venus. "And there's no money. I don't know what I can do for you, after all your help."

Venus chewed her lower lip. "Mama always said never to feed a stray kitten. You feed 'em, you stuck with 'em, she said."

"What's that even mean?" demanded Carl.

"Means let's get on the train, orphans, 'fore I makes up my mind to drown you like the pair o' strays you is."

"Stop right there!"

"Shit," muttered Venus, who was halfway up into the empty boxcar when the voice rang out across the yard. Marshall and Carl were still on the ground behind her. "Bulls," she observed.

Two men in dusty overcoats and mismatched caps strode toward them. The taller one had a long face decorated by a handlebar mustache that obscured a protrusive lower lip. He looked like he'd been belted in the mouth and the swelling had stuck. He had his hand on his belt, drawing his coat back. There was a glint of metal in the sun.

"They have guns," whispered Marshall.

"Always do," said Venus.

Drawing near, Belted Mouth stopped, kicking gravel as his boots dug in. "Lookin' for a free ride?" he asked.

"Naw," said Venus, "we was—"

"Ain't talkin' to you, boy. Talking to your masters here."

"There are no masters, sir," said Marshall.

For his trouble, Marshall received a cuff in the mouth. His lower lip, cut against his teeth, began to bleed.

"Wrong, boy," said the tall man. "I'm the master here, and you all do as you're told."

"We just wanted to see the train," said Carl. "Ain't never seen one before."

"Ain't never gonna see one again, ya don't stop yammerin'," said the second, shorter bull. He was older, grayer, and even his face was short, appearing to be a size too small for his skull. His chin was too close to his nose.

"Now you boys gonna get out o' here right now. You come back," he leveled the gun at Carl's forehead, "you gonna meet my pistol here, up close an' personal." He looked Venus up and down. "Might shoot yer colored friend anyhow, make sure today's lesson sticks."

"No," said Marshall, stepping protectively in front of Venus. "We understand. You don't have to hurt her."

"Her?" Both bulls' eyes went wide. Belted Mouth pressed his gun against the seam of Venus's ragged jacket and pushed it aside. As the barrel pressed soft flesh beneath, he nodded knowingly and said again, "Her." He wrapped an arm around Venus's waist, pulled her close against him, and grabbed her breast hard. He pushed her back against the boxcar's edge, into the door's opening. "You boys go on get out of here. I'll send your friend your way if there's anything left when we're done."

"No!" cried Marshall.

The little gray bull began to advance, but his cohort had frozen at Marshall's outburst. As Carl pulled his friend by the shoulder, trying to encourage him to run, Belted Mouth sighed, "Weren't plannin' on killin' no damn fool boy today, but—"

With his free hand, he raised his pistol, pointed at Marshall's heart.

"Run!" screamed Carl, pulling Marshall again.

There was a loud screech from the front of the train, the whistle of impending motion. The boxcar lurched, and Venus took advantage of the moment to thrust her knee into the groin of her assailant. He doubled over in pain, dropping the gun. Carl, abandoning thoughts of escape, rushed forward to kick him in the back of the head before he could rise again. Venus scooped up the fallen weapon.

The second bull tackled Marshall, pinning the skinny boy easily to the ground and raising a fist that, in two or three punches, would probably pulp Marshall's face, or crush his windpipe. Marshall closed his eyes and turned away, but the blow never landed. There was a crack, like a whip being unfurled, and Marshall's would-be killer fell backwards and off of him. Getting to his feet, Marshall saw a red spot, slick and growing, on the front of his shirt.

"Sweet Jesus," Marshall muttered. "Have mercy."

"Marshall, come on!" called Carl.

Marshall looked up from the dying man at his feet to see Carl scrambling onto the now-moving boxcar, his hand extended. Venus was already onboard and safe. Marshall ran, saying uselessly over his shoulder, "I'm sorry," to the corpse behind him. He extended his arm, grabbed Carl's hand, and used his knees to propel himself into the air and onto the moving car. As he landed on the hard, wooden floor, something grabbed his foot. With Carl's hands firmly gripping his shoulders now, Marshall looked to see the surviving bull, his face twisted in rage, holding onto the iron step of the car with one hand and Marshall's ankle with the other. His feet moved comically, trying to keep up as the car gained speed.

Venus, kneeling, reached out with the gun she still held and drove the butt of the grip into the bull's forehead. He screamed but did not release. He tightened his grip and yanked, trying to pull Marshall out of the car.

Venus struck again, harder this time. The pistol connected with a sickening crunch, and blood spurted from the impact point. The bull tried to say something, then gasped. His hand on Marshall's ankle relaxed, pulled free, and he fell backward into empty air, off the train. Marshall looked away.

"Sissy," muttered Venus, her breath still ragged. "Can't watch a man die when he done tried t' kill you?"

"Reckon he ain't as bloodthirsty as you," said Carl defensively.

Venus glared momentarily at Carl, then, as if she could contain herself no longer, burst into laughter. "He done all right for a uppity white boy." She placed a hand on Marshall's head and mussed his hair. "Thanks for standin' up for me." She looked at Carl and added, "Both of ya."

Carl helped Marshall to his feet, and the three moved away from the open door.

"What now?" asked Marshall.

"Now we head to the jungle," said Venus.

"No!" insisted Carl. "I ain't doin' it!"

"But—" Marshall began.

Carl threw himself down on the floor resolutely, arms crossed, as if daring the other two to move him. "I ain't goin' to no jungle."

"It's not a real jungle, fool," said Venus. "Ain't no lions or nothin'!"

"It's a hobo jungle, like Venus said," Marshall explained again. "A safe place where we can—"

"A safe place is California, where Phil said there's work! And there's orange trees, and open space. It never rains, and it's never cold."

"An' the mountains is made of candy!" jibed Venus.

Carl ignored her, speaking only to Marshall. "Even if we didn't have a place to live, we could just sleep out under the stars nights. You and me, Marshall, we could—"

"And what about Venus?" Marshall demanded. "Sure, you and me, we could just fade into the background all the way to the coast. Maybe even steal tickets and pretend we're passengers." He looked at the girl. "But a black girl with two white boys? We'd stick out like a sore thumb. And they'll be looking for us! We probably killed both of those policemen!"

"Thugs," said Carl. "We probably killed two thugs who was gonna kill us."

"Dammit, Carl—!"

"Whoa!" Carl's eyes, which had been closing as if in preparation for sleep, flew open. "Did you just swear?"

"You damned well drove me to it!"

"Past it, I'd say," said Venus.

Carl looked at her. "You promised to get us to Indiana. You done that and thank you. But now—"

"We promised to pay her," Marshall reminded him.

"But we couldn't. Circumstances beyond our control. Act o' God. If she wants to come to California, we'll make some money and—"

"I just said, if she tries to go with us, we'll all get caught."

"Then she better go hide in her jungle. Me, I'm goin' to California."

"Without me, you won't last a day," said Venus.

"We'll take our chances," said Carl.

Marshall shook his head. "No. We won't. I'm going with Venus."

For just a moment, Carl's mouth dropped open. He looked as though Marshall had punched him in the chest. His eyes looked moist. For just a moment. When the moment was gone, he said, "Fine. Safe travels."

"Carl!"

"What?" the boy asked irritably.

"You—you're no gentleman!"

Carl closed his eyes and settled his head back against the wall of the car. "Reckon I'm not."

At a stop whose name Marshall never learned, he and Venus climbed out of the car, fell down in a gully by the tracks until the train passed, and he followed her into the woods.

"River's this way," she said, beckoning. "I ain't been to this camp, but I know it's near the river, and not far from the tracks. They all are."

Marshall stopped, watching the receding train, moving off into the afternoon sun.

"What you lookin' at?" asked Venus.

"Nothing, I guess."

"You gonna cry, sissy?"

"No, I am not going to cry," he snapped at her. "I just—Carl was my family. I can't believe he just . . . left."

"Look to me like he stayed in one place, 'far as that went. You was the one got off the train."

Marshall swallowed. "It was the right thing to do."

"If you say so. Me, I never had time t' think about what'uz the right thing and what'uz the wrong thing. I just always does what I got to t' get through to the next stop."

"I suppose that's all Carl's doing too."

"Families doesn't always stay together, does they?"

Marshall laughed harshly. "Not mine."

"Do you reckon maybe a black girl and a white boy could be . . ." She stopped suddenly and looked away.

"What?" asked Marshall.

"Nothin'."

"But—"

"Drop it, sissy!" Her voice was cold. Marshall knew the subject was closed.

She tugged at his shoulder. "C'mon, it's gettin' dark. They'll put out the fire soon, and we won't get nothin' t' eat."

Indeed, shadows were lengthening in the woods. Sundown would be in an hour or so. Marshall followed the girl dressed as a boy, his feet crunching through old, dried leaves, and occasionally sticking in wet muck beneath them. "Why would they put the fire out at dark? Don't they want to keep warm?"

"Fool, the bulls can see a fire. So can the locals. And they loves to blame every little thing on us hoboes. You want to be safe, you don't attract no attention."

"Are you sure they'll feed us?"

"Of course they'll feed us. Hoboes feed each other. That's part of the life."

She stopped at a tree, traced her finger in its bark.

"What is it?" Marshall asked.

"Says it's safe to camp."

"I don't see any writing."

She seized his wrist, brought it to the tree, and traced his finger in a deep, carved groove. It went down, angled, went parallel with the ground, then angled back up again, forming a square with no top.

"That's a hobo mark."

"How do you—?"

"Shhh! Listen!"

Marshall obeyed, and heard a vague rumble of voices, very quiet, as if the speakers did not wish to be overheard. Their speech was occasionally punctuated with metallic clinks, and the pops of wood on a fire. As he heard them, he smelled smoke on the breeze.

He started toward the sounds, but Venus pulled him back. "Can't go empty-handed."

"But we don't have anything!"

She nodded at the ground. "Find some wood for the fire. I'm gonna hunt around."

Marshall, baffled, searched the surrounding ground for broken limbs. Most were too spindly to be of any real use, and many were wet and pulpy—no good for burning. He did not know much about the hobo life—he did not know anything!— but he knew how to gather firewood. He had learned at home— his real home—and learned well enough to avoid extra punishment at the asylum. A boy or girl bringing a too-spindly stick for the fire would find said stick applied to his or her backside in quick time.

As he was using his foot as a pry to break up a medium-sized, dry branch, Venus returned, two armloads of greens caught in her elbows. "Wild onions," she said. "Ain't much, but they's good in soup."

They started again toward the sound of voices and the smell of a campfire. "Are you sure they won't rob us?" Marshall asked.

"Don't nobody rob nobody in the jungle," said Venus. "If'n they tried, they'd get beat good and proper."

"By whom?"

"By everybody else there. Hoboes don't tolerate no foolishness. The camp is a safe place."

Laden with their offerings, they came upon a clearing in which a fire burned. Three ragged men sat around it, while others lay on bedrolls nearby. One man stood, shirtless, by a tree, glancing into a mirror mounted to the trunk, shaving with a straight razor and a bowl of water that steamed.

The men by the fire were sipping from tin cans and smacking their lips. Their makeshift cups obviously contained whatever was simmering in the kettle that hung on a rustic hanger over the fire. It smelled wonderful to Marshall. He knew that, in fact, it might smell like the outhouse the morning after a midnight storm, but he had not eaten in some time.

The old man stirring the kettle looked up. "You boys lost?"

"No," said Venus. "We come to stay the night." She held out the onions, and gestured to Marshall's supply of wood. "Looks like we in time to clean up after supper."

The man nodded thoughtfully. "You look awfully young."

Marshall began, "I'm fif—"

"We old enough," Venus interrupted him.

"You in trouble?"

"Maybe a little. Maybe some bulls didn't like the look o' my friend."

"Runaways?" pressed the hobo. "Left your folks to have an adventure?"

Venus shook her head. "Ain't got no folks. Him neither."

" 'Cause runaways get took home," the man went on.

"And you'd be welcome, if'n either of us had homes." She looked at Marshall. "My friend, he's kinda new. I'm teachin' him, on accounta he lost his people in the war." She slapped Marshall's shoulder. "He's green, but I'll whip 'im inta shape."

Again, the man nodded. A slow smile grew on his lips. "Kinda like you, boy. You'll do all right." He raised a pointed finger. "If you does the cleanup."

"We certainly will, sir," said Marshall.

The man narrowed his eyes once more and looked at Marshall as he might have at a traveling circus freak.

"My friend, he talks a little funny. I'm workin' on that."

"Well," said the old man, "let's get them onions cut up, and some o' that wood on the fire before we gotta put it out. You're just in time. I sent the other new boy to the river to get the water t' douse it."

"There's another new boy?" asked Marshall.

The old man nodded. "Scruffy boy," he observed. "Wild look in his eyes. Hair as red as hot coals, and eyes as black as cold ones. Didn't have a good feeling about him, but thought I should give him a break, after what he said."

Marshall's voice trembled as he asked, "What did he say?"

"Said he just needed a place to stay while he looked for his family."

**Steven Howell Wilson** has written science fiction and fantasy for DC Comics and mythological adventure for Crazy 8 Press's *ReDeus* series. His original science fiction audio drama, *The Arbiter Chronicles*, has earned the Mark Time Silver Medal and the Parsec Award. Prose adventures of the Arbiters are available from Firebringer Press. "The Colonel's Plan," Steve's weekly blog about the joys and sorrows of completing the

fifty-year-old house his late father designed, is available at www
.stevenhwilson.com.

★ ★ ★ ★ ★

# THE BELLS OF JUNIPER
## BY VONN MCKEE

★ ★ ★ ★ ★

Folks, the name's Ralph Carlisle and my sweet wife here says I need to set this little story down on paper before I go forgetting it. For posterity, she says. But I'm here to tell you that me losing track of this particular memory ain't likely to happen. No sir, not in this lifetime.

You see, that was the day—July the 12th, it was—in eighteen and sixty-nine, that I both killed a man and fell in love with a woman. To be honest, I couldn't tell you which one I done first. Didn't mean to do neither one. Well, I'm already getting ahead of myself.

Anyway, it started like this. I was in the store filling an order. Yep, I'm the proprietor of Carlisle's Mercantile and I reckon I shoulda done told you that. It was shaping up to be a regular old same-as-usual day when, about midmorning, I swore I heard the church bell ringing. Well, I found that curious so I stopped weighing Mrs. Lynch's coffee and cocked my head to listen. There was so much going on outside—wagons rolling by and folks walking on the boardwalks—that I decided I must've been hearing things. I knew for sure it wasn't Sunday.

You see, there ain't but two bells in Juniper, Wyoming, and after a year of working there on Front Street, I guess you could say my ear had got tuned to 'em both. The first bell is down at the train station and we hear it twice a week now that the last spike was drove in at Promontory last May. That opened up the rails all the way to California and turned Juniper into a right bustling little town.

Now, the other bell hangs up there on top of the First Methodist Church and that's the one I was thinking I heard. Preacher Crane's boy, Willie, rings it at ten o'clock every Sunday morning, and on special occasions. The ladies was some proud when that bell came in on the train all the way from Richmond. But I ain't here to tell you about that.

Anyhow, when I got up to the counter to write up Mrs. Lynch's bill, I heard the bell again and I knew something was sore amiss. Weren't no wedding or funeral going on or I would have known it. I saw through the window that people was looking up the street towards the sound. I made my apologies to Mrs. Lynch and excused myself. I yanked off my apron and charged out the door.

There was probably a dozen men running along with me. I didn't see or smell any smoke. Clifford Meeks, the undertaker, passed me like I was a lame mule. I might mention here that Clifford gets more excited about tragic events than is fitting and proper. I said, "What do you reckon is going on, Clifford?" But he was done out of earshot.

When we got to the church, what we saw stopped us all cold there at the front steps. The door was standing open and inside there was a woman slouched down on the floor crying and a big man standing over her pointing a revolver towards the top of her head. I realized that the woman had her arms wrapped tight around the bell rope that hung down inside the door. Every time the man would reach down and try to grab her arm, she would rock her head and shoulders back and forth and moan something—maybe no, no, no—and that would make the bell ring a couple of times.

Daniel Willingham was the first one of us to say anything since I guess all the rest of the men was dumbfounded like me. He hollered out, "You let her go, mister. No need to be a-pointin' a gun at nobody. Let her go, hear me?" But the man just looked at us, real crazy and mean-eyed, and said he'd shoot her if he wanted to, weren't none of our damn business. He said it right there standing in the church house. Well, the woman started wailing like a lamb with no mama and the bell started ringing again from her pulling on it.

"What'll we do?" I asked Daniel since he had kind of put hisself in charge by being the first one to speak out. But Daniel didn't look like he knew what our next move might be.

He said he didn't think we ought to shoot somebody inside the church and, besides that, he didn't have his gun on him. Daniel was still wearing his smithy apron.

That's when I said, "Well, it looks to me like *he's* about to shoot somebody inside the church so we'd best do something quick," and all of the men nodded.

The man with the gun looked nervous and called out, "This here's my wife. I caught her with another man."

The woman shook her head no and looked out towards us. Her face was all red and wet with crying but I noticed she was a pretty girl, maybe a lot younger than the man. It seemed like she put her eyes dead-center on me. "No, no," she was saying but it didn't make any sound. I figured right then the man was lying.

Matter of fact, now that I looked at him, I remembered him coming in the store about once a month to buy a bill of groceries. Nothing fancy, some tobacco and flour and such and, once, a few sewing notions and bolt of calico. I knew that calico wasn't likely for him so I figured he must have him a woman. But I never seen her come in, not even one time. Thought it strange. The man didn't like small talk either. Just paid his bill and left. Kind of man that looked like a mule eating briars, as my ma used to say. Well, he was worse than eating briars there in the church house that day.

179

Well, back to the story. That big man was a sight—his hair was all mussed up and he was breathing heavy—and he shook hisself sudden-like and turned away from us with a big roaring sound, grabbed the girl by the hair of the head, and twisted her face up towards him. I swear she turned whiter'n a china plate. Then he brought that revolver down slow and careful and pressed the barrel to her lips—almost like a kiss, now that I think about it.

I can't say that I remember just what happened next. All I know is that, in the space of a rattler strike, I was up there tackling that man down like he was a runaway calf. I know I had to have got up those steps somehow but I can't tell you how I did. Must've jumped 'em all in one bound.

Well, that fellow was a beefy one and had a good forty pounds on me but I somehow got a hold of his gun arm and was trying to back him away from that girl. I have thought many a time how lunk-headed I was to run up there with him holding a gun to her face. I can't hardly think about how bad that might have turned out.

Anyhow, I was just durn lucky, I guess, and caught him off his mark. But it wasn't two seconds before he bear-wrapped both arms around me and wrestled me down. Had me on one knee and was trying hard to work that revolver up to my skull.

I didn't think, I just did. Kinda like jumping the church steps. I threw my weight forwards to get my feet under me. Then I jumped up and twisted backwards all at the same time, kinda like a whirligig. He still had me but at least the bulk of him was behind me. I grabbed his wrist—he had big bear-paw hands too—and I was aiming to squeeze it hard enough to make him drop that iron. What an ox he was!

I squeezed and pushed but that barrel kept easing towards me. I could see the muzzle and I was thinking I'd never seen one up that close before and that I might not again.

I was in sore need of a miracle and durned if it didn't show up. Ole Daniel come charging in like a bull through the church door. He was being as fool-headed as me about breaking in on somebody with a gun almost to their head. But I was sure glad to see his homely mug anyhow. His surprise visit was just enough to throw the grizzly man off. His arm loosened up but I forgot to stop pulling and the gun kicked towards us both.

I heard a *boom* . . . and a bell ring!

I was on the floor and when my eyes could look straight, I saw the big man lying maybe a foot away from me. His eyes was open but there was a round hole just under his chin that was beginning to bleed. What I couldn't see until later was the top of his head. Or what there was left of it.

"Ralph, Ralph, are you hearin' me?" Daniel was shaking me.

"Daniel, of course I'm hearin' you and seein' you too, sorry to say. I know that can't be the face of St. Peter. Wouldn't nobody walk past that through them pearly gates."

Daniel pulled me up and started laughing and slapping me on the back. Guess he thought I could have been dead about then. I tell you he wasn't the only one.

We both remembered the girl and saw that she was standing back in the corner quiet and pale. She looked to me like one of them statues of Mary you see in them old missions. I said, "Let's get you outside," and I went over and put my hand on her shoulder. She was a little thing. I led her out the door trying to stay between her and the man's body but I reckoned she'd already seen. When we got out in the daylight, I saw there was a bruise where he'd been holding her wrist. Not only that but there was other dark places further up her arm that looked like they was healing up. Made me sick to my gut.

Well, that's the story—of that day anyhow. Preacher Crane's

wife insisted on taking the girl in until things settled down. Some of us offered to escort her back home, which was only a mile from town but hid back in a draw. She got all big-eyed and scared and said she didn't want to ever set foot back in that place again so we went out and got what belongings she said she'd like to have.

I got in a habit of dropping in to check on her now and then. The Cranes began inviting me for supper once a week. I started going to church for the first time since I was a youngster.

Though it wasn't my finger that pulled the trigger, I'll always feel like it was my doing that took a man's life. But I reckon it saved somebody else's too. I leave all the reconciling to the Good Lord.

And it wasn't just the girl's life that was saved neither. It didn't take the Cranes and everybody else long to figure out I was falling for her like a schoolboy. She was the gentlest, nicest human being I had ever met and it riled me to think that someone could ever raise a hand to her.

Sometimes when she's standing by the window, I still think she looks like a pretty church statue. Even prettier now that she smiles. Her name isn't Mary though. It's Emmeline. And I was one happy storekeeper the day the Juniper church bell rang for us on our wedding day—happy in spite of the fact that I had that blockheaded Daniel Willingham for a best man. I reckon he'll do though.

Oh, and what we figured out later was that the bullet (the one that lead-poisoned her stinking excuse for a husband) went straight on up into the belfry. Willie Crane saw the hole in the ceiling and climbed up to investigate. He said there was a skint mark up the side of the bell. I knew I wasn't hearing things!

If you want to hear more than that, you'll have to come on by the mercantile and get it from Miz Emmeline. My story writin' ends here, folks. You all have a fine day now.

Regards,
Ralph Carlisle

**Vonn McKee**, Louisiana-born and descended from "horse traders and southern belles," is a two-time Western Writers of America Spur finalist for short fiction. Now based in Nashville, she enjoys antiquing, destination-less driving, and writing stories of the West. Her website is vonnmckee.com.

★ ★ ★ ★ ★

# Frank Rule and
## the Tascosans
# by John Neely Davis

★ ★ ★ ★ ★

Frank Rule had pushed the insanity down into the depths of his being for so long, the craziness was feeling natural. He would not admit it to anyone—not that he had many opportunities up here in the desolation of the High Plains—but it was almost comforting.

Oh, Ellen still came to him in the stillness that permeated his house just before dawn, and her voice remained soft and almost musical. She talked of their future and her love for him, and he found solace in her words. However, as the horizon lightened with the rising sun, she went away and little fringes of madness accumulated at the outer edges of his thinking.

The Devil was a frequent, uninvited visitor into Frank's world, giving advice, taunting, goading. Recently, the rancher had succeeded in turning the demon away, but he knew the power of his adversary and that, in time, he would surrender to the relentless attacks of the beast.

Perhaps a more philosophical man could rationalize what was happening, but that was far beyond Frank's ability.

This morning Frank was doing one of his least favorite ranching duties, arm deep up in a brindle cow that seemed to insist on doing everything opposite from the rest of the herd. The lanky animal was unsuccessfully trying to give an out-of-season birth to a jug-headed calf fathered by a neighbor's fence-busting bull. Pulling a calf was exhausting under the best of circumstances. However, the cow had tired of her fruitless activity and, ignoring the fading labor pains, was munching contently on an armload of hay.

Frank tightened the cord around the calf's front feet and gave a final tug. The animal squirted out onto the ground and lay there for an instant, large eyes staring at the brightness of its new surroundings. The rancher wiped the newborn with a burlap bag and helped it stand. Holding the calf by the flanks, he helped the wobbly-legged animal toward its mother, who seemed to have little interest in her offspring.

Shirtless, Frank sat at the tack room door and, using the same burlap bag, cleaned afterbirth from his arms and hands.

*Hey, will you look at what's comin' down the road. You got company. And here you are all dressed up. Old Scratch thinks you're gonna make a helluva bad impression.*

Clenching his teeth, Frank shook his head. It had been a week since the Devil had talked to him.

*Whoa! Fancy. That man's got on a white shirt and is wearing a tie. And here you are, lookin' like something that has fallen outta a cow's innards.*

Frank walked across the stock lot and waited at the gate as a spic-and-span buggy pulled by a gray horse came down the rutted lane toward his homestead. The horse came to a stop, and a light swirl of red dust rose around the buggy, then settled on the driver.

"Good afternoon, sir," the nattily attired man said. "I believe you are the man I'm seeking. You are Frank Rule, aren't you?"

*Oh, he knows damn well who you are. He turned you down for a twenty-dollar loan last winter. Said you were a poor credit risk. Unsatisfactory collateral he said.*

"Yes, sir, I'm Frank Rule. And who would you be?"

*Atta boy. Put him in his place. He is riding in your territory now. Mr. High-Hat-Banker.*

The man stepped down from the buggy and shook the red grit from his calf-length duster. "You probably do not recall meeting with me last winter. It was about a loan. I'm Harald Donovan. Longsought Bank?"

"Yes, sir. I remember."

"Yes. Well, I want you to understand I've regretted the decision to not make the loan ever since I made it. I . . . I acted in haste. I've come out to make the loan. Today. Right now. No strings." The banker raised the buggy seat and withdrew a small canvas bag. "I can let you have it in fives or tens. Your choice."

*Whoa. Watch the sumbitch. He's fixin' to pee on your leg. Betting he's not come all the way out here just 'cause he's had a change of heart. He's after somethin'.*

"Mighty kind of you, Mr. Donovan. But I don't need the money now. I needed it last winter. Needed it to buy feed. Had a couple of cows starve. But, I'll get over that. Pastures are starting to come around now, and I reckon I'm in pretty good shape."

"Well, I'm glad things are working out for you. Just wanted you to know that anytime in the future I can be of service, Longsought Bank will more than welcome you."

*Get on with it. Quit beatin' around the damn bush.*

Donovan cleared his throat and then looked at Frank's barn and house. "Mighty nice little place you've got here." He removed his hat and revealed a bald scalp that might never have experienced unshaded sunlight. "Yes, sir, mighty nice."

*Okay. Enough of this. He needs to quit wasting our time. We've still got that wobbly calf in the barn.*

Using a thumbnail, Frank scraped dried afterbirth off his forearm. "Harald, I don't 'spect you come all the way out here just to talk about my little spread. What you got on your mind?"

*Yeah. What's goin' on under that bald head of hair?*

". . . and I never heard anything else," the banker concluded.

Frank leaned against a buggy wheel and studied the banker. "You never went over there?"

"Oh, heavens, no. There have been better men than me who rode into Tascosa horseback and were carried out flat on their back in a wagon. I wrote Sheriff Siringo. Waited and waited. Found out he was looking for that McCarty kid and his buddy Tom O'Folliard somewhere down in New Mexico Territory. I hired a couple of . . . couple of men who were supposed to be good at . . . getting young men out of trouble. They took my hundred dollars and—*poof*—never heard from them again."

*You see where he is going with this, don't you? Come out here, sugar-wouldn't-melt-in-his-mouth banker man.*

"So, your boy, believe you said his name was Cal, been goin' over to Tascosa looking to buy a ranch or sheep from some of them *pastores*. Didn't come back. That right?"

"Yes. He was on his third trip. Had no trouble before. Early on, I'd sent a couple of pretty tough fellows with him. I figured everything would be all right after he kinda got his feet on the ground. Figured he'd learned his way around."

*Helluva lot different figuring in a bank than figuring in a place like Tascosa. Gotta use a different instrument. Something that can do a whole lot more subtracting than adding. Like a gun!*

"So, why are you telling me all this?"

The banker clasped his hands and drew them in against his chest. "Yes. Well. I understand that you traced preacher Clark's wife down."

"Then you know I never brought her back. Preacher tell you that?"

"Yes. Yes, I'm aware of that. But you found her. I hear she ran off on her own. Cal's not like that. He is being held against his will. His mother thinks that, and I do, too. She . . . we want him back."

"And you want me to go get him?"

"Yes."

"What if he's dead?"

"Please don't say that. Even if he is, we still want him back."

"You willing to pay me?"

*Damn. Thought you would never get around to that. This old banker has more money than God. He has been sucking money outta poor ranchers like a skeeter drawing blood from a baby lying on a summertime pallet.*

"Yes. I will pay you."

"Whatever I ask?"

"Well, within reason. I'm not gonna be held up like I was some . . . Yes, I'll pay whatever you ask."

"I want a hundred dollars 'fore I leave." Frank thought about his past dealings with the banker. "Want it today. Hundred dollars when I get back if I've got your son." The rancher dragged his boot toe through the dirt and made two straight lines. "And I want fifty for every man I have to kill, and if I have to kill a woman, it'll be an extra twenty-five dollars." Frank smudged the lines with his boot. "If I don't bring your boy back alive, I'll still keep the hundred and you'll have to pay me for any killin' I had to do. Won't owe me nothing else."

The banker climbed back up into the buggy, raised the seat again, and removed a packet of bills wrapped in a piece of wagon sheet. He stepped to the ground and counted the bills out on the floor of the buggy. "There," he said. "In my business we always draw up a contract . . . something saying what each party is obligated to do when money changes hands."

Frank Rule glared at the banker, and the man looked away, avoiding the icy stare of the rancher.

Harald Donovan's voice was ragged like a man who needed

to swallow, a man whose voice was weak and crippled with stress and anxiety and fear. "But, I don't suppose under these . . . these circumstances . . ."

Frank almost felt pity, not quite, but almost. "I don't know 'zactly what the word circum . . . whatever you said means, but I'll shake your hand, and that's a lot better than my name on a piece of paper."

"Yes, certainly. Of course it is," the banker said after shaking Frank's hand. He fumbled in his duster pocket and withdrew two photographs. "Mrs. Donovan sent these two pictures of Cal. They are a couple of years old. Had them made on a trip down to Oneida. She thought it would aid you in your search. He's our only child, and we miss him. You will be careful and bring him back, won't you?"

Rule nodded. Somewhere out there in the vastness of the Llano Estacado, his own son was a captive. Or perhaps, after these ten years, he had become a Comanchero and adopted the ways of those fierce renegades. Ellen talked about him last night—he was seldom far from Frank's thoughts.

Banker Donovan climbed back into the buggy, pulled his gloves tight, and looked down at the bespectacled, rotund man he had just bargained with to find Cal. He opened his mouth to say something, but then thought better of it—anyway, Frank had stopped listening. The banker turned the buggy around in the scrubby pasture, slapped the reins across the horse's back, and, trailed by a veil-thin cloud of red dust, traveled west.

*You could have got a damned sight more money out of him. A whole lot more.*

It had taken three miserable days, and he had faced the swirling southwest wind as it ferried sand and tumbleweeds toward lands of the Cherokee Nation. On the second night after the gust settled, twice he imagined he saw a faint twinkling of scattered lights. But he could not be sure because the flatness of the country made estimating distance a fool's game. He squatted before a miserly fire, splurging with a second cup of coffee. Unless his bearings had wandered from the teaching of the army compass, he would reach the confluence of Atascosa Creek and the Canadian River tomorrow. He thought of the wind again and took comfort in knowing, at least, going home it would be at his back. If he got to go home.

He had been to Tascosa two years ago. It was a dusty Panhandle, cattle-trail village, two hundred forty-miles south of Dodge City, a thirty-four-hour, bone-jarring stagecoach trip. *Pastores,* sheepherders from overgrazed New Mexico, brought their herds here to forage in the broad *vegas* and take advantage of the well-watered springs. But the XIT and other large ranches were tiring of sheep and their habit of shearing the grass to ground level and spreading mange. Joseph Glidden's newly perfected barbed wire was spreading like locoweeds across the open range. It took no wise man to forecast that hostilities were imminent.

Tascosa was only three dozen houses strung out on either side of Spring Street, a dirt road that became a loblolly during the infrequent rains. On the east side of town, Charley Patton ran a blacksmith shop and livery stable next door to a laundry and barbershop run by a Negress, Lucy Williams. Across the street, Otis Taylor operated a combined grocery store and mortuary, and just past that, Homer Martin ran a boardinghouse. West of town, the Equity Bar and the Jenkins Saloon, usually inhabited by down-at-the-heels drifters and overnight freighters, sat side by side on the bank of the Canadian River. North of town, a small but growing cemetery squatted on a low hill—Tascosans called it Silent City. A quarter of a mile past that, two houses of ill repute, Jolene's and Bitsy's, were staffed with two dozen women whose looks ranged from kinda ugly to spectacularly ugly. Cowboys without the wherewithal to spend a few minutes savoring the female delights lounged on the whorehouse front porches, playing dominos and telling tales so preposterous that even the most gullible and green cowboy quickly discarded them.

Outside of town and scattered along Atascosa Creek, Mexican shepherds lived in plazas, small collections of native sandstone houses held together with adobe mortar.

An average day in Tascosa was dull; an average night, hair-raising.

To the southwest, the sun faded behind the never-ending horizon. Frank made good time today, mostly because he had gotten an early start. Just before dark last night, he had hobbled Red and the other mule and pitched his bedroll on the bank of a narrow arroyo. He enjoyed sleeping under the stars; it reminded him of the trip up from the New Mexico Territory. He and his wife had slept outside most nights—"communicating with God," Ellen said—while their son and daughter slept in the wagon.

Those good times were gone. Forever. The Indians took those times by killing Ellen and their daughter and kidnapping their son.

In the darkness, Frank fidgeted in his bedroll. He wanted Ellen to come and talk with him. Tell him of their plans, about having neighbors, sending their children to school, monthly trips into town to buy supplies.

But she didn't come. It frightened Frank. What if she never came again?

Restless, he had gotten up before dawn lightened the eastern sky, collected his mules, and headed west.

". . . four bits a night for the mules seems about right," Frank agreed with Charley Patton. "Reckon, you'll throw in free lodging for me in the hayloft?"

"Long as you don't eat no hay," the liveryman said.

Frank laughed. "No, I ain't much on victuals. Hay or any other kind. Gimme a cup of coffee and some bread, I'm good for fifty miles."

Charley opened the lot gate and waited for Frank to lead his mules inside. "You ought to fit right in around here," he said. "You can get food, such as it is, down at Homer Martin's place. But I wouldn't make a habit of it. It'll stunt your growth, I've been told. Some say it'll make your toenails turn black and fall off."

"Don't think I'll be around long enough for that. I've just come down here to get a feller. His daddy got worried about him. Wanted me to bring him back home."

"What's his name?"

Frank took the two photographs from his coat pocket and handed them to Charley. "Name's Donovan. Cal Donovan. You familiar with him?"

"Seen him. Been a while. That's his rig right over there. His pacing horse threw a shoe. I couldn't get to it right then, so he rented a saddle horse from me. I never saw him again."

"You reckon he skipped out with your horse?"

"No, wadn't that. I still got his rig and horse, lessen, of course, he stole it off somebody and it ain't really his. Anyway, my horse come back. Donovan feller didn't."

"He pay you when he left with your horse?"

"Yep. In advance. And he paid me for shoeing his horse, too. I think he meant to come back."

*Don't believe I've ever been hungry enough to eat something that looks like this. You'd be a whole lot better off goin' out on the creek*

*bank and doing your own damn cookin'. Eatin' crawdads and the*
*such.*

Frank looked at the stew and mentally agreed. In a way, he
had missed Old Scratch. Sometimes, the Devil could be
downright funny.

". . . then, I told him, 'sure I'll keep your room a couple of
nights.' " Homer Martin was raking crumbs from the table onto
the floor, much to the delight of two mice and a half-grown rat
obviously getting their share of daily bread.

Frank tried to ignore the rodents now in a wrestling match
over a half-eaten sourdough biscuit. "Then . . . he . . . he didn't
show up?"

"No, sir. Weekend come and I needed the room. There were
a couple of Dodge City freighters wanting a place to sleep. I
took Donovan's stuff outta his room and piled it in a shed in
the back. Didn't throw 'em out in the street, like most folks
would have done."

Frank moved the stew around in the bowl, looking for
something he might recognize. "Yeah. I get through eating supper I'll have a look if you don't care."

A pair of custom-made boots, two shirts, leather braces, broad-
striped trousers. Two hand-drawn maps, three unsigned deeds,
and a half-dozen blank bills of sale for sheep. No gun. No knife.
Folded and stuffed down in one leg of the trousers, Frank found
a pair of woman's drawers—didn't look like they had ever been
worn, but definitely red and definitely silk. He unfolded the
underwear and a note fell to the floor: Fifi from Cal.

*Whoa. Froggie went a-courtin' and he did ride. Mhmm. A sword*
*and pistol by his side. Mhmm.*

Frank slept well that night as a light rain pattered on the tin
roof of the hayloft. The pack of coyotes rejoicing at the edge of

the river did not interfere with his rest, nor did the five-shot gunfight at the Equity Bar. At daylight, a screech owl broke out in a quavering call and caused the rancher to leap from the hay burrow and wildly claw for his shotgun.

After rubbing the rheum from the corners of his eyes, Frank climbed down from the loft on a rickety ladder and interrupted Charley Patton's early morning routine of watering the livestock.

"Enough rain last night to settle the dust," the liveryman said.

Frank cleaned his glasses with his shirttail. "And I had enough roof to keep me dry. Sure beats sleeping in a bedroll under a mesquite bush. I was young, didn't mind it too much. Gets old pretty quick now."

"You have any luck last night down at Homer's?"

"Not really. Found Cal's clothes. Found out he'd paid two days ahead for a room, then never used it."

*Hey, tell him about them fancy drawers. That ought to get the old goat goin'.*

"Ain't surprised. Money didn't seem to mean much to him." Charley put a pinch of snuff behind his lower lip. "If I was you, I'd go down to the Equity Bar and the Jenkins Saloon. Show the man's picture around. Jenkins gets most of the cowboys; Equity gets folks that don't talk English. Somebody at one of them two places might have seen him. Getting anything past a bartender is like sneaking daylight past a rooster."

Rusty Jenkins stood behind the long wooden bar reading a two-month-old newspaper. He leaned forward to look at the photos Frank spread before him. "Don't know. Maybe. We get a lot of fellers in here. Some I see only once. He's right ordinary looking, 'cept he is dressed terrible fancy. Wish I could help you, but I can't recollect him right off. Might try over at the Equity. Talk with Badlegs Watson if I was you."

Frank crossed the alley and stepped onto the porch of the Equity Bar. A man in a wheelchair, wearing a dirty apron and a week-old salt-and-pepper beard, sat, arms resting on an overly ample belly. He watched a Mexican scrubbing the floor with soapy water and a stiff brush. He acknowledged Frank, *"Buenos días."*

Frank didn't respond.

The wheelchair-man grinned. *"¡Hola! ¿Cómo te va todo?"*

Frank shook his head and extended his hands, palms up.

"Said, good morning." Wheelchair-man smiled and revealed a mouth of picket-fence teeth. "Wouldn't you just know it, sumbitch got shot out here last night? Bled like a stuck hog. If you don't get that blood up 'fore it plumb dries, it'll stain just like oil. Every time it rains and the wood gets wet, blood will show up again. I've seen puke do the same thing."

"Knew that about blood; never heard that 'bout vomit," Frank said.

"Yeah, you run a saloon long as I have, you learn a bunch of stuff like that. Ain't worth nothing, but you learn it anyway. I'd whole lot druther a sumbitch get shot out in the street as inside or even out here on the porch. Not near as messy. You needin' a drink? Little hair of the dog what bit you?"

"No. Too early in the day for me. You Mr. Watson?"

"No, I'm Badlegs. Mr. Watson was my father." After Badlegs finished the joke, he went into a coughing spasm that ended with his face as red as a fall apple.

Frank introduced himself and showed Badlegs the photographs of Cal Donovan. "You seen this man?"

"Can't say as I have. Shore don't look like any customer I can recall. What's he done? Beat you outta money?"

"No, nothing like that. I was just trying to help his daddy out."

Badlegs nudged the Mexican with the wheelchair's footrest.

*"Diego, obtenga un balde de agua y enjuague el piso."*

The Mexican nodded and jumped from the porch down onto the packed street.

"Mr. Watson, I'll be around town for a couple of days. You see this man, let me know. I'd sure appreciate it."

The water pump down near the river stopped squeaking, and Diego rounded the corner of the saloon with a wooden bucket. He threw the water across the porch and watched the suds drain onto the red clay.

Badlegs held the photos out for Diego to look at them, *"Sacuda su cabeza."*

The Mexican shook his head, and the saloonkeeper handed the pictures back to Frank. "Mexican ain't seen him either. 'Bout the best I can do for you. Where you stayin'?"

"Down at Charley Patton's."

"You sleeping in the barn?"

Frank nodded.

"Dang!" Badlegs turned the wheelchair and rolled through the swinging doors into the darkness of the saloon.

*So, how about that Badlegs Watson feller! Reckon if he'd known we lived on the Rio Grande for twenty-five years, he'd have thought we might speak Spanish just about as well as Diego. Telling that Mexican to deny he'd ever seen Cal Donovan. Humph. We gonna put old Badlegs right at the top of our lying list. He's liable to wind up with something a whole lot worse than blood on his damn porch.*

Charley Patton wasn't around the livery. Frank saddled Red and rode northward toward the low hills and the cemetery. Some caring soul had built a picket fence around the graveyard, not to keep the inhabitants in but the sheep and cows out.

Frank tied his mule to the gatepost and then walked through the cemetery. Most graves were unmarked, just low, narrow six-foot-long mounds of dirt covering the remnants of people betrayed by nature or their own carelessness. Judging by the new growth of buffalo grass, he figured that the newest grave was over two months old and wondered if the man shot at the Equity last night might show up later today.

*Whoa, let's get outta here. Dead folks give me the willies. I like 'em alive so they can hop around when the fire gets hot. Fact is, I believe I recognized that name on the wood cross at the back of the damn graveyard.*

Frank stepped back up into the saddle and followed the dusty road as it cut across the hill toward the whorehouses.

*All right! This is more like it.*


Perched on sandstone piers, there was little to distinguish the two unpainted houses. Frank chose the one on the left, the one with a bedraggled cowboy sitting on the front steps.

"They ain't open yet," the cowboy said after identifying himself as Cletus from the Lazy Eight ranch. "Women stay up pretty late. Sometimes, Bitsy lets them sleep 'til after dinner. You'll have to come back, or you can sit here with me. Or you can try that 'un over there, Jolene's." Cletus lazily pointed to the house a little higher on the hill. "I'm kinda partial to this 'un. Little redheaded woman, ain't been here more'n six months works here. When I got the money, I see her. She's plumb rowdy, all right. Name's Fifi or something like that. Claims she is a French woman."

The cowboy shook his head when Frank showed him the photographs of Cal Donovan.


The front door was open at Jolene's as if welcoming a breeze to come inside and freshen things up a bit. No one waited on the porch. Inside, a tousled blonde-haired woman stood behind a makeshift bar constructed of three rough planks nailed across two wooden sawhorses. She was smoking a cigarette and eating a sandwich constructed of cornbread and fatback.

"Won't be open for another hour," the woman said. "But if you can't wait that long, I might . . ." her words trailed away, but Frank knew what she was saying.

She did not recognize Donovan's likeness.

*Hey, not too shabby. Not been in one of these places for a couple of weeks. What say we have a drink and see who else shows up? Don't never hurt to look.*

Two women, both dull-eyed and tired, came from behind a bead-curtained doorway, vigorously scratching beneath their wrinkled gowns. No, they hadn't seen him either.

*Sit down, Frank. We're not in a hurry. Or, at least, I'm not.*

The whore that seemed to have the greatest need to continue scratching followed Frank out onto the porch. "I could get in trouble for this, but . . ." she paused and pried something foreign from under the fingernails of her scratching hand, "but you might want to talk with that feller that chucks the rowdies out over at . . ." She looked toward Bitsy's but did not finish her sentence.

*Dang! Looks like we got outta there just in time. I'd have hated to see the next bunch of women that come out from behind that door. Believe, longer they come, worse they was gonna look.*

Frank rode past Bitsy's. Nothing had changed: doors still closed, Cletus still sat on the steps—by himself. Frank waved and the cowboy nodded, then touched thumb and forefinger to the front of his wide-brimmed hat.

"So, you finally got around to me." Lucy Williams moved to the single window of her one-room barbershop-laundry and examined the photographs. "You figured a black woman ain't gonna know doodly-squat 'bout what's happening here in Tascosa."

"No. No. It's not that. You was just the last person I come to."

"Um-hum. Yeah, see if you can make me believe that."

Frank took the photos from Lucy. "Not gonna try to make you believe nothing. That's the way it is. You was the last person. You'd been open this morning, you might have been the first person. Look at it this way. Somebody's got to be last. And today, it was you."

"Where you from, mister?"

"Longsought. On further up in the Panhandle."

"I know where that is. Got some kin that lives over there. You know any of the Manesses?"

Frank wrinkled his brow. "No, can't say as I do."

"That's a good answer." Lucy laughed, laced her large fingers together, rotated her hands, extended her arms, and cracked eight knuckles. "All my kin lives up in the Indian Territory, and they named Kizer, not Maness." She laughed again, cheeks billowing like summer clouds and forcing her eyes into slits. "Good to find out you don't lie 'bout little things. Man that'll lie 'bout little things will shorely lie about big things."

*Hey, old girl is pretty smart. Might make a good range detective.*

"I ain't known for lying," Frank said.

"No, I suppose you ain't. I know your young man—man in those pictures—or leastways I've seen him. Did his shirts a couple of times. Even give him a haircut and a shave once."

"How long ago?"

"Um. Twenty-three days ago. It was on a Tuesday."

"How can you remember that?"

Lucy snorted. "Well, I ain't dumb. I got a calendar and I can read. You read?"

Frank nodded. "Enough to get by."

The woman laughed. She was starting to understand the deadpan rancher. "He always paid me a little extra. And he was a clean man. Underwears wadn't never very dirty. Didn't hardly have to boil his shirts none. Just drag 'em over the rubboard couple of times, starch and iron them."

"When was the last time you saw him?"

"Nineteen days ago."

Frank counted the days on his fingers. "That would be a Saturday. I know. You got a calendar and you can read."

"You learn kinda quick for a cowboy from Longsought."

"Reckon I ought to say thank you for that compliment."

Lucy laughed again. "Don't be thanking me too quick."

Frank removed his glasses and huffed moisture on the lenses. Lucy handed him a clean cloth, and he wiped the dampness away. "You got such a good memory and all, anything happen about that time that was out of the ordinary?"

"Yeah. That big ugly man what keeps order up at Bitsy's brought a shirt in to be mended up and washed. Had couple of right bad-burned places in one sleeve and soot all over it. Liked to have never got it clean."

Frank thought about the whore at Jolene's, what she'd said or almost said. "I'm gonna bet the shirt was bloody, too."

"Dang, mister. For a white man, you're pretty smart."

Frank roused. He was getting accustomed to sleeping in Charley Patton's loft. Somewhere around midnight, gunfire woke him. But he turned in the hay, much like a dog making a bed on a buffalo robe, and went back to sleep. Near dawn, Ellen came and whispered to him. When this first happened, he struggled to wake because he wanted to talk with her—touch her—smell her. But, of course, she wasn't there, and it took days for the sadness to leave. He was smarter now. He enjoyed the dreams and did not try to leave the happiness of sleep when his wife visited.

After checking for scorpions and spiders, he pulled his boots on, then climbed down the shaky ladder to the open hallway of the barn. His mules pricked their ears forward and then watched as he forked hay and took it to their feed rack.

Yesterday, he had left his shotguns and the Henry in the loft wrapped in his bedroll; today he would carry the sawed-off .10-gauge, L.C. Smith double-barrel shotgun. Probably wouldn't need it, but a man can never tell.

In his shop, Charley was stirring the coals of his forge, leather apron already cinched around his narrow shanks. "You up and moving around, Frank Rule? Must have a pure heart to be able to sleep this late. Sun's just about to come up. Figured I'd not start hammering on these horseshoes 'til you come awake. But I was about to get tired of waitin' on you."

" 'Preciate you doing that. Letting me sleep. I'll try to return the favor someday."

"Betcha four-bits that'll never happen." Charley raised his farrier's hammer and struck the anvil; the clean *whannnng* sound rolled out into the freshness of the morning air. "Heard you spent most of yesterday snooping around, visiting whorehouses and the such."

Frank shook his head. "Not what you're thinking—the whorehouse part, I mean."

Charley pulled a cherry-red horseshoe from the forge and eyed its curvature. "Yep. That's what I used to tell my wife when she was alive. 'It ain't what you think, honey, me stopping by the whorehouse and all.' Never made much progress with that kinda tale. She was a hard woman to fool." He waited for that to sink in, then said, "Most of the time."

Frank saddled Red and led him out into the hallway. "What do you know about the man that works up at Bitsy's? Man that keeps things under control."

"His name is Kermit Bricknell. Folks call him Brick. Tough old boy. Throwed a rowdy halfway down the hill the other night.

204

Broke his collarbone and a bunch of ribs. If I had my druthers, I druther be kicked by a mule than hit by Bricknell."

"You think he would kill a man?"

"If the need come about, I believe he would. Quicker 'an a hiccup."

Frank grasped the saddle horn and put his left foot in the stirrup, "Going down to Homer Martin's to get a little bite of breakfast. I'd buy yours."

Charley shoved the horseshoe back in the coals before looking at Frank. "Not just no but hell no. I ain't gonna eat down there. Rather rassle with Brick than Homer's food."


Frank studied the watery scrambled eggs while Homer Martin rolled a cigarette one-handed and sat on the bench across the table from him. "Guess you heard what happen last night?" Homer said, after he got his cigarette going.

Frank tilted the plate so the liquid drained away from the eggs. "I heard shooting. That's all. Didn't know where or who."

"Over at the Equity. I hear tell, cowboy and a freighter got into it. Freighter died. And to top that, man got stabbed up at Bitsy's. Two dyin' in one night, 'bout average, I reckon."

Frank moved the eggs around on his plate, and they continued draining. "Was they local?"

"No. Freighter was outta Dodge. Man who got killed up at Bitsy's was from the Lazy Eight, big spread over on the New Mexico Territory border."

"Man from the Lazy Eight, was his name Cletus?"

"Dang," Homer said. "How did you know that?"


"Just wanted you to understand that you are the second stop I've made today. Didn't want to hurt your tender feelings." Frank stood in the backyard of Lucy's laundry and barbershop and watched the proprietress stir a black pot of sudsy water and clothes with a battling stick. "Reckon you ought to drag a little more fire around the pot, make that water hotter?"

Lucy stopped her stirring, looked at Frank, and mopped the sweat from her brow. "Reckon you ought to go help somebody that be needin' it. I've washed more clothes than you've ever seen."

"I thought everybody washed on Monday."

"Thought wrong. On Mondays, I wash everything that needs washing from Jolene's; Wednesdays everything from Bitsy's; Saturdays, just townfolks' clothes."

Frank moved across the backyard and sat on a wash bench beside a galvanized tub of clean water. "So, this being Wednesday, those clothes are from . . ."

". . . Bitsy's. Maybe you ain't as smart as I thought you was."

"Uh-uh, don't sell me short. I know there's eight days in a week."

Lucy went back to stirring the clothes. "You full of foolishness this morning, ain't you?"

"Well, let me try this. I'm guessing there's nothing in that pot but sheets and pillowcases—maybe a few washcloths and that many towels. Maybe some women's drawers."

"Yeah, you be pretty right. 'Cept there was something rolled up in the sheets this morning that ain't in the pot."

Frank laughed. "You want me to ask what, don't you?"

Using the battling stick, Lucy lifted a sheet from the boiling pot and dropped it into the tub of fresh water. "Up to you."

"I give up, what was it?"

"Man's shirt. It's soaking in a bucket of cold water in the house."

"And the reason you are soaking it is . . . ?"

"It was bloody."

"It's Bricknell's shirt, isn't it?"

"I believe it is pretty safe to say that, since ain't no man 'cept

Brick what lives up there with all them women. One other thing you might ought to know. He carries a nine-inch Bowie knife in a leather sheath cradled against his backbone. Just thought you might want to be acquainted with that."

"We ain't open." The voice was distant.

Frank knocked on the door again.

"Told you, dammit, we ain't open." The voice was closer, threatening.

Frank made a fist and pounded on the door, the hammering booming down the hall of the whorehouse like a spring thunderstorm.

The door was violently yanked inward. Brick stood in the entry, pantless, gut hanging over dingy drawers, barefoot, shirtless, hair tousled.

"I told you, dammit, we—" Brick stopped in mid-sentence. Initially, he was surprised that a Tascosan or any other man living in the Panhandle would have the nerve to cause such a disturbance at Bitsy's. The man standing before him wore spectacles and a parson's hat, and would not reach his shoulder in height, but he was broad and thick in his chest and his arms were oversized. And a sawed-off shotgun was clutched in his right hand.

Frank looked up at the man standing in the doorway. "I reckon I need to talk to the person what runs this place."

Brick eyed the shotgun. "Well, I reckon that would be me."

"No. I don't believe that's right. You're not the owner. You are just a flunky that tries to scare people. Maybe even bust up a still-wet-behind-the-ears cowboy named Cletus."

"You calling me a liar?"

"Yep, 'cause that's what you're doing right here to my very face. Now, I reckon you ought to let me talk with Bitsy. If there is really a woman by that name."

"You are not talking to anybody, 'cept me."

Frank raised the L.C. Smith, cocked both hammers, and jammed the gun barrel into Brick's navel.

"You're not scaring me," Brick said, his sentence ending on a note high as a teenaged girl.

"Not intending to scare you. Just want you to understand that I'm gonna talk with the woman that owns this place. Now, you may be dead first, but I'm still gonna do it."

*Way to go, Frank. Put a charge of buckshot in him. See how tough he is with his guts draggin' on the ground.*

Raising his hands to ear level, Brick took a half step backward, and slowly turned his head to the side, "Bits, man here to see you."


Unwavering, Frank stared into the woman's face, his eyes reluctant to explore other regions.

Bitsy might have been an attractive woman forty years ago. But most likely, not. In the dim light of the bordello's parlor, she sat on a four-person, stained sofa, smoking a long-stemmed pipe, and drinking from an oversized cup. Her dingy-red housecoat was featureless except for one pocket bulging with a Remington .41 double-barrel derringer. Buttonholes had expanded to a point they no longer served their intended purpose, so the robe gaped open, revealing tired breasts resting on an ungirded midsection laced with stretch marks.

*Damn, Frank. Wished you'd warned me. I'd have stayed outside. If I can't get this outta my mind, I'll not sleep a wink tonight.*

"You ain't some kind of preacher, are you?" she said, her voice raspy as the first-of-morning caw of a crow. "Aim to come in here and save souls? Disrupt my business? Cost me money?"

"No. Come trying to find this fellow," Frank said, pulling the two photographs from his coat pocket. He turned so Brick remained in his peripheral vision and extended the pictures toward the woman.

She took the pictures in her arthritic hands and shifted so that the light shown more favorably on Cal's likeness. "Sit down," she nodded toward the end of the sofa, "I don't bite." She did a half-moon grin and revealed pale, toothless gums.

Frank sat and leaned back against the arm of the sofa—he would have liked more distance.

*Whoa, reckon how long it's been since she seen a washrag?*

Bitsy studied the photos. "Brick, you ever see this fellow?"

Bricknell came from the shadows, briefly looked at the pictures, shook his head, and retreated to wherever he'd been.

Bitsy handed the photos back to Frank. "May have seen him. May not. What's he done?"

"Nothing. I've been employed by his daddy, Harald Donovan, over in Longsought. I've come to find the young man and take him home."

Bitsy showed Frank the toothless half-moon again. "What does this Harald Donovan do, pray tell, so that he goes about hiring men to hunt other men?"

Frank put the double-barrel shotgun across his lap and rested his hat over the stock. "I reckon banking, mostly."

"Banking! Well! I don't recall doing business with a banker. Not in a bank, I mean. Had plenty of bankers stop by, stayed an hour or two. Most was customers. One paid to just hide in a closet and peek through a part open door and watch the goings-on. Always found them to be mighty tight with a dollar. This Harald feller, he pay you on the front end?"

"Yeah, some."

"Good. Always a good idea to get the money first. I had a banker try to crawl outta a window one night. Wanted to play, didn't want to pay."

*Dang, that's pretty good—Wanted to play, didn't want to pay— I'm gonna remember that.*

Bitsy raised the coffee mug over her head, a crooked index finger through the ear of the dangling cup. "Brick, I'm ready for 'nother 'un. Mayhap you hit it a little harder with whiskey this time."

Frowning and staring at Frank, the bouncer crossed the floor with a large, blue enamel coffee pot and refilled Bitsy's cup. He upended a pint of whiskey over the cup, and the bottle gurgled three times before he turned it right-side up.

Bitsy took a drink and shuddered. "This banker, this Harald feller, you think he'd pay to get his son back?"

"No. I don't expect he would. That's my job to get the son back. And I don't pay for what I can do myself."

"Then, I think you might have a problem finding young Mr. Donovan."

Frank stood and placed the flat-brimmed parson's hat on his bald head. "Might be right. But I'll tell you one thing. If I find out that somebody knew where the boy is and didn't tell me—or that something has happened to him—I'm gonna be mighty aggravated. Folks generally pay to see that I'm not aggravated."

Bitsy looked at Frank. "My. My. Do we—Brick and me—take that as a threat?"

"No, ma'am. I don't hold in threatening. Found it to be a waste of everybody's time. Just letting you in on the way things are with me."

The woman ran a finger across the top of her smooth lower gum as if searching for something. "Brick, do you believe this man is trying to scare us?" The investigation was fruitless, so she traced the same route with her tongue.

Frank checked his coat pocket to see if it still contained the photographs. "Not my job to scare folks. I'll be leaving now."

Bitsy hobbled alongside Frank to the door, then watched as he climbed into the saddle and set out down the dusty road toward Tascosa. "Gotta bad feeling we ain't done with him. A bad feeling."

Two hours past midnight, Diego walked from the Equity Bar, a still-dripping mop in one hand and a kerosene lantern in the other. He stood on the porch and waited while Badlegs Watson padlocked the large wooden outer door.

"No later than nine," Badlegs shouted to Diego, although the Mexican was only six feet away. "You better be hearing me. None of this 'My wife was not feeling well' crap. That's getting old."

The dim lantern barely lit the narrow path the Mexican followed along the river. Once it entered a grove of cottonwood trees, the path became almost obscure. It had been a long day, and Diego dreaded the three-mile walk to the shepherd's camp.

"*¡Hola!*"

Diego had only heard the voice once, but he knew it was the man with the glasses, the man who questioned *el jefe* about the photographs. And he understood the two cold circles pressed against his neck were the business end of a double-barrel shotgun.

"*¿Hablas inglés?*"

"*Sí. Un poco,*" Diego whispered.

"*Bueno.* I'll bet your little bit of English is probably better than my Spanish. I have questions for you, and it is important that you be truthful with me. *¿Entender?*"

"*Sí.* Yes, I understand."

"The man in the picture I showed Watson. You know him, don't you?"

"*Sí,* I mean, yes."

"How?"

"He was *el jugador.*"

211

"I see. He was a gambler. Will you speak only English if I take the shotgun away from your neck?"

"Yes, it will be easier. I can think more better."

"The man's name is Cal. He gambled at Watson's?"

Diego nodded. "Yes. Many times."

Frank lowered the shotgun and continued, "Poker. Did he play poker?"

"*Sí*. But not very well. He lost his money."

"How much?"

Diego struggled with the answer. "Don't know how much. But it was all. And more."

"Who did he play poker with?"

"Señor Watson and sometimes, Señor Brick."

"Brick, that the man who works at Bitsy's?"

"Yes. That one. The big man."

"Is Brick a good player?"

"About the same as . . . the man, Señor Cal."

"Did Brick owe Watson money?"

"Yes. But . . . the man . . . Señor Cal, he owed more."

A light skift of clouds slid across the sky, temporarily shielding the two men from the moon's light.

"Do you know how much he owed?" Frank asked.

"No, but it was many dollars. Señor Watson became very angry. Pointed gun at Señor Cal."

"He shot him?"

The clouds moved on and the moon shown again on Diego's face. "No. But another day he told Señor Brick to take him . . . the man you call Cal . . . away. Kill him."

"Kill him? Watson paid Brick to do this?"

"No. He told Señor Brick that he would not owe him any money if he did this."

"So, Watson cancelled Brick's gambling debt if he would kill Cal?"

"Yes. I think that is the way for you to say it."

On the opposite riverbank, something thirstily lapped water, stopped, then moved almost noiselessly back into the cane thicket.

"Did you see him do it? Kill Cal?"

"No. But they left together one night, and I did not see the man . . . Señor Cal . . . again."

"Ever?"

"No. Never again."

"So, if he killed him, he had to bury him somewhere. You know where his grave is?"

Diego's voice was little more than a whisper. "I do not want your question."

"Oh, you'll answer me. I've got to know. The man who hired me will need to know. Will want to see his son's grave."

"Señor Brick didn't bury him. He took this man, Señor Cal, out to a *barranco* and burned him."

"Burned him in a ravine! What do you mean, he burned him?"

Diego put his hands across his eyes and shuddered. "My brother saw it. He had been to see his *novia* on the other side of the river. He was walking home. Saw Señor Brick wrap a sheep's *cuerpo* around Señor Cal, poured kerosene over them. Set them on fire."

"You've seen the bones?" Frank asked.

"No. The coyote and lobos carried them off."

"Nothing left?"

"Nada. No."

"Diego, do you have a family? Mother? Father? Children?"

"Yes, I have all this."

"Do you swear what you've told me on the heads of your family? And if I find that you have been untruthful, I will kill all your family. But I will let you live so you can be in sorrow for the rest of your days."

The Mexican knelt before Frank Rule and crossed himself. "I swear this on my faith and my *familia*."

Frank raised the shotgun and placed it against the kneeling man's forehead. "Have you told anyone else about this?"

Diego crossed himself again. "No, señor. Only you."

Frank removed a thin oilskin packet from his pocket. "I want you to have this money. But for you to keep it, you forget that we ever talked. Do you understand what I'm telling you?"

"Yes, I understand."

Frank moved the gun from the Mexican's forehead. "Remember your oath. Don't force me to come back to Tascosa and find you."

*I don't know 'bout this. Old Scratch thinks, maybe you should have killed him. Can't trust a Mexican far as you can kick him. You are turning into a namby-pamby, if you ask me, course you haven't asked me anything lately.*

The men who ate breakfast at Homer Martin's sat at the table until almost noon, drinking coffee, smoking, and discussing the happenings.

"Two in one night!"

"Yeah. Heard it happens in big towns, Dallas, Fort Worth, Dodge. But, hellfire, for it to happen here in Tascosa, I just don't get it."

"Could have been worse. Good thing for us, Bitsy and her girls all got out."

The oldest man at the table grinned. "Speak for yourself. I ain't had no use for the such in ten years. That kind of women, I mean."

"Hear tell that Fifi got to Brick, but she couldn't rouse 'im. She told the sheriff that Brick's throat might have been cut. Said there was blood, but in all that smoke and runnin' and screamin' and hollerin', she just couldn't be sure."

"Um-hum, I'll bet it was hell among the yearlings. All them whores tryin' to get outta there at the same time. Charley Patton said the roof caved in about two minutes after the building caught on fire."

"Otis Taylor tells that the Equity was roaring like a wintertime fireplace when he got there. Said him and Rusty Jenkins tried to get in but it was just too damn hot. They could see Badlegs, crawling around on the floor, bellowing like a calf that was gettin' pulled down by a pack of wolves. Said his face looked like somebody had beat it with a two-by-four. Then this morning, they found his wheelchair out in the river behind the saloon."

"His wheelchair out in the river! Why, I never saw the man outta that thing. He couldn't walk a step."

"Yeah, strange goings-on. Never had a building burn down, and then have two in one night. But reckon it ain't all bad, we got rid of Badlegs and Brick."

Frank Rule tied the pacing horse and Cal's rig in front of the two-story bank. Inside, Harald Donovan sat at a plain desk in the corner of the lobby. When Frank came in, the banker stood and crossed the wooden floor with long strides, his face expectant as a child anticipating a birthday gift. "You've found Cal!" The banker continued past Frank, opened the door, and stood staring at his son's horse and rig.

Frank shouldered past the banker and stood in the street. "It was . . . it didn't turn out like I'd hoped."

"But you brought him back?"

"No. No, I didn't."

Harald looked in the back of the rig. "This is his rig. That's his clothes."

"Yes, he left the rig with a blacksmith and the clothes at a boardinghouse in Tascosa."

The banker held onto the top of the rig's back wheel, his

body slumped, and he stared down at the dusty street. "But you found him, and he'll be coming along later. That's it, be coming along later. Or you carried him by the house, and he is with his mama right now." His words were hopeful, but his voice was not.

"No. Sorry to tell you, your boy is dead."

Donovan moved to Frank and placed his hands on the rancher's shoulders. "Did you see the body?"

Frank pulled away from the banker's grasp and shook his head. "No. I didn't."

"Then you're not sure?"

Frank shook his head again and, this time, looked across the prairie at the buffalo grass swaying from an unseen force. "I'm sure. You don't need to question me no more. It'll be easier on you if you just take what I'm saying. Let it go at that."

"But his mother will want to—"

"No. Not from me. Make up whatever you want to. Tell her what you think might give her peace. But, you will never have no more proof than my word."

"Then if there's nothing else you will tell me, I guess our business is finished." Harald's lips were tight, thin, and little more than a slash across his face. He turned, gathered his son's clothing from the buggy, and moved toward the bank's door.

"Wait." Frank's voice was so low that Harald was not even sure the rancher had spoken. "You owe me money. A hundred dollars more."

The banker placed his son's clothing back in the buggy. "That's not our deal. You didn't bring our son back. So I don't owe you anything else."

"Yes, you do. Our deal was that if I had to kill a man, I'd get fifty dollars more. I killed two men that needed killin'. That comes to a hundred dollars."

Harald shook his head. "You don't have a contract saying

that. This is robbery. I'll not pay it."

Frank stared at the banker. "We shook hands on the deal. You either pay me the hundred dollars, or I take your lying hand—the one what shook mine—with me."

Panic and fear, the kind a pack rat has just before the rattler strikes, ignited in the banker's eyes. "I would have to make arrangements."

Rule pointed to the bank. "Lots of money in there."

Harald shook his head. "But it's not mine; it's the bank's. I can't just walk in there and scoop up a hundred dollars."

*Liar, liar, pants on fire. What's good for a liar? Brimstone and fire. Watch him, Frank. You know how he is with money. Old-man banker is tighter than Dick's hatband.*

"Might be true. But you can do it, and you better do it. I'll sit out here on this bench for an hour, 'spect you to come back out with the money. You don't, I'll come inside. I'll have what you owe me. A deal's a deal."

Harald gathered his son's clothes again and, without looking at Frank, went inside the bank, passing no closer to the rancher than necessary. He sat at his desk, opened a drawer, and made notations in a thin leather-bound book. Occasionally he looked through the window, hoping the sturdy, bespectacled man wearing the parson's hat was gone.

*I'm keeping my eyes on him. Remember what Bitsy said. "Want to play but don't want to pay." He's just the kind that will try to crawl out through the back window. I'll tell you if he tries that. You can head him off, fill his sorry ass full of buckshot. Make the world a better place and make getting loans a lot easier. Why, I might even be able to get a loan myself.*

A teller came from the bank, barely glanced at Frank, and continued his way through the twilight along the wooden sidewalk. One by one, lights in the bank faded and, minutes later, Harald came out, masking his anger by making a great pretense of locking the bank's front door. "Here's your damned money." He shoved a sealed envelope at Frank. "You don't have to count it. It's all there. Don't ever come near me again."

Frank folded the envelope and put it in his coat pocket. "I'll not worry about counting the dollars. It'll all be there or I'll be back. You don't want that. And don't forget, this last time I didn't come to you, you came to me."

Frank stepped up into the saddle and, leading his other mule, turned northward. The wind had shifted and skeletons of dead tumbleweeds came bounding past him. It would be near midnight when he got home and looked after his livestock.

After that, there would be only the empty house filled with memories of Ellen. She had died years ago; it seemed like only yesterday.

He rode through the dusk wondering how much the banker loved his son or even if he loved him at all. He thought about his own son, captive, dead, or perhaps wandering somewhere out on the High Plains. He'd sell his soul for the return of his boy.

*You'd sell your soul, would you? What makes you think I don't already own it. Or at least, most of it.*

Frank slumped in the saddle, and his eyelids hooded against the blowing sand.

Maybe Ellen would come tonight.

**John Neely Davis**, a writer of western and Appalachian fiction, lives in Franklin, Tennessee, with his wife, Jayne. His most recent western novel, *The Chapman Legacy*, was released by Five Star in June of 2018.

# A Century of the
# American Frontier
## *1875–1885*

* * * * *

# WHEN TULLY CAME TO TOWN
## BY RICHARD PROSCH

* * * * *

The sight of Rex Tully standing in the rain-soaked street of Randolph City, his heavy boots and slick denim trousers caked with rust-colored mud, made Smith Oberlin's stomach lurch.

And his heart raced the tick of his pocket watch.

Tully!

Roughneck and loudmouth.

Sneak-thief and womanizer!

The last time Smith had seen him—back in Wyoming—Tully had promised to fill Smith's guts with lead.

What could he want in Randolph City?

Was he looking for Smith?

And why now of all times? With the press broke down and the newspaper facing a deadline.

Smith ducked back into the shadow of Gerty's General Store, tasting the bacon and beans he'd had for lunch across the street at the Stockman's Café, clutching the paper-wrapped package he carried tight to his chest.

Maybe Tully hadn't seen him.

"You okay, Smith?" said Matt Gerty coming around the store's counter behind him.

No.

"Y-yes," said Smith. "Yes, I'm fine."

Smith closed his eyes and breathed deep, letting the familiar smells of the shop slow his pulse. Rich, oiled leather, spicy sawdust and dried fruit—raisins and dates—mixed with the woody smell of assorted nuts in an oak barrel. Over all came the full, warm scent of a spring rain wafting in from the street through windows propped open with cedar dowel sticks.

Smith exhaled, pushing away the fear. Opened his eyes.

The image of Tully, raw-boned and lanky, pockmarked and soaked to the skin, his long mustache drooling over a fat upper lip, was still there.

Eyes squeezed shut, Smith took another few breaths.

His watch clicked away a lazy half-minute, then another.

When he looked again, Smith saw sunshine breaking through the clouds and Gerty hovering at his side.

Outside, the street was empty.

Tully had moved on.

"Good old Gerty," said Smith, clucking his tongue. He put a hand on the older man's shoulder. "I'm quite all right."

"You weren't all right just a minute ago."

"A momentary, ah . . . indigestion."

"Indigestion? Got just the thing." And even as Smith opened his mouth to object, the proprietor slipped behind the tall square counter with its bins of beans and seeds toward a row of brown bottled liniments and glittering cure-alls.

"I'd rather not," said Smith. "I do have a printing press to repair." He held up the just-purchased package. "Mustn't keep old Brownstown waiting."

Smith poked his head out the door once more, eyes darting this way and that. "At least not any more than I have to," he said.

North Street, running east and west in front of Gerty's General, was clear with only a single old-timer tottering out of the café, moving toward the livery stable in the opposite direction of Tully's march.

"If you're sure . . . ?"

Smith made another quick scan and nodded obediently. "Sure

as an April shower," he said, half to himself.

Certain that the street was clear, or at least free of Rex Tully, he squared his shoulders and put a boot to the saturated boardwalk. With a fast wave goodbye, he turned to the left, and, after another quick left, scurried down a row of busy emporiums, watching his reflection in the store windows. Heavy package in hand, his lanky frame, sandy brown crop of hair, and schoolmaster's physique slid past the busy hitching posts and street full of bustling customers.

A pleasant spring Saturday surely brought folks to town.

But why—thought Smith—oh, why did it have to bring Rex Tully?

A man who'd shoot Smith Oberlin on sight.

Smith recalled the last time they'd been together.

A ranch in Wyoming.

There had been a fight. Smith had made a remark about a girl. Tully took offense.

In memory, he heard Tully's warning: "I ever see you again, I'll dump so much lead into your guts you'll sink on dry land."

Two years and a thousand miles ago.

Now here was Rex Tully in Smith's Nebraska hometown.

And today of all days—with the added strain of a broken press crippling the next edition of the *Randolph City Monitor* and Smith under a deadline to finish his newest story.

Just two steps from Ben Brownstown's two-story frame building, home of Randolph City's only newspaper, Smith's stomach lurched again.

Striding up the street, sloshing through a swirling gray puddle directly toward him, came Rex Tully.

Wearing a gun.

Smith ducked into the *Monitor* office with only seconds to spare.

Through a front window, Smith watched his nemesis pound up the street toward the general store.

"Cowardice?" said Smith. "No, I wouldn't exactly call it that."

He handed Brownstown the iron wrench, now unwrapped, that he'd procured at Gerty's store.

"I'd call it . . . a prudent reluctance to engage the man without all of the facts in hand," he added.

Twisting around the frame of the big printing press, the old publisher snorted as he fit the wrench to a stuck lug nut on a heavy support beam for the middle paper roller. The roller's main bearing was a tangle of metal filings. "Fancy way of sayin' you're scared," said Brownstone.

He gave the wrench a tug with no result.

"I simply want to know why he's in town before engaging him," said Smith.

"You think he's looking for you?"

"I don't know," Smith said. "But it's awfully odd, don't you think? Why here? Why now?"

Brownstown grunted, pulled on the wrench until his face turned the color of fresh beets, then let it fall to the hard wood floor of the office with a clank.

He kicked the machine.

"You'll be the death of me," he told it.

The nut, bent frame, and frozen roller remained stoic and noncommittal.

Brownstown uncurled himself from the monstrosity, stood straight, and wiped his forehead with a grease-covered rag. He kicked the wrench over to Smith.

"You give it a try."

"What? Me?"

"You got your mind too much on this Tully. Not enough on work."

Smith shrugged, retrieved the wrench.

"I mean it," Brownstone continued, "Even if we get this press up and running, you've got that wagon train story to write. How's it coming along?"

"I've done some general research on the families involved with the Floran wagon train. Traipsed around the prairie some, even followed the trail for some miles across the plains."

"But have you got anything down on paper?"

"Let me give it a go."

Smith snaked through a pair of iron rods and smacked the wrench onto the nut and the clank echoed back from the high ornamental tin ceiling through three lazy belt-driven ceiling fans.

"We don't get this roller spinning, there's no paper this week," said Brownstown, reminding Smith of their predicament.

"Or next week, or the week after," Smith recited in harmony as Brownstown continued on.

"What we really need is a machinist."

"Call Angus Wegner," said Smith.

"Wegner's a blacksmith. I need somebody who knows gears and levers. Somebody who can take this thing apart and put it back together better than we can."

"Funny," said Smith, fumbling again with the wrench. "The best machinist I know is Rex Tully."

"Again with this man? You're obsessed, son."

"I mean it," said Smith, pulling away from the press. "Back in Wyoming, I saw Tully fix everything from wagon wheels to pipe organs. For all his bad habits, the man's got a real knack with tools."

"Would he do it? Would he fix the press?"

"I expect that if the price was right, Rex Tully would try just about anything. And he'd deliver. In that sense he was a fair man."

Brownstown nodded, his mind made up. He handed Smith a blue shop cloth.

"Go find him."

Smith handed back the cloth. "Like hell."

"This machine won't fix itself. And apparently neither can we."

"Ben, please understand."

Brownstown put both hands on Smith's shoulders. "We need to get the press fixed, Smith. Both our livelihoods depend on it."

Smith cleared his throat.

"I understand your fear," said Brownstown. "But if this man can help us, isn't it worth a try?"

The older man's level gaze was unwavering.

Smith answered. "I'll need to arm myself." Then he wagged a finger. "And I'll have you responsible for all of my doctor bills."

"I doubt this fellow would draw on you in broad daylight."

"You don't know Tully."

Smith tossed the cloth aside and walked to his desk where he retrieved a heavy pepperbox pistol.

"Most foolhardy thing I've ever done for this paper," he said. "And mark my words, I've done some foolish things."

Brownstown waved him away with a dismissive left hand. He was already back to studying the broken press.

Pushing the gun into the waistband of his trousers, Smith turned and left the building.

"Rude fella, this man you described," said Bill Carpenter. "Didn't say two words to me." The livery owner adjusted his bent spectacles and straightened his big felt hat, quietly working a plug of tobacco in his cheek. "Can't say I cared for his looks, but his horse is in good shape. Seems well cared for. Just muddy." Carpenter shrugged. "With the rain last night, what can you expect?"

"He didn't say why he was here?"

Carpenter spit into the hay-covered dirt of the livery floor. "Nope."

Smith leaned on the rough oak station next to Carpenter. The livery barn was wide open, with only two equestrian residents in a pair of rear stalls. A black horse that Smith recognized as belonging to the stable.

"The buckskin must be Tully's," he said.

"Yeah, that's the one your stranger rode in on," said Bill, retrieving a broom from its place near the doorframe. "Like I said, he's in good shape. Covered with mud. They both were."

"Any word where he came in from?"

"He didn't tell me. I'd say west. Mud covering him and the horse was red. Wish I could tell you more. He came in with a single canvas bag. Paid me cash for a stall."

Smith toed the dust, drew a question mark, kicked it away.

"For how long?"

"No more than a week. That's just how he put it."

In Smith Oberlin's mind, fear was giving way to curiosity.

"Tell me this," he said. "Did he take the money from a pocket or from the bag?"

"Bag," said Carpenter.

That fit with the man Smith remembered. Tully never carried money on his person.

Carpenter swept a path away from Smith toward a gutter dug into the livery floor. "Paid more than he needed to. Gave me a twenty-dollar piece."

"Did you get the impression he had more where that came from? Did it seem he was carrying much money?"

Carpenter leaned on the broom. "I'd reckon that's a good bet. Heard some jingling when he reached inside the bag."

"A man with a bag full of money might not want to carry it

around," said Smith.

"Hotel would be your next obvious stop." Carpenter chuckled. "But, hell. If I had that much money, I'd take it to the bank."

Smith grinned and reached out to shake Carpenter's hand. "Thanks, Bill," he said. "I owe you one."

Back on the street, Smith followed Bill Carpenter's suggestion.

From the general store, Smith had seen Tully muddy and wet from his ride. Not at all a man who'd checked into a hotel and had a chance to dry off.

Neither had he carried a canvas bag like Carpenter had described.

Maybe he *had* stopped at the bank.

Keeping an eye over his shoulder, he made it to the Randolph City Savings and Loan.

Inside the clean room with its whitewashed walls and walnut trim, Melvin Russell invited Smith to join him at the rear of the bank beside his desk.

"I really shouldn't," said Smith. "I've just been to the livery and my shoes are rather dirty. No sense me tracking up the place."

Russell rose from behind his desk, and stroked his bushy white mustache.

"You're a considerate man, Mr. Oberlin, quite considerate. Why, I was just telling Mr. Brownstown the other day how fortunate we are to have you in Randolph City."

"Thanks, I—"

"No, no," said Russell. "The thanks are mine. And ours—all of us that call this little oasis on the prairie home. Now," he said with both hands on the counter. "How can we help you?"

"I'm looking for a gentleman who may have been in here today. Drooping mustache, muddy attire—"

"Looking for a gentleman? Why didn't you say so?" Russell winked. "Of course, I can't divulge anything confidential, but we'll do our best to help out one of Randolph City's favorite sons."

"That's dandy," said Smith, cocking an eyebrow. "I think."

"Oh, think nothing of it. Nothing indeed. Can I get you a coffee? Perhaps a cookie? Mrs. McCallum recently brought in a tin, and well—I believe she's still in back." Russell turned and called through a rear door. "Meg? Bring Smith Oberlin one of your cookies and some coffee from the stove."

Smith chewed his bottom lip. Russell had always been friendly enough when crossing paths with Smith, but the two weren't exactly friends. Since this was the most words they had ever traded, Smith couldn't help wondering why the banker was treating him so well.

From a back room, rolled the widow McCallum as though on wheels. Dressed in her Sunday best and carrying a pink parasol against the rain, the woman had nothing better to do than pass the time of day wherever gossip led, the bank, post office or *Monitor* building.

So Smith wasn't surprised to see her.

Wherever the laundry was aired, Meg McCallum was there.

"Sweets for the sweet," she sang, dumping two penny-size cookies onto the counter.

"Oops, I forgot the coffee." She returned to the back room.

Smith glanced at the clock on the wall above the counter, then took in Russell's smiling gaze.

A notepad, inkwell, and pen lay at odd angles to one another on the counter.

"This man, Tully, you see—"

"Let's wait for that coffee," said Russell.

"You have an admirable commitment to hospitality," said Smith.

"Anything for our good citizens, Mr. Oberlin. May I call you Smith?"

He nudged the pen and pad, lining them up with the inkwell.

When Meg McCallum returned, two tin cups in hand, she gave one to Russell and the other she placed carefully on the counter before Smith.

"You boys just go about your business," she said.

"How can I help you?" said Russell.

Before he could be again interrupted, Smith gave them Tully's description, then told them about Bill Carpenter's twenty-dollar coin and the warbag. "Sound familiar?" he asked.

Russell cleared his throat.

"Well, naturally, sir," he said. "Naturally."

Smith drummed his fingers on the counter.

"So you admit he's a customer?"

"I admit a man matching your description was here just before lunch, opened an account, and that he seemed amiable in nature."

"He was wearing a gun, wasn't he?" said Smith. "Did that seem amiable to you?"

"A lot of good men wear guns, Mr. Oberlin." Russell leaned over the counter, peering down at Smith's waistband where the butt of the pepperbox was plainly visible.

Smith drummed his fingers some more.

"So he didn't give his name?"

"I'm sure you know his name." Russell slurped from his cup and set it down.

"You seem to think I know more than I do about the man's business."

"And why not?" said Russell. "He gave your name as a reference for his deposit."

Smith sat back on his heels.

"He didn't seem so amiable to me," said Meg.

"Why don't you get us some more cookies, Meg," said Russell.

"And of course, you know about the girl," said Meg.

"I don't think that's relevant to Mr. Oberlin's interests," said Russell with a stern voice.

"Why not? This stranger, whatever his name is, asked us directly about the girl. I wouldn't consider that part confidential."

Smith knew there wasn't much Meg McCallum considered truly confidential.

He took the bait and ran with it.

"What did he say, Mrs. McCallum?"

"He asked if we had the acquaintance of a young woman named Lynn."

"No last name?"

"Lynn Bertrand," said Mrs. McCallum.

"And do we?" said Smith.

"We most definitely do not," said Russell. For some reason, the subject seemed to be making the banker more nervous by the minute. "If you won't get those cookies, I will," he said, leaving the counter.

Meg McCallum leaned over into the space Russell vacated. Cupping her hand to her mouth, her words came to Smith in a knowing hiss.

"We got the impression that young Lynn Bertrand is a girl in trouble," she said.

"Ooohh," Smith whispered back. That explained the banker's attack of the nerves. "But why is the old man being so nice to me?"

"Like we said, the stranger used your name as a reference when he opened the account," said Meg, still whispering. "Why, he deposited nearly twenty-five-thousand dollars!"

★　★　★　★　★

Smith returned to the street, determination nipping his heels.

The newspaper man shoved aside the fearful boy.

There was a story here, and Smith wanted to get to the bottom of it.

Rex Tully was driven by money and women.

Twenty-five-thousand dollars was a lot of money.

The other element seemed to be this girl, Lynn Bertrand.

No, Smith corrected himself. This *troubled* girl.

He followed a hunch and walked straight to Betty Fischer's Boarding House.

As it turned out, the madame was in.

Dressed in a cool blue satin dress that hugged every curve, Betty Fischer's greeting was a breath of evening shadow. Her long, ebony hair a nighttime contrast to its resting place of sunlit bare shoulders.

Betty always tried to fluster young Smith, but he gave as good as he got.

"You changed the color of your hair?" he said.

"I don't think so."

Smith snapped his fingers. "Must've been a different girl."

"Probably those naughty tintypes you boys pass around on poker night."

"Betty, I need your help," said Smith, abruptly all business.

"I've waited weeks for you to realize it."

"I'm looking for a man."

Betty rolled her eyes. "That could be arranged. But I must say, I'm surprised."

Smith stepped in close enough to smell Betty's heady lavender perfume.

"Betty," he whispered. "A man who might've been here. A stranger asking questions."

"No men here today except the usual."

"Big fellow," said Smith. "Long, unkempt mustache. Wearing a gun."

Betty smiled. "A dream walking."

"Melvin Russell gave me the impression he left a large sum of cash with the bank today."

"How large?"

"Pretty big."

"When it comes to size, Melvin tends to exaggerate. Believe me." Betty wrapped a lock of hair around her index finger.

"He's not exaggerating, Betty."

"I don't think—Wait!"

"Yes?"

"This big money man, was he covered in mud? Like he just came in off the prairie?"

"He was," said Smith.

"Then he *was* here," said Betty. "I barely noticed because I was doing some cleanup in back, but he came in and I overheard him ask one of the girls about somebody named Lynn."

"He asked about Lynn?"

"I thought that's what I heard?" said Betty. "Does the name mean anything to you?"

"It might."

"The way he said it was like he was real eager to find her." Betty lowered her voice. "Like he was desperate."

"Did you hear anything else?"

"Apparently this Lynn was . . . well . . ."

Her words trailed off, and Smith cocked his head.

"What, Betty?"

"He said it like she was more than a friend, and he made it pretty clear that's the case."

"How so?"

"Apparently Lynn is . . . in a family way." Betty smiled with mischief. "If you get my meaning."

"I get your meaning, indeed," said Smith. "And it's silly for you of all people to be coy."

"He left in a real hurry," said Betty.

"Did he say where he was going?"

She shook her head. "No."

"And you don't know where Miss Lynn might be?"

Betty shook her head. "I don't know anybody named Lynn. Neither do the girls. I wish I could be more help."

For a brief moment Smith questioned her with his eyes. He'd come to Betty's boarding house because of her reputation for helping lost souls.

But he sensed she was telling the truth about Lynn Bertrand.

Smith bent and kissed Betty's cheek.

"You've been a great deal of help," said Smith.

"Come back," Betty whispered, "when you're not looking for a man."

On the street again, moving back in the direction of the newspaper office, Smith reviewed the situation.

It wasn't unlike a news story, or even one of the many wild western tales he'd read in the periodicals published back east.

Of course, such sordid details as had obviously befallen Tully were usually smoothed over for the readers' delicate tastes.

Apparently, Big Rex Tully, the boasting philanderer, had made one conquest too many.

The poor recipient of trouble, this girl called Lynn, had fled the region as so many are forced to do. She could have traveled in any direction, but perhaps with summer coming on, she came to Nebraska where there'd be plenty of seasonal kitchen and garden work.

Now Tully was on her trail . . . with twenty-five-thousand dollars.

Smith wondered why.

To help or to hinder?

To redeem the girl's honor, and perhaps salvage his own?

Or to force her into final silence?

As in any narrative, he needed to take the next step.

He marched straight to the courthouse, halfway hoping now that he'd meet Tully head-on.

But it didn't happen.

He did, however, get all the answers he needed.

And it left him feeling like a heel.


Out of breath from an all-out run up the boardwalk, Smith pushed open the *Monitor* office door with a fast shove and almost tripped on the threshold.

"Brownstown," he cried. "We've got to find Rex Tully."

But before he could finish, a crusty rasp of a voice cut him off.

"Smith Oberlin?"

Instinctively, Smith reached for the pepperbox, pulled it from his waistband, and swung it around in the direction of Rex Tully.

The man was crouched beside the printing press, surrounded by tools and miscellaneous parts. His fist clamped around a polished Colt revolver, he issued a stern warning.

"Drop the peashooter, Smith."

Smith's eyes held Tully's gaze; he didn't lower his gun.

Tully had aged in the two years since Smith had seen him last. Or maybe it was just that he was still covered in drying mud.

But no, Smith thought, the eyes were tired, the beard and mustache more unkempt than ever.

"I know why you're here," said Smith.

"Back in Wyoming," said Tully, "I gave you a warning. Do you remember?"

"You said the next time we met, you'd fill my guts with lead."

"I meant it."

"What's it about, this beef between the two of you?" said Brownstown.

"I've got the information you want," said Smith.

Tully blinked.

"Isn't that why you're here at the newspaper office? After covering half of Randolph City asking about Lynn Bertrand? Isn't there still something you're looking for?"

"Lower your guns, both of you," Brownstown said.

"Smith and me used to work on a ranch together," said Tully. "He was always making the smart remark. The know-it-all comment."

Smith smiled. "I can't exactly deny it."

"One day he made a comment about my family. My sister."

"In fairness, I never met the girl." Smith rolled his eyes. "It was a general insult leveled at the man's family."

"At the women in my family."

"All right, yes, fine." Smith shrugged. "I was angry. We both were."

"I'm asking you both—for the last time—to put down your weapons."

"You shoot me," said Smith, "and you'll never find what you're looking for."

"I'll take my chances."

But even as Tully began to squeeze the trigger, Brownstown brought the wrench down hard on the man's wrist.

The six-shooter clattered across the floor.

"Doggone, it! You sonnuva—" Tully rolled ahead, holding his arm and whining,

Smith walked forward, keeping the pepperbox straight out in front of him.

"Now," said Smith. "Let's make another deal."

"That's enough, Smith," said Brownstown. "He's no danger

to you now."

Tully rolled onto his knees, sat back rubbing his wrist. "I'd rather deal with the devil."

"What makes you think you aren't?" said Smith, lowering his gun. He tossed the pepperbox onto his desk and placed both hands on his hips while he examined the printing press.

For once, Tully kept quiet.

"You were always quite the machinist, Tully. Back in Wyoming, you could fix anything. I want you to fix Mr. Brownstown's press."

Tully cursed under his breath, then said. "What's in it for me?"

"I told you. I know why you're here in Randolph City. I know about Lynn Bertrand. Fix the press, and I'll take you to her."

Wide eyed, Tully stammered. "Y-you know about Lynn. How?"

"Who's this Lynn?" said Brownstown.

Smith picked up Tully's gun and tossed it onto his desk where it landed beside his pepperbox.

"Lynn is Mr. Tully's sister," said Smith, putting his hand out to Tully. "And in the past half hour, I've gotten to know her quite well."

"I don't understand," said Tully.

"I'm sorry," said Smith. "For my slur back in Wyoming. For my terrible, terrible words. I apologize."

Tully let Smith help him up.

"I was wrong, Tully. Your sister was the best of us all."


After Tully got the press working, Ben Brownstown stayed at the *Monitor* office while Smith and Tully rode the black gelding and the buckskin stallion five miles northeast of town.

Smith followed the signs he'd left during his study of the Floran wagon train, bringing them through wet creeks and sharp hedgerows of multiflora rose and Russian thistles.

On a high hill under a clear blue sky, he reined in his horse and invited Tully to dismount.

They walked a few yards to the summit where several yards of spring grass were fenced off with wood pickets.

They walked through the cemetery gate.

Among several squares of flint embedded into the topsoil, one was of interest to the men.

*Madelynn Bertrand. Born 1853 Died 1873*

Tully's eyes were red and his jaw clenched and unclenched.

He looked at Smith.

Smith nodded and Tully knelt down, brushing the marker with his fingers.

"She came to town with the Floran wagon train," said Smith.

"I knew that much myself," said Tully. "I just didn't know where she was."

"The money you brought along," said Smith. "It was for her?"

Tully nodded. "An inheritance. Our old dad died back in Illinois. It was up to me to divvy things up. Last letter I got from Lynn said her and her husband, Jan, was here, near the little settlement of Randolph City."

"Not so little now. It's growing."

"I thought I'd find her alive."

"The Floran train passed through here in late August on their way west—woefully behind schedule. Lynn was with child, having a rough go of it. She and her husband, Jan Bertrand, made camp here with a local settler and his wife, hoping that bed rest would cure all. Sadly, she and the child both passed."

"How did you know where she was?"

"Once I saw her name in the locals records of the deceased, with you listed as her brother, I made the connection with the burial place."

Tully stood.

"One question," said Smith. "Why did you give banker Russell my name as a reference?"

Tully chuckled. "Better the devil you know," he said. "When I said the account was for the family of Jan Bertrand, the banker didn't recognize the name."

"There's nobody in Randolph City with that name now."

"So after Lynn passed, Jan went back to the wagon party?"

"Or just simply left town. No way to know where he is now."

"Anyhow, Smith, I knew you were in Randolph City," said Tully. "Some of the boys at the ranch still read that crap you write for the story magazines. They sort of keep up with you."

"Tell them I appreciate that," said Smith.

"Send 'em a wire if you want." Tully slapped Smith on the back. "I can't tell 'em."

"You can't?"

"Hell, Smith. What little I been in Randolph City, I like it here."

"You do?"

For the first time in two years, Smith saw Tully smile the big, obnoxious tooth-filled smile he'd learned to be wary of.

"I'll be putting down roots here," he said. "I'm staying."

Smith swallowed hard.

At least we'll have a reliable press man, he thought.

"Now," said Tully, turning away from the grave. "Tell me more about this Betty Fischer and her boarding house."

Or, thought Smith, maybe we won't.

After growing up on a Nebraska farm, **Richard Prosch** worked as a professional writer and artist in Wyoming and South Carolina. In 2016, Richard won the Spur Award for short fiction given by Western Writers of America. He lives in Missouri with his family. Visit him online at RichardProsch.com.

★ ★ ★ ★ ★

# THE CAVES OF
# VESPER MOUNTAIN
# BY GREG HUNT

★ ★ ★ ★ ★

It was dusk now, and the thick ominous clouds above promised more bad weather on its way. Ridge Parkman knew he would soon have to find someplace to hunker down overnight, whether or not his companion returned from his latest scouting excursion or not. But surely, they would at least be able to find each other in the morning.

Making up his mind at last, he turned his horse off the road and up the cut of a shallow, half-frozen creek. General Grant was a husky, sure-footed animal, and found purchase on the stony ground even though the light was nearly gone. A couple of hundred yards into the forest, he found a spot where a wide slab of rock extended out over a flat patch of dry ground. It was tall enough to shelter the General and promised some protection from the stiff wind blowing in from the west. It would have to do.

He gathered a couple of armloads of deadfall to build a small fire, then unsaddled General Grant and laid out his bedroll in a niche toward the back of the overhang. The fire might be a bad idea, but he had been yearning for a hot cup of coffee for the past few frigid hours, and decided it was worth the risk.

Since midday yesterday when this escapade started, not a dang thing had gone his way. He had been up in Springfield at the time, testifying against a woman-stealer he had chased to ground, and was looking forward to a hot meal and a warm hotel bed before heading back north. But then the telegram from Captain Wooten in Kansas City arrived, dispatching him south to Cable Springs, where a rowdy gang of heathens had raided the town. The captain had made it clear that he didn't want to set eyes on Marshal Ridge Parkman again until the leader of the gang, Jethro Swope, was swinging from a rope or otherwise out of business permanently.

Parkman made the twenty-mile ride south that same day.

Everything continued to run foul when he reached Cable Springs, starting with a past-his-prime town marshal named Tom Brigance in Cable Springs who wasn't about to round up a posse and take out after the gang who had just robbed their bank, ravaged several other businesses in town, and left five corpses in their wake—four citizens and one yellow dog. Still, Parkman understood the marshal's take on things. The last time Jethro Swope's outfit raided the town two years before, Brigance had mustered what manpower he could, and lit out on their trail. But they never did come close to catching a single outlaw because of the shoot-and-run ambushes that Swope had strung out behind to discourage any pursuit. Even two or three men with rifles could slow down a posse several times their number, then dissolve into the woods before anything could be done about it.

After that chase, Brigance had returned to town three days later with two of his men dead across their saddles, and two more bloodied. This time, chances were slim that anyone would be eager to saddle up and ride out again, even if the town marshal had wanted to, which he didn't. By the time a U.S. marshal showed up, Ridge Parkman in particular, Brigance was relieved to back away and let a federal lawman carry the water.

When Parkman realized that he would be riding out alone this time, the plan he came up with was simple enough. Cut off the head. He'd do his best to quietly track Swope until he went to ground with few or none of his men still around, then kill or capture him, as circumstances allowed. Afterward, local lawmen could deal with the remaining members of Swope's gang, or not, as they saw fit. And that would have to satisfy the captain's orders.

At the last minute, a man named Mel Carroll, a lean, somber character, a local farmer with a hard, determined look but little to say, had volunteered to come along, explaining that he intended to hound Jethro Swope to the grave whether or not Parkman wanted to partner up with him. Carroll knew the territory here in the mountains of southwest Missouri well, whereas Parkman did not, and Carroll's brother-in-law had been shot dead during the raid. Parkman welcomed the help. He offered to swear Carroll in as a deputy, but Carroll said that a badge on his chest wouldn't make any difference to him.

When they left Cable Springs, the day was pleasant enough for early February, but Carroll was already talking about worse weather on the way. Later in the day, as they probed deeper into the remote, hilly territory south of the town, thick gray clouds began to roll in and the storm hit. It started with a steady rain that froze on everything it touched and kept the forested hills filled with the brittle noise of crackling tree branches. Next came the hail, big round chunks that hurt when they whacked a man and kept the horses spooked. The snow came finally, blowing and swirling in from the west, not stopping until it layered several inches on top of the ice and hail.

Mel Carroll had spent most of the time scouting ahead, knowing that any men that Swope left behind weren't likely to ambush a single rider when they were expecting a full-out posse to come riding down the road at any time. But there had been no ambushes so far. Parkman figured that by now, three days after the raid, Swope was probably feeling secure in the knowledge that even if there had been a posse behind him, they were already on their way back home. But Parkman and Carroll were still cautious.

The iron pot of beans and jerky was nearly ready to eat when Parkman heard the distant crunch of horse's hooves breaking through the ice of the creek, coming from the same direction he had ridden. He was pretty sure of who it was, but still slipped into a cluster of brush, beyond the light of the fire.

"That fire sure is a welcome sight, Marshal," Mel Carroll called out from the darkness nearby.

"And so are you, Mel," Parkman said. He uncocked the hammer of his Colt and holstered it as he returned to the fire. "The coffee's boiled, and there's beans a'plenty if you can stomach my cooking."

Over supper, Carroll began to tell Parkman what he had discovered farther down the road. "The snow had pretty much covered up all the tracks on the road, but I did find a place a mile or two down where it looked like six or eight horses had cut off into the forest."

"There was twelve or fifteen of them back in Cable Springs, so the town marshal said. If there's only half that many left, Swope must be splitting up his gang," Parkman said. "He's an old bushwhacker from back in the war, and that's how Quantrill used to do it when the Bluecoats were after him. Sometimes he'd even peel away on his own and let the Yankees ride on after the rest of his band."

"They seem to be heading southeast into some rugged territory that stretches all the way down into Arkansas. Those mountains would be a good place to hole up 'til they see if anybody's still after them."

"Maybe Swope will get cocky and careless if he decided he got away clean."

"And then comes our turn," Carroll said, spitting into the fire.

It was late afternoon the next day when all hell broke loose for the first time.

The tracks they had been following since they left the road that morning became clearer as they rode along on a game trail deep into the foothills of the mountains ahead. These Ozark Mountains weren't as tall and ragged as the Rockies and the other high-country ranges Parkman had traveled through out west, but they sure were as rugged, and the trails were just as steep and twisting.

When they heard voices ahead, on the other side of a jumble of ragged boulders, both halted their horses, dismounted, and readied their weapons. The voices continued, indicating that their preparations hadn't been heard. One of the men up ahead was moaning and cursing, obviously in pain, and another one seemed to be trying to convince him that he'd be okay.

Parkman and Carroll talked in whispers. "Just two of them, you figure?" Carroll asked.

"Just two talking," Parkman answered in a low voice. "But there could be others. With all of that yowling, one of them must be hurt for sure. Let's go at them from two sides, and maybe we'll be lucky enough to take at least one of them alive."

"Suits me."

"Do you want one of these?" Parkman asked, raising his Colt. "I've got an extra in my saddlebag."

"I'm used to this scattergun. It clears a wide swath, and I can reload faster than you'd think."

As Carroll slipped around the edge of the jumble of rocks to the right, Parkman eased forward along the trail as far as he dared go without being seen. Then, when he figured he had given his companion time enough to get in place, he leaned his head and his revolver far enough around a boulder to cover the small clearing where the men were.

The man who had been cussing and complaining lay on his back, with one leg twisted unnaturally. Another man knelt beside him, and a third one remained mounted on the far side of the clearing. Two horses waited nearby, one favoring a front leg.

"We can do it the easy way, fellows," Parkman called out gruffly, "as long as you don't try to fill your hands."

But there was no easy way for men like these. They knew that if they were taken alive, nothing but a dancing loop of rope waited for them back in Cable Springs. The kneeling man was the first to take a chance, but a blast from Carroll's shotgun and a .45 slug from Parkman both found him about the same time. The mounted man slapped his heels into his horse's flanks, and the animal bolted away into the brush. Parkman slung a couple of wild shots in that general direction, but it wasn't until Carroll emptied his second barrel that the escaping man let out with a surprised yip. Jittery by then, the other two horses galloped away behind the escapee.

The remaining outlaw, still prostrate on the ground, had been fumbling around trying to lay a hand on his pistol, but it must have fallen out of his holster when he went down. Parkman saw it a few feet away, then walked over and kicked it a little farther.

"Damned if you don't look familiar. Your name's Parkman, ain't it?" the injured man said, ignoring his pain for a moment. "I knew you and your kinfolk too up north of Independence. I rode with some of them in Quantrill's bunch, back during the rebellion."

Parkman stepped closer to get a better look. "Gillum, isn't it? Something Gillum? I recall we did meet a couple of times."

"Claude Gillum," the man said, seeming to see a sliver of hope in the middle of this mess. "I rode with your cousins, John and Daniel, for two years, right up to the last hurrah outside

Westport, and then for a little while after with the James brothers."

"I remember," Parkman said coldly. "But all that doesn't buy you any favors, Gillum. Not after what you and the rest of Swope's bunch did up there in Cable Springs."

"I didn't hurt nobody," Gillum said. "I was guarding the far end of town while all the shooting was going on, and I never broke leather."

"You're a lying dog," Carroll growled, feeding two fresh loads into his shotgun as he walked over to them. "I seen you out front of the bank. I can't say you're the one who shot my brother-in-law, but I can testify that I saw you with a smoking gun in your hand."

"There's not much we can do for you, Claude," Parkman said. "But if you'll tell us where Jethro Swope is heading, we'll build you a fire and leave you some food before we ride on."

"I ain't the kind to do something lowdown like that to a compadre like Jethro Swope," the injured man said defiantly. "And anyway, I don't fancy hobbling around the rest of my life on only one good leg. I'd druther wait in hell for a hunnert years for the two of you to show up than . . ."

The blast of Carroll's shotgun interrupted whatever solemn vow Gillum was about to make. Parkman snapped his head around to his companion, hardly prepared for such a sudden execution.

"There's a druther for you," Carroll said, sending a squirt of tobacco juice down on the dead man's face. He stepped forward and pulled the dead man's hand from under his side, revealing to Parkman the small hideout gun Gillum had been trying to put into play. Then, without saying more, he turned and crossed the clearing to the spot where the third man had escaped. Carroll disappeared into the brush for a couple of minutes, then came back to report as they mounted up.

"There's a few drops of blood on the leaves alongside the trail, so I guess we stung him at least."

"But not bad enough to knock him out of the saddle."

"Nope. But maybe if his horse caught some of that buckshot, it'll slow them down a bit."

Jethro Swope had put together a comfortable little nest for himself a dozen steps back into the cave, and was looking forward to the best night's sleep he'd had since before the raid. With a fire nearby to keep him almost warm, he was leaning back against his saddle, and had his blanket spread across his legs. He held a revolver in one hand, and a half-full wine bottle in the other. Most of his men had gone for the whiskey when they raided the saloon in Cable Springs, but Swope favored the luxury of wine when he could get his hands on some.

He raised his pistol when he heard voices outside the cave entrance where the sentries were posted, then rested it back down on the blanket when he realized there was no excitement or any hint of danger in the conversation. It was probably just Gillum and his bunch coming back to report, he thought. And he felt confident that the news would be good. Between the snow that covered their backtrail, the misery of the cold, harsh nights, and the rugged country they were heading into, he figured that any posse that came after them was already on their way back to town. But then, maybe there never had been a posse, he thought with a crooked grin, not after the lesson his gang had taught them the last time.

Swope lifted the wine bottle to his mouth and took a swallow as he watched two figures enter the cave and walk toward him. He was disappointed to see that neither of them was Claude Gillum, his longtime friend. The man on the right was Abel Branch, his second in command, and the other was one of the three men he had sent out that morning to scout the trail behind them. It couldn't be a good sign that Gillum was nowhere in sight.

The man approaching with Abel Branch had a pronounced limp, and his right arm dangled at his side like a worthless appendage. His shoulders sagged and his hat was missing.

"Spankler's got some bad news to deliver," Branch announced. "Seems like Gillum and Kane both got shot up a few hours ago back down the trail. Spankler here caught a scattering of buckshot, but he got away."

"And the buckshot hit you in the backside?" Swope asked gruffly. "Why not in the front?"

"After I emptied my gun, I had to hightail it out of there or I'd have gone down too," Spankler explained. "There was just too many of them. Six or eight, maybe, and prob'ly more back down the trail. They caught us plumb off guard."

"Wasn't it supposed to be the other way around, peabrain? Didn't I tell the three of you that if you saw a posse coming up the trail, you were supposed to pick off a few of them with your rifles, and then scatter into the woods? So how in hell did they manage to ambush you instead?"

"We would've done like you said, Mister Swope. But things was already going bad even before they jumped us." Spankler was so jittery that his hands were shaking and his high-strung voice was a sure sign that he was lying his way through this whole tale. "Claude's horse twisted a hoof on the rocks, and when he went down, he fell right on top of Claude's leg. That leg was mashed like a fritter, and Claude took to squalling 'cause of the pain. The posse was not far back, and I guess that's how they knew we were there. They came in shooting, and we fought them off for a while, but there was just too many of them."

"And that's how you caught that buckshot in your hind end? By fighting them off?" By then, Swope was so aggravated and frustrated that he considered just dropping this inbred moron where he stood. He felt like it might almost be an act of mercy but he knew the rest of the men in his gang would frown on it. Bloody Bill used to get away with such things once in a while . . . but that was then, and he wasn't Bloody Bill Anderson.

"So, when you hightailed it, the first thing you did was head straight here so that posse would have a fresh trail to follow in the morning?"

"I figured you might want to know," Spankler mumbled, seeming to realize his own mistake even as he spoke.

As Spankler stumbled away Swope noticed the bloody scattering of buckshot wounds across his back and right arm. Branch sat down on the ground near Swope and pulled a small brown bottle out of his coat pocket. He was a rotgut man.

"I guess we'll have to hightail it," Branch said.

"Looks like it," Swope agreed. "At first light for sure, or maybe even earlier if the moon comes up and the clouds don't hide it. I'll pay the other men off in a while, and tell them to scatter in the winds. That might keep the posse confused long enough for us to get lost deeper into the mountains."

"Yeah, maybe." There was no confidence in Branch's voice.

After a while, Jethro Swope wandered to the edge of the rock-strewn clearing outside the mouth of the cave to settle his nerves. An uneasy feeling plagued him, the kind of feeling that experience had taught him to heed. Maybe it was finally time to get out of this business and head out to California, like he'd been thinking about doing for years. All it took was just to do it, but there was always that nagging thought that he needed to put together just a little bigger stake to make a good start out west.

This wasn't like the old days. He could still put together a big enough crew to take over a remote little berg like Cable Springs for a short time, but it wasn't like it once had been, back during the war when the bushwhackers rode out by the hundreds. He had been at Lawrence and Centralia when they thundered into town like avenging devils, taking what they wanted, killing who they wanted, and leaving only chaos, corpses, and towering blazes in their wake. He was just a common thief and a hunted criminal now, with no claim to a higher cause behind what he did.

Everything seemed wrong about how the Cable Springs raid unfolded, starting with the caliber of the men he rounded up for the job. The best never showed up anymore, men he could trust, men who knew what it was like to live by the way of the gun. Now it was the weasels and scalawags and morons who answered his call, men like that cowardly fool Spankler, who wouldn't have lasted a week riding under the black flag of Bill Quantrill or Bloody Bill Anderson.

Then there was the nearly empty vault in the Cable Springs Savings and Investor's Bank, which he had counted on for ten thousand dollars or more to make this whole enterprise worth the time and effort it took to put together. Once he paid off his motley band, there would scarcely be enough left to cover his expenses and keep him fed for the next few months.

He was almost embarrassed by the pointless savagery of a few of his men. It was one thing to shoot it out with other armed men, but there had been no resistance in Cable Springs this go-around. So why had there been a scattering of dead and wounded in the bank and in the streets when they rode away? He thought bitterly that if he could have found out who shot that poor old yellow dog, he might have gladly gunned the bastard down himself. What kind of man shot a dog just for running alongside them and barking?

Now there was the matter of whoever was on their backtrail. If Spankler's report was even close to the truth, there might be a lot of them, scattered out like buckshot through the forests and mountains nearby, and it worried him that there was no good way to tell. All he knew at this point was that whoever was back there must be good, a lot craftier and more determined than the backwoods trash that he had riding with him.

Swope heard footsteps behind him and turned to see Abel Branch approaching. "So, what do you think, Abel?"

"I admit, it sure ain't like the other time when we hit Cable Springs," Branch said.

"Remember how we hit that posse three times in two days, and the third time they turned and scattered like a sack of rats?" Swope said. "Just like Bloody Bill would have done it. Aren't there any of the good ones still left from the old days?" He took a gulp of wine from the bottle, then passed it over to his companion.

"Mayhaps, it's only you and me now, Jethro."


"When Ham came back after the war, there wasn't much left of their family place but ashes and bare ground and fields full of unmarked graves. There'd been a big fight there, just like at my place. It took his daddy's life, and after, I brought his mama and two sisters back to what was left of my farm. I married the older girl, Rochelle."

It was the most Mel Carroll had talked since they partnered up three days before, and Ridge Parkman just stayed quiet and listened.

"He was a good man, God fearing, hardworking, and always patient and kind to his addle-brained mother. Within five years he had the place shaped up again, even though he was still turning up bones in his cornfields, just like me. He married one of the Butterfield girls. They had three little ones running around, and another in the oven. If I ever had a best friend besides a dog or a mule or my woman, I guess Ham would have been it."

Parkman glanced over to see if he might be joking, but saw

no sign of it. There was scarcely any humor in Mel Carroll's makeup, especially on this bitter mission. Carroll rearranged a log at the edge of the fire so it would burn better, then spit a cord of tobacco juice expertly into the flames.

"We was in Cable Springs for the stock auction. Ham had a fine young Angus bull to sell, and I brought along a brace of two-year-old mules I was ready to part with. Soon as we made our sales, Ham walked down to the bank to turn our vouchers into cash money, and that's where he was when Swope's outfit rode in. His guns was in the wagon. I'm sure he'd of given them what-for if he'd been armed, but he must have tried even unarmed, and got himself killed for it."

"Sorry to hear that, Mel," Parkman said. "Sometimes life just don't seem fair, does it? To survive all through the war and start up a new life. And then this . . ."

"The Bible says vengeance belongs to God," Mel said, "but in this part of the country, we figure sometimes we have to help Him out a bit."

"I suppose that's not much different than how we feel in my line of work. We just call it justice instead."

They had stopped for the night when it got too hard to track the lone survivor of the shootout, but Carroll had risen well before dawn, eager to get going again.

They both drained the dregs of their morning coffee from their metal cups, knowing it was the last, and wrapped the remains of last night's pone in cloth for later. They had provisioned themselves for four or five days when they left Cable Springs, and they were about to run out of everything. Pretty soon they'd be living off the land. Parkman wiped the skillet, coffee pot, and cups clean with handfuls of snow, then stowed them away in a canvas pack. Carroll went over to the horses and checked their cinches.

"We've got a clear trail to follow, and we'll need to make the best of it while we can," Carroll said. "We could get more snow after dinnertime."

As they mounted and started up the steep game trail once more, Parkman scanned what lay ahead. A stark winter landscape of rolling forested hills, daunting stone cliffs, and occasional peaks loomed on all sides.

"We should have gone west, Jethro," Abel Branch mumbled sullenly. "Or south on the post road down into Arkansas."

"With a posse on our trail?" Swope scoffed.

"There's just two of us now, and we could lose them easy enough."

"They've stayed with us this long, and I want to get lost out there someplace where they never could follow us. You know this country, Abel, and I'm counting on you to lead us plumb to the far side of nowhere."

"I know it all right." There was an odd tone to Branch's voice that Swope couldn't remember hearing before. "Maybe I know it too well. That there's Vesper Mountain up ahead."

"So?"

"It's some of the roughest country you ever imagined. No trails in and none out. Cracks in the rock that go straight down to hell, and caves that can swallow a man up whole. The talk I heard all my life goes way back to Indian tales, about men that went in there and never come back out again."

"Sounds like a perfect hideout," Swope said, trying to lighten things up. "Maybe we should build a cabin back in there someplace."

"Laugh if you want . . ."

Parkman unloaded and unsaddled the horses while Carroll scouted around and read the sign near the gaping mouth of the cave. When he came back from a short jaunt into the surrounding woods, he was carrying an armload of deadfall for the evening fire.

"They must have spent a night here. There's a little clearing down the hill a piece where they kept their horses, and we might as well do the same. There's a patch of dead grass the wind swept clear that they can nibble on, and a little stream running too fast to freeze over."

As Parkman scraped together the remnants of the fire the outlaws had built and blew up a small flame from the smoldering coals, Carroll turned and stared off into the distance. "Looks like they rode due east from here," he noted. "I was hoping they'd go just about any other direction instead."

"Why's that?"

"It's rough country over there. Rough and dangerous. You can't see it from here, but there's a place over there called Vesper Mountain that folks in these parts know to stay clear of." His voice trailed off, and he seemed caught up in his own thoughts.

"Maybe Swope's got a hideout back in there someplace," Parkman suggested.

"Not likely. If he'd ever gone in there once and made it back out, he wouldn't be wanting to go in again."

"That bad, huh? Have you ever been there, Mel?"

"Just into the edge of it. Some horse soldiers chased me in there back during the war, and I hid out there for a night. But I think if I had to do it again, I'd take my chances with the soldiers."

"But if Swope goes in there . . ."

"I know. I s'pose we'll have to go after him, won't we?"

Later as Parkman was frying up the last of the bacon and keeping an eye on the biscuits baking in a cast-iron pot next to the fire, he told his companion, "This is it for me, the last of the food I brought along. You got anything left?"

"Some jerky, and a sack of beans. In the morning I'll put the beans in my canteen to soak, and then we can cook them at suppertime."

"And after that?"

"The Lord will provide, I suppose."

Parkman lifted the lid on the pot and checked the biscuits. They were charred on the bottom and doughy on top, but edible, more or less. Carroll didn't complain. It would be good to sleep in the cave tonight. They could build the fire up to stay warm, and if any snow fell overnight, at least they wouldn't wake up buried in it. After they finished eating, Parkman rolled a smoke for himself, then handed the makings over to Mel Carroll, who packed some of the tobacco in his cob pipe.

Finally, the marshal decided to broach the topic that had been on his mind all through supper. "You know, Mel, you're a puzzling man."

"When Rochelle says something like that, I know it means trouble," Carroll said.

"It's like this. Back in Cable Springs, you're the only man that stepped up when you saw I was going out after Swope and his bunch, even with all the odds against us. You're a courageous man, no doubt about it." Carroll sat across the fire, leaning against a boulder, looking at Parkman and waiting for him to make his point. "But a while ago, when you were talking about Vesper Mountain, there was some kind of look in your eyes. It's hard to explain what I saw."

"Every man carries around fears inside of himself that he don't know are there unless a particular thing happens to him. And then, just knowing that's inside of you is like having it chained to your leg. You'll never be free of it again."

"I guess I don't know what you're talking about. I've been afraid lots of time in my life, but not that kind of afraid."

Carroll turned his gaze away, out into the night, the forest, and probably the past. "I don't never talk about it to anybody, not even to my wife when I used to wake up at night once in a while, wet as an otter, yelling out all kinds of nonsense. But I will tell you this. I think I went mostly crazy that night out toward Vesper Mountain, and I ain't sure I ever came all the way back. There's dangers that you understand, and those you don't, and it's the last ones that keep a man tossing on the tick at night."

Parkman waited a moment, still feeling like he didn't completely believe or understand what his companion was talking about. It sounded like sheer superstition to him. "And yet you're still willing to ride with me tomorrow to the place that did that to you."

Mel Carroll cocked his head, and a crooked almost-grin reshaped his features for an instant. "They killed my kin," he said, as if that explained it all.

Now, with only Abel Branch remaining, the deeper they forged into this rugged country, the more confident Swope felt that he could quickly leave the posse behind. Surely, they'd lose the trail in this raw, rugged wilderness.

"We've rode together for a long time, haven't we, Jethro? Been through plenty of bad scrapes together." Abel Branch was riding ahead, carefully picking his way uphill through a tangle of boulders, fallen rocks, and jagged fissures.

"Many a mile, and many a fight," Swope agreed.

"And you know I ain't a cowardly man. I've always been loyal to you, haven't I? But there comes a time . . ." He fell silent for a moment, as if he didn't quite know how to turn his thoughts into words.

"Get to it, Abel. If you want to part ways, just come right out with it."

Ahead was a grade so steep that Abel's horse threatened to balk at climbing it. "I've never been to the cave up there myself," he said. "But I heard another man speak of it, and we seen it ourselves from back down the trail. If your mind's still set on it, you can make it up there alone. But I swear on my daddy's grave, I can't bring myself to go along. The whole idea of it's got me so worked up I'm about to wet my britches."

"We wouldn't want that. Cut loose and head on home, Abel," Swope said.

"And you won't hold it against me? I still get my share?"

They paused for a moment while Swope loosened the straps on a saddlebag and pulled out the canvas satchel from the bank. He counted out the money he owed his companion and handed it over. Abel Branch stuffed it inside his coat without counting it.

"Keep one eye open even when you're sleeping, Jethro, and keep your guns cocked. Don't stay around these parts any longer than you have to."

"You know I will."

The two men shook hands, and Branch turned his horse toward their backtrail. Swope watched him go, haunted by some strange feeling that this was the last that they would ever see of one another.

Sundown was approaching, and it would be dark in an hour or less. A wind was blowing steadily from the west, bringing the serious nighttime cold with it. Mel Carroll turned up the collar of his coat and held the front together to keep the wind from blowing in.

The circling buzzards high in the sky alerted them that there was carrion up ahead. With each patient pass, the smoothly gliding creatures descended a little more. They were in no hurry. The larger animals below on the ground would have to eat their fill before the broad-winged, crook-necked birds got their turn.

Carroll and Parkman heard the wild hogs up ahead before

they actually saw them. Their frenzied grunting and squealing were familiar to Carroll, and he knew they were feeding. It would be smarter to backtrack and cut a wide trail around them, but that wasn't possible on this bewildering, stone-strewn mountainside. There was no guarantee that there was another way around, and even if they found one, there was a good chance they would lose the faint trail they were following.

"Check your loads and let's have at 'em," Carroll said to the marshal. "It don't sound like more than three or four." As Mel cocked the hammers on his double-barrel, Parkman drew his Colt from its holster and pulled a second handgun from inside his coat. "Keep shooting 'til they're all stone dead. They're thick-skulled and they don't go down easy."

The hogs were feeding in their own rambunctious way on the fresh carcass of a horse, crowding and squalling and slashing at one another with their long, curved tusks as they greedily tore away chunks of meat and swallowed them down. They didn't seem to notice the appearance of the two riders until the shooting started. Mel downed one with both loads of buckshot and quickly began to reload. Parkman finished another one off with a succession of shots across its skull and shoulder. But the third, also wounded but not yet ready to die, spun and charged. The marshal killed it within feet of the horses, but not before Mel's horse reared in panic, pawing the air with its front hooves. Mel Carroll tumbled backward in a disheveled heap on the ground.

Parkman was already reloading. "You all right, Mel?"

"Not sure yet." The hip he had landed on hurt like blazes, and he noticed that one of his arms was no help as he struggled clumsily to his feet. Sharp pain was beginning to shoot up his arm and shoulder.

"That must be the fellow who was riding the horse," Parkman said. He pointed at a body several feet away, bent awkwardly across a fallen tree. He lay face up, his backbone clearly snapped. They both went over to take a look.

"I know this man," Mel said. "Name's Abel Branch. He settled a few miles east of my place after the war. I didn't know he rode with Swope, though." To his and Parkman's surprise, the corpse's eyes fluttered, then opened. He looked around for a moment, then his gaze settled on the two men looking down at him.

"Who's that?" the man asked.

"It's Mel Carroll," Mel said. "We thought you was dead already, Abel."

"Not quite yet, Mel. You riding with the posse?"

"Tom Brigance wouldn't put together a posse because of what Swope did to them last time, so it's just me and the marshal here."

"You mean it's only been the two of you all along? Well I'll be damned."

"I had to come along because yours and Swope's bunch killed Ham Adderly in the bank holdup. He's my brother-in-law, and he didn't even have a gun on him. No sense in it, and I had to avenge him for Rochelle's sake, and her family's."

"Yep, I was there when he got shot, and I felt bad about it right off. I was sorry about him, and sorry for that poor ol' dog too. Ham smart-mouthed the wrong man, and got a bullet for it."

"Are you hurting bad, Abel?"

"Nope. I don't feel nothin'. Can't move nothin'. I heard the hogs over there eating my horse, and I figured I was next."

"Yep, and there's buzzards that'll be along shortly." Carroll knelt beside the paralyzed man, his gaze cold. "For my money, you ain't getting no worse than you deserve, you son of a bitch. Ham had a wife and three little ones, and now they'll have it hard for a long time to come."

Branch's eyes sagged closed, and for a moment Carroll thought he had died. He scanned the man's mutilated body. Branch's back was curved across the log like the blade of a scythe, and his neck was twisted awkwardly.

"I knew it warn't right what we was fixin' to do," Branch said at last, his eyes opening slowly like a man just waking. "But my family was most near starving, and it was my own fault. Folks told me we was too far north and it wasn't hot enough to grow cotton, but I set my mind to give it a try. I had that good bottomland and it seemed to make sense at the time. But the whole crop failed."

"Yep. Corn's the thing in these hills. Corn, and maybe some wheat if the soil's right for it."

"I know that now." Branch's eyes fluttered and rolled back like he was dizzy. His breathing was shallow and seemed to stop briefly, but then he gained control again. "I ain't got the right to ask, Mel," he said, "but I always heard you was a good man. They's a roll of money in my jacket, three hundred dollars, and I'm hoping you might have the charity to take it to Delilah. She and the children might starve without it."

Carroll scoffed at the notion. "If I was to give the money to anyone, it would be Ham Adderly's wife and children, not yours. If your brood was in need, you should have been there yourself to see to them, not riding off with the likes of Jethro Swope to steal and murder. The Good Book's got something to say about the children paying for the sins of the fathers."

For the first time, Parkman intervened. He knelt on the other side of the man's broken remains and reached inside his coat for the money. "This goes back to the bank in Cable Springs," he said. "And I agree with Mr. Carroll. You can start your trip to hell knowing that whatever hardship your family goes through is on you." His voice was hard, bereft of sympathy. "But I will make you one bargain. You tell me what you can about where

Swope is, and where he's heading, and I'll make sure you don't have to lay here helpless when the wild animals hereabouts make a meal of you. The buzzards start with the eyes. I've seen it."

Carroll watched Branch's eyes as they shifted from Parkman to him, and then back to the marshal. Even though the muscles of his face were still, his eyes seemed filled with terror at the thought of it.

"He was bound for a cave up yonder on the side of Vesper Mountain," Branch said at last. "I can't say where exactly 'cause I never been there and wouldn't go now. Folks I knew and trusted always said it's best to stay out of these parts."

"I've heard the same my whole life," Carroll said.

"So what were his plans after he got to the cave?" the marshal asked.

"He said he'd hole up there 'til the posse gave up and turned back, and then he'd head south. He's got kin down in Arkansas someplace."

Parkman nodded his head, then he and Carroll rose to their feet. They both backed up a few feet so the blood wouldn't splatter on them when the marshal kept his bargain with Abel Branch.


"I can feel the break up under your skin," Parkman said. Carroll gritted his teeth against the pain as the marshal probed the flesh of his arm one last time. The growing pain in his right arm was convincing him that his injury was worse than he first thought, but he hadn't mentioned it to his companion until they were settled in for the night.

Neither of them wanted to make camp in a spot where a dead man, a dead horse, and three dead hogs were lying close around, so they had ridden a short piece back down the trail to a spot where there was some deadfall for a fire and a protruding slab of rock that would serve as scant shelter when the weather turned bad again. Tonight, they kept the horses in close so they wouldn't suffer the same fate as Abel Branch's animal had.

The two men sat side by side near the fire, and Carroll's injured arm lay across Parkman's legs. One end of the broken bone pushed up against the skin of his forearm like a huge boil, and it was twisted unnaturally.

"Can you set it?" Carroll asked.

"I wouldn't even try," Parkman said. "It feels all splintery inside and turned wrong." The broken bones had not punctured the skin, but his arm was already swelling and turning red. It was bleeding in there, and no way to stop it. "Lucky for you I thought to check that man's saddlebags," he added, handing a small dark whiskey bottle over to Carroll. "I've got a feeling you're going to want plenty of that before we get you back to Cable Springs."

"But first we go up the mountain and finish off that skunk, Jethro Swope. Right?"

Parkman was silent.

"Right?" Carroll repeated.

"You need a doctor who can cut that arm open and put the bones back together like they belong, and then sew you up. You could lose that arm, Mel. Or something even worse."

Mel Carroll gritted his teeth again, this time out of frustration instead of pain. He stared out into the night at the moonlit slopes of Vesper Mountain. "But he's just right up there," he said, his voice filled with frustration and defeat.

"I know," Parkman said. "But this is an easy call for me. Jethro Swope will get his when the right time comes. My worst problem will be trying to explain all this to the captain when I get back."

His life was reduced to darkness, and pain, and terror.

He was deep into the cave now, too deep for light or cold or any outside sound to penetrate. Those things had quit looking for him, seeming to know that if they roved beyond the dim glow of outside light behind them, they might end up as lost as he was. His eyes ached from staring into the impenetrable darkness, desperate for any hint of light, but all he saw was an occasional fleeting pinprick glow, created by his own mind, perhaps to give him an instant of hope where there was none.

The only sound was a distant gurgling ripple of flowing water, like the noise of an energetic stream trickling down a mountainside. He would have liked to locate it and get a drink, imagining how good the cold water would taste. But it mocked his efforts to find it, sometimes over here, sometimes over there, seeming to move around like a malicious sprite. The last time he tried to find it, his leg had slipped down into a slash in the rock and he fell forward. He heard the bone snap, and felt the pain lance up the length of his leg. After that he could barely crawl, and he gave up on getting himself a drink of water.

Cable Springs would be his last robbery. A man like him never had as much money as he wanted, but this experience was surely a sign. He had enough. His slowing brain skipped right on past how he would get out of here, straight on to the part about traveling west across the open plains and towering mountains, not stopping until the waves of an endless ocean lapped at his feet.

The pain wasn't quite as bad when he sat very still with his back against the smooth stone wall. With every breath his chest felt like drying strips of leather were tightening around him, and odd sounds came out of him, like a man asleep and snoring. He understood that things were busted inside, and he could feel warm trickles of blood flowing down his back and into his pants. The back of his head was sticky with blood, and when he probed with his fingers across a small protruding bone, everything inside of his skull caught fire.

Women, and good food, and good wine. He'd heard it never got cold out there in California.

No man, not even a carnival show giant, ever grew that tall, nor had the strength to pick a man up with one arm and throw him against a rock wall ten feet away. But that huge, brutish thing did. It had all happened quicker than a man could blink, just as he passed around a little turn in the cave entrance. He remembered the stink and the yellow-gray hair and the petrifying growls and snarls in the shadowy chamber. He remembered tumbling through the air like a leaf in the wind and slamming into pain worse than anything he could have ever imagined. And he remembered the mindless terror.

It all got fuzzy and confusing after that, staggering into the dark away from the grunts and growls behind him, tripping and falling and stumbling blindly into unseen rocky hazards. And finally, when he fell one last time and was too spent and damaged to get up again, all he heard were his own moans and gasps.

Buy a little saloon. Maybe get married again, or else just keep a clean, decent whore handy. Make a baby, a son to replace the one they took away up in Liberty . . .

At first, resting there on the stone floor, full of relief in knowing that no one, or nothing, was still after him, it took him a moment to understand the full meaning of it all. Those sounds behind him had been his last connection to any notion of direction. There was no forward or back, no understanding of which way would lead him out of the cave, and which would take him deeper into the belly of the mountain.

The howling was the worst. The loud, shrill shrieks didn't come close to anything he had ever heard before. There was no relation to the varied cries of the big cats he was familiar with, nor did it sound anything like the grunts and growls of bears or hogs. There was something hauntingly human about it, although he could not imagine any human throat ever issuing those soul-racking sounds. All he was sure of was that when those noises echoed back from time to time through the coal-dark recesses of the cave, it was like hearing Satan bawl out his name.

The money he had hidden away was right there waiting, buried behind the foundation rocks at his uncle's abandoned cabin near Fayetteville. All gold, because paper rotted. Just waiting. The kind of woman that smiled when she looked at you. Maybe a back room for gambling. A train huffing and smoking beside a station ramp, ready to carry a man away out west. He'd remember his name again by the time he got out there.

A bloody yellow dog lying in a mud puddle. Dead just for doing what dogs do.

There was no real thing called time anymore.

**Greg Hunt** has published over twenty Western, frontier, and historical novels. A lifelong writer, he has also worked as a newspaper reporter and editor, a technical and freelance writer, and a marketing analyst. He also served in Vietnam as an intelligence agent and Vietnamese linguist. Greg now lives in the Memphis area with his wife, Vernice.

★ ★ ★ ★ ★

# HOBNAIL
## BY LOREN D. ESTLEMAN

★ ★ ★ ★ ★

The town of Hobnail boomed.

Not, like so many cities of frontier legend, because of precious metals or cattle or, later, oil, but on the basis of something far more precious in that burned-out country. Despite the wisdom of the ancient philosophers, it was not lead that could be transmuted into gold. An entire population could survive without ever laying eyes on a double eagle or a pocket watch ringed in the yellow stuff of legend, but it could not last ten days without that thing that covers nine-tenths of our spinning planet.

Josephus Gannon was a swamper. He scoured wagon trails for bottles, sticks of furniture, and other nonessential items shed by pioneers when the going got rugged, trading them for victuals or drink or a night's lodging in town. One day in this pursuit, he got a skullful of sun and wandered off the rutted road into uncharted desert. Groping around for his bearings, he stepped into a soft plot of ground and turned his ankle.

Had the reason been what he suspected, a prairie dog town undermined by verminous rodents, he'd have perished there for lack of transport and thirst, and gone unrecorded by history. But when he sat down to assess the damage and saw that his boot was plastered with mud, he knew his future was assured, and with it, his fortune.

The boot's sole was studded with hobnails. Gannon was a simple man and staked his claim to that previously worthless plot of earth under that name.

It got better: The water was warm, almost piping hot.

It was potable, of course, once it was allowed to cool. But the heat and effervescence of its geologic origins promised at least a century of tourists desperate to partake of the healing waters.

In those days when "The Great American Desert" was accepted as gospel, whole civilizations sprang up wherever a man spat, like cottonwoods. What began as a rude dugout, suitably provisioned with water from the underground spring and prairie hens ripe for the taking, grew swiftly into a metropolis: Investors poured in, hired horse-drawn dredges, and transformed Gannon's Sink into Olympia Hot Springs almost overnight.

But the real secret of Hobnail's first flush of glory had only partly to do with slaking one's thirst or soaking away one's inflictions. We can grant that particular burst of genius to Henry Ward Beecher Pruitt, its first chief constable.

The date is disputed, even the year; but most accounts favor 1881, when the name of Jorge Castillo rivaled General Lew Wallace's epic novel *Ben-Hur*, if not in bookstalls and general mercantiles throughout the U.S., then certainly by way of wanted readers posted on telegraph poles and the walls of barns from San Antonio to Sacramento. A reward of $10,000—back then a life's lease on the pleasures of the flesh—was offered for the Mexican Devil's capture, dead or alive. The enterprises of the Wells and Fargo and Butterfield stagecoach lines and the Union Pacific Railroad had pooled their interests to make good on the pledge, as Castillo and his gang had been looting their treasuries for the better part of a decade.

For years, the gang had prospered by raiding targets in Texas and New Mexico Territory, then fleeing back to old Mexico. There they dispersed among scattered villages whose residents favored well-behaved visitors over sworn authority. Questions from strangers met only with blank stares and the local incomprehensible dialect; machetes, if the interrogation grew irksome. But the Castillistas became victims of their own success. The Texas Rangers, dormant since the conquest of the Comanche Nation in 1875, reconvened with the specific purpose of apprehending the road agent and his cohorts, and a treaty was struck between Washington, D.C., and Mexico City calling for the federales to root out the brigands "by means best left to these authorities." In time, real and suspected accomplices decorated so many cottonwoods on both sides of the border that the waggish press dubbed the gang "the Christmas ball bandits."

The survivors cast themselves in all directions; some east to the Atlantic seaboard, some north to Canada, others sailing as far away as Europe and (it was rumored) Japan. There an Occidental referred to as "the Yankee Samurai" badgered the ancient trade roads for silks and spices for months until he was overtaken by mounted forces commanded by a former shogun and hacked to pieces.

Much of this is unsubstantiated, but it's a matter of record that a gaunt and exhausted Jorge Castillo straggled into Hobnail astride a broken-winded mule not long after H. W. B. Pruitt was sworn in as peace officer, and laid down a handful of pennies—likely all that remained of his swag—to share a flea-infested attic with a half-dozen other vagabonds already in residence.

He was recognized from his well-advertised likeness by one of his fellow wayfarers, who promptly put in to Pruitt's office with the intention of collecting the reward. Instead, the man was charged with vagrancy and handed over to a prison road gang.

Pruitt was a visionary. Rather than settle for ten thousand in one lump sum, he saw the opportunity to rake in many times that by offering the hospitality and shelter of Hobnail to fleeing felons in return for a cut of their take and the pledge that they would commit no crimes within a hundred miles of the town. He dispatched two deputies to conduct the half-starving bandido from his filthy bunk to his office and put the matter to him.

Castillo shrugged. "But, *el jefe, es imposible*! I was forced to trade my guns in El Paso for that miserable beast I rode to this place; and I doubt very much it will carry me another mile, much less one hundred!"

"Ask for Campbell, the manager of the Olympia Hotel, on Gannon Street; he's my brother-in-law." Pruitt scribbled on a writing-block, tore off the sheet, and handed it to him. "This instructs him to advance you two hundred dollars. Buy a good rifle and pistol, a sound horse, and a decent set of clothes; no one would take you seriously in those rags. This is a loan, which I'll add to what I expect you to share with me from your first— let's call it a transaction."

He waggled a finger. "Mind you, if you are not back here with the proceeds in ten days, you will be tracked down and dealt with on the spot. Dick Running Horse, who runs the livery, scouted for General Crook. He can read sign across a field of polished granite and will be only too happy to split the ten thousand with me in return for delivering your head in a jar to Austin."

The thief pulled his forelock. "You have my word, señor."

"I'll accept that when I have eighty percent of your take."

"*Ochenta!* But that is highway robbery!"

The constable grinned behind his moustaches. "Right you are, partner."

Castillo came through, of course; with fifteen hundred dollars in gold seized from an Overland strongbox in Palo Pinto. If he retained reservations about the inequity of the cut, he was reassured by his stay in the Olympia Hotel, Hobnail's first and most luxurious place of lodging, with room service and the most skilled sporting women the thriving resort town had to offer. It all came at the price of his twenty percent, but he was undisturbed by lawmen who came from outside to inquire after the marauder's whereabouts. It was the first time in many months he felt at ease remaining in one spot for more than a few days.

Unfortunately for him, his pioneering status came to an abrupt end when the money ran out and he exited a bank in Sweetwater square into a field of fire belonging to the local committee of public vigilance. His bullet-torn corpse was packed in ice and shipped to the capital. Back in Sweetwater, men came to blows over how the reward should be split among thirteen armed citizens.

By this time, events in Hobnail were going swimmingly under what became known (to those who were aware of it) as "the Pruitt System." Communications along the Outlaw Trail traveled swifter than Western Union. Others came in to take advantage of the opportunity. Floyd Donegan, a former Confederate guerrilla who'd extended his war on the Union long past Appomattox, carried the fifteen thousand dollars' bounty on his hide into a standing reservation on the second floor of the Olympia. In between visits he would launch a personal crime wave in such far-flung places as Brownwood, Lampasas, and Comanche Creek. Soon after, he vanished into history—slain, most likely, in some undiscovered stretch of desert for what was in his possession by commonplace cutthroats, ignorant of their victim's identity and the value of his lifeless shell.

Parades of lesser fugitives came to "take the cure"; these enjoyed their freedom in the more modest surroundings of the Railroad Arms and various boardinghouses until they, too, passed into obscurity, the state prison at Huntsville, or the noose.

As might have been expected from men of low character, there were some who took unfair advantage. Cherokee Jack Swanson shook Pruitt's hand and at the first opportunity stuck up the local train station for several hundred dollars' worth of federal securities, and returned downtown, under the impression that his flour-sack hood would shield him from discovery. Within hours, Pruitt's deputies entered the Celestial Gardens spa and shot him in the head as he was soaking up the waters in a complete state of nature. The constable, always magnanimous with his men, shared equally with them the five thousand dollars paid for Jack's capture dead or alive. Other cheats, upon whom the reward wasn't worth the expense of ammunition and the effort of disposing the bodies, were apprehended, bound, and dumped in the desert, either to succumb to heat and thirst or to wander into the hands of their pursuers. The combination of theirs and Cherokee Jack's fates was sufficient to keep others in line.

But career criminals weren't the only ones to stray from the program. In the fall of 1884, a rookie deputy named Logan was overheard, over his fifth whiskey in the Lucky Boot Saloon, boasting of his plan to kick open Bass Ballenger's door in the Olympia, shoot him in the foot, and haul him in his buckboard to San Angelo, where he was wanted for robbery-murder, then decamp to New Orleans with five thousand dollars in cash. He passed out soon after divulging his intentions, to awake with a gunnysack over his head and his wrists bound behind him. In that condition he was transported in his own buckboard across the county line and off-loaded into a patch of mescal. How he fared after that—survived, dead of thirst, or slaughtered by Comancheros for his goods—brightened many a conversation among his former fellow deputies for months. Any other inside outrages against the System guttered out at the start whenever Logan's name came up.

Needless to detail, Henry Ward Beecher Pruitt grew fat in his job; and his job was secure. Those citizens who suspected, or were even fully aware of, Pruitt's methods, gloried in Hobnail's reputation as the city with the lowest crime rate west of the Mississippi; or so it was reported in *Harper's Weekly* and *The New York Herald*. Tourists, and especially settlers hoping for a safe place to raise their families, arrived by the trainload, contributing to the wealth of merchants and the treasury. The constable was re-elected automatically, with none foolhardy enough to waste money and time bothering to oppose him.

All things, however, are finite, and good ones the most perishable. In 1890, with the West settled, the forces of law and order trading the hit-and-miss methods of hot lead and breakneck horsemanship for solid detective work, and the seats of justice established within mere miles of one another, the days of wild outlawry neared an end. The gangs had failed to move with the times and had paid dearly for their lack of vision. Some hung from proper scaffolds, others broke rocks in Huntsville. The flood of fugitives seeking asylum slowed to a trickle.

One day in this season of change, a canvas-clad, cheroot-smoking hoyden going by the name Bess Browder galloped into town. She was preceded by a flurry of gaudy popular novels celebrating her daylight assaults on banks, trains, and freight offices across the Southwest. Circulars came by the bale, pledging a whopping $25,000 for her delivery to justice.

True to her reputation, she marched boldly into Pruitt's office, deposited a jingling sack stenciled BANK OF ALBU-QUERQUE on his desk, and demanded sanctuary until the trail cooled sufficiently to allow her to decamp to old Mexico. The constable was as impressed with her appearance as he was with the cascade of double eagles that spilled onto his blotter when he upended the sack. She was even prettier than the illustrations in her fanciful biographies, with chestnut locks spilling to her shoulders from under her sweat-stained slouch hat, an oval face, robin's-egg-blue eyes, skin burnt but clear, and a trim athletic figure that even the sack coat and leathern breeches could not dissemble.

He stood to proffer his hand—a courtesy he'd never extended his male guests—and said he'd make arrangements for the bridal suite at the Olympia.

"I'm no man's bride," she said. "A hot bath, a warm meal, and a proper bed will suit me down to the ground. I've had my life's portion of rat-filled barns and cold sowbelly."

Still, he installed her in the hotel's finest accommodations, with an adjoining bath and limitless privileges in the dining room, where ham was served in champagne sauce with ice cream for dessert and a different French wine with every course. Both Pruitt and the manager were relieved when each time she appeared in public she was outfitted in the latest eastern fashions, unpacked from her worn valise and set right by the laundry and valet. In feathered hats, silk skirts, patent-leather shoes, and corsets, she could keep company with the finest ladies in New York, Chicago, and San Francisco.

At the end of six weeks—considering the number of people sharing in the largesse and the constable's own elevated tastes—the contribution she'd made to the Pruitt System began to run low. It was time for a fresh infusion.

To broach this delicate matter, he brushed and put on his dress uniform—dove gray, with bright silver buttons and Napoleonic epaulets, topped by a fore-and-aft admiral's cap crested with an ostrich plume—and presented himself at her door. She admitted him, attired in a comely dressing gown that matched her eyes and paper slippers. Over piping-hot tea and fresh warm scones, they discussed the proposition.

"Naturally," she said, "I won't burden you with my plans. I will require a good mount, as the one I came in on has seen his best days, a box of .44 cartridges, and an advance of five hundred dollars to cover incidentals and the unexpected. I assure you the good citizens of Hobnail will be more than satisfied with the return on this investment."

"Of that I have no doubt. Er, would you do me the honor—?" He presented her with the latest panegyric to appear in print, a red-and-yellow-bound copy of *Bold Bess, the Pirate Princess,* attributed to one J. Shoemaker and published by the Parker Press of St. Louis, Missouri. Laughing throatily, she rose from the settee they shared, sat down at an elegant writing desk, dipped a pen, and on the title page wrote, in an elegant hand: "To Henry Ward Beecher Pruitt, with pleasurable anticipation of things to come. Bess Browder."

The details were worked out. Expressing reservations about the possibility of another duplicitous Deputy Logan rearing his head (How, he wondered, had *that* bit of information found its way out of town?), Bess insisted that Pruitt share their agreement with no one. They would meet, alone, behind Dick Running Horse's livery just before sunup, when all the businesses were closed. The constable would be leading the promised horse, saddled and provisioned, and deliver the five hundred in cartwheel dollars, whereupon she would ride out, to return in not more than two weeks with the proceeds.

To all this he had no objections. For some time, he'd bridled against the increasing demands from his deputies, Campbell the Olympia manager, Running Horse, and others who had to be let in on what was surely no longer a secret. The spread of civilization would continue to dwindle the System's profits, and the notion of retiring East with what he'd socked away had been with him since the official closing of the frontier. A fresh injection, courtesy of the Pirate Princess, was just what was needed to turn the thought into reality. Once again, the pair shook hands; once again, he was surprised by the tensile strength of his lovely partner's grip. He bowed. She curtsied. What strange twist of frontier fate, he mused on his way back to his office, had turned so refined a young lady into bandit royalty? A drunken brute of a father, a wastrel of a husband, forcing her into the twilight life to make ends meet? He shook his head. "Ah, 'tis an imperfect world, populated with such shiftless men."

Shortly before dark, he collected his own mount, a sleek blue roan, from the livery, and placed upon it his own blanket and fine saddle. Dick Running Horse's seamed face showed nothing of what was behind it. "I'll be closing up in an hour. Won't hang round waiting on you to return it."

"It won't be tonight." Pruitt slapped his great round belly. "I'm getting fat as a hog; so's Old Mike here. Camp in the desert overnight, shoot a jackrabbit for my supper, race some coyotes for an hour or so come morning, and burn some of the suet off us both."

"Mike's fit already. Take more than a scrawny meal and a gallop to turn you into a greyhound."

Disgruntled, he led the roan away. The liveryman's insult made him feel better about deceiving him. To have asked for a strange horse would have invited more questions and suspicion. Better Dick think him an old fool than a cheat. You never knew what unscrupulous behavior a half-breed was capable of.

Darkness crept toward dawn. It was November. The desert heat had long since drained away into the sand, making him grateful for the fleece that lined his old leather coat and the woolen lumberjack's cap with the flaps down over his ears and tied under his chin. His breath crawled in the chill air. He was early:

The back wall of the livery, untouched by the sun's first glow, cut a blank square out of the spray of stars. He tethered the roan and inspected the saddlebags containing canned goods and salt pork, the five hundred in their plain sacks, and the water bags slung from the horn. Satisfied, he dug his fists deep in his pockets and stamped his feet to keep them from turning into inert sledges. The soft life had made him impatient with discomfort. Before sunup! What did so unspecific a time mean to a woman, a breed well known for its disregard of the clock?

Just then a light step displaced gravel. Turning toward the sound, he saw a figure approaching from the corner. Immediately his humor lifted. The newcomer's dark attire contrasted against the spreading tails of a white linen duster that reflected starlight. The silhouette was indisputably feminine. As she drew near enough for him to make out details, he was struck once again by her beauty. In a man's worn slouch hat and the shapeless garments of trail riding, she was quite as comely as when decked out in feathers and silk. Could it be he was falling in love? After twelve years a widower, he'd thought he was past all that.

He was moved to impress her. Slapping the roan's strong neck, he said, "Best in the stable; in Texas, if you'll forgive the boast. It's my own, along with provisions sufficient and *three* boxes of .44s in the boot. Nothing too good for our association."

"I'll be the judge; if you'll forgive the impertinence. Strike a match so I can inspect its teeth."

He reached inside his coat, taking his eyes off her as he did so. Something swished. Before he could react, a bright blue light burst in his skull. His knees gave way. He was out before he hit the ground.

When he awoke, his brain athrob, he was lying on his stomach. He tried to push himself up. He lacked the use of his hands, bound as they were behind his back. Blinking away tears, he saw Bess Browder standing over him, holstering a long-barreled Colt, the polished wooden butt of which he was painfully familiar.

"Wha-what's this then?" His voice was hoarse, as if it hadn't had use in days. He was sure he hadn't been senseless more than a few minutes. "The money's here, just as arranged."

"The Agency will see what it can do about returning it to its lawful owners." Even in the present circumstances, one could not fail to notice the refined quality of her voice.

Bewilderment turned to indignation. He struggled against his fetters, cold steel against his wrists. Then what she'd said registered. He lay still. "Agency?"

She produced something shiny from inside her rough coat. His vision had cleared enough to make out the wide-open eye embossed upon the shield and the word PINKERTON NATIONAL DETECTIVE AGENCY.

"I'm a beginner," she said. "The office in San Francisco put me into the field after a crash training course, in light of my special circumstances." Her voice deepened. "Henry Ward Beecher Pruitt, I'm placing you under arrest for malfeasance in office and as an accomplice after the fact to forty-six counts of armed robbery and murder, and one count of murder in the first degree."

"I never did murder!" In his confusion, he failed to take note of the fact that he had implicitly confessed to the other crimes.

"You directed your deputies to do it for you, but Cherokee Jack Swanson's dead just the same. I imagine at least one of them will be only too eager to testify against you in return for a life's sentence in Huntsville instead of a short rope and a long drop."

"Who in thunder is Cherokee Jack Swanson?"

"No one. He took the name to protect his family, or what's

left of it. He was born Jacob Shoemaker. I felt it fitting to use it for a *nom de plume* when I wrote all those dime dreadfuls about Bess Browder. My publishers were so caught with the sales potential they agreed to print up a few dozen wanted readers bearing my likeness. I have the Messrs. Pinkerton to thank for the money I brought as bait."

While he was laboring his hellish head to sort this out, she placed two fingers in her mouth and blew a shrill whistle. A brace of broad-shouldered men materialized at her side from the darkness. He recognized them as local teamsters.

"Volunteers," she said. "Not everyone in town approves of the Pruitt System." To them: "I'll hold the horse. Throw this sack of offal aboard his fine mount and we'll start for the U.S. marshal's office in Dallas." She favored the prisoner with a saintly smile. "It's a hard ride, I admit, facedown across the saddle; but no less arduous than the poor souls you pitched into the desert, on foot and without supplies or provisions."

"What are they to you?"

"Them? Not much, apart from Christian sympathy. You can mark time in your death cell considering the folly of killing the brother of a woman who matched him in ruthless intelligence. Elizabeth Shoemaker, your escort." She touched the brim of her greasy slouch. "This is all I have to remind me of Jacob. It found its way to me through one of your disgraced deputies— you remember Logan?—along with all the information I needed to apply for a position with the Agency."

**Loren D. Estleman** has published more than eighty novels and two hundred short stories in the areas of mystery, western, and mainstream. He has received more than twenty national honors, including four lifetime achievement awards.

★ ★ ★ ★ ★

# THE ASSASSIN
## BY PATRICK DEAREN

★ ★ ★ ★ ★

The assassin crouched in the shadows of brushy mesquites and surveyed the sagging house ahead. Through a mist falling from a black sky, he noted the large covered porch with skirting, as well as the screened windows that cast muted light across a series of flat rocks leading from the weathered steps.

Thunder roared and shook the tinseled leaves above him, causing a beaded spray to sprinkle his coat. A sudden gust tossed the pliant limbs, but he held his position on the soggy ground even as thorns raked his face.

He was very cold and tired, but it didn't matter. His eyes narrowed as he measured the width of the little clearing. From the brush line to the drip of the porch eaves, it was about twenty paces, maybe twenty-five.

He couldn't see anyone through the twin windows, but he knew they were there. He didn't know their names nor did he care.

Lightning flashed, illuminating the scene for an instant. It was a white, box-and-strip house with cracked paint and warped cedar shingles, an isolated home nestled in the mesquite-covered hills of rugged West Texas rangeland.

His blood ran hot in his forehead. He hated them—them and their home and the horses in the adjacent pen and everything they touched. The smell of them seemed to choke the night, just like the ozone stirred by the storm.

He watched the rain fall through the lamplight and ripple the puddles of water outside the pen where the small bay and big Appaloosa stirred. He had first seen the two horses many miles away, right after it had happened. He had chased after the animals as long as the dust plume had been in sight. Even afterward, when there had been nothing but craggy rangeland ahead, he had followed the tracks down the pitted wagon road.

And now he crouched there quietly, watching . . . waiting. The riders would come out sometime. Sooner or later they would push open that door and step out on the porch.

And he would be ready.

His eyes wandered past the muddy yard and small house, even beyond the dark hills in the distance. He would give them no more chance than they had given her. The mist blurred his vision as he remembered how they had ruthlessly attacked her and left her to die in a pool of blood beneath the swollen sun.

Hate and vengeance clouded his eyes. They would pay.

He padded stealthily out of the shadows and approached the house. A bolt of sky fire lighted the yard for an instant, and he grew still on the ground, almost as if he were a part of it.

The roar of thunder passed, and he continued on, a low shadow slinking through the night. The assassin had never killed a man before, but he knew he would this time. He was sure he would, because of the terrible, terrible thing they had done to her.

As his angle to a window changed, he caught sight of a young woman inside the house. She sat slowly rocking as she clutched something small and white to her breast.

Theirs, he thought. The child of the man who had taken so much from him.

His gaze shifted to the elevated porch only yards ahead. He stopped for a moment, studying the black shadows at one end—

shadows that lurked within reach of the rotting plank floor. He crept on across the puddles until the dark veil crawled over him. He huddled there, intuitively assessing the porch and measuring distance. It wasn't far to the screen door that banged in the wind—he could be at it in moments when the time came.

He licked his lips in anticipation, the quiet fury in his eyes burning deeper.

The tin skirting of the porch crowded him, and as he shifted position, he bumped it hard, the clatter like counterpoint to the crack of thunder and whistle of wind. He checked the door, piercing it with a stare as he waited and wondered. Suddenly it screeched open, and he crouched lower in the shadows, but not so low that he couldn't see the screen as it framed a silhouette that included a long object that must have been a lever-action carbine.

The man stood alone in the threshold for long seconds, facing night and storm. All the while, the assassin stayed frozen with the patience he had long nurtured. Then another form appeared in the doorway, a slender one that exuded strong perfume that wafted into his nostrils. He hated it, for he had caught that same fragrance over the bloody pool. In the young woman's arms was a small, blanketed form that must have smelled like its mother, and he hated the tiny figure also.

A tentative, girlish voice broke the whisper of wind and patter of rain. "What's wrong, Johnny? How come you got the gun?"

The man in the screen turned. The lamplight fell on his face, and the assassin noted the browned skin and dark hair and jutting chin he had seen once before on that day. It was a cruel face, indeed—fiendish and yet so very human.

The man nodded to the darkness. "Somethin's out there."

The girl shrank a step and hugged the baby to her breast.

"Don't scare me that way! Not after what you—not after today, the—"

"I heard somebody. I know I did." He looked back into the storm and gripped the carbine tighter.

The girl shuddered and moved closer, begging for the arm that he slipped about her. "Come on in. May-maybe it was just the wind, darlin'. Shut the door and come on in!"

Still, he surveyed the blackness, but now with his forearm against the screen door. "Who in the . . . ? I'm gonna have a look-see."

"No, Johnny! Stay inside!" she implored. "Don't be lookin' for trouble!"

"Be back in a minute. Stay put."

The woman continued to plead, but the man pushed open the screen and stepped out, the Winchester carbine ready at his hip. Now the assassin hugged the shadows at the porch base even closer, especially as the planks creaked with footsteps that ended almost above his head.

He knew the man scanned the stormy night, ready to wield that potent weapon at any quick movement, any sudden noise. But the assassin made no such mistake; he stayed motionless, allowing no greater sound than the pounding of his blood.

Finally, he heard the footsteps resume, the creaks growing fainter, but only after they ceased entirely did he risk a look. The man now stood at the porch's far end, the light from the window bathing his back.

With anxious eyes, the assassin saw the young woman push open the screen and step indecisively onto the porch, the baby still sleeping in her arms. On spring-loaded legs, the assassin tensed.

"Come on in, Johnny!" she begged. "Please! I'm scared!"

The man looked over his shoulder at her, and then turned again to the darkness. He took a deep breath. "I'd've sworn I heard somebody. I'd've sworn somethin' was out h—"

The assassin sprang for the porch. The woman started at the sound and whirled. In a split second her eyes widened as if witnessing hell, but the scream on her lips died in a muffled cry as he fell upon her.

Yes, they would pay.

The woman went down. The one she called Johnny spun and cried the terrified cry that she had been unable to voice. Brandishing the Winchester, the man lunged across the porch as the assassin tore the infant from the woman's grasp. The carbine boomed, a wild shot that creased the assassin's shoulder and ricocheted into the night.

The searing bullet was unlike any pain the assassin had ever felt, but he didn't care. For with a great bound, the puma was off the porch and dashing through the shadows, in his mouth the grisly mass of flesh that had been the child of the man who had killed his mate.

Winner of the Spur Award for his novel *The Big Drift*, **Patrick Dearen** is the author of fourteen novels and ten nonfiction books. His new novel, *Apache Lament*, is based on the events surrounding the last free-ranging Mescalero Apaches in Texas, an era that ended with an 1881 fight with Texas Rangers. See patrickdearen.com for more information.

# A CENTURY OF THE AMERICAN FRONTIER 1885–1900

★ ★ ★ ★ ★

# Apaches Survive
# BY HARPER COURTLAND

★ ★ ★ ★ ★

Rose awakened at noon to pounding on the door to her crib—just a tiny room with a bed, the sort where the cheapest whores stayed, those who were older or broken down to the point where they couldn't command higher fees. Hoping to find a daytime customer, she dragged a comb through her hair and pinched her cheeks before opening the door to find the potbellied crib owner scowling at her. "It's time to move on, Rose," he said. "You aren't making enough money to stay here." Behind him, a stringy-haired brunette in a soiled red dress stood smirking at her.

"But you said I could stay through the winter," Rose said, taken aback. "What am I supposed to do when the cold sets in?"

"Not my problem," he said, hooking a thumb under his suspenders. "I meant you could stay if you brought in enough money. Now, hurry up and get out because this young lady's ready to move in." Having no choice, Rose gathered her few belongings and vacated the space.

Not knowing what else to do, she set up a makeshift camp in a piñon thicket outside of town.

Near midnight, Rose hadn't eaten all day. She pulled her shawl tighter around her shoulders. It had been a hot late September day in Kingston, New Mexico, but the desert night air was chilly. Standing in the alley between the Three-Legged Dog

Saloon and a hardware store, she heard a man's boots approaching on the wooden sidewalk. When he reached the place where the sidewalk ended, she called out, "Hello, dearie. Could I offer you some entertainment this evening?" She stepped out of the alley, keeping to the shadows to make it harder for him to see her face. The man, tall and stout, maybe fifty years old, kept moving toward her without saying anything. When he reached her, thinking she had a customer, she touched his arm, but he shoved her and said, "Get away from me, you hag."

She would have fallen but her shoulder slammed into the rough corner of the hardware store. "You could have just said no," she hissed. She wished she could cut him with the knife strapped to her leg. When he was gone, she rubbed her shoulder, which would surely bruise, and sat down on an old crate in the moonlight.

*Maybe that was just what I needed, a bit of pain to take my mind off my hunger.* A fresh round of laughter rose inside the Three-Legged Dog and spilled into the street. Rose stood when a lanky man left the saloon, but she sat back down when she saw the chubby whore in a blue dress at his side. Her motion drew his attention, though. "Well, hello, darling—have a round on me," he called, tossing a coin over near her feet.

"Why'd you do that, Walter?" the whore asked. "Do you think she has nothing to steal?"

The man stopped for a moment and rubbed his chin. "It's good practice," he said. "Haven't you heard the saying, 'Do unto others as—' "

"But it isn't fair," she whined. "You make *me* work for my money."

"Ah, yes," he said. "That's tragic." He reached into his pocket and handed the greasy-faced woman some cash.

Rose waited until they moved on to pick up the half-dollar the man had thrown to her. She wanted a whiskey, as the man had suggested, but she took it into the saloon and ordered a beer, a bowl of hot chili, and two biscuits to tuck into her pockets for later. Upon leaving the saloon, she slipped back into the alley, passed through it, and headed out of town, moving like the mist after a rain.

Upon arriving at the piñon thicket, she checked to see that everything was still there—her blanket, a comb, a small mirror, a tin cup, a gunny sack, a whetstone, a box of matches, a cooking pot, a bowl, and a spoon. She wrapped herself in the thin blanket, got settled, and ran her hands along her threadbare dress. It frightened her to think of the oncoming winter.

Rose didn't know why she'd kept the mirror. She didn't want to follow the progression of lines in her face or see the gaps where two teeth were missing. She wanted to forget that her honey-colored hair was almost half-gray. The only thing on her face that reminded her of her childhood was the red, berry-shaped birthmark on her left cheek. She was thirty-four years old, but her youth and good looks were spent.

But she could take pride in simply being alive. She knew many whores never survived into their thirties. Whores died of diseases, at the hands of violent men, from drinking too much, from drug use, and, often, by their own hands. She knew exposure could also kill working girls when they were thrown outdoors, but she thought, *I'm an Apache. Apaches survive.*

She wasn't an Apache, of course. In truth, her life had been stolen from her twice: first, when a band of Apaches had taken her during a raid on a wagon train when she was four years old and, second, when she was fourteen and the U.S. Army had taken her from that Apache band's encampment. The Apache woman she'd been given to as a slave had named her *Alch-isé,* which means "the little one." She had beaten her until she learned to do her chores properly, but eventually she softened to her and treated her more like a daughter than a slave. So

Rose had learned how to be silent, how to gather nuts, roots, and berries, how to trap and skin a rabbit, how to make stew with deer meat, and how to make fry bread. And she had grown content with her life among the Apaches.

One morning, she'd awakened to gunfire, horses' hooves pounding the earth, and the smells of blood and death. She had run from a wickiup into the confusion outside, and a soldier had snatched her up onto his saddle and taken her out of the carnage.

Later, she'd been placed in an orphanage where the keepers forced her to relearn English and beat her for crying and begging to return to the Apaches. But why shouldn't she cry? The Apaches considered her a woman after she had started her menstrual cycles, and she had been promised to Dark Wolf, a young warrior. A few more weeks in their camp, and she would have been an Apache wife with all the honor and respect of her position as such. Her white rescuers only saw her as a foolish and ungrateful child.

Looking back, she couldn't understand why it had taken her more than a year to find the courage to steal a butcher's knife and slip away from that orphanage to search for her Apache family. A couple of miners found her, and she soon learned that white people expected the worst of her since she'd lived among Indians, but it hadn't been Apaches that took her virginity forcibly. Upon losing it, she knew she would be considered "soiled goods" in either culture and took up the one profession she saw fit for herself.

Rose sighed and tried to shake off the memories. Her life had become a mess she couldn't fix. Even so, she had once known how to live off the land. She could do it again.

The next morning, Rose found a stream, bathed, and ate one of her biscuits before heading for the Black Range Mountains.

Reaching the base of the mountains, she wound her way up a narrow pass, enjoying the songs of little canyon wrens until she was startled by a light brown, mongrel dog, which stepped out from behind a rock and growled at her. She stopped and retrieved the knife she kept strapped to her leg because, even though the dog was very thin, it was large and probably weighed almost as much as she did. She and the dog sized each other up for a moment before the dog came nearer to her and sniffed the air.

Rose sighed, took the remaining biscuit from her pocket, and said, "Come here, girl." She broke the biscuit in pieces and fed it to the dog until it was gone. It seemed crazy to feed a dog when she had so little, but as the man who'd tossed her a half-dollar the night before had said, giving was good practice. Addressing the dog, she said, "I'm going to name you Misty because your hair is colored just like that of a girl I knew in my younger days." Misty nudged her hand, apparently wanting to be petted, and gave her a doggy smile.

As they walked along, Rose gathered whatever she found along the wayside, including a few wild onions and some wild carrots. It was well past noon when Rose left the canyon trail and followed deer paths under the cover of trees. She was glad she had fed the dog because Misty moved with her more silently than she would have expected, and she felt safer with the dog at her side. They came to a place where the ground was covered with acorns, so Rose decided to rest there for a while, thinking she'd gather some later. As Rose drowsed, she felt Misty lunge forward without barking first or making any sound. When the dog returned, she laid a gray squirrel at Rose's feet.

"Good girl," Rose whispered. "Let's be quiet and see if you can do that again." In less than an hour, they had two squirrels, and Rose gathered some acorns and decided they must move on. Soon, she found a good place to camp by a natural spring and set about dressing the squirrels and stewing them in her pot with the acorns, wild carrots, and wild onions. The site was excellent for camping, especially for travelers with horses because there was a huge clearing on one side covered with grama grass. She sat about gathering grass to sleep on, but then she heard Misty growling at the other side of the clearing and went to see why.

An Apache warrior sat up in the grass, knife in hand. "Stop!" she yelled in Apache. "I'll kill you if you kill my dog!"

Drawing closer, she realized she had threatened her old Apache band's great leader, Goyahkla, "the one who yawns," better known among whites as Geronimo. She could tell he was very weak and sick because he was sweating and the hand holding his knife trembled slightly. Though she expected a sharp rebuke, Goyahkla wheezed a laugh and fell back into a horizontal position. She ran to get her cup and filled it with cold water for him.

He tried to pull himself up again when she came with the water, but she shook her head and lifted him, wedging her knee behind his back. He was burning with fever, so she laid him back after he drank, cut some cloth from her skirt, and wet it with spring water.

As she smoothed the cold, wet cloth over his face and neck, he touched the birthmark on her cheek and said, "I had not thought to see you again, Alch-ísé. Do things go well with you?"

Tears came to her eyes because she was overwhelmed that this heroic man remembered her name after so many years had passed. For a moment, she couldn't speak, and then she said, "The white man's world isn't kind to me."

"It isn't kind to me, either," he said. "But the spirit world is good. I performed a sing for my healing a little while ago, and soon I'll be better." He closed his eyes and drifted into sleep.

Rose hurried to cut more grass for herself and for Goyahkla.

Before the sun began to set, she filled her bowl with stew and took it to him with another cup of water. This time, he was able to sit on his own to eat and drink. A troubled look came over him, and he asked, "I left my pony hidden before approaching the water supply, thinking I might ambush anyone here, but I found no one. Being feverish, I thought to rest a few minutes and awakened in this state hours later. Will you water my pony and bring him here where he can eat grass?"

"Of course, where is he?"

"About five stone throws up that ridge," he said, pointing to an area beyond the spring. Though Rose was hungry, too, she left to find the pony before it became too dark. On the way back, she found a creosote bush and cut some of it to make a tincture for Goyahkla's fever. She let the pony drink at the spring, but she did not let it overdrink because she didn't know how long it had been without water.

Once she had the pony hobbled in the grass, she returned to her cooking pot. Of what was left of the stew, she poured a portion on a flat stone for Misty, and she ate the rest straight from the pot. After washing the pot, she began boiling the creosote. Darkness had fallen when she took a bundle of grass, rolled Goyahkla onto his side, and stuffed it under him. Then she applied some of the tincture to his chest and wrapped her blanket around him. "I'll check on you during the night. Call for me if you need anything," she said.

She settled onto a bundle of grama grass and cuddled with Misty to keep warm. Around midnight, she took another cup of water to Goyahkla, bathed him, and applied more creosote tincture to his chest. Well before dawn, she awakened and found Goyahkla moving about the camp, preparing to leave. Getting up, she said, "You should rest."

Goyahkla shook his head. "Sickness has already delayed me too long. My sing and your stew and your care have broken the fever. I have important business. I must go." He handed her the blanket and said, "I was going to put it over you before I left, but I see you are too much of an Apache for that to happen without waking you. You say the white man's world isn't kind to you. You're welcome to come back to us, though you must know the bluecoats continue to hound us. If you stay near this spring, I'll send someone for you within a matter of days. Will you do it?"

"I will. I wish to come home." She stood there a moment with a question on her lips, afraid to ask it. As a holy man in their tribe, she supposed he sensed it, for he turned and asked, "What is it?"

"The warrior Dark Wolf. Did he survive the attack on our encampment?"

"He did. He has a wife and three fine sons."

She felt tears stream down her face, but she made no sound. "I'm glad for him," she said after a moment passed.

Goyahkla replied, "Perhaps he would welcome a second wife now." Rose nodded and turned her face away from him. "Why do you turn from me?"

"Because I'm old and ugly."

Goyahkla touched her hand and said, "No need to turn from me or any man. You're a fine woman. Dark Wolf will likely see you as that beautiful girl he knew—and he has changed, too. He still speaks of you at times." Goyahkla mounted his pony and repeated their plan, "Wait here. I'll send for you and your dog."

It felt good to be living as an Apache again, but within three days, a fever came on Rose. By midafternoon, she was burning hot and weak. She knew she'd be unable to protect herself if hostile travelers came to the spring, so with the last of her strength, she dragged her gunny sack over to where Goyahkla had lain hidden in the grass and prepared for the hard time to come. She filled her cooking pot with drinking water and covered it with its lid, placing it by her bed of grass. For a while, she lay there dreaming and clinging to her dog through periods of light and dark, for how long, she did not know. She was dimly aware that Misty left her at times, but she always returned.

Once she heard wheezing and thought Misty had gotten sick, so she held her more tightly and dreamed she was a young girl again, waiting in a wickiup for Dark Wolf to come to her for the first time. Another time, she heard a gurgling sound and assumed her dog was worse. "Let me rest just a bit longer, and I'll get up and find something for you to eat," she whispered before drifting into the depths of dreams again where she was strong and healthy. It seemed she could be anything in the dream world. Soon, she found a fierce desire to become a shapeshifter, so she sat on the edge of a broad overlook and scanned the valley below as her body changed to that of an eagle.

Beside her, Misty growled and Alch-ísé thought she heard voices near her as she spread her wings. She felt her body being lifted from the ground effortlessly, and then she was flying out over the valley, thinking, *Apaches Survive.*

**Melissa Watkins Starr,** writing as **Harper Courtland**, is a native of Eden, North Carolina. She is a former news reporter and a cancer survivor. She works as a writer/editor from her home in Virginia. Her first novel, *Indiscretions Along Virtue Avenue,* was released by Five Star Publishing in December 2019.

★ ★ ★ ★ ★

SPANISH DAGGER

BY W. MICHAEL FARMER

★ ★ ★ ★ ★

The sun straight overhead, a dust devil appeared out of nowhere to rattle and twist the mesquites and creosotes. Soon disappearing, its intensity left Oats with a sense of foreboding that grew as he saw the distant dust streamer from a horseman heading for him. He pulled Old Joe to a stop. Checking his revolver's load, he threw a leg around his saddle horn, and waited. He soon recognized Tomás Bonito spurring Blackie and slapping him with the reins as lather flew from his neck and withers. Uncurling his leg, Oats sent Old Joe off at a run toward them.

Their horses hung their heads in exhaustion as they walked up the canyon toward the spring and past the neat little house by the corral. Cattle, enjoying the good grass, paid them little attention. Oats saw Jordon stretched out in the shade of an overhang at the spring. His hat was pulled down low over his forehead, a large rounded rock his pillow. His legs were crossed at the ankles; a horsehair quirt he was braiding rested on his chest; his gun was holstered; his gun hand with its fingers partly curled rested on the ground.

Oats tied Old Joe to a piñon and climbed down. Jordon's face was peaceful, close to smiling, eyes closed. He looked like he was taking a nap except for the black, half-inch diameter hole between his eyes.

Nausea burned in Oats's throat; water crept to the edge of his eyes. He dropped down by Jordon and leaned forward to stare at the ground while he swallowed down the bile. The nausea and tears gave way to howls of anger filling his soul. The chaos in his mind ended with a vow that his best friend since they were little boys was going to have justice.

Oats and Tomás circled the body, studying every square inch of ground until they found a place fifty feet away where the grass was bent and bruised. Close by was a pair of boot tracks in the crusty sand, damp from the spring's water. Ten feet from the tracks, a horse had stamped around while tied to a piñon. Another ten yards up the canyon, the tracks showed the horse already in a full run.

They followed the tracks up the canyon until they crossed the ridge into the next canyon and disappeared—a clean getaway. It was Tomás who first saw the little string of hide and blood on the Spanish dagger point fifty yards down the trail from the body. The shooter had run his horse by the sharp, pointed blade of the cactus. There was just enough hair on the hide to make Oats think the horse was white or gray. He ran his fingers over the little piece of hide and dried blood trying to remember who in the basin had a white or gray horse. There were at least twenty, maybe more. He didn't care. He'd check them all.

Tomás helped him wrap Jordon in a blanket. Oats found the slug that killed Jordon pancaked against the bloodstained rock he had used for a pillow. It was three quarters of an inch in diameter with rough splayed edges and grit from the rock smashed into the back surface. He washed it off in the spring and put it in his pocket, and wore it on his watch fob for the next fifty years.

On the way home, they stopped in Canto. Oats sent a telegram to his little sister and mother shopping for a wedding dress in El Paso. He agonized over the words, but found no easy way to tell them to come home right away and that the wedding dress wasn't needed.

The next day, he met Clemmy and Mary at the train. Clemmy's eyes were red and swollen, Mary grim and quiet. They buried Jordon the next day after sitting with his coffin all night. Clemmy wept in soft sobs until the spring in her soul ran dry. Mary stared at the coffin box in the flickering candlelight, her heart lower than a stone falling in a black well. She remembered all the men she had buried in her life. Men who were killed accidently by animals, the land, or weather, but none had been murdered.

The minister gave a fine sermon; everyone in town turned out for the burial service. Jordon had been an iron-nerved young man they all liked and respected. Even as the minister spoke, Oats was looking out the church window at the five gray and white horses ridden to the funeral. None of them were cut—he didn't really expect them to be.

Gloom settled over the Oats ranch house. They all did their work but said little, each immersed in thoughts of Jordon and what might have been. Oats struggled to keep his anger from boiling over and filling his guts with dynamite ready to explode as he tried to get his mind around how to find who had filled his life with such misery.

He expected the sheriff to come investigate. When Asante hadn't put in an appearance, Oats saddled Old Joe and rode the fifty miles into Felicidad. Asante had his boots upon his big rolltop desk ready for his afternoon siesta when Oats appeared in the doorway. Holding his palm out and flexing his fingers to motion him in, the sheriff tilted his hat back. "Howdy Oats. Just gittin' ready for my siesta. Yuh lookin' for me?"

"Afternoon, Sheriff. I came to ask what you planned to do about Jordon's murder. I expected you or a deputy to be doin' an investigation by now."

Asante folded his hands, shook his head, and put on his solemn face. "Decided against one—waste of time." He saw

Oats's scowl and held up his hands palms out. "Don't get me wrong, it ain't like Jordon don't deserve to have his murderer caught. But there weren't no witnesses, no suspects at all, nothin' to give us a clue. There just ain't anything I can do. Yuh wanta convict in court, yuh gotta have a charge clearly proved. Yuh got it—a charge clearly proved? Ain't a chance in hell we'd prove anybody done it with what we know." Asante shrugged and turned his ear toward him listening for an answer. "Is there?"

Oats's jaw muscles rippled. "No, Sheriff, I guess there ain't." He turned back to the street leaving Asante staring after him.

On the ride home, Oats recalled that a body had been found two years earlier. An owner of a trading post on the reservation had been killed—shot between the eyes while he slept. The shooter had not been caught. Word among the cowboys around their cooking fires was that José Serna had been the killer. Oats, Jordon, and Serna got along well—there was no apparent reason why Serna would murder Jordon. Besides, Serna rode a sorrel. But Serna was now very friendly with Nate Wells. Nate Wells, six-three, mean, no-good. He was the middle son of Charlie Wells, operator of the biggest ranch in the basin. Charlie had tried to run the little ranchers off their homesteads and block their access to the free range. Many of them left rather than stand up to him. Charlie and his backers took over the deserted homesteads giving them more water with which to control thousands of acres of free range.

Jordon didn't blink when the Wells clan—Charlie, his three sons, a son-in-law, and Charlie's brother, Israel, and his four sons—tried to run him off. At the fall roundup, Jordon faced down Nate over who owned what cattle and he enforced the branding rules when the mavericks were branded. Nate didn't like it a bit. He swore he'd get even. When Jordon and Charlie

Wells crossed paths in Canto, Charlie tried to bully Jordon into giving him compensation for the mavericks Nate had lost in the branding argument. Jordon wouldn't have it and backed Charlie down when their hands settled on revolvers. Nate's favorite horse was a black and white pinto. Killing someone while they slept was just Nate's style; he settled into Oats's mind as the prime suspect for Jordon's murderer.

A week passed. Oats took the wagon and drove into Canto to get supplies. Tying the team at Torrey Lofton's Mercantile, he saw Nate's pinto tied to the hitching rail stomping at flies in front of the saloon a couple of doors down. Casually walking down the street, he stopped and looked the pinto over. There was a cut in a white patch of hide. The horse snorted and its muscles quivered as Oats gently ran his hand by the cut. It was tender, just beginning to heal. The cut was about the right height for the bloody Spanish dagger at Jordon's place. Hearing Nate's loud, raucous laughter in the saloon, Oats stared toward the saloon doors before turning back to Lofton's.

The next day, Oats and Tomás rode over to the Wells ranch. They found Nate's pinto in a pasture far from the ranch house and borrowed it for the afternoon. The return to the little ranch in the canyon, filled with bittersweet memories, and the corpses of a thousand plans, was as hard as anything Oats ever did. Asking Tomás to lead the pinto by the Spanish dagger, he dismounted and stood to one side to watch how the bloody tip matched against the cut. At first, Tomás had a hard time coaxing the pinto close enough to the dagger point for Oats to tell; it kept shying away each time it was led near the cactus. Finally, they put Oats's shirt over its eyes and were able to lead it close enough to almost touch the offending spike. The match of spike height and cut on the pinto was flawless. There was little doubt the horse's rider had murdered Jordon. Still, Oats didn't have enough evidence to take to the district attorney for a charge clearly proved.


Nate Wells was a blowhard. He bragged about everything he did or owned. Oats decided that if Wells had murdered Jordon, then he probably bragged about it to the men who worked for Charlie.

Oats began stopping off at the night fires of the Wells's free-range cowboys to have a little coffee, talk water supplies and grazing, and swap stories. At first the men didn't say much when he was around, but after a visit or two, they took Oats as a friend and began loosening up.

One night while finishing a cup of Arbuckle's, he listened to an argument over how good a man needed to be with a revolver to survive on the free range. Pete Cowans maintained that a man needed to be fast, but accuracy was far more important; he was instantly rebutted by Jeb Fortis who said it didn't do you any good to carry a gun at all if you were shot in your sleep by your enemies. The silence that fell around the fire was instant. Heads turned toward Oats who sat with his coffee listening and saying nothing. In a couple of minutes, the argument had regained full steam. Fortis, saying nothing else, kept glancing at Oats who showed no emotion over what was being discussed.

The next day Oats found Fortis trying to get a calf out of a mudhole while the mother stood at the edge bawling for the life of her baby. After struggling in the wet goo that sucked strength out of hard muscles and made getting a hold on the calf like trying to catch a greased pig, Oats and Fortis managed to pull it free and return it to the side of its mother.

Sitting down in the shade of a mesquite to rest, they shared a canteen and Fortis rolled a smoke.

"I shore appreciate yuh helpin' me out with that calf, Mr. Oats. I'd been in that mudhole for near to an hour and hadn't made much progress."

Oats grinned. "Glad I came along. Sometimes the littlest ones can give you the most trouble. Besides I wanted to talk to you about what you said yesterday evenin' about being shot in your sleep. I'm sure you know about Jordon bein' shot when he was asleep. Just wonderin' if you knew any more about it."

Fortis looked at the ground and shook his head. "I don't want no trouble, Mr. Oats."

"You ain't gonna get in no trouble if I have anything to do with it. I want to know who did it. You ain't got to do anything that'll get you in trouble with anybody."

Fortis sighed and stared off down the cattle path. "You promise this ain't goin' no further than me and yuh?"

Oats held up his right hand as if to swear he was speaking the truth. "You ain't gonna git in trouble with nobody."

Fortis nodded, but wouldn't look at him. Staring at the ground between his boots, he said, "When we was playing cards in the bunkhouse, Nate bragged that he killed Jordon. He said somethin' like, 'By damn I caught that son of a bitch sleepin' and plugged his ass. He ain't gonna bother my daddy no more, that's for shore.' "

Oats clenched his teeth and looked Fortis in the eye. "Who else was at that card game?"

"Well, sir, let me think . . . Pete Cowans was there, Jack Quade, Brownie Newman, Nate Wells, and Ty Hulst. I think that was all."

Oats nodded and stared out toward the mountains in the brown haze. "Cowans seems like a pretty good man, smart in an argument. Do you like him? Has he got spine?"

Fortis took a draw and blew the smoke into the whispering breeze. "Yes, sir, I'd say he's a pretty fair hand. Ain't got a fast gun, but like he was sayin' last evenin', he's accurate and all the years I've knowed him, he ain't never backed away from a threat."

Oats lay back in the shade resting on his elbow, thinking. After a while he said, "You know, I've been trying to find me a couple of top hands for a while now. You and Cowans look like you might fill the bill. Tell you what I'll do. I'll give you five dollars a month more than what old Wells is payin' if you'll come work for me. What d' you say?"

Fortis's jaw dropped. "Five dollars a month more than Wells pays! Mr. Oats, yuh can count me in and yuh can bet I'll work my tail off for yuh too. I don't like old man Wells and those hard-assed sons of his at all, especially Nate. They treat their hands like they's dirt. I can't speak for Cowans, but I'm sure he'd be interested. When do yuh want me to start?"

Oats smiled. "Wait until next payday. Doesn't Wells pay at the end of the month? That's next Friday. You tell Cowans the deal and to think about it. I'll drop by your fire in a day or two and discuss it with him privately."

Fortis grinned and nodded as he stubbed his cigarette.

Cowans was eager to accept Oats's offer when they talked. He didn't like the Wellses and was already thinking about leaving.

A couple of weeks after Fortis and Cowans moved into his bunkhouse, Oats had a come-to-Jesus meeting with them.

"Boys, I'm worried about you stayin' alive."

They frowned, looked at each other and then him. Cowans spoke up. "Just 'xactly what do yuh mean, Mr. Oats?"

"Everybody in this basin knows that Jordon and me was best friends and that I'm lookin' for his murderer. Everybody thinks I plan to shoot it out with who done it. But, I ain't. I'm lettin' the law hang who done it. Sheriff says I got to have a 'charge clearly proved.' That means witnesses. Both you boys heard

Nate Wells say he shot Jordon when he was asleep."

Cowans, his teeth clenched in rage, turned to Fortis. "Yuh stupid idiot! Why in hell couldn't yuh keep yore damned mouth shut? Now we're in it for shore!"

Fortis was shaking his head. "But Mr. Oats said what I told him weren't goin' no further than me or him. Didn't yuh say that, Mr. Oats?"

Oats looked at them with hooded eyes. "What I said was you ain't gonna get in trouble with nobody. I want to keep you boys alive and Nate Wells hanged. It ain't me that's spreadin' stories about you boys talkin'. Nate and Charlie ain't fools. Soon as you boys came to work for me they started askin' themselves why I'd hire you two over some other good hands. Then Nate is gonna remember that poker game you was both in and him running his mouth. He's gonna add it up and figure he'll put you down the first chance he gits. Now, boys, I'm swearin' on my mama's good name that ain't gonna happen if you'll promise me you'll give evidence to the grand jury in a couple of months and in a trial if he's indicted. What do you say?"

Cowans and Fortis looked at each other and then stared at Oats in the deepening silence. Cowans slowly nodded. "Reckon we ain't got much choice if we want to go on livin' do we, Mr. Oats?"

"No, you ain't."

For the next two months, Cowans and Fortis worked around the corral and barn doing chores and keeping watch for threatening riders. None ever came. The night before the grand jury was to meet, they along with Oats saddled their horses in the gathering dusk and rode all night along desert trails, avoiding the main road, to reach Felicidad before sunrise.

Oats, Cowans, and Fortis met with the district attorney early that morning. He asked many questions, often asking them to repeat themselves to be sure he understood what they were say-ing, and he took copious notes. When time drew near for the grand jury proceedings to begin, he asked them to stay around town and be available when he needed to call them.

As the hours waiting passed into days, Oats began to wonder what was taking so long. Why hadn't they been called? The hope for justice that burned in his soul began to dim.

The grand jury adjourned about noon the last day they met. Sheriff Asante was the first man out the door. He smiled and nodded as he walked past Oats and his witnesses. The district attorney was the last one to leave. He saw Oats and shook his head. "Your case wasn't called this session. Maybe next time."

Oats knew the case was never going to be called. He didn't say a word on the ride home.

A rider from Toby Stewart's ranch found Nate Wells in the big ranch house and handed him a note. It read:

Mr. Wells,
    Four days ago, your black and white pinto showed up in our pasture. I'm tired of feeding it. Please pick him up in the next day or two.

Thanks,
Mrs. Toby Stewart

Nate thanked the rider and said, "Tell Mrs. Stewart I'll be over to pick up that damned troublesome jarhead before din-nertime tomorrow and that I apologize for not getting him sooner. I didn't even know he was gone."

The next morning, Nate saddled up after breakfast and told his wife he'd be back before dinner. When she told him she was worried that he was riding into a lion's den, after all Toby Stew-art was Oats's half-brother, Nate laughed. "Oats and Stewart? I ain't afraid of nobody, much less them little desert rats. I'll be back by dinner. Have it ready."

Nate didn't return home by dinner, as he promised. Being young and newly married, Nate's wife was pacing the floor late in the afternoon when Charlie Wells came through the front door after a business trip to El Paso. He saw her puffy, tear-streaked face. "What's the matter, daughter? You look like you lost yore washin' in a dust storm."

Snuffling, she said, "Nate went over to Toby Stewart's place to get his horse. He was supposed to have been back hours ago. It ain't like him to miss his dinner. Paw, I'm scared somethin' has happened to him."

Charlie flew into a rage. "That fool idiot! Don't he know Stewart and Oats are half-brothers! That gang of thieves and outlaws will kill him if he's alone." He stuck his head out the front door and bellowed for his foreman.


The sun had turned the sky to a brilliant orange glow that painted puffy clouds on the horizon a dark fire red. Toby Stewart was enjoying the peaceful evening sitting with his wife on the porch steps of their ranch house. They were watching Nate Wells's black and white pinto cavort in their corral where they'd put him in expectation that Nate would pick him up earlier that day. Toby was disgusted. Good neighbors kept their word.

At first, they thought the low rumble was thunder in the distance, but the falling light was bright enough to show a dust cloud rolling toward them, hard riding horsemen.

"Toby, do you want me to get your rifle?"

"Naw, it's probably Nate come to claim his horse in grand style. Stay here with me."

Charlie Wells thundered up to Toby's front steps at the head of twenty-five men, their rifles at the ready. His face twisted in rage, he roared, "Where the hell is Nate?"

Toby frowned and looked at his wife. "He ain't been here. We were expectin' him before dinner. That's his horse over there. I don't know where he is."

Charlie turned to his foreman. "Take that son of a bitch inside. He's gonna tell me where Nate is or he ain't gonna see the light of another day."

Charlie spent most of the night "interrogating" Toby. All night Toby swore he didn't have any idea where Nate was. The grandfather clock in the corner was striking four when Charlie growled, "Hang the son of a bitch."

Charlie's son-in-law stepped between Toby and the men with a noose they'd just finished. "Wait a minute, Charlie! What if he ain't lying? What if you hang an innocent man? Your friends and Asante will have to do something and at the very least that's gonna mean jail time. If this man's guilty, we'll find it out and hang him then. You can't do this now. Use your head and think about what you're doin'."

Charlie did think about it as he glared at his son-in-law and then paced the floor for a while before he spoke. "All right, Stewart, you ain't gonna get hanged this night. I can wait. But just look at this here floor. It's got my son's blood all over it. You burned your own house to get rid of the evidence. Get this murderin' bastard and his wife out in the yard and then burn it, boys."

The son-in-law started to speak, but Charlie held up his hand palm out and shook his head.

Charlie and his men spent two weeks searching the range and every ranch in the basin for some sign of Nate. On the third week, an old prospector told Charlie he thought he saw buzzards picking at something buried in the sands.

They found the bones exactly where the prospector said they might be. The skeleton was from a tall man; his boots, fancy and practically new, a gold watch chain and Navajo silver and turquoise bracelet, and a revolver and holster were all that were left. The revolver had been fired twice; the remaining chambers were still loaded. The skull had two bullet holes an inch apart in the left temple.

When Charlie saw the watch chain and bracelet, he knew he had found Nate. As his anger came to a rolling boil, he directed his men to collect his son's remains and swore he would wipe out Oats, Toby Stewart, and any man that stood with them.

Charlie Wells spent the next two months chasing Oats, Toby Stewart, and their friends with a warrant he had gotten from the judge in Felicidad. He never caught them. Oats's trail would disappear up canyons. When Charlie's riders turned back to try and pick it up again, the Oats riders would be sitting their horses not far behind the posse on its back trail. Oats's ability to disappear off a trail and then reappear in a position where he could easily murder the entire posse spooked Charlie's men. They began wondering when Oats would stop running and start shooting. Soon the posse began to lose members as the riders decided discretion was the better part of valor and quit, but all the family men refused to leave the posse. Without riders or bosses to maintain and oversee Charlie's ranching operation, it suffered from neglect and steadily lost money for the businessmen with whom Charlie had herds on shares. As Charlie's riders dwindled down to a small handful, so did his investors. It finally dawned on Charlie that he was never going to catch Oats and that his focus on the chase had led to the ruin of his ranch. It was time to move on to greener pastures and let the law hang Oats and his friends.

When he learned that Charlie Wells's ranch was up for sale and he was leaving the country, Oats rode into Felicidad, turned himself into Asante, and posted bond until the trial. Wells's backers paid a prominent attorney, Allison Tenet, one of the best in the territory, to assist the district attorney in Oats's prosecution for murder.

Tenet conducted a thorough investigation and claimed to have found an old Mexican who had worked for Toby Stewart at the time of Nate's disappearance. The Mexican said he had seen Oats, Tomás Bonito, Toby Stewart, and two men he did not know tie Nate to a post behind Stewart's barn and shoot him to death. Tenet even claimed to have the bullet-riddled post the old man claimed Oats and the others tied Nate Wells to while they filled him full of lead.

Oats hired his own attorney, a young man who had fire in his belly and was not intimidated by the reputation of Allison Tenet.

The courtroom was packed when the old Mexican took the stand. To Tenet's surprise and disgust, the old man eyed the defendant and shook his head at all questions. He denied he'd ever seen anyone tied to a post and shot to death by Señor Oats and the others. Tenet went after the old man for more than three hours but could not make him change his story. Oats's attorney didn't even cross-examine him. The rest of the prosecution witnesses established that Oats had motive for killing Nate Wells, but that was true for half the men living in the basin.

The defense established that on the day Nate disappeared, Oats was in El Paso on business. It took the jury less than ten minutes to declare Oats not guilty.

After the verdict, two crowds formed. One was around Oats surrounded by his neighbors to offer congratulations, and one was around Sheriff Asante surrounded by Charlie Wells and his investors. They were quick to let the sheriff know how angry they were. It was obvious that that verdict was due to the sorry evidence he provided the prosecuting attorneys, and he wasn't getting their support in the next election.

Red in the face and still smarting from the verbal abuse from Charlie and his backers, Asante came up to Oats outside the courtroom, thrust out his chin, and said through clenched teeth, "Yuh got away with it this time, Oats. But next time, by God, yuh'll hang!"

Oats looked Asante in the eye. He nodded and carefully measured his words, a smile flickering at the edges of his lips. "I reckon I will sheriff, when you have a charge clearly proved."

Asante's face became brighter red. He said nothing before he turned and stomped off toward his office.

**W. Michael Farmer** has published short stories in anthologies, and award-winning essays. His historical fiction novels have won Will Rogers Medallion Awards and New Mexico–Arizona Book Awards for Adventure–Drama, Historical Fiction, and History.

★ ★ ★ ★ ★

# THE WAY OF THE WEST
## BY L. J. MARTIN

★ ★ ★ ★ ★

"Aye, Mr. Hogart, I hear you perfectly well, and I understand you, but I still think it's about as good an idea as ticklin' a mule's heel to cure your toothache." Big John Newcomber spat a stream of tobacco juice in the dust to punctuate his point.

"Come on inside and let's gnaw a cup of coffee," Hogart said, trying his best to sound like the men who worked for him.

The owner of the recently renamed Bar H, Harold L. Hogart, reared back in his chair, stuffed his fat banker's cigar in his mouth, and narrowed his eyes. He wasn't a banker, but he was the next thing to it; he was an investor. And he had invested in the Bar H a year ago after old man Wells lost it to the Merchant's and Farmer's Bank—but then, old man Wells wasn't the only one to lose a ranch in 1886. All hoped this year would be a lot better.

The two men took a seat at the plank table that served the bunkhouse. And Hogart did his best to sound the empire builder. "You and I have gotten along fine so far, Newcomber, I hope to continue the relationship. . . . But you've got to abide by my wishes, and his mother and I wish to have our son accompany you on this drive."

"I've already got a half-dozen whelps green as gourds, Mr. Hogart—"

"Then another won't matter much. Wilbur will be ready and waiting at sunup. He's eighteen, older than some of your hands, and perfectly capable. We want him to have this experience before he leaves for college in the East."

So it was settled. John Newcomber had his back up over the whole affair, but he said nothing knowing from long experience as a *segundo*, foreman, that it was hard to put a foot in a shut mouth, and besides, it's usually your own throat you slice with a sharp tongue—and he wasn't about to walk away from a good job when even a poor one was nigh impossible to find. Still and all if he could change the man's mind, he'd give it a go, but he knew that trying to make a point when Hogart thought otherwise was like trying to measure water with a sieve. He'd end up all wet with nothing to show for it. Hogart was slick as calf slobber, but he was the boss.

Ah Choo, the cook, who was nicknamed Sneezy for obvious reasons, filled the two men's coffee cups, but was thinking of his honorable ancestors as he did so—which he had a tendency to do when he had to face unpleasant tasks. He was the bunkhouse cook at the Bar H, not the main house cook. That was Mrs. O'Malior's job. The two of them spatted like a pair of cats whose tails had been tied together before they were tossed over a clothesline. And this afternoon, Sneezy had to go to the main house to round out his chuck for the month-long trip ahead. He did not look forward to the afternoon's chore, nor to having John Newcomber, who he had to be as close to for the next month as a tick in a lamb's tail, start on a long drive with a burr already festerin' under his saddle.

Mr. Hogart finished the varnish Sneezy called coffee, acted as if he enjoyed it, then rose and extended his hand to Newcomber. "You know how important this trip is to the Bar H, John. These cattle have to be in Mojave by the 16th of September in order to fulfill the contract with Harley Brothers' Packing. A day late and those robber barons will want to renegotiate, and the price I have now will just barely cover this year's costs. Be there on time."

"God willin' and the creek don't rise . . . and some tenderfoot don't stampede the stock, we'll make it. Dry year or no." He couldn't help putting the dig in to the boss's withers like a cocklebur, but it rolled off Hogart like rain off an oiled slicker, not that there'd been enough rain this year to test the theory.

Hogart left the bunkhouse, and John Newcomber stood at a window staring out through the dirty glass, shaking his head. "This is gonna be like startin' a long trip with a sore-backed horse and hole in yer boot sole," he mumbled, more to himself than to Sneezy.

"Pardon, Mr. Maycom'er?" the little cook asked.

"Nothin', Sneezy. Pack a lot o' liniment and bandages, an' a Bible if you own one. I got a bad feelin' about this go."

"Yes, sir, Mr. Maycom'er, sir. Renament and ban'ages and the Christian book, snap snap."

Morning dawned fresh and breezy; with the Sierras at the ranch's back and the Whites—also the better part of fourteen-thousand feet above sea level—between it and the rising sun, it took a while before the sun touched the Owen's Valley bottom with its warmth. It was the better part of two-hundred-fifty miles down the valley and across a piece of the Mojave Desert to reach the rail station at Mojave, and to be comfortable, they'd have to average ten miles a day to keep the schedule. Ten miles should be easy, all things being equal. But John Newcomber had driven stock long enough to know that all things never stayed equal for long.

Sneezy had rung the chuck bell at 3:30 a.m., a half hour earlier than usual, so he could feed the men the last of the eggs and milk they'd see for a good while, and still get a jump on the herd. He wanted to stay ahead of them if he could, at least on this first day—or he'd be eating dust the rest of the drive. And the four-up of mules he had pulling the chuckwagon would keep ahead of the herd, given no major trouble.

True to his father's word, just as Sneezy whipped up the chuckwagon team to get a jump on the drovers, Wilbur Hogart pranced up on one of the Hogarts' blooded thoroughbreds, a dun-colored horse with fine long bones that stood sixteen hands. It was a pleasurable animal to look at, but . . . He carried a quirt and wore a fine new Palo Alto fawn-colored hat, twill pants, a starched city shirt, and English riding boots—on his hip gleamed a new Smith and Wesson chrome-plated .38 in a polished black holster. The bedroll he had tied behind the saddle couldn't have carried more than one blanket and one change of clothes. John Newcomber stood cinching up his sorrel quarter horse as Wilbur's animal proudly single-stepped over to the hitching rail.

"John," the young man said, "I'm ready—"

"You'll call me Mr. Newcomber while you're working for me," the Bar H *segundo* said quietly, his voice matching the cold-granite of his chiseled face—but Wilbur heard him clearly enough. The young man's eyes and nostrils flared a little, but he said nothing in reply. "Understood?" Newcomber asked, unsatisfied with the boy's silence, his own voice a trifle louder.

"As you wish, Mr. Newcomber," the boy replied, stressing the *mister* in a manner that rang of sarcasm. John left it at that, knowing it would be a long trip and that time and the trail would work out most of Wilbur Hogart's kinks. Hard work had a way of doing that to a man, or breaking him, if he wasn't much of one to start with. John really had no way of knowing if Wilbur Hogart had any sand, but time and the trail would tell.

"Dad said I was to ride point," Wilbur added, rubbing salt in the spot Harold L. Hogart had already galled on John's back.

"You'll ride drag, like all new hands do, Mr. Hogart." John Newcomber swung up in the saddle, forking the sorrel and waiting for him to kick up his heels with the first saddle pressure of the morning—he didn't, but John knew the sorrel was saving it for later. He took the time to switch his attention and give Wilbur a hard look.

The boy glared at him. "Dad said—"

"Wilbur, let's get something straight right up-front. Your daddy's not going on this trip, and if I hear you say one more time, 'daddy said,' I'll not take kindly to it and I might lose my temper. I've got a deep well of temper, Wilbur, and I can lose it every hour of every day and not run out. It's been tested. That's the kind of trip this might be, Wilbur, if you say 'daddy said' ever ag'in."

"But—"

"There ain't no buts about it, Wilbur."

"Yes, sir," Wilbur said, to his credit, and reined the tall dun-colored horse away.

Sally Fishbine had ridden for the Bar H for fourteen years, the first thirteen when it was the Lazy Loop, and the last one under John Newcomber. He reined his bandy-legged gray over beside John and paced him out to what they called the creek pasture, where the eight hundred fifty seven head, by yesterday's count, of Hereford mix—with Mexican Brahma—were gathered. The rest of the hands, a dozen of them, were holding the cattle and getting their minds right for the drive.

"Salvatore," John said quietly as they gigged the horses toward the creek pasture, "is the weather a'gonna hold?"

"Bones say it is," he said, stretching. About that time John's sorrel decided he was awake enough to shake loose, and began a bone-jarring humpbacked dance. "Step lively!" John shouted, giving the big horse his spurs and whipping him across the ears with the rein tails at the same time. The sorrel settled, and John knew from long experience that that was it for the rest of the day.

"I swear, you two are like an old married couple . . . got to have yer spat or you can't get the blood to pumpin'," Sally said, rolling a smoke with one hand as his own mount plodded along.

"Both of us got to show how young we still are," John said, reaching forward and patting the big horse on the neck. "If'n I didn't pop 'is ears ever' morning, he'd think I didn't care for 'im."

They picked the pace up to a cantor, with Wilbur Hogart keeping a respectful twenty paces behind. Wilbur had learned to ride English, in Oakland at the Hogarts' breeding ranch, across the bay from their home in San Francisco, and he could sit a saddle with the best of them by the time he was sixteen, and rode jumpers, but it was different from western riding— considerably different in that you handed the horse to a groom when finished for the day, and you finished for the day whenever you tired of the animal and the exercise. Still, he knew he was equal to anything the country and John Newcomber could throw at him—at least he was quite sure he was.

They crested a rise and looked down into creek canyon, and close to a thousand bald-faced and mixed-breed cattle lowed and grazed while a dozen cowhands waited the chance to earn their dollar a day and found.

Stub Jefferson had ridden in the year before, and John Newcomber had hired him on without so much as a second glance. His rig, and the way the black cowboy sat the saddle and kept his own council, was enough of a resume for John.

Sergio and Hector Sanchez, a pair of young brothers up from San Diego, were hired on just for the drive. John knew nothing about them, other than they rode fine stock and carried the woven leather reatas of the vaquero, and theirs were well tallowed and stretched to seventy feet with the weight of many a cow.

Old Tuck Holland had been working cattle on the east side of the Sierras for as long as John could remember. He had tales both older and taller than the Sierras and would tell 'em until they chopped ice in Death Valley, if you'd listen. His age was indeterminable but he had to be on the shady side of seventy. He looked so puny he'd have to lean against a post to spit to keep from blowing himself down; but he was tough as whang leather, had a face carved and etched like a peach pit by sun, sand, and wind, and spent most of his time looking back to see if the younger hands were keepin' up. And they were struggling along wondering why he made it all look so plumb easy.

Colorado, which was the only name he gave and consequently was the only name used for him, was redheaded befittin' his name, bow-legged enough that a pig could charge twixt his knees while he was clickin' his heels, and loud; but he pulled his own weight. He too had been hired on just for the duration of the drive.

Pudgy Dickerson was the last of the hands hired on, and John had to bail him out of the Bishop jail in order to do so, but he needed a hand and the rest of the able-bodied men in the valley had run off to another silver strike in the high country—another whiff of bull dung as far as John Newcomber was concerned. But particularly when times were tough men seemed to jump at the chance for easy money. It normally turned out to be grit and grime and beans and backache, but still they chased the will o' the wisp.

The remuda man was Enrico Torres, as good a man with horses as John had ever seen. He pushed three dozen head of rank half-broke stock so the cowhands could trade off a couple of times a day. It was hard country between the north end of the Owen's Valley and Mojave. Some spots of good grass and sweet water, but more than enough hard-as-the-hubs-of-hell ancient lava flows and flash floods, cactus and snakes, and heat if the weather decided it wanted to run late, or snow if it ran early. And it usually decided to do one or the other—and sometimes both—when a herd was being shoved to market. It was hard on horses and men, and hard as hell on a good attitude.

They pushed the herd out, jittery, but then all of them were when a drive began and before they settled into the routine. The men found their positions, all unassigned except for Stub Jefferson, the black cowhand who was riding point, and the Sanchez brothers, who were assigned drag with Wilbur Hogart and quickly took up positions flanking and staying out of the dust. The Sanchez boys had ridden enough drag to know they could stay out of most of it on the flanks, and still do their job. So they gave Wilbur the position of honor . . . or so they told him . . . dead center trailing the herd.

John Newcomber floated from position to position, judging the men he didn't know, watching the herd, eyeballing the weather, and worrying—that was his job.

They hadn't gone three miles before Wilbur Hogart let his horse drift over close enough to Hector Sanchez so he could call out to him. "I'm Wil Hogart," he called.

Hector looked over and nodded, and touched the brim of his sweat-solied sombrero.

"What's a fella to do about the privy?" he shouted again.

Hector looked at him, a little confused.

"I need to pee," Wilbur said.

"Sí," Hector repeated, "the señor needs to 'pee.' " He reined over closer to the fancy-looking gringo, who didn't look quite so fancy now that he was covered with a half-inch of dust. "Well, señor, you ride sidesaddle to accomplish that task."

"Sidesaddle?" Wilbur questioned. "You're funnin' me, *amigo.* I meant do you take the drag while I drop out, or just what?"

"Señor Newcomber will be very angry if you stop to water the sagebrush, señor. It is the tried and trusted sidesaddle method—"

"Fill in for me, señor," Wilbur said, and reined away to find a bush, which was no problem as the country was chaparral covered.

"Sidesaddle," Hector said to himself, then laughed aloud. He couldn't wait to tell his brother.

"Sidesaddle," Wilbur repeated to himself, pleased that he had not fallen for the obvious prank of the other rider. He knew he would be the butt of many attempts, but was wise to them.

He dismounted and unbuttoned his trousers and began to relieve himself, just as the grass under his attacking stream came alive in the most terrible buzzing and thrashing Wilbur had ever heard. He stumbled back and pawed at the Smith and Wesson when he realized it was a four-foot rattler he had the misfortune to awaken from his repose in the sun.

Wilbur emptied the six-shooter, managing to scare the snake into retreating even faster than he already was, but not managing to kill it.

Still, Wilbur was satisfied with himself—until he heard the men begin to yell, and felt the vibration of nearly four thousand hooves begin to beat in rhythmic stampede.

"My God," Wilbur said aloud to himself. "Did I . . . ?"

He raced for the thoroughbred, mounted, and rode after the advancing wave of cattle and men, and into a wall of dust as he had never seen.

The cattle ran for three miles, then the heat and the sun dissuaded them and they slowed, and finally, no longer hearing the explosions that had set them off, stilled and grazed.

John Newcomber sent Stub and Sally back along the flanks to pick up any strays, and checked with each of his men to make sure they were present and accounted for.

Wilbur Hogart, who sat at the rear of the herd, catching his breath as the thoroughbred stood and hung his head sucking in wind, was the last man he approached.

"You managed to keep from getting ground up," Newcomber

greeted him.

"Yes, sir."

"Let me see that firearm," Newcomber said, his face turning to granite.

"It was a snake, Mr. Newco—"

"You shot at some poor ol' snake who was trying his best to get the hell out of the way!"

"He was only a couple of feet away, makin' a terrible noise."

"Give me that weapon."

"Dad said—"

"What did I tell you about that 'dad said,' " Newcomber snapped.

Wilbur looked red faced, but quieted and reached down and slipped the Smith and Wesson out of its holster and handed it over. Newcomber slipped it into his saddlebag. He eyed the boy up and down shaking his head. "Don't make any more trouble, Wilbur. You just cost the Bar H about a thousand dollars in lost weight. At a dollar and a half a day, not that you're worth that, it'd take you some time to pay it back should Mr. Hogart want his due."

"A thousand dollars?"

"A thousand dollars . . . that is if we get all the steers back."

John reined the sorrel away.

Wilbur sat chewing on that for a while, when Stub and Sally approached, pushing a half-dozen head that had strayed during the stampede. They reined over next to him as the strays rejoined the herd, kicking up their heels like a reunion of old friends.

"You the *jefe's* pup?" Sally asked.

Wil gigged his horse over and extended his hand. "I'm Wil Hogart." Sally shook with him, but Stub just touched his hat brim, and Wil said "Howdy."

"Did the boss tell you about Oscar?" Sally asked.

"Oscar?" Wilbur said.

"Oscar, the new hand with the six kids and the crippled wife."

"He didn't say—"

"Oscar got stomped under." Sally said, keeping a straight face. Stub eyed him but, as always, kept his own council.

"Stomped under?" Wilbur asked.

"Ain't enough of 'im left to bury," Sally said, shaking his head sadly.

"You mean—"

"Oscar's cold as a mother-in-law's kiss, boy." Sally looked as if he was about to break into tears.

"It's all my fault," Wilbur said, his face fallen.

"Don't know about that," Sally said. "It's the Lord's place to judge reckless behavior . . . the kind what causes the good to die young. Yer misbegotten ways will be laid out a'fore St. Peter soon enough. You may not even survive this drive. Many won't. Maybe you'll meet Oscar in heaven and can explain to him why you got him stomped into salsa. Well, it's nice to make yer acquaintance." He reined away. Both he and Stub were doing their best not to break into uproarious laughter, and in doing so, their shoulders quaked. Wilbur thought they were both in the throes of grief.

"Aren't we going to bury him?" Wilbur called after them.

Stub turned back, wiping the tears of laughter from his eyes. "He's already stomped so deep he'll take root and sprout." He turned away, and the shoulders shook again.

Wilbur Hogart had never felt so terrible. What kind of a man was John Newcomber to worry about running off a thousand dollars' worth of fat, and not even mention a man who had been stomped to death?

The word traveled quickly among the men, and all stayed away from Wilbur for the rest of the afternoon—knowing they would break into laughter if they rode up beside the dejected boy, and give it away. Wilbur clomped along behind the herd, his eyes and ears filled with dust, his mind filled with remorse.

They caught up with where Sneezy had made camp, an agreed spot ten miles from the home place on the edge of Bar H property and on the bank of a fair cold creek, lined with willows, a couple of spreading sycamores, and a few Jeffery pines.

Wilbur was the last to the camp, and the men parted from a group as he rode in—Wilbur presumed it was because he was approaching, and that they didn't want to have anything to do with the man who'd caused Oscar's death. Not that he knew who Oscar was. He'd only met a couple of the men, and Oscar had not been one of them.

Wilbur dropped the saddle from the thoroughbred and turned him out with the remuda, then walked straight over to John Newcomber.

"They told me about Oscar," he said, his weight shifting from foot to foot. "I want to go back and pick up his body. A Christian—"

John Newcomber gave him a dubious look and started to say something, but was interrupted.

Sally stood nearby and offered quickly, "Oscar wanted the coyotes and other critters to have him, boy." Sally removed his hat and placed it across his heart. "It was his last wish. He always was a kind soul to the little critters. And it's the way of the west. We'll say a few words about him after we bean up."

Wilbur was still unsatisfied, but didn't know what to say. It was a custom he'd never heard off, but little would surprise him with what he knew of cattle drives and drovers.

"The coyotes?" he finally managed to mumble in amazement. His gaze wandered from man to man, but none would meet his and none offered to disagree with what he thought was a pagan practice.

"Oscar was a religious soul, but he was the outdoors type . . . thought these here mountains was his . . . what do ya call them fancy churches . . . his cathedral. He wanted to be spread all over these mountains," Sally added. "Nothing like a band of the Lord's scavengers to spread a body about. Crows and buzzards and such fly for miles doing their business and the coyotes and skunks and wolves'll deposit him in all the places he loved—not in exactly the way I'd personally favor it, but he'll get spread. Ashes to ashes, dirt to dirt, dung to dung, so to speak."

Wilbur thought he was going to be sick to his stomach. All the men turned away, and some were obviously overtaken with grief. They held hands to face and shook, or turned away. He walked away from the camp and into a clump of river willows and found a rock by the creek and sat, watching the water tumble by, wondering what would happen to "Oscar's" six starving children. He sat there until he heard Sneezy bang the bottom of an iron skillet, and hurried to get his beans—grief and remorse was one thing, hunger was another.

The men ate in relative silence. Once in a while, one would mention one or another of Oscar's children, or his crippled wife.

The men cleaned up the biscuits, bacon, and beans, and hauled their tins to Sneezy. Darkness was creeping over the camp, and chill setting in. The drive would take them from fifty-five-hundred feet elevation on the slopes of the Sierra, which rose to fourteen-thousand feet behind them, down to less than two-thousand feet at the railroad corrals at the town of Mojave.

"Time for the ceremony," Sally said. "Gather round, boys."

All the men gathered in a circle, standing, drinking their coffee, gnawin' chaw, smoking roll-your-owns. "Now, what do you remember about Oscar?" Sally said. "You start, Stub."

Stub removed his hat and scratched his woolly head. "Well, I ain't much on reminiscence, so to speak, but I might remember something, given as how Oscar was such a fine fella." He took a long draw on the tin cup, then began. "You know that ol' Oscar used to run the Rocking W down near San Berdo. He was countin' cattle there for a buyer from San Francisco, and knew the W didn't have enough cattle to meet the contract, so ol' Oscar set his countin' chute up against a small hill. The buyer set up on the top rail and went to markin' off the stock. Ol' Oscar had the boys drive those heifers and steers round and round that hill till the buyer counted what he needed, then drove the herd off to the yards. The W got paid for nigh five-hundred head . . . twice. Oscar saved the Rocking W, which the bank was sure to grab."

The boys laughed at that, but Wilbur found it to be down right dishonest. He smiled tightly.

"How 'bout you, Tuck?" Sally encouraged the old cowhand.

"Well, Oscar was a tough ol' bird." Tuck scratched his wrinkled chin and its stubble of a day's growth of beard. "One time the foreman of the Three Rivers Ranch bet him a season's pay that he couldn't make love to an Indian squaw, kill a grizzly bear, and drink a fifth of whiskey in one day . . . and the foreman knew where the bear's den was and knew an ol' squaw who was a mite friendly to all the Three River's hands, were they to bring her a bag o' beans or sugar. Well Oscar took that bet, but the thing was, he drank the fifth a' rye first, then . . . a little confused with the firewater an' all . . . he shot the ol' squaw dead as a stone. The hard part was holdin' that griz down . . . but he did an' that's why some bears here about is such sonsa'bitches."

The boys laughed and slapped their thighs.

Wilbur began to get a little suspicious.

"How about you, Colorado?" Sally asked the pock-faced redheaded cowhand. He sat away from the others, sharpening a ten-inch knife on an Arkansas whetstone.

"I never much cared about tellin' tales," he said, and spit a mouthful of tobacco juice, then went back to his work on the blade.

"You, Pudgy," Sally asked the man John Newcomber had bailed out of the Bishop jail to join the drive.

"Nobody," Pudgy began, "could ever find his way home, good as old Oscar. One time over at the Whiskey Holler' saloon in Virginia City, old Oscar went up to the bar with a bunch of hands he'd just finished a drive with, and they got to drinkin' and drinkin'. A couple of the boys, realizing how drunk ol' Oscar was, went out to his nag and turned the saddle around—they didn't want him riding into trouble. Oscar, hanging onto that poor ol' nag's tail, rode clean to Sacramento before he sobered up and realized he was facing backward. He never could find his way to Sacramento after that, unless he reversed his saddle. But he was always real good at knowin' where he'd been."

By this time Wilbur was red in the face.

"We need to cheer up," Hector Sanchez said, after he quit holding his sides from laughing. "A little friendly competition. Who's the newest hombre to sign on?" Hector asked.

"Must be ol' snake killer," Sally said, putting an arm around Wilbur's shoulders. "You get to go first."

"Wait a minute," Wilbur said. "Did any of you fellas even know this Oscar fella? In fact, was there even any Oscar at all?"

"I've knowed a few Oscars in my day," Sally said. "How about you, Stub?"

"Cain't say as how I ever knowed an Oscar."

All the men broke into laughter, slapping their thighs. Wilbur reddened again, and he felt the heat on the back of his neck. He didn't know whether to get angry and stomp away or offer to fight, so he just stood and got a silly grin on his face.

"Ain't you proud you didn't cause nobody to get hurt with that fool stunt?" Sally said, more serious than not.

Tuck cut in before Wilbur could answer. "Give the boy a chance to show he's as good as the rest a' ya." Old Tuck looked serious. "Ya'll been funnin' him enough."

Hector stepped over in front of Wilbur. "Can you swing an axe, Señor Hogart?"

"I imagine."

"Good, then we have the notch cutting contest."

"Notch cutting?"

"Sure, every drive has the notch cuttin' contest."

John Newcomber walked away shaking his head, but was unseen by Wilbur who was anxious to redeem himself for being stupid enough to be taken in with the stomped-in rider story.

"Notch cutting," Hector said. "You go first, so the rest of us know what we have to beat."

Sneezy had already fetched the double bladed axe out of the chuckwagon and offered it to Hector. "Come on, over here." He led Wilbur to a fallen log, two foot in diameter.

"This is a good log for notch cutting," Hector said, and the other men agreed with him. He lined Wilbur up in front of the log. "Get your distance, *amigo*," he suggested, and Hector adjusted his distance from the log.

"Now, here is the rub, *amigo*." Hector stepped behind Wilbur and encircled his head with his red-checkered bandanna.

"Hold on, now," Wilbur tried to protest.

"This is how it is done, *amigo*. Blindfolded. You can do it."

Wilbur allowed himself to have the blindfold put on.

"Wait until I give the signal," Hector said. "Your hat, *amigo*," he said, and removed Wilbur's new fawn-colored, now dusty, wide-brimmed hat. "You will do better without the hat."

"One, two, three, go," Hector called and, and the men yelled their encouragement.

Wilbur, with vigor born of embarrassment and a desire to show these men he was equal to any of them, swung the axe five times before Hector yelled for him to stop. "Time is up, *amigo.*"

Wilbur reached up and removed the blindfold, anxious to see how much of a notch he'd cut. And he'd cut three fine ones . . . in his hat. His new Palo Alto lay in front of the log, its crown split, its brim with two wide splits.

"*Carambra,*" Hector said, a sorrowful look on his face, "you have cut the notch right where I put your *sombrero* for safe keeping."

The men roared with laughter.

"You win the contest, Wilber," Tuck said. "The prize is a free millinery redesign. That's now what's known as an Owen's Valley special."

Wilbur's mother had bought him that hat, just for this trip. The anger began to crawl up Wilbur's backbone, and to the men's surprise, he cast the axe aside and went after Hector Sanchez with his fists. Hector was quick as a snake, and backpedaled as Wilbur took four or five healthy swings, then Hector charged in low and tackled him and drove him to his back. He got astride him and pinned him down. Wilbur was red in the face and spittin' mad, but he couldn't move.

"Hey, *amigo,* you can't take a joke?" Hector asked.

"Let me up and I'll show you."

"I think I hold you here awhile until the pot she don't boil so much," Hector said.

"Let him up," John Newcomber said, crossing the clearing from where he'd been leaning against a log, taking it all in. "And Mr. Hogart, you will find your bedroll and a place to bed down. The fun is over."

"You might think it's fun."

"I notched my hat, as did most every man here. It'll pass and you'll see the humor in it."

"The hell I will."

Hector unloaded off of him, and Wilbur regained his feet, spun on his heel, and stomped away.

"Remember the Alamo," he said under his breath, but no one heard.

He found a spot away from the others for his bedroll, and ignored the feigned compliments to his hat the next morning as the men ate beans and cornbread by the dawning light. He turned in his tin and got a handful of jerky and hard biscuits for his noon meal, and was the first to saddle up for the day's work.

The wrangler, Enrico Torres, cut out a new horse for him—ignoring Wilbur's suggestions that he ride his own thoroughbred with a terse, "Horse has to last the trip, and you will get a new *caballo* at least twice a day, sometimes thrice, from here on."

The ragged-looking buckskin selected by Torres stood and allowed the currycomb, then the saddle and bridle, but went into a stiff-legged bounce as soon as Wilbur forked him. As much as the boy fought to control the animal, he turned and bounced right through the middle of Sneezy's camp, kicking fire, and ash, and dust in every direction. The Chinese cook scattered for cover, cursing in Oriental jabber, then sailed a pot lid after the boy and high-jumping horse as they moved on into the chaparral.

But to the surprise of all who watched in amusement, Wilbur stuck in the saddle.

He tipped his hat after he got control of the animal, yelled, "Sorry, Sneezy," then gigged away the snorting horse, keeping the animal's chin pulled to its chest, to take up his position riding drag.

"Not bad for a stall-fed tenderfoot," Enrico said to Sally and Stub, who were currying their animals nearby. "His ridin' ability is a bit better than his sense of humor."

"Spent his first day admiring his shadow, cause there was no mirror handy," Stub said. "I thought at first he might be studyin' to be a half-wit, but I believe he might just end this trip knowin' dung from wild honey. He's game enough, and has more sand than I figgered."

"I donno," Sally offered. "It seems to me he's taken too much of a liking to thick tablecloths and thin soup, but we'll see . . . we will see. My bones is goin' to achin', weather's a' comin'."

Before noon, the sky turned from deep bright blue to flat pewter and the temperature plunged forty degrees. The wind whipped down out of the Sierras, and men pulled coats from rolls behind their saddles.

Wilbur Hogart had a coat, but a light one that served as little more than a windbreaker, and the gloves he pulled from his saddlebag were kid leather—not working gloves, nor warm. Before long, he was cold to the bone, hunkered over like a ninety-year-old man, and shivering in the saddle. To add injury to insult, the hole in the crown of his hat leaked water, and his head was soaked.

Hector Sanchez had kept his distance and the two young men had no more than exchanged glances.

By midmorning, flakes of snow began to drift. Both Enrico and Hector Sanchez had pulled heavy *serapes* from the rolls at the back of their saddles, and their wide sombreros kept the snow from their shoulders. A steer began to fade back from a position between Hector and Wilbur, and both men moved to haze it back into the herd.

As they did so, Hector spoke for the first time that day. "You do not have a heavy coat?"

"I'm not cold," Wilbur managed through teeth gritted to keep them from chattering.

"I see that, *amigo*," Hector said, and smiled and reined away.

"Greaser," Wilbur said under his breath, and pulled the light jacket closer as he moved back to his position. At least the dust

347

had stopped.

After a moment, Hector again moved closer and yelled to Wilbur. "I must leave for a *momentito*. Cover the flank."

Wilbur said nothing, even though he heard. He watched the Mexican gig his horse and lope away, then laughed to himself. If the herd did fade and stray on Hector's side, Hector would get a dressing down from Newcomber. He ignored the herd on Hector's flank and tended only those cattle directly ahead of him.

But as fate and the cold would have it, the herd did not stray but rather bunched closer, and Hector soon returned. He drifted over to Wilbur and tossed him a bundle. "It was Oscar's *serape*." He laughed and slapped his thighs. "He needs it no longer so he left it to me. It is not because I am generous, *amigo*. If you continue to knock your teeth together like the castanets, you will cause another stampede. And more work for us all."

Wilbur held the wool *serape* in his hands and stared at the young Mexican, saying nothing.

"Ayee! You stick your *cabeza* . . . your head through the slit, tenderfeets."

"Though the slit," Wilbur repeated. And without hesitation, learned the use of the *serape*. The same one he had seen Hector use as a blanket the night before.

"*Sí, amigo*," Hector said, and spun his horse to return to his position.

"*Gracias, amigo*," Wilbur called after him.

"*Da nada*, Wil," Hector said, and gave the spurs to his horse. "You have mastered the *serape*, a difficult task. Tomorrow, if the weather is better, I will teach you the use of the reata . . . it should be nothing for a man who can chop a notch as you can."

"Tomorrow, if the weather is better," Wil called after him, and wondered what new trick Hector had up his sleeve and he knew that if Hector was fresh out, the others weren't. He wondered if he could borrow a needle and thread from Sneezy to sew up his hat—if Sneezy wasn't still wanting to sail pot lids at him for riding through the middle of camp.

But he was sure Sneezy had long forgotten the incident.

The wind picked up again. But he didn't care. He was warm, for the first time that day.

He removed his hat, eyed it skeptically, and began to chuckle.

**L. J. Martin** is the bestselling author of over fifty western, crime, and thriller novels. He lives in Montana and winters in California. Check out more from his website: www.ljmartin .com.

★ ★ ★ ★ ★

# Return to Laurel
## by John D. Nesbitt

★ ★ ★ ★ ★

The print shop I was looking for lay on a side street a few blocks from downtown North Platte. My route took me past a row of meat markets and green grocers. At a little before eight in the morning, a row of delivery wagons stood in the street, each one backed up to the sidewalk with a team of horses turned at an angle. When I walked down the same sidewalk the evening before, to make sure of the location, the street was calm and quiet. Now the area was bustling, with men and boys unloading sacks of potatoes, crates of melons, and bushel baskets of fresh corn in pale green husks. One wagon had a box of dressed chickens, white and yellow, on a bed of crushed ice. I paused at the last wagon, where two men in newsboy caps and shirtsleeves were grappling with a block of ice the size of a coffin. They slid it onto a cart that had small wheels with wide iron rims, then hauled the cart into the dark interior of a shop that sold fish.

Down the street a ways, I found Empire Printing and went inside. The clock on the wall showed a few minutes before eight. A man wearing a gray apron was working at a stack of burlap bags, brushing black ink across a tin stencil. As he set aside a printed bag, I saw the word "BEANS" in capital letters, with "50 Lbs. Net Weight" below the word. Along the walls I saw bills and posters on display, advertising horse sales, theatrical productions, and a traveling wax museum.

The man set his brush in an inkpot and turned to me. He had long, straight hair and thick spectacles, and he had a few

353

dots of ink spatter on his face.

"Yessir. Help you?"

"My name's Henry Tresh. I have an appointment with Mr. Haines."

"He's in his office. Come on back."

He led me to an office with a window looking out onto the work area. Inside, a man sat behind an oak desk. Off to his side, a woman dressed all in gray sat with her hands in her lap.

The man rose. He was in later middle age, with weight showing in his face and his upper body. He had thinning brown hair, a trimmed mustache, and a pale complexion. As he reached across the desk, he said, "Mr. Tresh. I'm Edwin Haines, and this is my wife." We shook hands.

I took off my hat, nodded to the woman, and said. "Pleased to meet you both."

"Have a seat," said Mr. Haines.

I took one of the two wooden chairs on my side.

"We appreciate your traveling this far to visit with us." He settled into his seat and picked up a polished steel letter knife. Looking at it as much as at me, he said, "It's very difficult for us to get away. My business has me tied down."

"I understand. Travel is part of my business, at times."

"I'm sure you're wondering why we wrote to you all the way out in Cheyenne, Wyoming."

I shrugged. "I assume people have their reasons."

"You could say we have two. One is that we understand you have had some success at finding missing persons. We read the story of how you found the girl in Laramie City. Alive."

"I consider myself very lucky. And in her case, thankful as well."

"And the second reason is that the work we would like you to do is in Wyoming. Close to the center of the state."

"I see." I glanced at Mrs. Haines and back at him.

He stared at the letter knife, frowned, and looked up at me. "Mr. Tresh, it's our son. His name is Arthur. He went missing quite a while back."

"I'm sorry to hear that." I nodded toward Mrs. Haines to include her. She continued to sit with her hands folded and her mouth firm.

Mr. Haines let out a heavy breath. "It's been almost twenty years, and there's never been a day without anxiety for us."

"Have you tried looking for him before now?"

He spoke in a weary voice. "It's so far away, and Wyoming is such a vast area. And to tell you the truth, we didn't know where to begin until just recently. We didn't know the name of the town where he was last seen."

I let him speak. I assumed that if he wanted me to do this piece of work, he would tell me the name of the town without my asking.

"You see, he got into trouble because of a girl. Don't get me wrong. He didn't get the girl into trouble in that sense. But he took off with her."

"They did not elope," said Mrs. Haines.

"No, they didn't," said her husband. "They didn't get married or anything like that. They just ran off together, on a kind of adventure. Something happened, we don't know what, but the girl showed up again, and Arthur didn't."

"She must have given you some explanation."

"She has never cooperated with us. Any time we've tracked her down, she goes somewhere else. And she won't talk."

"It's all her fault from the beginning," said Mrs. Haines. "Arthur would not have gotten into any kind of trouble if it weren't for her."

"Very well," I said. "I have an idea of the case. Perhaps we should determine whether I'm going to work for you."

"Of course," said Mr. Haines. "We need to tend to the business details." He held the letter opener by the point as he tapped the back of his other hand. "We'd like to know your fees."

"Not to be too blunt, but I need a hundred dollars minimum for my time, plus my travel expenses. If my work goes beyond two weeks, my fee continues at three dollars a day."

"I see. When does your time begin?"

"It already did. When I left Cheyenne."

Mr. Haines took a long breath, glanced at his wife, and said, "I suppose we should."

"Very good," I said. "If the girl lives anywhere near, I can begin by talking to her. What's her name, by the way?"

"Bella Collingsworth. But I don't know where you can find her."

"How old is she now? You say this was about twenty years ago?"

"Yes. Arthur would be thirty-eight now, and this girl, who is no longer a girl, would be about thirty-seven."

"And her last known address?"

"It was in Broken Bow, but that was years ago. She's moved around. We thought you might make more efficient use of your time if you went to the town where Arthur disappeared. As I said, it's been but recently that we learned the name of the place, and that's why we wrote to you."

I saw that I was going to have to ask after all. "Very well. If you could tell me the name of the town, I'll have a place to start."

Mr. Haines looked at his wife and back at me. "This is a very important undertaking for us."

"I understand. And I'll do the best I can."

"Laurel," he said, turning again to his wife. For a moment I thought he was speaking to her, until he met my eyes and said, "The name of the town is Laurel."

I found the town named Laurel, first on the map and then on the rolling plains, a day's ride north of Douglas on Walker Creek, not far from Thunder Basin. Like many such towns, it sat on a main trail and drew most of its business from the surrounding ranch country. I took a room at the Blue Star Hotel and lingered a few minutes to visit with the person at the desk.

She was an attractive woman, with dark brown hair, brown eyes, and a clear complexion. She wore a woman's business suit consisting of a dark blue wool jacket and skirt with a white blouse. I guessed her to be about my age, somewhere around thirty-five.

"I hope you enjoy your stay in our town," she said as she handed me the key. "If there's a way I can help, please let me know."

"I appreciate it. You might be able to recommend someone. I'm interested in the possibility of doing a little hunting. Perhaps antelope but more interested in deer."

"You don't have to go far for antelope. As for deer, there are some breaks and pine ridges over to the east, and from what I understand, that's where they find deer. If you want someone to take you out, I know of one young fellow who does that sort of thing. His name is Clay Cooper."

"Good to know. I'll tell you, I've heard a story of a huge buck deer, with a great set of antlers, that someone killed in this area about twenty years ago."

"Clay would be too young to know much about that, and he didn't grow up here."

"I'm sure there are some old-timers. Someone might even have a photograph."

"No telling. But if you want to talk to someone who's been here a long time, there's Mr. Boynton, the druggist. He's rather knowledgeable on a variety of subjects, and he's something of a town historian, though he hasn't written it down, as far as I know."

"Mr. Boynton."

"Yes. Hugh Boynton. They call him the old bachelor."

I met her eyes and gave her my best smile. "Thank you. You've been very helpful."

"And the young man's name is Clay Cooper."

"Right. I caught that."

"You'll find him at the blacksmith shop. If you need a horse shoed, he's good at that."

"Thank you again."

I found Clay Cooper by following the sound of metal on metal. I came to a low wooden building with most of the white paint worn off. Inside, a slender young man of about twenty-five was beating a short-handled sledgehammer on an iron rod. He wore a leather apron and a cloth skullcap, both grimy. He looked up from his work and smiled.

"Howdy."

"Good afternoon. The lady at the hotel says you're a man who knows his business."

"That's nice of her." He looked past me. "What do you need done?"

"Nothing at the moment. But with fall in the air, I'm thinking of doing some hunting."

"There's some of that around. Deer, I guess?"

"I could try for an antelope, but what drew me here was the deer. I heard a story about a legendary deer that someone killed in this area about twenty years ago."

Clay shook his head. "Haven't heard of it. But there's some big ones out there in the breaks. Hard to git. That's how they come to be so big."

"I believe it. The lady at the hotel—"

"Miss Glover."

"Yes. She told me that the one person in town who knew all the old stories was a Mr. Boynton."

"Oh, the old bachelor." Clay gave a short laugh. "They say he knows just about everything."

"If he's anything like Miss Glover, he might be able to—"

"Ha. He's nothing like Miss Glover. Though they know each other."

"Being an old bachelor, he's probably not her gentleman caller."

"Ha-ha. Far from it. But he's got the biggest house in town, and she's got the best business." Clay gave me a sly look. "Got an eye for her?"

"Nothing more than normal. And she seems pretty reserved."

"Oh, she's all right. She's just a little above most people here. She's been out in the world, had some kind of an upset, and came back here to run the hotel when her father died. If she doesn't keep a distance—well, even as it is, she has to cool off every teamster or cowpuncher who's got four bits for a room. She's not your common kind of heifer."

"All for the best, I'm sure."

"So when do you want to hunt?"

"What do you think? You know more about this country than I do."

"Cottonwood leaves are just beginnin' to turn yellow. I'd say in another week or two. If you kill a nice buck, you want to be sure his horns are out of velvet."

"Oh, yes." I glanced around the shop and came back to the smith. "And what about Mr. Boynton? Miss Glover said he's a druggist."

"He's only in his shop when someone needs him. You can usually find him at home."

"In the biggest house in town."

"That's right." Clay pointed with his thumb over his shoulder. "You can't miss it. Big wooden house on a stone foundation. Gray with white trim."

Clay Cooper was right about not missing the house. I saw it from a block away, stately with two dormer windows, scrolled white woodwork, and a stone foundation painted white. I guessed that the house had a cellar or basement, which with the main floor and then the attic made for a large house for an old bachelor.

The front yard on either side of the walkway had a series of flower beds, with taller plants like daisies and zinnias growing in the plots closer to the house, while lower plants of the pansy and petunia variety grew in front. Closest to the street, the earth had been worked up in a strip about six feet wide and twenty feet long. A man was jabbing at the dirt with the tip of a garden spade, breaking the clods into smaller pieces. As I approached, he looked up and paused in his work.

He was an older man, about sixty, above average in height, with a not very firm physique. He was wearing a drab work shirt with a low collar and three buttons. It fit him close, so that his sagging chest muscles showed like breasts. His shoulders sloped, and his waist spread, like that of a man who spent most of his time in a stout chair, yet here he was, working on a sunny fall afternoon.

He wore lightweight leather gloves. Holding the shovel handle with one hand, he rubbed his forehead with the other. "Good afternoon," he said.

"How do you do?"

"Well enough for an old man."

"Getting some exercise. That's good." I stopped at about twelve feet from him. His short-brimmed hat cast a light shadow on his face, but I could see him now.

His face was thick with age, full and not wrinkled. He had pale eyes with heavy brows above and bags beneath. His blond hair had gone not to gray but to the colorless hue of dead grass in winter. He was clean-shaven, and his small, yellowing teeth showed when he spoke.

"It's that time of year to plant the tulip bulbs."

I looked at the ground and nodded.

"Visitor?"

"Yes. For me, it's that time of year to think about hunting."

"This is a place for it, though I haven't ever taken an interest in it myself."

A strange, cawing sound drew my attention toward the front steps of the house. Sitting in the shade in front of the door was a large wicker cage, with a dark form shifting inside.

"Is that a crow?" I asked.

"Yes, that's Henry. I named him after a cockatiel that belonged to a lady friend of mine, many years ago. He would whistle and say, 'Henry is a pretty boy.' "

"This bird doesn't talk, does he?"

"No. They say that if you split a crow's tongue, you can get him to say a few things. But I wouldn't know how to go about it."

I recalled a house in Cheyenne where the owners set a parrot and its cage in the shade of the house on warm afternoons. I said, "He's good company, though."

"Of sorts." The man looked me over. "So you're here to hunt?"

"Here to see about it. By the way, my name's Henry Tresh." I stepped forward and offered my hand.

He had a firm handshake. "My name's Hugh. Hugh Boynton. I'm the old man in this town."

"You don't look so old to me."

"Nice of you to say so. But I don't fool anyone."

"Well, it's a pleasure to meet you. I suppose I should be on my way. Not interfere with your work anymore."

"I'm done for today."

"Oh. And what's next?"

"Daffodils. No rest for the wicked." He stepped back and laid his hand on a short-handled manure fork that I had not noticed. It was stuck in the ground at the edge of the tulip bed. He pulled the fork loose with a quick jerk, rested it on the ground, and rubbed with his shoe to clean the tines. With a placid expression he smiled and said, "It's good to meet you as well, Henry. Enjoy your stay in our town. And good luck with your hunting."

"Thank you, and good luck to you, Mr. Boynton."

"Hugh. Call me Hugh."

I found my way to the Shanty, the one saloon in town, that evening. If the barkeep had thicker spectacles, he could have passed for the twin brother of the printer's devil in North Platte. As he poured me a glass of whiskey, he told me his name was Mike.

I told him my name was Henry. He asked what brought me to town, and I told my usual story about looking into the prospects of hunting. He left me alone, and I fell into my own thoughts. I wondered about Hugh Boynton and the restraint he showed in conversation. Nine people out of ten would have said something about my name being the same as a pet crow's. It seemed to me that he hadn't missed the opportunity to mention that he had a lady friend. I thought of his tulip bulbs, nestled in their bed, waiting for the first snow.

Movement at my right caused me to turn and look. A fellow about my age, wearing a short-billed cap that was ridged up in front, tapped on the bar with the edge of a silver dollar.

"Gimme a whiskey," he said. He stretched out his arm and

drew it back, in a restless sort of way. He raised his hand and pulled on the back of his neck, then pushed up his cap so that it sat cockeyed on his head. He had whitish blond hair, cropped close, so that the lumps on his cranium were visible. The shortness of his hair reminded me of what they call a jail dock, and I recalled reading about phrenologists and their interest in measuring criminals' heads.

"Have you got the makin's?" he asked.

"No," I answered. "I don't smoke."

"Just as well." He stretched out his arm again. "Son of a bitch. What does a fella have to do to get a drink?"

Mike appeared with a relaxed smile and his eyes half-closed. "You say you want a drink?"

"I guess I do. Seems like I been here an hour."

"You'll be all right. Whiskey?"

"That's what I said earlier."

Mike set a glass on the bar and poured enough for a lumberjack. "Passin' through?" he asked.

"Maybe."

Mike pointed at me with his thumb. "He's here to hunt."

The newcomer tipped his head and looked at me sideways. "What do you hunt?"

"Nothing yet. But I'm thinking about deer."

He drank a slug of whiskey. "I used to hunt. Then I got smart. Found out I could stay in bed on cold mornings." He rotated his glass. "What do you do for a living?"

"I delivered groceries for several years. I'd like to go into business for myself. I'm thinking about the printing business."

"That's what I should do. Print money."

"I think there are some restrictions on that."

"There's restrictions on everything. That is, on things you like."

Mike wiped the bar top with his cloth. "I'm Mike, and this is

Henry. We're all easygoing here. What's your name?"

"Ned." He had large blue eyes with puffy lower eyelids, and he rolled his head to gaze at me. "So you delivered groceries."

"That's right. I delivered ice for a while, also, but I didn't like carrying the heavy blocks."

"You remind me of a guy named Deadwood Dick."

I had heard the word "guy" before, and it struck me as the kind of slang that people used in poolrooms. "I don't know anything about him," I said.

"There's not much to know."

"What kind of work do you do?" asked Mike.

"I've worked as a stone mason."

"That's good work." Mike smiled. "You know, they're planning to build a new prison in Rawlins."

"They can have it. I'd rather work on a bank."

"It'll be a while till they build a bank in this town."

Ned snorted. "I'd say so."

"Are you here for the scenery, then?" Mike polished the same spot on the bar as before.

"You ask a lot of questions." Ned rotated his glass a quarter of a turn and knocked off the rest of his drink.

"Care for another splash of firewater?"

Ned pushed his glass forward. "Rawlins. I wouldn't live there if they paid my rent."

Mike kept his eyes on the whiskey as he poured. "What's your idea of a good town?"

"Ogallala."

"Isn't that the one that the drovers used to call the Gomorrah of the Plains?"

"Six whorehouses for every saloon. And no one asks questions."

I sat by the window at breakfast the next morning and stared at the street, which among other things was a main trail running north and south. I thought about Ned from the night before, and I wondered if he came from the north or the south. One might assume the south, as the two towns he claimed to know about lay quite a distance to the southwest and the southeast—both railroad towns, for that matter, which went along with his hard manner. But he could have come from the north on this trip. One thing I had learned in my line of work was not to make assumptions and not to make details fit an idea I had already formed. Keep the idea open.

Along with that rule came another I also had to remind myself of. I did not have to like someone in order to do my work. In the Haines case so far, the only people I had liked were Miss Glover and the young blacksmith. Bartender Mike did not cipher very much one way or the other. As for Mr. and Mrs. Haines, Hugh Boynton, and Ned of the close-cropped hair, I did not think so much about whether I liked or disliked any of them. I grouped them according to another principle, the extent to which I thought they told the truth. I seemed to have met them in descending order.

In addition, the town of Laurel gave me an uncertain feeling. For as much as it seemed like a place where people followed normal tasks such as beating on hot metal, planting tulip bulbs, and serving fried potatoes, it also seemed like a place where something dark could have happened.

I turned my thoughts to a brighter topic, Miss Glover. I did not expect to see her until later in the day, as the reception desk was attended by a clerk with high cheekbones and an upturned nose. I had given him my key when I came to breakfast.

When I finished my meal, I asked for the key and went back to my room to while away some time reading a book.

The sun warmed the day, and the afternoon was a replica of the one before. I went out for a stroll, walking on the east side of town first, then crossing the thoroughfare and ambling toward the gray house with dormer windows, white trim, and a painted stone foundation.

Out front, on the other side of the walkway from the tulip bed, the old bachelor was digging up another plot. He was dressed in the same clothes as the day before, showing his soft form. He was wearing his light work gloves, and I recalled his firm handshake.

As he put his weight on the shovel head, it sank into the ground. He lifted a spadeful of dirt, turned it over, and cut it twice with the blade. He kept at his work until I drew near, although I suspected he saw me coming. Nearby, the manure fork with thick tines was stuck in the ground, and next to it sat a basket full of yellowish-brown flower bulbs.

"Good afternoon," he said. "Out for a walk, I see."

"Wonderful day for it. Good to see you back at your work."

"Today's the day for daffodils."

"Have you had the first frost here?"

"Yes, but not a very heavy one. My zinnias are still hanging on." He waved his arm toward the house.

At a distance, I could see tinges where the frost had nipped the leaves and outer petals. I said, "Zinnias bring hummingbirds, don't they?"

"That they do. And it's a pleasure. Of course at my age, those are the pleasures that are left. The small ones. A glass of wine, a hummingbird on an August afternoon."

"When do you get your first snow?"

"There's no set date, of course, but usually after the first of October."

"That must be a source of pleasure, too, to look out the window and think of all those little fellows slumbering beneath a blanket of snow."

"I don't know if I'm that poetic. Or deep."

"Maybe it's the book I was reading this morning."

"Do you stay at the Blue Star?"

"Yes, I do."

"Very good establishment. Excellent hostess, Miss Glover. I'm glad to count her among my friends—not that I have many to count."

I expected him to mention his age again, but he didn't.

"Have you met Clay Cooper?" he asked.

"Yes, I have. Miss Glover recommended him."

"He's a good lad. If anyone can help you find a deer, it's him."

"It's still up to me to pull the trigger, of course."

"I don't know anything about that. When I was in school, studying to be an apothecary, we took a couple of science courses where we had to collect our own specimens. Something like a pill bug didn't bother me, but I didn't like killing the higher forms, like butterflies."

"Some of the great ornithologists brought down beautiful birds—hawks, eagles, owls—all in the interests of science, of course."

"I'll stick to my mortar and pestle."

"Let Audubon and Burroughs kill the herons and the chicken hawks."

"Put it as you may." He stabbed at a clod with his shovel.

"I can tell I'm keeping you from your work. And I should be moving along. I need my exercise, too."

"Oh, don't take me too seriously. Sometimes I'm an irritable old coot. But it's good to talk to people with ideas from the outside."

"I doubt that any of my ideas are that new." I took a step. "Good luck with your gardening."

"And good luck to you in your hunting, Henry."

"Thanks." I went on my way in the warm afternoon.


I found Miss Glover at the reception desk when I returned to the hotel. She was wearing a lavender-colored dress with a neck scarf of a darker shade, and her dark brown hair was pinned up in neat coils.

"Good afternoon," she said. "I hope you're enjoying your stay."

"I am. I met young Mr. Cooper, at your recommendation, and I also met your friend Mr. Boynton."

"I suppose he's my friend. I don't know him that well. Was he familiar with the story of the big deer?"

"He doesn't care to talk very much about hunting. He seems to be more interested in butterflies, hummingbirds, and daffodils."

"You make him seem like a gentle old soul. I don't know that side of him."

"I can't say that I do, either. He's not the type you get to know right away. A bit brusque. But he's civil enough."

"I would agree."

"By the way, and this comes from an entirely different source, do you know of someone named Deadwood Dick?"

Miss Glover frowned. "That's the name of a dime novel character."

"Oh." My spirits sank a little. "I can't say that I look into that sort of literature."

"Neither do I, but I've heard of that character—maybe because we're not far from the Black Hills. Not that those stories are based very much in reality anyway."

"Well, right now I'm reading *The Portrait of a Lady,* and I can't say that it has much to do with daily life as I know it, but it does have a level of reality and seriousness."

"Oh, yes. James is good, even when he's so precious about life among the Europeans. There's still something in it for us."

I wondered if she had met her Gilbert Osmond, as Isabel Archer did in the story. "I agree," I said. "As for Deadwood Dick, I met a fellow who said I reminded him of someone by that name."

Miss Glover drew back her head and gave me an appraising look. "I'd think you'd need a more gaudy outfit, with two revolvers, an embroidered jacket, an ornate sombrero, and flowing mustachios."

"I had the impression he meant a real person."

"Oh. Maybe he did. A nickname." She flicked her eyebrows as if to brush away the topic. "And how does it go for the hunting itself?"

"As I said, I spoke with Clay Cooper. He says the time would be right in another week or so."

Miss Glover spoke in a lower tone. "That is what you came for, isn't it? Deer hunting?"

"Well, yes." I met her brown eyes, and I felt a level of confidence that did not include much romance. In a tone that matched hers, I said, "But I have other interests."

"Other kinds of hunting?"

I nodded one way and the other. "Not butterflies." I met her eyes again. "Maybe information."

"I had a sense of something like that."

I thought I must look like a duck out of water in this town. But I was here, and I needed to follow through. "I'd be willing to hear anything you might have to share."

In an even lower voice, she said, "There's a woman staying in this hotel who's scared to death. Won't go out of her room. I don't know what she's waiting for. But in a small town like this, if one person's looking and one person's hiding, there might be a connection."

"I'm not looking for a woman, at least not in that sense, but you're right. There might be something. What's her name?"

"She goes by Sarah Ewing. If that's her real name, mine is Isabel Archer."

I nodded in recognition, then said, "What would be the best way for me to talk to her?"

"Well, she won't come down to the dining room, that's for sure. If I take you to her room, that's against hotel rules. Same as if she goes to yours. But there's a suite of rooms not in use on the second floor. You could meet in the sitting room part of it."

I sat in a wooden armchair for a long while, trying to keep still, until the door opened. I stood up as Miss Glover came in with another woman behind her. Miss Glover stepped aside and ushered the woman forward.

"Mr. Tresh, this is Miss Ewing. Miss Ewing, this is Mr. Tresh, the gentleman I mentioned."

The woman had a clouded face and squinting eyes. She made a tentative nod.

Miss Glover stepped back. "I'll leave you two to visit. If you need anything, just pull the bell." She turned and walked out, closing the door behind her.

I faced the woman again. She was of average height for a woman and neither thin nor stout. She looked as if she had had a good figure but had not won the battle against time and a hard life, for her shoulders, bosom, and waist all sagged. Her light brown hair had begun to turn gray. The clouded effect I had noticed was due to swelling and blotching, familiar signs among people who drank more than a glass of wine while appreciating the hummingbirds. She raised one hand to rub her nose as she sniffed, and then she spoke in a hoarse voice.

"The landlady said you wanted to talk to me."

"I appreciate your willingness to visit. You might know something that will help me. I might be able to help you in return. Miss Glover suggested that you might be in a predicament."

"I'm a decent woman, Mister—"

"Tresh. Henry Tresh. Though I don't think my name matters."

"I haven't heard it before."

"Have you heard of Deadwood Dick?"

Her face went motionless as her eyes opened.

"Don't be startled," I said. "Please sit down." When both of us were seated with the table between us, I continued. "I came here in the employment of an older couple in North Platte. I don't suppose that surprises you."

She shook her head.

"And just to be clear, I would guess your name is Bella Collingsworth."

"One name is as good as another in a place like this."

"Then who is Deadwood Dick?"

"I think you know."

"I assure you I don't."

"Well, he's like you, I guess. He was someone Arthur's parents hired to try to find him—or what happened to him."

I felt as if I had the wind knocked out of me. "They didn't tell me they hired someone else. Where is he?"

"We think he's dead."

I paused. "Then let's go back a couple of steps. How do you know about him?"

"Well, they hired him. They offered him a reward. He came and found me in Broken Bow. He asked a thousand questions, and he told me what he was up to. I thought he talked too much about what he was doing, but it must have worked, because he got out of me something I had never told anyone else, and that was the name of this town."

"And once he got it, he left?"

"That's right. I felt like a fool, but it wasn't the first time. Or the last."

"What was his name, by the way?"

"Dickerson. First name was Paul, I think, but I'm not sure."

"So he went on his way."

"Yes, and I went into hiding. I didn't know what to do. Then after a while I decided to mention it to a friend of mine. He thought we could beat Dickerson to the reward, but he had a head start on us."

"You say 'we.' Is the other person named Ned?"

"Yes, sir."

"Last name, just to be complete?"

"What does it matter?"

"I never know. But it would help, and it might even help me help you."

After a few seconds, she said, "It's Brower. Ned Brower."

"Thanks. Let's go ahead. Did the two of you travel here together?"

"No. He came first and laid low, and then I showed up."

"You've talked to him since you've been here?"

"Yes."

"And that's why you think Dickerson is dead?"

She hesitated. "Yes. He disappeared before Ned got here."

I brought out a pint bottle of whiskey from inside my jacket. "Do you care for any of this?"

Her eyebrows went up. "I don't like to drink it out of the bottle."

"It's all right. I won't contaminate it by drinking any of it myself."

"I didn't mean that."

"Nothing personal taken." I set the bottle on the table

between us.

She unscrewed the cap and lifted the bottle to her lips. She did not seem like an altogether coarse woman, and I felt sympathy for her. That's a mistake in my line of work, but I can't get rid of the soft spot I have for women—most of all women who have had a fall.

When I thought she had braved herself with a swig, I said, "Let's go back again. To the first time you came to Laurel."

She shook her head. "I don't know if I can."

"Look," I said. "I'm not after a reward. These people are paying me a flat fee, so what I want is the truth. Incidental to that is justice for Arthur, if it can be found, and justice for you."

"For me?"

"His mother told me they blamed it all on you from the beginning."

"They did. And I can't ever hope to change that."

"So you just came for the reward."

"It was Ned's idea. I would never have come back on my own. Never."

I motioned with my hand. "Go ahead."

She took a second drink, and I thought I could see the warmth flowing through her.

"Let's give it another try," I said. "We're on the top floor of this hotel, and only one person in the world knows where we are. It's these four walls." I waved my hand.

She shook her head as before. "I've never wanted to tell anyone this story, but something tells me I should. I hope I don't hate myself for it, but it's no worse than how I've felt all this time."

"I'm not here to judge, and I'm not here to get an advantage over you. If you can tell the story, I'm here to listen."

Her chest went up and down as she took a deep breath. "All right. I think I'd better." Her hand moved toward the bottle, then stopped. "It happened like this. Arthur and I took off on a lark together. That's what he called it, a lark. I don't want to blame everything on him, but it was his idea, and he stole the money from his father. We took the train from North Platte, then another from Cheyenne up this way. By then, Arthur said he was tired of the train, so we ended up on this road, and we ran out of money when we came to this town." She reached for the bottle and laid her hand on it.

"Go ahead," I said.

She took a drink from the bottle, capped it, and set it aside. "We met an older man—old to us, at least. He invited us to go to his house, so we did. He served us a meal, which all seemed normal, and then he gave us some wine. I think he put something in the wine. As I recall, he was a druggist. It made me woozy with less than half a glass, and it made Arthur silly."

She paused, as if she had to get her nerve up. "The old man started playing with him, like sitting next to him on the couch and patting his leg. Instead of moving away, Arthur started giggling. Flirting, it seemed like. I asked him what he was doing, and he said they were just having fun. It didn't seem new to him. But it scared me. I didn't know what old men did to pretty boys—I still don't know what they do, but back then, I didn't even know they did it. So I got scared. I was afraid of the old man, afraid of what they were going to do, afraid of Arthur knowing I knew—afraid of everything. So I ran. Then I was afraid of what Arthur would do when he caught me, and when he didn't come back to North Platte, I was afraid of what the old man would do if I ever said anything. I never mentioned the name of this town, and I never wanted to come back."

I let out a breath and widened my eyes. "And here you are."

"Yes, like the biggest fool in the world."

"You came for the reward, you said."

"Ned wanted to, and I went along. But I don't want to have

anything to do with any of this now."

I frowned. "Then what do you want?"

She leveled her gaze on me. "I want to get out of this town."

"Can't you just tell Ned?"

"I don't know if he wants to go, and I don't know if he would think I was going back on him. I thought I could trust him, but I'm not so sure of that now." She breathed with her mouth open. "I wish I had twenty dollars. I'd leave on the stage, and no one would ever be troubled by me again."

I said, "I don't have twenty dollars on me, but I'll see if I can find it." After a second's thought, I said, "You don't think Ned would tell the old bachelor you're in town, do you?"

"I don't think so, but Dickerson might have mentioned my name, and the old man could do something to me sooner or later."

"Well, it's enough to be worried about. Ned could make a slip."

"Do you think you can find twenty dollars?"

"I'll try." I knew where it was in my bag. I didn't like the idea of having to pay out a considerable portion of my fee, but I could see I was headed in that direction.

"Mister, I'll—"

"Don't worry about the money. I'll ask Miss Glover to help me get in touch with you later tonight. The hard part will be getting you onto the stage without anyone seeing you, but that can be done. I assume you don't want Ned to know."

"Not at all. I just want to get away."


I stood by myself at the bar in the Shanty. Night had fallen, and Mike had the company of two cowpunchers who had ridden in from the country north of Fort Fetterman. They were telling stories and laughing it up about the famous Hog Ranch down that way. The taller of the two punchers was doing card tricks.

I had plenty to think about, though I was not astonished by anything Bella had told me. I had her in the group of people I considered believable, and everything she told me confirmed my impressions of Arthur's parents, the old bachelor, and Ned Brower. What I needed to do was plan out a sequence of steps I should take, plus alternatives in case some part went wrong. At present, the first critical moment entailed getting Bella onto the southbound stagecoach when it came through at ten the next morning.

Mike drifted into my line of vision. "Ready for another?"

"One more."

As he poured the whiskey, Mike tipped his head. "They say one of Bill Cody's men is in the country, looking to buy horses for the show."

"They should be able to find some."

"You'd think." Mike tucked the cork into the bottle. "Where's your friend?"

"I didn't know I had any."

"That jailbird-lookin' fellow who came in here last night."

"Ned? I haven't seen him." I was hoping to sound out Ned that evening, but I didn't say so much to Mike. "Why do you call him my friend?"

"Just kidding. He came in right after you did, and he left not too far behind you."

"If he had any interest in me, he didn't learn much. I came here from the hotel and went straight back, which is what I plan to do this evening. Thanks for the word, though."

"Don't mention it." Mike drifted back to the two cowpunchers and their stories about the Hog Ranch.

I left the Shanty with two ideas in mind. One was not to look over my shoulder or seem too cautious, and the other was to give twenty dollars to Bella Collingsworth. When I walked into the hotel, Miss Glover was standing at her station, wearing a wine-colored jacket along with her lavender outfit. She looked up from reading the newspaper and folded it.

"Good evening," she said as she handed me my key.

"The same to you." Lowering my voice, I said, "I'd like to ask you to do me a favor. I would like to convey some money to Sarah Ewing so that she can leave on the stage in the morning."

"You want me to deliver it?"

"If you would." I set a stack of four five-dollar gold pieces on the counter and held my cupped hand above them.

She bit her lower lip. "I'd rather not be carrying money in that way. But I can take you to her door. As long as you don't go in, there shouldn't be anything wrong as far as rules go."

I settled my hand over the coins. "That should work well enough. Thank you." I recalled a humorous saying about a certain kind of hotel in which a man did not go into a lady's room, but if he did, he did not sit on her bed. And if he did sit on her bed, they each kept one foot on the floor. I appreciated Miss Glover's drawing the line at the door itself.

I followed her down the hallway. Halfway to my room, which was on the left, she stopped at a door on the right. She rapped with the backs of her fingernails on the panel.

After rapping a second time, she stood closer to the door and spoke through it. "Miss Ewing. Sarah."

Miss Glover looked at me, raised her eyebrows, and said, "Perhaps we should go in." She produced a key from her jacket pocket and opened the door.

Soft light from the hallway spilled into the dark room. "Let me light a lamp." Miss Glover moved to a bureau, found a match, and lit an oil lamp. As light spread in the room, she said, "Uh-oh."

Bella Collingsworth lay on the floor on the right side of the bed as I stood at the doorway looking in.

"Come in and close the door," said Miss Glover. She led the way with the lamp and stood by, lighting the scene, as I knelt by the body.

Bella lay slumped, with her head on her left shoulder and with her left arm stretched out. I touched her neck with the back of my fingers. I felt no pulse, no body warmth.

"I think she's been dead for a while," I said. "A couple of hours or more. Do you mind holding the lamp closer?"

The face did not tell me much. Even in death, her features looked blotched and swollen and troubled. But I did not see any bruises or lacerations. I leaned close. I could not pick up an odor of chloroform or ether, though I knew those substances did not linger for a long time. Then something caught my eye. On the inside of her forearm, just below the crook of the elbow, a dark red dot showed where a bead of blood had dried.

I stood up. "It's best not to move the body or anything in the room until someone from the law has been here."

"Do you have any idea of who might have done this?" She had a dead serious expression on her face, and I thought she showed good repose.

"Call me superstitious," I said, "but I'd rather not say anything out loud until the law arrives. How soon do you think that could be?"

"They would have to come from Douglas. I can send a wire first thing in the morning. The office here in town is closed by now."

"Well, if you can, in the meanwhile, try to let on as if nothing has happened."

"What are you going to do?"

"The first thing is to get a pistol out of my bag. Then I think I'll sit by the door in my room and keep an ear tuned for footsteps. How would they have gotten in?"

"I think someone could pick the lock on the back door. I

can't say it hasn't been done before, but I haven't had any trouble. Until now."

"I'm sorry to see it. Sorry for her."

We left the room, and Miss Glover locked the door behind us. We shared a wordless glance, then went our separate ways.

I tried to walk with as little noise as possible. The hallway had a thin carpet that absorbed some of the sound. As I walked, I tried to keep my thoughts in a straight line. Everything went back to Arthur. He was the source of this trouble, from the time he stole his father's money until now. Everyone wanted to find him—his parents, the ineffective Dickerson, Ned, Bella, and myself. I thought it remarkable that so many people wanted to find something that did not seem like much of a treasure. And at this point, I didn't care so much about finding him as I did about bringing the old perpetrator to justice. I did not think he should get away with whatever he did to Arthur, whatever he did to my predecessor, and what he did or had someone do to Bella Collingsworth. I did not even like him trading on the good image of having lady friends. I caught myself on that thought. I needed to keep my eye on the object, and that was to help bring this criminal to justice.

I reached my room with little noise. I unlocked the door and left it ajar as I found a match and struck it. As I lit the lamp and turned up the flame, the door closed.

The glow of the lamplight fell on the hard features and billed cap of Ned Brower. He stood with his thumbs in his belt and a pistol on his hip.

"Hello, Jack," I said.

"The name's Ned."

"What brings you here?"

"I thought you might like to know how to find Deadwood Dick."

His comment struck me as being off center. "I can't say that

I'm interested. I don't even know who he is."

"Do you think anyone is fooled by your story of coming here to hunt deer?"

"There's only one person in this town whose opinion I care about."

"Well, aren't you sweet?" In a smooth motion, he pulled his six-gun and held it on me. "Don't take off your hat, partner. We're going for a walk."

"I tell you, I don't have an idea about Deadwood Dick."

"Never mind him. There's a man who wants to talk to you."

The night was dark and the streets were deserted as he marched me to the house with the dormer windows. I could see them with their white trim, like two eyes looking out into the night.

I had a hunch that Ned did not know what had happened to Bella, and I thought it best not to say anything until I knew how things stood between him and his new boss. I said, "You're just helping this guy get away with what he did to Arthur."

"Arthur," he said, in the same tone he had use to mention Rawlins. "He was as useless as tits on a boar. Bella says his own father said so."

"Still," I said.

"Yeah, yeah." He poked me with the gun, so I didn't say anything more as we followed the walkway between the flower beds.

Ned gave a light rap on the door, and the old bachelor let us in. He was not dressed in his work clothes but in what I took to be his evening attire. He was wearing a pink silk shirt, untucked with square tails. It fit him like a tent, falling from his flabby chest to his spreading girth.

He closed the door behind us. "This way." He crossed the room and led us down a hallway. He stopped to light a lantern, then opened a door. Dark steps disappeared into the cellar.

Holding the lantern forward, Boynton went down the stairs first. I followed, with Ned Brower's gun barrel poking me in the ribs.

The cellar had a packed dirt floor and a low ceiling. Boynton was not wearing a hat, and the joists cleared his head by an inch.

He led the way to a front corner of the cellar and held the lantern up. The light fell upon a wooden cage, a stout structure with a board floor and with vertical two-by-three studs about four inches apart.

"In here." He held the door open, followed us in, and reached out to slide the latch. He hung the lantern on a nail on one of the uprights, and I saw that he had a couple of items on the floor. One was a jar with a cork stopper, and the other was a small, cylindrical steel object I did not recognize at the moment.

Boynton reached down and picked up the jar along with a white cloth that lay behind it. He twisted out the stopper and put it in the waist pocket of his shirt. He tipped the jar to soak the cloth.

"Get your arms around him," he said. "This won't take a minute."

My heart was beating in my throat. I thought, *Chloroform. Then the needle.*

"You'll have to hold this." Ned motioned with the gun.

Boynton set the jar on the floor, and with the clean white cloth in his right hand, he took the pistol in his left.

As Ned began to lock his arms around me, I stomped on his toe. He yelped and jerked, and I dropped like dead weight with my feet out in front of me. It broke his hold on me, and I rolled free. As I came up, he lunged and hooked his arm around my head. I shoved, and the wall of the cage shook. Boynton fired the pistol.

Ned let out another yelp and grabbed his midsection with both hands. I turned toward Boynton, who did not seem very adept with the gun in his left hand. I punched him in the jaw as hard as I could, and he dropped the gun. I kicked it, and it slid across the wooden floor and rattled its way out between two studs.

Ned was on all fours, with blood dripping on the floorboards.

"Help me, you dolt," said Boynton, but Ned did not stir. Boynton came at me, large as a bear, with his arms reaching out.

I jumped to one side and then another until I had a chance to hit him again. His head went back, but he didn't stop. He backed me into a corner, got his arms around me, and tightened his grip.

He was stronger than I would ever have imagined, and I knew that he was driven to subdue me. I had to summon up just as strong a will not to let him. I thrashed and kicked. He lifted me from the floor, and I kept struggling. Then I drove my knee into his groin, and he lost his hold.

I ducked down and scrambled out of the way. I saw Ned, stupefied, still on all fours, but now he had a sheath knife in his right hand. I stepped on his hand, broke his grasp, and pulled the knife away.

I straightened up and looked for Boynton. I had lost track of him. Now I found him. He had crossed the cage and picked up the steel object, a four-inch cylinder with a two-inch needle sticking out of it. He had the white cloth in his left hand.

He came at me steady, not rushing and not feinting. He had his left arm out to catch me, and he held his right arm cocked and ready to plunge the needle. His mouth was open, and I could see his little yellow teeth.

He moved forward, and I jumped away, but he cut off my space. He was working me into a corner again. I shuffled to my right, then back to my left, and struck with the knife. A streak of blood appeared on the heel of his hand, and he dropped the syringe. I kicked it, and he clubbed me with his left hand. Then he moved in on me and got me in his grip again.

He hung on to me, hugging, and moved the cloth up to the side of my face. I tried to push away. He swung me to one side, off my feet, and we crashed into the wall of the cage. The lantern fell and smashed. I felt my feet touch the floor again as he began to tighten his squeeze.

I pushed the knife upward between us. His abdomen felt soft, like the dugs of an old bitch dog, and warm fluid spilled on my hand. He fell away, and I saw my hand as red as if I had gutted a deer.

He lay on his back, and both the syringe and the cloth were out of his reach. Flames were rising from the wooden floor. I turned my attention to Ned again.

He had his head turned to the side, toward Boynton, and his voice was coarser than usual. "You stupid son of a bitch," he rasped. "A soft-petered, clumsy old toad."

"Save your breath," I said. "If he's not dead, he will be in a minute."

"Good. Now nobody gets the reward."

"I doubt there's a reward anymore, but it probably doesn't matter." I knelt next to him. "Why in the hell did you turn on us?"

"I didn't turn on anyone. He said he had Bella, and he would tell me where she was if I brought you."

"Who picked the lock on my room?"

"He did, though I could have done it myself."

"You're the fool," I said. "The old bachelor put her on ice, and then he played you like a fish on the line. Now this place is on fire, and I don't know if I can get you up those steps."

"I don't think I can make it." He sank to his elbows and

made a deep, heaving cough. "Tell Jemmy goodbye."

I imagined Jemmy was a name, but I thought he might have meant either Jimmy or Jenny. "I'll do that," I said.

Ned Brower spilled over onto his side, and his cap slipped off his head.

The flames were spreading, and the low cellar was beginning to fill with smoke. Crouching, I moved over to check on Boynton. The old bachelor was dead.

I found the latch on the door and opened it, then went back, left the knife on the floor, and picked up my hat. I did not look for the pistol. I hurried up the wooden steps to the kitchen, where I washed my hands.

Smoke was billowing up the stairwell, and the main floor was in a haze. I ran out into the street and took deep breaths of fresh air. Before long, firelight was dancing behind the curtained windows.

*Let it burn,* I thought. *Let the son of a bitch burn.*


In the light of day, the townspeople found four graves in the back part of the cellar. Mike the bartender was able to identify the most recent remains as those of a man named Dickerson, who had been in town for a short while.

"He asked a lot of questions," Mike said.

The other remains were too old to identify. The townsfolk went on, recalling one time and another when someone came through looking for a missing person—way more than the two that I thought were unaccounted for. As for which set was Arthur's, I would have guessed the one on the left, as Dickerson was on the right. But then I told myself that I was making an assumption, for I did not know at what point in the old bachelor's career Arthur made his appearance.

It was not until someone asked about Boynton's crow that I

became less theoretical. I had run right past poor Henry in the smoke. His was one life I could have saved.

I took leave of Miss Glover on my last day in town. She was wearing a tan dress, and she had a red ribbon in her hair.

I said, "Goodbye, Miss Glover. It's been good to know you."

"You know my name," she said.

In the course of giving our statements to the sheriff, I had learned that Miss Glover's name was Angela. "Yes," I said, "and it's not Isabel Archer."

"It seems like an unfeeling thing to have said, in light of what happened later. I don't think she was such a bad woman."

"Neither do I. And I don't think she deserved what he did to her. But at least there was some justice after all."

"And where do you go now?"

"I told Arthur's parents I would report to them in person. They pay for my travel, so it's not a loss on my part. I just have to work on the wording. After that, I suppose I go back to Cheyenne and keep on trying to make a living."

"Don't be afraid to come back this way sometime. We could play a game of backgammon."

The uncertain feeling I had had about the town seemed to have gone away, thanks in part, perhaps, to the burning of the old bachelor's house. Here we were, talking about normal things.

"I've never played the game," I said, "but I could learn. That in itself could be a reason for me to return."

**John D. Nesbitt** lives in the plains country of Wyoming, where he teaches English and Spanish at Eastern Wyoming College. He writes western, contemporary, mystery, and retro/noir fiction as well as nonfiction and poetry. John has won many awards for his work, including two awards from the Wyoming State

Historical Society (for fiction), two awards from Wyoming Writers for encouragement of other writers and service to the organization, two Wyoming Arts Council literary fellowships (one for fiction, one for nonfiction), four Will Rogers Medallion Awards, and four Spur awards from Western Writers of America. His recent books include *Dark Prairie* and *Death in Cantera*, frontier mysteries with Five Star.

# ABOUT THE EDITOR

**Hazel Rumney** has lived most of her life in Maine, although she also spent a number of years in Spain and California while her husband was in the military. She has worked in the publishing business for almost thirty years. Retiring in 2011, she and her husband traveled throughout the United States visiting many famous and not-so-famous western sites before returning to Thorndike, Maine, where they now live. In 2012, Hazel reentered the publishing world as an editor for Five Star Publishing, a part of Cengage Learning. During her tenure with Five Star, she has developed and delivered titles that have won Western Fictioneers Peacemaker Awards, Will Rogers Medallion Awards, and Western Writers of America Spur Awards, including the double Spur Award–winning novel *Wild Ran the Rivers* by James D. Crownover. Western fiction is Hazel's favorite genre to enjoy. She has been reading the genre for more than five decades.

The employees of Five Star Publishing hope you have enjoyed this book.

Our Five Star novels explore little-known chapters from America's history, stories told from unique perspectives that will entertain a broad range of readers.

Other Five Star books are available at your local library, bookstore, all major book distributors, and directly from Five Star/Gale.

Connect with Five Star Publishing

Visit us on Facebook:
  https://www.facebook.com/FiveStarCengage

Email:
  FiveStar@cengage.com

For information about titles and placing orders:
  (800) 223-1244
  gale.orders@cengage.com

To share your comments, write to us:
  Five Star Publishing
  Attn: Publisher
  10 Water St., Suite 310
  Waterville, ME 04901